DADDY DEADEST

"Oh, Dad, oh, Daddy, oh, please, Daddy, wake up . . . . We were going to go fishing. . . ."

But Joey knew it was no use. The unimaginable had happened. The arms that gave him hugs and quieted his fears and decorated the Christmas tree would not move again.

Joey noticed the fly that had alit on his dad's arm. The insect was buzzing and rolling. Joey's heart skipped and a cold ferocity ravaged his chest.

"You . . . you . . . you . . ." Joey growled. "You . . . you dammit . . . you sumbitch . . . I'm gonna get . . . you! Gonna . . . git . . . YOU!"

The child knelt down and cupped his hand over the fly so it could not escape when he crushed it.

But that did not end it.

Evil had only just begun to rise from the depths of darkness to fill the sunlit air with terror and the peaceful valley with death. . . .

Stanley R. Moore

AN ONYX BOOK

NEW AMERICAN LIBRARY

PUBLISHER'S NOTE

This book is a work of fiction. Names, characters, places, and incidents either are the product of the author's imagination or are used fictitiously, and any resemblance to actual persons, living or dead, events, or locales is entirely coincidental.

 ONYX TRADEMARK REG. U.S. PAT. OFF. AND FOREIGN COUNTRIES REGISTERED TRADEMARK—MARCA REGISTRADA HECHO EN DRESDEN, TN, U.S.A.

SIGNET, SIGNET CLASSIC, MENTOR, ONYX, PLUME, MERIDIAN and NAL BOOKS are published by NAL PENGUIN INC., 1633 Broadway, New York, New York 10019

First Printing, January, 1989

1 2 3 4 5 6 7 8 9

PRINTED IN THE UNITED STATES OF AMERICA

This book is dedicated to
the memory of
Detective Sergeant Ed Haslam,
late of the Anaheim Police Department

Part One

FROM SATURDAY TO MONDAY

When sorrows come, they come not single spies,
But in battalions.

1

No one imagined it. It had never happened before. And because people could not imagine it, they could not avert it.

Yet it was not without warning. In the fourteenth century a similar agent killed one of every three people in Europe. In more than a decade in our time, there had been ample warnings, ample deaths, ample time to imagine it . . . or something like it.

Peter Bilyeux would later reflect that calamity is most often a product of the least thought. But, cruising in the patrol car that Saturday morning, the only calamity to occupy his thoughts was domestic. His wife was going mad, and his job was not helping her. Pete's torment was that he loved both his wife and his job.

So when Pete saw Al Murdock leading his young son into the trees, he had no inkling what lay in store for so many in so short a time, nor how his own mind and body would be ransacked by the following Saturday.

Al Murdock's troubles were different, and about to be worse. It was said that if trout could be taken anywhere in the county, they were Al's for the taking. He neither liked to eat trout nor did he hold anything against them. The taste inspired him to apathy. If Lissy had a yen for fish, she and Al ate them. If not, Al threw them back. Al just liked fishing. Some said he thought like a fish. It took his mind off things and kept his worries from marauding his sensitive stomach. But even the prospect of the day's fishing could not keep him from mulling the previous week's work and his manager, one Black Fang Webster, whose voice came back to Al this Saturday morning.

"Murdock, come in here," Black Fang had called from his doorway, in the tone of a man educated beyond his capacity to learn. "Who made these ghastly entries, man?" he asked, holding an offending ledger. Automated banking had not yet come to the hamlet of Thomas Valley.

"Gloria did, Jack. The new girl," Al said. It was an in-joke at the bank to refer to Jack Webster as Black Fang behind his back. He gained this epithet from the loss of his lower incisor teeth as a youth. While in the Navy Supply Corps he had a fixed bridge capped onto his canine teeth, filling the void between at government expense. Time caused this bridge to darken the canine teeth to a hue matching his disposition toward subordinates.

"And who supervised her?"

"Well, Jeanette, I suppose," Al replied.

"You suppose? You suppose? And who supervised Jeanette?"

"Well, I guess I'm responsible, Jack," Al said. He felt that his glasses were getting foggy. He slipped them off, blinked against the blurry sight of his boss, wiped the lenses, and replaced them in time to see the infamous lower fangs glisten.

"At least you're willing to admit responsibility," Webster said. "A precious good thing too, Murdock, or you'd get your walking papers. Simply look at this, man."

Al Murdock looked and calculated rapidly in his mind and could find nothing wrong but the penmanship. "Sorry, Jack," he said, "but I . . . uh . . . I . . . can't see it . . ."

"Can't see it? Can't see it?! It's not the arithmetic that's wrong, damn it, man, it's these jejune hieroglyphics, no doubt the product of a degenerate educational system. This is slovenly work, Murdock, slovenly work done by a slip of a girl supervised by a slattern who can't keep her blouse tucked in, who in turn is supervised by you. Put yourself in my place, Murdock. Suppose someone from central were to come by and audit this trash. What would you say if you were me and that happened? Be fair!"

"I . . . I don't know, Jack. I'm sorry."

"Damned right you're sorry, man," Webster said.

"You're going to be even sorrier if you don't discharge that wretched little Gloria at closing time on Friday. I want this dismissal to serve as an example."

On the whole, Al would rather have been back in Vietnam. At least the enemy didn't invade his stomach as Black Fang did.

There was something else, too, that nagged at him. A year or so after Webster took over the branch, he started sending Al to central headquarters in Harrisburg, the Pennsylvania state capital, on Tuesdays and Thursdays after closing. These were small errands that Webster said would nonetheless improve the image of the Thomas Valley branch with top management. The trip took two hours or so, then meetings would take an hour or two, and then it took another couple of hours to get home.

Not long after these journeys began, Lissy told Al she didn't want any more kids and started taking the pill. Lissy had managed to keep her looks and her figure, which was abundant, and Al thought her decision might make her feel more free in lovemaking, which she always enjoyed. But it didn't. Sometimes a whole month would go by when Lissy said she had forgotten to take her pill and didn't want to take chances.

Al came to connect this disruption in their love life—rightly or wrongly, he wasn't sure—with other things. With the way Lissy and Black Fang looked at each other when she stopped by the bank. With something Emily had once said about Mommy going out. With what was said went on between other people at the Sunset Motel off the interstate.

Al wasn't stupid but he didn't want to distress his stomach with a subject he could do nothing about. No, he would go fishing and let the week slip downstream with the waters of Owl Creek.

He awoke before the clock radio went off. Lissy rolled over restlessly. As he dressed he wondered if he ought to take one of the kids along. He decided he'd take little Joey. It was Joey's last summer before kindergarten and he adored fishing with Al.

Joey grumbled at first but when he heard about fishing Al could sense his eyes widen in the pre-dawn gloom.

Al left Lissy a note and got their gear and they tumbled

into the Chevy wagon and drove down the Elmsford
Road. They stopped at Ed & Edna's Diner and got a hot
breakfast and Al had his thermos filled with good black
coffee.

A topaz wash from eastern hilltops flooded their faces
and cast long shadows as Al fumbled for a country-music
station on the car radio. He dialed past the Farm Report
and lingered over the evangelical station long enough to
elicit a question from Joey, who had gone to sleep the
previous night watching a western on TV.

"Dad?" Joey asked.

"Yes, son?"

"Did God come before the cowboys?"

Al chuckled and looked at his five-year-old son and
rumpled the boy's hair. They exchanged smiles. If the
week had been a bad one, surely the weekend could be
a good one.

"Yes, son, I guess there was God before there were
cowboys."

"How come, Dad? Are you sure, I mean?"

Deputy Sheriff Pete Bilyeux, a native of Thomas Valley, was cruising by on the Elmsford Road when Al and
Joey left the Chevy by the bridge and walked hand-in-
hand down toward the creek. Bilyeux honked and waved,
and they waved in return.

The ground fog was burning off, but the dewy grasses
and bushes dampened their boots and trouser legs.

They walked a mile and a half past oaks and elms and
hickories and thickets of forsythia that would vaunt gar-
ish yellow fingers the following March. Al took some
comfort in the thought that by then perhaps Black Fang
would get transferred to a bigger branch or maybe have
a heart attack.

They set their gear down in the shade of wild rhododendrons on a bank where the creek widened into a pool
of primeval black. Here they sat and watched. Al told
Joey to be very still as they waited for the telltale disturbances of trout snapping at insects on the surface—caddis
flies, mosquitoes, whatever.

There were plenty of flies around this morning. Al
hoped this might encourage the trout to venture upward
to a surface he feared was already growing too warm for

them. He was pleased to see this surface soon punctuated by the dimples of striking fish.

Al helped Joey tie an artificial caddis fly onto his line and was at pains to remind him that this fly was made of deer and rabbit fur and wasn't real and wouldn't be hurt. He knew Joey worried about such things. The day was heating even in the shade where they sat, and Al took off his jacket and rolled up his sleeves from arms beginning to sweat.

A real fly, smaller than a caddis and probably old because it was flitting erratically, alighted on Al's discarded jacket.

"Well, Mr. Fly," Al said as he tied an artificial fly to his line, "come to think of it, it'd be cheaper if I used you for bait instead of buying these things."

The fly buzzed more loudly than most flies do, flew into the air, then landed awkwardly on Al's naked forearm.

"Shoo, fly," Al told it.

Joey knew his dad was being funny for his benefit when he talked to the fly, and it made Joey laugh.

He stopped laughing when his dad screamed and clutched at his arm and fell back with the fly still on him. What Joey saw next he could scarcely believe. He had never seen anything like it on TV.

His dad stopped screaming and looked terrified. His chest and belly convulsed as they tried and failed to provide him with oxygen. Choking and rattling noises forced their way from his throat. His arms and legs flailed as those of a hanged man.

"Dad? Dad? You okay, Dad? Dad! DAD! *Don't do that, Dad!*"

Joey's dad had looked at him once, just after he screamed, trying to reassure the little boy. But in seconds the eyes looked away, bulged, stared upward, then began to look at something deep inside and far away.

Within a minute Al Murdock's skin took on a bluish cast, his body lay still, and his eyes closed to reveal only a hint of glimmering tears dammed within slits of white marble.

Joey knew by instinct that his dad was dead even if he was not sure what death was. He began to cry.

"Oh, Dad, oh, Daddy, oh, please, Daddy, please wake up . . . We were going to go fishing . . . Oh, please . . . get up, Dad . . . please . . ."

But Joey knew it was no use. The unimaginable had happened. The arms that gave him hugs and quieted his fears and decorated the Christmas tree would not move again.

Joey noticed the fly that had alit on his dad's arm. The insect was buzzing and rolling on the ground as if unable to fly. Joey's heart skipped and a cold ferocity ravaged his chest. His skin prickled as he looked down on his father's murderer.

"You . . . you . . . you . . ." Joey growled as he circled the ground on which the fly wallowed. "You . . . you, dammit . . . you sumbitch . . . you sumbitch basset. I'm gonna git you! Gonna . . . git . . . YOU!"

Joey knelt down and cupped his hand over the fly so it could not escape when he crushed it.

It was the first time it ever happened to anyone.

2

Although not truly residents because their diner and the small house behind it lay more than two miles outside the town line, Ed and Edna were Thomas Valley institutions. Ed was a sort of horror connoisseur and was always happy to tell anyone about the time when, at the age of eleven, he was bitten by a copperhead. This was especially true if he had taken a pull or two from the quart of rye he kept in the kitchen, which he could be expected to do regularly even at his present age of sixty-two.

This Saturday around noon Deputy Sheriff Pete Bilyeux stopped in for a cheeseburger and before he had taken his

NIGHTSHADE 17

first bite was treated to Ed's rendition of the bite of the copperhead.

Edna, typically, wore a dour expression as she wandered the diner wiping and dusting and swatting at flies. "When you gonna fix the screen, Ed?" she said.

Ed ignored her and continued talking. "Was out balancing barefoot on an old log. Tripped and fell off the damned thing and landed right on top of the sumbitch, all orange and diamonds like and layin' coiled up just awaitin' for some dumbass kid like me to sink his teeth into. He let out the Christawfullest hiss and nailed me. Felt like Babe Ruth had slugged me in the leg with a ball bat with a couple of spikes in it, 'cept it stung like blue bloody hell at the same time . . ."

Slap went Edna's flyswatter. "Shoot," she said, "missed him. Should've dove at him outa the sun like a Jap Zero. Hey, Ed, when you gonna fix that screen?"

"I ran home like a striped-assed ape yellin' my fool head off," Ed continued. "I told Ma I was bit by a copperhead and she yelled for Pa. They made me lay down and Ma held me while Pa opened his Barlow knife. By this time my whole lower leg had swole to twicet its regular size above where the snake had bit, and it was all black-and-blue, like . . ."

Slap went Edna's flyswatter. Edna was now caught up in the metaphor of aerial combat. "Got the little devil," she said. "That makes four today. One more and I'm an ace. Hey, Ed, when you gonna fix that damn screen?" She picked up the dead fly with a rag and dumped the rag and the corpse into a trash pail.

"Pa cut my leg," Ed went on, "and I don't know what hurt worse't, the snakebite or Pa cuttin'. Then Pa sucked on the cuts and I was ahurtin' like a whore headed for hellfire and I begin to git all dizzy like. But Pa kept asuckin' and cussin' and spittin' the gooey bloody pus all over the floor. I like to died from all the pain. Then Pa gits up and cranks up the old Ford and heads for a phone to call the doctor. When the doctor come, I was afeelin' like my head was black-and-blue too and I was sick to the stummick and fevered and all . . ."

Slap went Edna's flyswatter again. "Hah! That makes five! Hey, Ed, did you know you was married to the ace flykiller of Elmsford County? When *are* you gonna fix that screen? Next thing you know we'll have the board of health after us.''

''The doc takes a look at me and shines his light in my eyes and tells them to make me set up all night soakin' my leg in a tub of ice water and ammonia and gives me two aspirin and says he'll be back in the morning but for my folks to call if I died so's he could save the trip. Well, I was sicker'n a drunk sailor in a cyclone for a couple of days and then I got better, 'n that's that. 'Scuse me, I gotta tend to the kitchen for a minute.''

''Hey, you old lush,'' Edna said, ''come back here and set to work fixin' that screen.''

Pete laughed to himself and paid up and got back in the car and drove the western part of his beat. He wrote a speeding ticket to a pretty girl with a dopey demeanor who was doing seventy-nine in a Corvette with New York plates. Then he wrote a warning to Old Lady Peterson, who always had trouble remembering whether you should stop on the green and go on the red or vice versa, never mind the fine distinctions between left and right and the points of the compass. He wrote another warning to a man who had shot a bear out of season and was trying to cram the carcass into the trunk of his Toyota. He let him off as a matter of policy, though he impounded the bear and the man's ammunition. The sheriff's office was inclined to be lenient with bear poachers lately. The bears had been making a comeback after being close to extinction for a generation. Now they often raided people's garbage cans.

On the last leg of his eight-to-four shift Pete drove over the Owl Creek Bridge and noticed Al Murdock's Chevy wagon still parked in the same place. Old Al must be reeling them in. Getting more than his quota, too, and probably stashing the excess in the little boy's creel.

Pete Bilyeux would not find out until the next day that a missing-persons report had been phoned in to the desk at 11:04 P.M. on Joey Murdock. The mother was worried the husband might have left her and kidnapped the boy and gone on to another state. At 2:47 A.M. the desk called Mrs. Murdock back to report the car had been found at Owl Creek Bridge and the deputy had called out to Al

and Joey on an electronic megaphone and got no response. The car had not been disturbed and the two had
probably fished too long and late and decided to camp
for the night. The desk would send a man out in the
morning to look if Al and Joey weren't back by then,
which they surely would be.

3

*The earth trembled and the mountaintops spat fire
and the very heavens shrieked forth their wrath upon
the land. The unthinkable had occurred. It was the
expulsion of a god.*

*Quetzalcoatl, feathered serpent, god of light and
good, had been banished from Tula. It was because
of the treachery of Tezcatlipoca, god of darkness,
that his catastrophe was visited upon the Toltec.*

*And so did Quetzalcoatl wander for many seasons.
At last he stopped at the place where the earth meets
the great waters. This was the god's home.*

*This benevolent god uncoiled his girth and did
stretch his plumage of iridescent bronze-green, crimson, white, and shimmering emerald. Then did Quetzalcoatl speak unto his people in a voice of such
force that its magnitude did make the limbs of trees
bend and the clay of lanterns shatter.*

*"Know ye, children of Tula, how I have been be-
trayed. I go now to slumber in sublime warmth. I
shall return at a time when the moon sets in full day.
It is now ye who must deracinate the Evil Ones even
unto that time.*

*"These Evil Ones are the minions of Tezcatlipoca
and are known to take many habitations and forms.
They may shape themselves as humankind, as stones,
or beasts of any sort—yea, even unto the fly of the*

*air. Tezcatlipoca remains forever secure as long as
these his slaves remain at large among ye.*

*"That ye may come to destroy the Evil Ones, I tell
ye this final thing: that the heart of evil is in the
heart of life."*

*Then did this great god command the sun to lift
him to its bosom of divine flames. And so it came to
pass that the generations of Toltec, then Maya, then
Aztec grieved under the wicked god Tezcatlipoca. Yet
they never forgot Quetzalcoatl. Valiantly they en-
deavored to root out evils from the hearts of life.
Alas, it proved never enough. Yea, the Aztec were
nigh invincible. Yet neither could they remove the
heart of evil in the heart of life. Great glories to
Quetzalcoatl were made. Scores of thousands of living hearts were rent from writhing breasts, and this
was surely good for many Evil Ones perished there-
with. The skulls of those who once did contain these
hearts littered the very streets, so diligent were the
Aztec. Yet even unto today the evil spell remains un-
broken. The Evil Ones and the evil god Tezcatlipoca
lust on unto the day Quetzalcoatl shall be restored
to glory when the full moon sets in daylight.*

Enid Bilyeux thought and thought and thought about
this fable. She knew it was meant to be some kind of
parable or allegory. After all, nobody in her right mind
believes in gods in this day and age, let alone those that
are snakes that parade around in feathers.

But with each letter she got from Adair in Teotihuacán
there was another interpretation of the legend more re-
vealing and cogent to both of them.

She had told this story to a few of the doctors and to
Pete, more to elicit their responses than to reveal her
thoughts. They all said it was a myth such as all societies
had. Nobody thought it had much to do with her problems. But then nobody knew about her and Adair either,
though Pete might have had some inkling of it. Poor stuttering Pete. So solid, so stolid, so dumb to imagine himself of poetic nature. She, Enid, was the poet. Enid
chuckled to herself with the letter on her lap.

But she knew Pete wasn't easy to fool. He was every-

where and saw and heard and mentally recorded everything. He understood Quetzalcoatl, miniature stone god
atop the mantelpiece, and to appease and amuse Enid,
he made to this divinity offerings of dandelion blooms,
Queen Anne's lace, violets, and day lilies that he plucked
from the roadside when he stopped his old two-stroke
Suzuki motorcycle on the way home from the substation.

Of course, Pete was a good man, Enid knew. She would
do nothing in life or death to hurt him. She swore it to
herself. He'd had too much pain already and had borne
it with too much grace. This made her feel guilty and
frightened when she thought of what she had done to the
animals. She hoped Pete never suspected it.

She sat in the armchair with Adair's letter on her lap
and rocked back and forth. Her thoughts took her to times
with Adair, and her ears began to feel warm, then the
sides of her neck and the backs of her hands.

It was the only thing that had saved them in the foster
home. Their older sister, Elspeth, had tried to save them
but the law would not provide for it. Now Elspeth is
fighting arthritis and, worse yet, is living in Scranton,
the wife of a dentist.

Adair, oh, Adair, why have we been cut apart?

Our minds were together and our hearts were together
and our flesh was together and we have been disjoined.
Oh, God, why did it have to happen?

She knew she shouldn't do it and she cursed her mind
as she did it anyway. It happened every time she got a
letter from Adair. Her hands became his—gentle, sweet,
kind, probing, touching—making her warm and moist.

Afterward she felt unclean. Sanity must be imposed,
Enid thought.

I'll take a shower, Enid decided. Yes, that'll straighten
things out. But first let me think for a minute.

Once again she thought of Adair's interpretations of the
ancient rituals. Oh, Adair, forbidden lover, forbidden
self, maker of the melting warmth of two become one.

Yes, the story of Quetzalcoatl and Tezcatlipoca was
meaningful. It gave them both a process of control as,
when you sleep and dream, you sometimes have lucid
moments that permit you to vanquish the outcome of the
dream. Definitions of elements of the story afforded them

both with new definitions of thought, grains of mortar to anchor intellectual bastions impenetrable to the invasion of insanity. But they had also built walls around their minds.

Enid took off the housecoat she had worn when she thought of the flesh. The housecoat must be unclean. She put it in the shower and turned on the water. Then she walked naked to the washing machine and started to get in it. She caught herself and giggled at her absentmindedness and set all aright by going back to the shower and donning her housecoat and getting well-bathed with it on.

Then she got the body of the cat out of the closet and walked into the woods and threw it in a ditch. She wrapped the cat's heart in a Baggie and wrapped that in aluminum foil and put it in the freezer.

It was three-thirty on Saturday afternoon and Pete would soon be riding home on his Suzuki.

Poor Pete. Poor Adair. They were Enid's loves. But there were two things wrong. Pete was inarticulate, and Adair was Enid's twin brother.

Just before Joey Murdock closed his hand around the fly to crush it, a cold viper of thought seized him by the heart.

If the fly could kill his father, it could kill him too.

He jerked his hand away and stood up to catch his breath and think. The fly wallowed on the ground in the crook of his dead father's arm. Joey could feel his heart pounding in anger and terror.

You can kill a fly, Joey, you've done it before. But this fly is poisonous. Don't let it get away, Joey, it killed Dad.

"You basset, you sumbitch basset." Joey lifted his foot and brought his heel down hard on the fly again and again until the fly was crushed and buried deep in a small pit. Then Joey looked at his father and began to cry again.

"Oh, Dad, oh, Dad, I killed it. Everything's okay now. Wake up now, Dad. Oh, please, wake up . . ."

Joey sat by his father and patted the dead chest and put his arm over the dead shoulder and waited for soldiers or somebody to come and make everything all right.

* * *

Pete Bilyeux was a resentful man who didn't know quite who or what to blame for the things he resented. So he resorted to the stratagem of forgetting his resentments, much as you would take a repugnant cheese given you by a dear friend on your birthday and tuck it away in the refrigerator until it became moldy and had to be thrown out.

Early in life he learned he was never going to be good at expressing himself. He had difficulty writing coherent sentences, and half the things he tried to say, especially in his adolescence, came out the opposite of what he meant. He still often inverted his words and stammered. So he stopped trying to be understood. He resented this very much because he was not a stupid person.

He resented his father, whom he had deeply loved, for getting killed in the line of duty in a high-speed chase on the turnpike just when Pete needed him most. He resented the trainee who had goofed and caused Pete to flunk the eye exam for the state police. He resented the red tape he had to go through to get re-tested because he thought he might have expected better from his father's old outfit. He resented getting drafted before he could take the exam again.

And he resented the ghoulish phantasmagoria of his year as a military policeman in Vietnam. He could not understand why the land he loved had turned his buddies into junkies who shot up a lot of attractive peasants who were bent on destroying one another without outside assistance. Most of all, he resented himself for standing by impotently when the little man was summarily executed in Saigon. This invaded his dreams still.

But Pete saw no point in cherishing his resentments, so he tucked them away and played the role of stolid fellow.

Yet he had a secret life, a life of poet without pen. If he could not express, then he would ingest. He would observe and take it in with unabated greed: sight, sound, scent, taste, touch, concepts and crossword puzzles, insights and jokes, absorptions epic and tiny from the idea of infinity to the discomfiture of a fat man stooping to tie his shoelace. In the solitude of his soul, Pete Bilyeux sat in a corner of the Dublin pub of life and was amused.

He did much reading but disparaged most modern fiction as too fictitious. He believed in Samuel Johnson's observation that "books without the knowledge of life are useless." He enjoyed Kafka, which he regarded as high comedy. He delighted in the books of James Joyce, which he actually understood. And he gloried in Shakespeare, perhaps partly because quoting the poetry was one of the two occasions when he could be sure he would not stammer. Contentment to him was an evening with McSorley's Cream Ale, a good book or the public television channel, and Enid.

He loved Enid more than anything and worried about her more than anything.

When Pete went into the kitchen from the garage, he knew that Enid had got another letter from Adair. There was water all over the floor of the laundry area, no food cooking, and no Enid.

"Hi, hon," he called. "H-hon, where are you?"

There was no answer. Pete went into the living room and found Enid sitting in her chair staring at the stone pre-Columbian god on the mantelpiece. No doubt Adair was sitting around in Mexico staring at the twin of this same silly idol. They each had identical ones. Sometimes Pete wondered if they were telepathic. How had they ever got hooked on that bullshit? Quetzalcoatl, indeed.

"Oh, hi, honey," Enid said. "I'm sorry. Enid's just having another one of her lost-in-the-clouds-of-contemplation days."

They kissed.

"That's okay, hon. W-want me to help cook? I got some onions at the farm stand," Pete said, giving her the bag.

"Onions?" Enid said, and looked in the bag. Laughter brought her out of her mood. "Tomatoes, you mean, you silly aphasic darling." She laughed again.

Pete was always getting words mixed up like that. But, what the hell, both onions and tomatoes were for chopping.

"Did you take your medicine today, hon?"

"Yes, dear, Enid took her medicine like a good girl.

Enid also took her pill," she said with a twinkle that let Pete know he could expect a pleasant evening.

They made supper and ate and enjoyed a typically one-sided conversation. Later, Pete opened a bottle of Mc-Sorley's and Enid sipped burgundy and they sat and watched public television.

The last show was about evolution, and this particular weekly segment dealt with insects. "If the birth of the world were to have occurred on a January first," the narrator concluded, "then the insect had arrived by November. The dinosaur died out by Christmas and man came along about midnight on December thirty-first. In the thousands of years of human time, man has driven many creatures to extinction. Gone forever are the great auk, the passenger pigeon. In jeopardy are many whales, falcons, condors, eagles, great cats, elephants—and, of course, man himself. Yet in these few geological minutes—for all man's ruthless efficacy in dealing with his prey and pests—not a single species of insect has met extinction at human hands. Good night until next week."

"Hmm," Pete mumbled, and turned off the TV.

"Strange, isn't it?" Enid said. "Quetzalcoatl said that even flies can be repositories of evil. Certainly all those nasty bugs do what we consider evil to the others as well as us. The spider eats the fly. The praying mantis eats practically every insect, not to mention her husband," she said with a clever wink. "Think of it. In the blades of the grass you mow lie tiny creatures with monstrous pincers, hideous arms, crushing jaws, stinging tails, what have you, all hell-bent on doing evil to the others. It's Armageddon amid the dandelions."

"Hmm. That's a good, uh, a good l-line. You ought to write it down," Pete said.

"I have," Enid said.

Pete chuckled and got up and turned Quetzalcoatl's face to the wall and looked at Enid.

She laughed and gave him her sexy look.

They went to bed and Enid was all over him, wild, sensuous, artfully calling forth her repertoire of tricks.

Everything was fine until morning.

* * *

Joey Murdock had picked up his father's floppy old fishing hat to swat at the flies that hovered over him and lit and walked on his dead father. They even tried to get into his dad's ears and nose and mouth.

Joey killed them. He would not suffer them to land on him or his father. *Whack*. They would be dead or scared away if they tried.

But there were so many of them. They darted and buzzed and got into everything. They even walked upside down on fishing poles. And they weren't afraid.

Joey waited and waited for the soldiers to come and rescue his father and him as they always did on TV. But they didn't come and Joey's head hurt from all his feelings and he was hungry and thirsty and tired.

Once when it got too hot he went down to the creek and drank from the black pool. It was then that a fly landed on the nape of his neck and Joey screamed and slapped at it and nearly choked with his face in the water.

Joey began to worry that nobody would come. Maybe he should go home and tell Mom what happened. He hoped she wouldn't be mad at him and give him a spanking. He couldn't think of anything he had done wrong, but he felt that way a lot when things he did turned out wrong and he got spanked. Maybe he should walk back to the car. He thought he remembered the way. He could wait by the car for a policeman. Or he could just walk home along the road.

But he would have to leave Dad alone, and the flies would keep killing Dad again and again. No, Joey couldn't let that happen. He would stay with his dad.

The air grew cooler and the day grew darker and Joey began to cry as he fought off the flies. He yelled at them so much he could feel his throat getting sore. He had called to all the birds who came by and asked them to take messages and some of them chirped and said they would.

But still the soldiers didn't come and it was getting dark. Once, Joey felt the pull of drowsy eyelids and let his eyes close.

A fly landed on his face and bit him and he screamed and knew he was lucky the fly had not bitten him hard enough to kill him too. He would have to get out from under the flies. He would have to spend the night in some shelter. He could now barely see.

He stumbled to his feet and looked for a place where something would be over his head. Then he found it. That bunch of bushes his dad had called the wild rhododingdongs.

Joey crawled deep inside the thicket and covered his face with his jacket and put his hands in his pockets and went to sleep.

He slept untroubled by dreams until he felt himself rolling in the night to keep warm. Where was Dad? Where was Mom? Where were Amy and Emily?

Suddenly there came a loud and hideous sound. A ghost with a voice like an awful man was howling in the distance. Joey leapt to his feet and rubbed his eyes. He could feel his heart troubling the walls of his chest. Part of the moon was out and he was surrounded by shadows and phantoms of huge and ghastly mien.

The sound came again. Once he thought he heard the ghost bawl his dad's name and his own.

He feared he would be next to die and he ran into this Saturday's monstrous night calling for his father and mother.

The bodies were taken to County Hospital in Elmsford for routine autopsies. Old Doc Dimoch knew it was heart failure for both. It was a sad Sunday morning for the doctor. He had known old Mrs. Peterson for years, had gone to school with her, had grown up with her, and some old-timers say may have had even more to do with her than that. Dr. Dimoch got the call about eight o'clock that morning from Mrs. Peterson's oldest son, with whose family she had lived. The doctor told them to give her mouth-to-mouth and push on her chest, but they knew she was dead. Doc Dimoch got there in five minutes, and sure enough, the poor old dear had been gone at least since sunup.

Stacey Riley was different. As soon as the doctor got home from the Petersons, his wife told him to get to the Rileys' house; their baby might be dead.

She was, and had been for a half-hour or so. The Rileys were black people. The father owned the most successful garage in Thomas Valley, and it had taken him and his wife years to conceive Stacey and she was their first and now she was dead at the age of one. Mr. and Mrs. Riley were quiet and sat in a chair together in the baby's room holding the limp little girl with a crimson ribbon in her hair. The only sounds were of throats fighting to choke back sobs. They were hard-working people, now with hard-bitten mouths. They looked like the pictures you see of parents holding children killed in war. Doc Dimoch suspected the worst and most insidious: crib death— fortunately rare, and rarer yet in girls. He explained it as best he could to the Rileys and knew it would be wise if he visited them a few times again because he knew all parents blame themselves unnecessarily for this mysteri- ous murderer of infants. The doctor wrapped Stacey in a blanket and took the tiny bundle to Elmsford. He knew the sooner she was out of the house, the easier for the parents. As the front door closed he could feel the hearts of the Rileys leaking in great hot gushes, and he heard them begin to moan behind the door. He would not send either family a bill.

The autopsies confirmed that Mrs. Peterson and little Stacey had died of cardiac arrest. The former probably due to the complications of old age, the latter no doubt due to the indefinable Sudden Infant Death Syndrome (SIDS). There was no pathological reason for the deaths other than heart failure. Nor had there been any pulmo- nary involvement. Both had died in adequately ventilated rooms, sleeping near open windows.

Debbie Winegarden thought it might be now or never. You can't stay a virgin all your life. Reed Hamilton was after her you-know-what, and if he didn't get it, so long, Reed, that's what. Reed was gorgeous. The most gor- geous boy she'd ever known. Not a boy, really, more a man. Long, soft blond hair tumbling around a chiseled face with azure eyes at once knowing, merry, and hurt.

Debbie had gone through her junior year still a virgin and had never heard the last of it from her friends.

But until now she had never had a boyfriend who was truly interested in her as a person. Some clumsy kisses and clutches in movie theaters and drive-ins and they never called again.

Debbie slipped into her mother's room and touched some droplets of My Sin on her neck, arms, armpits, and the insides of her thighs. The rest of the family was at church, but Debbie had pleaded a headache in order to keep her rendezvous with Reed. The last touch of perfume did not arouse her as touching near there usually did. Instead, it made her tremble and feel cold. She looked at herself before her mother's full-length mirror and was disgusted. Damned fat tummy bulging over the top of her panties. Damned fat thighs. Damned fat arms. Damned zits. She covered them with makeup. Why couldn't she be sixteen and svelte like other girls? But maybe it was just baby fat. Her mother said so.

Still, Debbie had a pretty face and nice breasts. She looked in the mirror to smile the smile Reed called her chipmunk smile, and remembered to brush her teeth.

She wasn't sure she could do it. The closer she came, the less sexy she felt, the more scared. She wasn't ready. Or was she?

Besides, Reed could go all the way with any girl he wanted, and had with a great many. This was well-known. She should be different for Reed, not just any old slut. But what if he lost interest? Debbie had been shocked to hear Reed had recently gone out with that skinny Janet Forman while he was supposed to be hers.

The horn honked and Debbie went down and got into Reed's black TransAm with a golden eagle on its hood.

Reed lit cigarettes for both and let the tires peel and knew precisely what he would do.

The hard part would be to seem sad and serious because he was happy as a tomcat with a baby bird that had just fallen from a tree. Already he could feel himself stiff. Number ten, number ten, his thoughts sang to himself. Nobody in the county had ever scored ten virgins by senior year. She may be a little on the dumpy side, but what the hell, there weren't that many eligible virgins left.

God, but it felt powerful to screw a virgin. Make 'em come and they'll do anything for you.

"Where are we going, honey?" Debbie asked.

"Oh . . ." Reed said. "Oh, I don't know. I just want to get out. I feel trapped."

"What's wrong?" Debbie had noticed that Reed didn't call her sweets as he usually did.

"I'll tell you later."

Reed stopped the car at a wide spot in the Elmsford Road on the hill overlooking Owl Creek. "Let's get out," he said, looking at her with those terribly hurt blue eyes.

"Okay, honey." Debbie knew from the hurt look that she was truly different, and she felt so sorry for Reed.

"Let's go for a walk, Debbie. I . . . I think it's time we had a private conversation."

Reed got a blanket from the back seat and tucked it under his arm and they walked up the hill along a path that led through dense woods. Reed didn't hold Debbie's hand. She could feel her fears rich with adrenaline.

"Reed, what is wrong?"

Reed spread the blanket in the shadow of a maple. He lit cigarettes for them and they sat and Reed smoked and looked at the sky in his best imitation of James Dean. A hot Sunday noon, alone under a clear sky, the smell of warm dust, the buzzing of flies—perfect. "I . . . I'm . . . I'm just having some thoughts about our relationship, Debbie." He turned his James Dean look to Debbie and saw it stab her in the face. Perfect. She looked like an injured calf, tears creeping into the corners of her eyes. She would be his veal. Made in the shade, laid in the shade, number ten, his thoughts chirruped.

"Is . . . is that why you went out with Janet Forman, Reed?"

The perfect response. Reed exhaled smoke slowly and sadly and turned old James loose on Debbie again. A fly landed on the blanket and Debbie absently brushed it away.

Reed shook his head no. "Janet can never mean as much to me as you, Debbie, nobody could. It's . . . it's just that we don't have a mature relationship."

Debbie felt herself flushing with heat and drained with cold at once. "A mature relationship?" she said.

Reed looked off and blew more smoke and stubbed out his cigarette. A fly lit on his sleeve and he shrugged it off. He turned his face to Debbie again. So mature. So handsome. So wise. So sad. "Men and women are two parts of the same togetherness, Debbie." He lay on his side and looked up at Debbie kneeling on the blanket wearing an expression of utter confusion. "I am a man, Debbie, you are a woman. A woman. We were meant to be together. Anything else just isn't natural. Debbie, do you know how a man feels when his mate deprives him of her love?"

Debbie felt her pulse throbbing and shook her head no.

"It's pain, Debbie, pain. Two kinds of pain. A terrible physical pain that beats and pounds deep inside your manhood. It hurts for days after your lover doesn't give you her love . . ."

"Is that what they call the blue balls?" Debbie asked, her lower lip beginning to quiver.

Reed nodded sagely. Coming right along, she was. "That's not the worst part, Debbie. The worst part is wanting to give everything to someone who doesn't want to give as much to you . . ."

"Oh, Reed . . ."

They were both beginning to perspire from the warmth of the day and the conversation.

A fly landed on Reed's ear. Debbie reached out and brushed it off and took his head between her hands. "Oh, Reed . . ." she said, and kissed him deeply with her tongue as Reed had taught her, albeit with rather too much ferocity for his taste.

They kissed long and held each other. Debbie shivered with the fear of what was to come, but she no longer felt sexless. Her heart beat wildly and she felt herself growing moist.

She let Reed take off her blouse and bra. He took off his shirt and they kissed again. He caressed her breasts professionally and teased the nipples to further erection. He blew his hot breath into her ear and licked the inside of the ear and could feel her melting.

"Oh, darling sweets, I'm aching for you, please, oh, please don't leave me in such pain . . . We need each other so much, so much, here, touch it, hold it . . ." He guided her hand to the erect penis he had deftly withdrawn.

Debbie timidly put her hand on it. She had no idea the

things got so big. How could that get inside her? But, then, a baby could come out the same place. "Will it hurt, honey?" she asked.

"No, darling sweets. Well, maybe a little at first, then it'll feel better than anything in the world. Oh, Debbie, it's going to feel so good, so good for the both of us."

Reed stood up and took the rest of his clothes off. Oh, God, Debbie thought, a marble statue come to life. Oh, this is going to be the most important day of my life. I'll be different for Reed. She took off her shoes and jeans and panties and lay back. Reed lay on top of her and they kissed again.

"Will you be careful, honey?" Debbie said.

"Oh, yes, darling sweets, so careful, careful for you . . ."

"But I don't know what to do."

"I'll show you, darling sweets, don't worry, I'll show you everything, you'll do real good . . ."

"Ouch," she said as he first began to penetrate. "Oh!"

"It'll feel better, sweets. There, now, doesn't that feel good? Oh, you're perfect, sweets, you feel just perfect and you're doing real good. There, now, doesn't that feel good?"

"Ooooh . . . ha . . . ha . . . Yes, it feels terrific . . . good . . . good . . ."

Reed maneuvered into a position of better leverage and noticed a fly alight on her sweating neck but was too busy to shoo it off.

"AAAAAH!" Debbie screamed. "AAAHH . . . aaaAAAHHH!"

Her eyes bulged and her mouth gaped and she was out of control, lurching fiercely against Reed.

Wow, Reed thought, am I ever the cocksman. A thirty-second come, and her first time at that. She's a hot one. May even keep her around for a while. God, even her arms and legs are thrashing. Just keep cool and hold off, Reed, he thought, give her a couple more comes and she's your slave.

Suddenly Debbie's body went stiff and immobile. She seemed to be choking and not getting enough breath. Jesus, Reed thought, better take it a little easy.

Debbie's eyes showed something behind them and it

was horror. Then her eyelids dropped and her body went limp.

Just as quickly Reed realized there was something terribly wrong. He grew limp and withdrew. Holy Christ, maybe it's a heart attack, or epilepsy, or something.

The fly buzzed away from Debbie's neck and circled overhead.

Reed opened her mouth. He made sure she hadn't swallowed her tongue and began blowing air into her and thumping on her chest as he had been taught in first-aid class.

"Debbie? Debbie? *Debbie! Wake up!"*

My God, my God, he thought, I may have killed her! Oh, God, don't let her die, don't let her die, I didn't want to kill her, I swear to God and to Jesus I didn't want to kill her!

The fly buzzed lazily over Reed's back.

Desperately he blew air into her lungs and shook her and pounded with the base of his fist on the blue-gray skin between her breasts.

It was no use. Minutes went by and nothing happened.

My God, Reed thought, my God, oh, my God, I've killed her! She's dead!

Reed stood up and tried to think of what to do. The fly tried to land on his shoulder and he brushed it angrily away. He knew it was too late for any kind of help. But what to do?

He threw on his clothes and tried to think. He looked at the naked forlorn body and for the first time felt something for her.

"Oh, Debbie, oh, Debbie, oh, sweets, I'm so sorry, so sorry . . ." he sobbed.

The fly landed on his shirt. He flicked it away with an irritated snap of the fingers. It fell to the ground and in Reed's jumbled emotions he furiously stamped it into the earth.

God, I've killed her, he thought, I've killed her and they're going to send me up for it. But I didn't mean to kill her, I didn't mean to. Will they understand? Jesus, what are her parents going to say? They're going to say rape and murder, that's what! Christ, I may get the chair!

Reed tried to remember whether Pennsylvania had capital punishment.

No! No! I didn't mean to kill her. I didn't want to do anything but screw her, for God's sake.

Reed thought about it for a few minutes, then rolled Debbie and her clothes in the blanket. Then he found some sandy soil and a sharp stick and he dug a grave.

When Pete Bilyeux arrived at the substation in the morning, Gary Busch was just coming off and looked glad to see him.

"You know Al Murdock and his kid, Joey, don't you, Pete?"

"Yeah, sure."

"Well, they're missing. Been out looking for them the better part of the night. Car's a Chevy wagon parked down by Owl Creek."

"I know. I, uh, saw them," Pete said.

"When was that?"

"Uh, yesterday morning about this t-time."

"Well, you've got your work cut out for you, old buddy."

Pete logged in, then put his foot into the gas of the white Pontiac patrol car and flashed the gumball on the roof. Within seven minutes he was next to the Murdock Chevy. He got out and called into the megaphone.

"Al? Al? *Al?* Joey?"

There was no answer.

He remembered the direction they had taken. The ground was still damp from Friday's rain and he soon picked up two pairs of footprints going down toward the creek.

He followed them, lost them, and found and followed them again, past the trees and the thickets of forsythia and into the patch of wild rhododendrons.

Then he saw it.

"Oh, Jesus," he said, and caught his breath and bit his lip. He ran to the bank of the black pool toward what looked like a bundle of old clothes.

It was Al. Pete reached for the wrist for a pulse, but the arm was long stiff. Two flies worried Al's nostrils and

Pete brushed them away with his broad-brimmed uniform hat.

"Joey! Joey! Jooooey!" Pete called.

There was no answer.

Pete unclipped his portable radio. "Portable one-one to KEF three-oh-three. Do you read me?" He let his thumb off the button and there was no sound but for the crackle of static and the buzzing of flies. "P-portable One-One to KEF three-oh-three. Repeat. D-do you read me?" The distance was too far for the portable and he would have to walk back to use the car radio.

He looked around the body. Two fishing poles, one a man's and one a child's, lay with tackle nearby.

The only strange thing he noticed was the deep imprint of a child's boot in the crook between the dead man's torso and his outstretched arm, as if something had been repeatedly trod into the ground.

He followed a faint pair of child's footprints into the rhododendrons and then lost them for good.

"Joey! Joooey! *Jooooey,*" he called into the megaphone.

He searched for about an hour, called some more, and had no success.

He walked the mile-and-a-half back to the car calling for Joey along the way. The sun was now white and higher and beginning to be hot. The Elmsford Road was quiet and desolate on this Sunday morning. Squirrels romped on it with impunity. Gone were the familiar whirs of engines and the *slap-slap-slap* of tires. The only sounds were the droning of flies, two of which alit on the patrol car's trunk as he approached. It was a lonely, lovely summer morning that forbode something.

He wondered where the kid could have gone.

Suddenly there was a violent clattering sound.

Bomb! Bomb! Get down!

Pete dived for the ground and held his arms over his head and waited for the blast. He had plenty of experience with this sort of thing in 'Nam, and plenty of bombs had gone off.

But not this time. Just as quickly as the clattering had started, it stopped. Pete waited a couple of minutes and got up and dusted himself off.

He looked under the car, inside it, and around it. There were no signs of anything, no trace of footprints except his own. He felt foolish as he had the time in Saigon when the man suddenly abandoned his ricksha and ran away into the crowd. Everyone else ran away too, sure that the ricksha man was an enemy who had just planted a bomb. As it turned out, to the general embarrassment, the man was only chasing a wheel that had run wild off his ricksha.

But what in hell could that noise have been?

Some crazy electronic thing in the car maybe. Pete would have to look into it later. He had an emergency on his hands.

"Car One-One to KEF three-oh-three."

"Yeah, Pete, what's happening?"

"I just found the Murdock kid, Billy, I'm sorry, I, uh, mean I just found Al M-m-murdock. He's dead and I can't find the kid."

"He's dead? What happened, Pete?"

"Beats me, Billy. Looks natural like, uh, a heart attack or something . . . Hey, uh, Billy?"

"Yeah?"

"Better, uh, phone and see if the kid could have wandered home. Don't, uh, tell the mother. No I mean, uh, jjjjust tell the mother we're only checking in. No use scaring her. She'll tell you if the kid came home. Then you can, uh, send someone around to break the news in person."

"I hear you, Pete. Good thinking. Stand by."

A couple of minutes later Billy called back to say that as far as Mrs. Murdock knew both of them were still missing.

"Okay, Billy, l-let's see if we can get Charlie Sevenpines over here as quick as we can."

Charlie Sevenpines was an Indian often used by the police for his skills in tracking. Pete and he had twice found lost children together.

Billy called back. "I just called Charlie's wife, Pete. Are you ready for this?"

"What?"

"He's been out in Arizona acting in a Mazola Corn Oil

commercial. The missus says he's flying into Philly tonight.''

"Shit. Let's see if we can, uh, get him out here in the
morning. Guess you'd better, uh, call Harrisburg for
choppers.''

"Right. I'm going to have to get the old man's ass out
of the sack to get permission.''

"Let's do it.''

It was not until midafternoon that state police helicopters arrived and began searching. Photographs were taken
and Al's body was brought out and taken to County Hospital for an autopsy. Pete searched all day, by foot and
later by car along the back roads, and could not find Joey.
At four o'clock Pete drove to the substation so his relief
could have the car. Pete would continue looking for Joey
on his Suzuki until it grew dark.

Billy Gianotti was walking out of the station with his
perpetual cigar clamped in his jaws. He stopped when he
saw Pete pull in.

"Pete, looks like we've got us another body.''

4

Reed Hamilton went home and lay down on his bed to
think. He was glad no one else was in the house.

He knew if he just thought carefully about it all, it
would be all right. Did I do the right thing? Sure. I did
everything I could to save her life. Should I have gone to
get help? Hell, it was too late already. She had a heart
attack and nothing would help. But isn't it unusual for a
sixteen-year-old girl to have a heart attack? Sure, but a
few years ago a senior boy died of a heart attack while
playing basketball, and everyone knew Angie Markert
had a bad heart and had to take medicine and there was
no messing around with her. Was it right to bury Debbie

like that and not tell anyone? Hell, to tell anyone would be suicide. They'd say it was rape and murder.

And that is what they did say.

When Reed heard the helicopters he was surprised they were searching so soon and he knew he had only minutes to get away.

Pete Bilyeux was prepared for the worst when he heard another body had been found. He was sure it was Joey that Billy Gianotti meant, and was both relieved and shocked to hear it was someone else.

"Looks like a sex murder," Billy said. "The choppers out looking for the Murdock kid spotted the grave. State police sent some guys to dig and found her wrapped up naked in a blanket. Not a mark on her. Probably strangled. Couldn't have happened longer than a few hours ago. None of our guys have gone up yet to identify her. Want to go with me, Pete?"

"Yeah, I guess I should."

They rode in Billy's personal pickup truck. Billy would file to be reimbursed for the mileage, and for comp time.

"Any s-s-suspects?" Pete said.

"Nope. You know, Pete, we might have a maniac out there."

"Jesus."

Pete tried to remember the last homicide in Thomas Valley. Indeed, nothing like it had happened in forty years.

Some state troopers were taking casts of tire prints where Reed had stopped the car, and of footprints leading up the path. Two pairs of prints were pointed uphill, and one pair pointed down. It was apparent to Pete that they had walked side-by-side and that the victim's footprints were regular and showed no sign of physical duress.

"Hey, Pete, where you going?" Billy asked when they reached the spot, gesturing to where troopers were photographing the body.

Pete motioned for Billy to wait, and followed the prints to the maple tree. He noticed the disturbances on the wild grasses and dead leaves left by the blanket and the weight of the two bodies. He noticed the cigarettes that

had been stubbed out. Marlboro, not marijuana. He saw
that the smaller footprints had never walked away but that
the larger ones had been walking all around the place.
His skin prickled and he wasn't sure why when he discovered the deep print of a large foot in the ground much
as the print he took to have been that of Joey Murdock.
He would find out if the troopers had made a cast of it,
and that done, he would come back and dig. A fly buzzed
over Pete's head and he wafted it away. Then he followed
the path made by the blanket as it had been dragged to
the grave.

The body lay fully covered in the blanket. Introductions were made among the deputies and the troopers and
they bantered in police argot with the false heartiness of
uneasy boys urinating in the snow of a cold and moonlit
night.

"D-did you guys dust that stick for prints?" Pete said,
pointing to a sturdy sharp stick lying nearby.

"Hell, no," said a trooper sergeant. "What do you
think we dug her out with?"

Wonderful, Pete thought. So why do so many murder-
ers get away? Well.

"Okay. There's a hell of a deep f-f-footprint up by that
maple tree. I'd like to, uh, fool with it after you guys
have got a cast. Did you get one?"

The troopers looked at one another and shrugged.

"Uh, do you mind?" Pete asked.

"No. Hell, why not?" the sergeant said, and nodded
for a man to do it.

A fly lit on the sergeant's nose and he slapped irritably
at it and was more irritated when he struck his own face.
The fly flew away.

"Kind of like to try to identify her, boys," Billy said.

"Sure," the sergeant said, and pulled back the blanket.

Pitiful, Pete thought, she looked so pitiful. He had seen
many dead children and youngsters in Vietnam and had
always tried to steel himself from the feeling and had
always failed. He knew her first name was Debbie, Debbie Somethingorother with several syllables in a last name
that would come to him in a minute or two. Debbie the

sweet little girl, Debbie of the sparkling eyes, Debbie now with dirt clinging to her eyelids.

"I don't know her, Pete," Billy aid. "I mean, I seen her but I don't know her name."

"I do. It's D-D-Debbie, uh, Beergarden, no, Winegarden, I mean . . . Let's have a look at her."

Pete took off the blanket and examined the body with as much professional disinterest as he could muster. Skin cool but not cold, blue-gray in color. Limbs growing stiff but still pliable. Mouth parted and full of dirt, tongue slightly distended.

Pete pulled back the eyelids. The eyes were widely dilated. Perhaps it was drugs.

There were a few zits on the chin and neck and the usual rash at the base of the buttocks. Everyone seems to have this rash. Now why is that, I wonder? Pete thought.

He felt over her head and smoothed her hair as he did it. No palpable cranial damage. Not a drop of blood anywhere. No bruises. No marks of hands or rope or anything on the neck. None of the distended eyeballs or skin hemorrhaging that tell of strangulation. No observable knife wounds. Certainly no bullet exit wounds and probably no entry wounds. A girl in apparent good health had walked willingly with someone, probably a boy, from a car to a secluded spot where they both lay on a blanket and where the girl died—most likely of natural causes or some kind of toxicity, quite possibly drug-related. Pete would be interested in seeing the autopsy report.

"Well, Sherlock, what's the score?" the state-police sergeant asked.

"Jesus, will you look at the size of those jugs," another trooper said as Pete lay Debbie's body on her back. Pete grimaced into the ground and quickly covered Debbie's corpse with the dirty blanket. Death should not be companion to humiliation.

"I don't, uh, think that, uh, this girl was m-murdered."

"You gotta be out of your fucking mind," the sergeant said.

"Let's get her autopsied ASAP," Pete said. "Did you finish with that cast by the maple tree?"

"Yeah."

"Thanks a lot, uh, guys," Pete said. "See you later. Oh, would you mind do me one more thing, one, uh, more, okay?"

"Right, Sherlock, it's your turf."

"Would you radio the sssubstation desk and have them phone my wife and tell them I'll be, uh, late, and ask them to priest the phone to Father Fierro at Holy Name—Debbie was a Catholic—and he should meet me at the substation ASAP, okay?"

"Gotcha, Sherlock."

"Thanks, guys. We, uh, going back to work with those choppers? We got a lost kid to find, you know."

"Right, Sherlock."

"L-let me know when I can do something for you guys, okay?" Pete hoped the sarcasm would sink in. He was used to their sort of condescension from childhood. He went back with Billy to the maple tree and began to dig with his fingers in the deep footprint.

Flies, many of them, buzzed loudly and lazily and drunkenly in the shade of the maple. Pete felt sweat soak the armpits of his uniform shirt and trickle down the back of his neck from beneath his hairline. Flies circled his head.

"Sh-shoo, you bastards," he told them.

Joey had run and tripped and fallen and had got up and run and tripped many times and ran on, haunted by the shrieking banshee voice in the night.

He ran through copses and thickets and patches of stinging brambles that tore at his clothing and at his face and made him taste his own salt blood. He clawed his way over rocks, ran on pebbles and over mud and hardpan earth. He ran until the night was silent again but for the call of night birds, the chirruping of crickets, and the baying of distant animals.

The Sunday sun with timid crimson fingers began its creep over an eastern hill and Joey was tired, very tired and very hungry. He looked for a place to rest and found it in a burrow in the side of a hill where the flies, which were soon to come, could not attack him from above. The floor of the burrow was littered with the tiny bones of small animals. Joey covered himself with his jacket and went back to sleep and dreamed a child's nightmares of death.

In a fearful rush, Reed packed his duffel with everything he could think he might want, ever.

Chuggachuggachugga, flapflapflap, went the helicopters in the distance coming closer to where Reed knew they ought to come.

He slipped into his father's room and found the wallet and left it with only three dollars.

Reed eased the black TransAm with gold eagle on hood down the gravel driveway. At the paved road he downshifted to first and let the clutch out softly to make less noise. Then he shifted directly into third to quiet tire squeal and so the *whumpawhumpa* of the trick exhaust would be less audible. He had trained himself well in evasion, having evaded many, but not all, policemen. He soothed the TransAm down Allen Street, past Third Street, past Fourth Street, past the OK Garage, and down Fremont Street with eyes spellbound on the rearview mirror and with ears fascinated with the helicopter engines overhead.

When he reached the ramps of the interstate, he paused. Next right, Youngstown; Next left, New York, read the signs.

Youngstown would be about 150 miles, just across the Ohio line. New York, well, that would be about 175 miles to the New Jersey line, then another 80 miles or so into the big dirty city, where Reed would be less likely to attract attention. The cops sleep on the job there, he had heard. The gas gauge read five-eighths full.

Yes, Reed would go to New York, where he wouldn't be noticed. He babied the TransAm onto the interstate in second gear and had a good look around before the car was on the cam. Stealth begone. Satisfied of a clear shot, he pressed his foot down hard on the accelerator, heard the sucking of air into the carburetor, felt the rumble of the supertuned V-8 engine and its exhaust, sensed his body thrust backward, and watched the tachometer needle leap toward the red line. He shifted to third and watched the tach needle climb again and the speedo nee-

dle reach the peg. He developed a plan. He would race
the interstate for a half-hour or so, then get off and cruise
the back roads until he crossed into Jersey. By then it
would be getting dark and he would get back on the interstate for a straight shot through Jersey to the George
Washington Bridge and freedom.

Pete Bilyeux dug carefully in the deep footprint by the
maple tree and found nothing.

Father Fierro owned the same old Mercedes diesel for
the better part of twenty years and loved every cubic cen-
timeter of its metallic soul. It was the best car he had
since his nineteen-year-old Studebaker had collapsed.

He listened to what Pete told him on the way to the
Winegarden house and clucked and make deprecating
sounds and crossed himself and murmured prayers.

"Oh, God, oh, God, thy hand works in strange ways,
strange ways . . ." Pete heard him say, and reflected on
it.

The priest asked the Winegardens to send the younger
children out of the room. Pete knew the parents guessed
why the pair had come. The tension charged the room.
He could feel their hearts pall and the air fill with an
electric plasma as just before a thunderstorm..

Father Fierro told them that Debbie had been taken to
the bosom of Jesus, and a little of how she had been
found.

Mrs. Winegarden's face paled and Mr. Winegarden's
flushed when they heard of the shallow grave.

"You . . . you mean she was *murdered?*" Mrs. Winegarden said.

"Uh, not, uh, necessarily," Pete said. "Parb-probably
not, in fact. Mr. and Mrs. Winegarden, I, I, uh, have to
ask some painful questions. Okay?"

"Anything that will help, Deputy," Mrs. Winegarden
sobbed.

"Well, uh, well, will you tell me if Debbie had ever
used drugs, I m-m-mean any kind of drugs, like medicines or, uh, frivolous drugs even?"

Both parents shook their heads no and Pete could feel
their indignation. Well, they could be wrong.

"Did she have a boyfriend?" Pete asked.

"No," Mr. Winegarden said, with a touch of pride in the innocence of his offspring.

"Well . . . well," Mrs. Winegarden said, "Debbie had talked of seeing a young man named Reed Hamilton . . ." She broke into tears.

"May I telephone, I, uh, mean may I use your telephone?"

They nodded yes. Pete looked at Father Fierro as though to nudge him and walked into the kitchen trying to keep the fall of his heavy boots on oak and linoleum from sounding too ominous to the Winegardens and their sequestered younger children.

Vince Egert was manning the desk and it was agreed to find Reed Hamilton with all speed. An all-points bulletin would be circulated if necessary.

"V-Vinnie, uh, if you do that, be sure to make it clear that he's not likely to be armed. I don't dangerous—I mean, I don't think he's dangerous. We don't want him to get hurt, okay?" Pete had known Reed from the Police Athletic League, knew of his churlish hobby and considered him less a criminal than a cad.

"Right, Pete, we'll get the word out," Egert said.

Mr. Winegarden was loading a Winchester semi-automatic shotgun when Pete slipped back into the room.

Pete smiled with closed mouth and looked into the man's wounded eyes.

"Mr. Winegarden, please put that thing away. Please. It's not going to do anybody any good and an innocent person might be hurt. Did you know that more people are killed by guns accidentally than deliberately?" Pete looked into the father's eyes and smiled gently, and as usual was awed by his own ability to be coherent in emergencies.

The man started to shake with the shotgun in his hands. It was a good piece, finely engraved with dogs and hunting scenes.

"Please, Mr. Winegarden. It won't bring Debbie back."

The father withdrew the cartridges from the gun and locked it up and sat down with his face in his hands and wept.

The four knelt and said prayers. Then Pete and the

priest left them with the awful task of explaining it to the
younger children and making the arrangements and living
with it for the rest of their lives.

Father Fierro interrupted the silence on the drive back
to the substation. Night had fallen. "Haven't seen much
of you and the missus at Mass lately, Pete."

"Well, uh, well, uh, you know pppolice work, Father,
you know how it is . . ."

"Is there anything wrong between you and the missus?"

"No."

"Are you sure, Pete?"

"No. I mean, yes, there's not something wrong. I don't
think so . . ."

"Well, let me know if I can help. I'm not far away,
Pete."

"Thanks."

They rode on through the blackness. Summer ground
fogs lay in the dips and gullies and shied from the nose
of the old Mercedes and licked its iron flanks.

The fluorescent exterior lights of the substation shone
a mile away. Pete shivered in the night chill and broke
the silence without quite knowing why.

"Father, do you know about exorcisms?"

"I'm only a country priest."

"Sorry," Pete said.

"Is there something you want exorcised?"

Four people had died suddenly in twenty-four hours in
Thomas Valley, a place in which four deaths a year was
about average. A little boy was lost in the night. And
Enid was going mad.

Pete thought about the priest's question. "Yes," Pete
said. "Can you exorcise a T-toltec god or two?"

The priest looked at Pete rather strangely.

It was about ten o'clock on Sunday night when Father
Fierro dropped Pete at the substation.

Vince Egert was flailing at the desk handling telephone
calls and the radio as a disc jockey who had accidentally
played an X-rated record on the Sunday sermon show.

"No, Mayor, no, sir," Vinnie was saying. "I'm sorry
we can't find the sheriff. Sunday is his bowling league
night and—" Vinnie was interrupted and Pete could hear

the mayor cursing through the receiver. "Yes, Mayor . . . yes, sir . . . yes, we'll have him call you as soon as we get hold of him . . ."

Three more people had died in Thomas Valley and suddenly the world was turning inside out.

Reed Hamilton slipped off the interstate as soon as it crossed the west fork of the Susquehanna River. He had gone farther than planned, but the road was clear and he was more than two counties and seventy-five miles from Thomas Valley.

He slunk along the back roads through towns with names like Washingtonville, Jerseytown, and Milville. It was in Milville that he caught sight of the first police car, a local yokel parked off the road. The muscles of the back of Reed's neck tensed as though awaiting the fall of a blade. He cruised by at thirty-three miles per hour in a thirty-five zone and he could feel the cop's eyes on him.

He had been traveling northeast. At the next town he turned off onto a lesser county road and made due east. He would do anything to avoid a big town until New York. So he followed a course described by the hind leg of a dog and found himself pulling into a town with the improbable name of Normal as the sun set.

The gauge read a little more than a quarter tankful of gasoline, and Reed calculated that just might get him across the Delaware River into New Jersey. Then he thought of what a disaster it would be if he ran out of gas.

The humming of flies and Halloween dreams wakened Joey in the afternoon. He was protected in his burrow but he was hungry and thirsty and he had to get home.

There were bushes and low-lying trees at the bottom of a vale in front of him. They would protect him from the flies overhead. That's where he would walk.

He trudged slowly, craning his neck in all directions to look out for flies. This wood was a nice place, dark and bosky and cool with branches just over his head. It was his size and he walked easily in it even if his feet were hurting.

Suddenly he heard it and his skin grew cold and his

chest felt robbed of breath. A fly, a big one, was coming
up from behind. He turned to face it and heard more big
flies. He sat down to fight them to the end, but he could
not see them. The sound of one of the big flies grew
louder.

Then it became distorted. It was not a fly It made a
noise like an electric saw or a hurt car or something. It
was a machine and it was coming closer and it was going
to be on top of him!

He looked up and saw through the trees the shadow of
a giant bird of prey slithering by overhead. The clatter it
made was thunderous and a hot wind beat down from it
onto Joey.

Then the thing went away, but not far away. It rattled
around in circles in the sky.

Joey decided to go look at it. It was going farther away
now and he would have time to hide if the thing threatened him. He crept to the edge of the line of trees and
bushes.

A fly landed on Joey's arm and he screamed and killed
it with his dad's hat and ran back into his jungle.

He walked for a long time through the jungle and gave
messages to birds, squirrels, a raccoon, a cute little
skunk, and a furry thing that looked like a fat squirrel
without a tail.

Then the big noise came back.

It was moving fast up the little valley of Joey's jungle.
He waited for the thing to go by and then ran to the edge
of the jungle to see it.

It was a helicopter! A helicopter just like on TV! Joey
didn't know helicopters made so much noise. It was much
more noise than they made on TV. He could see men in
the helicopter. Maybe they were the soldiers come to rescue him and Dad.

Joey ran into the open and waved his dad's hat at the
helicopter and jumped up and down. He saw the big
round-and-round thing on the helicopter's top and the little round-and-round thing on the helicopter's dragonfly
tail, which was pointed in Joey's direction. Joey waved
and jumped and yelled at the helicopter, but it went away.

The helicopter didn't care about Dad and Joey. Nobody

cared about Dad and Joey. Dad and Joey would have to look out for themselves in their separate ways.

This made Joey feel hurt and angry, but it also made him feel better about himself. He could take care of himself, all right, even if he was hungry. He drank at a small brook and got up and felt better and walked in the dark secret jungle that few flies knew about.

The jungle went in its valley up a hill and got smaller as it rose. Then in the gloom of dusk Joey saw a strange jagged shape. The wheels were torn and what remained of the tires showed big ugly brown strings. But it was a car, sure enough. Joey took a stick and poked inside the tangle of old springs and dirty padding and jumbled seats and broken glass. He was worried that a snake or a spider or some bad animal might be in it, but no such things were.

Still, Joey didn't like the looks of the inside of the rusty old car. There were things in it that could cut him, and besides, it would be easy for a fly to get inside.

So Joey poked his stick in the small crawling space under the car for a long time. There did not seem to be anything bad there. Then he thought he heard a fly buzzing. He couldn't be sure. So he crawled under the car and hugged himself and went to sleep.

When Enid got the call that Pete would be late, she had just put the casserole in the oven and timed it. She was crestfallen, if not surprised. Things like this had happened before. Pete was a policeman and serious about his work, and Enid admired him for that, usually.

But it had been such a lovely day. She felt better than she had in years. She had taken her pad and her pencils and walked through the woods and had felt the power of the sun tease her shoulders. She liked the way her hair felt clean and light as she brushed it against the wind.

She had sat on a rock and written poems. She started with iambic pentameter for discipline. Then she started fiddling with hexameters and trochees. Then she went on with the random scansions of one of her favorites, Robinson Jeffers. She wrote through lunchtime and well past it and didn't feel hungry, enrapt as she was in what the man called—who was it?—emotion reflected in tranquillity.

When the day began to grow on, she wrote a sonnet to love that broke all the rules of sonnets, if not of love. It began with a couplet and ended in free verse. What a pity you can't earn a living as a poet in this day and age, she reflected. She and Pete deserved better than to be stuck out in the middle of nowhere with no person of any sentience to talk to. But what could an orphan expect? Maybe one day Pete would take some vacation time and they would visit New York. They would go to The Museum of Modern Art, to some of the little boutique museums, to poetry readings at the great Fifth Avenue Library, to bookstores like the Strand, Mendoza's, Shakespeare & Company, the Gotham, and Barnes & Noble, of course, of course. Still, it had been a beautiful day, a frabjous day, callooh, callay, she chortled in her joy. Enid had not wasted a feather of thought on Quetzalcoatl or Tezcatlipoca or Adair, and she had not killed a thing, not even a fly.

When she got the call that Pete would be late she turned the oven down to warm and gobbled a Valium and went to play the television game. She flipped the channels on the remote control and maneuvered the audio so she could improvise her own commercial messages. To the airline commercial she sang, "Die the fiendish skies of the blighted." To the commercial with the wretched little man exhorting people not to twit the toilet tissue, she added, "Squeeze it and get a fistful of shit." To the tampon commercial she advised the lady to "Stick it in your ear, kid."

Enid raised hell with the television on into the night until she heard the *rap-rap-rap* of the two-stroke Suzuki coming home.

Pete tried to apologize and to be sweet and sexy, but Enid thought he was stupid—no, not stupid, dumb, dumb's a better word, more apt; dumb, he can't speak. She loved the Yiddish word she had learned for it: *shtum*. She laughed inside when she thought of this word and then felt cruel and guilty.

Pete looked pale and hangdog and talked even less than usual, the *shtum*. They munched on the desiccated casserole that the *shtum* made her ruin just when things were going well. Pete sipped his McSorley's. Enid sipped her burgundy and wondered what Quetzalcoatl would think if she ripped out Pete's living heart.

Reed Hamilton had to urinate so badly he idly wondered if he could pee in the gas tank of the TransAm and give it just enough of what it needed to get to the Jersey side of the Delaware.

He had not cast water for several hours and was feeling it intimately. He squirmed on the seat and clutched and squeezed at his parts to make the pain go away and his tortured bladder hold. The last sign he saw was dim, even under the high beams, and read "New Jersey 17 miles."

At last the bridge came into view. Reed gripped his privates and downshifted to second and looked carefully for white cars. He dug in his pockets for change for the automatic toll arm and nearly urinated on the seat. The change dropped, the arm went up, and he crossed.

On the Jersey side, he stopped the car in neutral, brake on, lights off, opened the door, and let go. Oh, freedom, oh. Back in the car, the gas needle read below empty. He nursed the TransAm to the only gas station in sight. A sign beside the station read, "Last Chance for Gas at NJ Prices." Reed was appalled. The price was twenty cents a gallon less in Pennsylvania. But it was Reed's last chance. So he stood in front of his license plate and tried to avoid the eyes of the attendant as the boy filled the tank.

This kid looked at him suspiciously and Reed wondered whether he ought to hit him with something and blast out of that place. The alternative might be the electric chair.

The dials of the gas pump flipped crazily. Ten dollars came and went. Reed felt for the money he had taken from his father's wallet. Seventy-nine dollars was all he had, including his own money. Never mind, Reed thought, when I get to New York I'll sell the car to some joker for quick cash and change my name and live in Greenwich Village.

The TransAm rumbled out of the New Jersey gas station and Reed felt hungry and thirsty and tired. His en-

ergy had gone the way of his urine. He spotted the
friendly arches of a McDonald's and eased the TransAm
into a parking lot toward a spot where the lights shone
least. He backed into the spot for a quick exit.

He ordered and took his food to the car and wolfed
down two Big Macs slathered with ketchup and drank a
couple of big Cokes. The world was all right again and
his eyes felt warm and drowsy.

In the slumber between sleep and wakefulness Joey
was back in his own bed and everything was fine except
he was very hungry for breakfast. He rolled over to catch
a little more sleep and bumped his elbow on the bottom
of the old car. Then he remembered where he was and
he remembered the flies and was awake.

He peered out and saw a morning covered with ground
fog. That was good because the flies couldn't see him to
kill him. His stomach growled bitterly at itself and the
dull hunger of the last two days began to be pain. He had
seen many wild berries and fruits on his journey. He
knew some of them were poisonous but not which ones,
so he didn't eat any.

Instead, when his stomach bothered him, he would go
to find water in a brook or pond. That would make him
feel better, but not for long.

He would have to find a road or a place where people
would see him, and that meant exposing himself to flies.
He would leave his jacket over his head and make a mask
of it to see out.

He walked carefully for a long time going higher and
higher uphill as his jungle dwindled and finally gave out.
He could see farther as he got higher and the mist began
to burn away under the sun. At last he reached the top of
the hill he was climbing and could see all around for
miles. In the distance he could still hear the faint clatter
of helicopters, but he couldn't see them. He was glad he
didn't see or hear any flies.

Then he saw the house.

It was across a little valley and stood in a large meadow
atop a hill. The people in the house would take care of
Joey. They would give him something to eat. They would
call for people to come help him.

He ran into the valley and up the hill as fast as he could go until he couldn't run anymore and had to walk.

Breathless, he tramped up the hill until he could see the house.

There was something wrong with the house. The yard was littered with all kinds of junk. There was no glass in the windows and the front door hung agape by a single hinge. But maybe it had a telephone. Joey knew how to use a telephone. Dad had taught him. He would dial "O" and ask the operator for help.

The first fly he saw that day landed on Joey's arm and he swatted it away with his dad's hat and ran across the creaking boards of the porch of the house.

It was dark inside and he paused at the door to let his eyes adjust so he could find a telephone.

He walked in. Suddenly they were all over him. The house smelled like a dirty toilet and it was alive with flies, buzzing, swarming, darting. There were hundreds of them.

Joey screamed in terror and ran out. He could hear the flies dancing over him, attacking him to kill him. He could also hear a helicopter and he looked frantically around but couldn't see it. It didn't care about him anyway. Nobody cared about him except the flies, which were trying to bite Joey and kill Joey.

He ran around the house with his enemies in pursuit. He would have to find something quickly, something to get under or inside.

Then he found it.

An old refrigerator lay on its back behind the house. Trembling with the horror of the flies droning over him, Joey opened the refrigerator door and tore the racks out and clambered inside and shut the door on himself.

5

"Thou criest unto me. Who is it that uses me thus," spoke the one.

"The same, O Lord, I am forlorn," spoke the other.

"Thou mockest me. Thou art but lorn," spoke the one.

"Even so, terrible Lord, yet I pray thee for deliverance from evil thou hast vested in my land," spoke the other.

"Pray on until thy breath exhaust and know this, that I invest nothing with nothing, thou vesteth it all. Know also this, that without evil there cannot be good and without good there cannot be evil, it is the law. And without god there cannot be man, yet without man there shall be god. This, too, is the law," spoke the one.

"It is now thou who mockest me, O dread god," spoke the other. *"I know not of what thou speakest."*

"Be that as it might and perish a fool." So spoke Tezcatlipoca, the one.

Pete could feel Enid thrashing next to him on the bed. As a diver beneath dark waters gropes toward the coruscating mirror above, he emerged from the cool of sleep into a warm tide that made his eyes sting.

"Hon, uh, you all right?" he said. He touched Enid gently on her naked shoulder, and her skin was cool and moist. The room was dark and he could see nothing but the digits of the Radio Shack clock radio telling him it was the wrong time to be awake. He felt a chill when he got out from under the covers and went to shut the window from night air creeping as the exhalation of ghosts.

"Enid . . . Enid?" Pete shook her shoulder and she screamed. "Hon, what's wrong?"

"Aah! Aaa! *Aaaaaaaaaa!*"

"Enid! Enid!"

"Oh! Oh . . . oh, God . . . I'm sorry, I'm sorry . . ." Enid sat up clutching at her abdomen as though she had appendicitis. She kicked under the covers and moaned.

"Enid? Enid, what's wrong?"

Enid collapsed backward on the bed.

Pete turned on the lamp and saw her dark eyes gaping in terror. Gently he stroked her perspiring forehead. "Hon, hon, l-let me, uh, get your m-m-medicine."

"Yeah," she said, staring at the ceiling. "Yes, please, honey, Enid's having another one of her nights."

Pete stumbled into the fluorescence of the imitation marble bathroom and opened the medicine chest. Eyes still hot with unfinished sleep, he forced himself to read and repeat to himself three times the wording on the label. Satisfied he was correct, he returned to the bedroom with the appropriate dosage and water.

Enid lay prone and spread-eagled on top of the sheets, her face turned toward Pete's pillow and her eyes glimmering. The lamp cast teasing shadows along the arch of her back that disappeared in the highlight of her white buttocks and lingered again on the backs of her thighs nearly to the twin sinews standing in the crooks on the opposite side of her knees.

Pete felt himself aroused and did not want to be this night.

Enid rolled over and sat up and gulped the medicine and seemed to find instant relief. The tips of her breasts brushed against the hair on Pete's chest and then pushed themselves in against him. She held his shoulders and pressed herself to him and shuddered.

They made love and soon Enid went to a quiet sleep.

Pete tried to will himself back to sleep and then realized the folly of this and got up and got a McSorley's from the refrigerator and poured it into a glass and sat up in bed and drank. Still he could not sleep, so he went to the kitchen and poured another McSorley's. He got out the big caffè espresso machine they had got as a wedding present from Adair, and loaded it with Medaglia d'Oro, for the day that was nearly there. He would have much to do, but he must not think about it. He must nap and save his energies for the things he would have to do before dawn. He warmed some milk in a pan. Warm milk always got him to sleep. He got out two thermos bottles and filled them with hot water and capped them. He would dump them empty in the morning just before he poured in the espresso. The coffee would stay hot longer that way. He got out vitamins for both Enid and him and put them in shot glasses on the His and Hers place mats. He took a gram of Vitamin C with his milk. The back of his neck felt tense and he feared catching a cold. He would have to think about something else to get some sleep. He drank all his milk and shuffled toward bed with the rest of his McSorley's and made himself tell himself jokes about the man trying to lug the bear into the Toyota, and at last knew he'd sleep.

He was dreaming and he knew he was dreaming and he knew what the dream would be and knew he had no power to stop it.

The place of hot rain and steaming ground and bright overcast and verdure with edges and corners rotting as ancient canvas came to him again. He rode with a friend in a pulse of warm air with a hot tight thing clutching his chest. The bird that bore them pitched and yawed and heaved against invisible claws of evil. Starry dots swift as flyspecks spattered the translucent cocoon in which they rode. They flinched from the dots drowned noiseless by the cacophony of the bird screeching for salve to soothe its aching digits. His friend nudged him as if to tell a joke. His friend turned toward him and grinned and bled dark deep blood from his nose and then from his ears and then vomited blood all over.

Pete was transported to the place of execution. He could not in this sleep smell the sweet salt abattoir odor of inside blood gone outside, nor could he smell the hot rot, nor the nitrate gases, nor the rank mildew of the time that passed for winter, for Tet. Neither could he smell the garbage, nor the human filth, nor the fetid urine cast on old stone. They dragged a man to the gibbet, the guillotine, the rack, the iron maiden, the electric chair, the burning barrel, the flaming necklace, to the pit where he would be buried alive and the cross where he would be crucified upside down. There was another man with a camera there. Pete told that man he must make a picture of this. People must see and know this. Pete stood aside and looked at himself. No, he was not the man who would be killed. Or maybe he was. Stuttering Pete Bilyeux stood in olive drab and waited with the rest. The little man who became this day's victim looked like a middle-class Filipino in a tacky barong Tagalog or a faded Hawaiian aloha shirt. When they dragged him in the ARVNs, he saluted the officer in charge, who drew a pistol and pointed it at the side of the Filipino-looking man's head. The victim was enthralled with something inner and did not seem to comprehend. The officer ceremoniously cocked the pistol pointed at the man's head and smiled, also ceremoniously. Pete screamed in his mind at the man with the camera to shoot a picture. In this dream, Pete unslung his M-16, fixed the bayonet, and threw it to his shoulder. An expert marksman, never before or since had he shot anything but paper targets. The ARVNs in the place were scandalized and pointed their M-16s and M-14s and their M1911A1s, all American, at all-American Peter Bilyeux, Sergeant, MP, USAR, Roman Catholic, Blood Type O+, Serial Number 564-44-4187, of Thomas Valley, Pennsylvania—or maybe they didn't. Nothing that happened in this place was real but marijuana smoke and mildew.

Pete cocked the M-16 and brought it to bear on the officer with the pistol, a French pistol, perhaps designed by a descendant of Pete's ancestors, or perhaps it never happened. Yes, Pete rolled over in his sleep and sensed the clock radio ready to toll the day and wished it never happened. The officer grinned and chuckled to himself while the victim shuffled his feet and looked down. Pete screamed in his mind or maybe with his voice, but either way knew he was mute, calling for the cameraman to shoot first. Then they would know the truth. All would know it.

Pete tangled the sling in his left arm to steady the right arm to aim the M-16. The officer giggled at the victim, who now wobbled on his feet. Pete flipped the safety of the M-16 to OFF and the little lever to full AUTO.

"Make a decision, son, make a decision," Pete's father had told him. "Half the time you'll be right, half the time you'll be wrong. But you'll always be wrong if you don't do something."

His father had spoken his last as Pete's legs were caught . . . No! It was his father's legs that had been caught under the dash panel of the state-police car on the turnpike when the gasoline erupted on him that night. It had been a closed-coffin funeral for a man who had been real and was now burnt pork butt in a hole.

"Make a decision, son, make a decision."

The man with the camera worked away at it.

BASS. Breath-Aim-Slack-Squeeze. Pete knew well what marksmen are taught. Take a breath and hold it, aim with careful deliberation, take up the slack in your trigger and slack half your breath out, squeeze the trigger as you would an orange. You'll never know when the thing will go off and so never throw off your aim. You'll be the perfect killing machine. Pete was good at this when shooting at black dots on paper but not so good when it came to insulting the flesh of a living being.

The officer thrust the pistol against the man's temple and jerked the trigger.

The victim grimaced against the mechanical sounds of the gun. The report went off in his ear as the copper-jacketed projectile struck his skull. The victim winced in slow motion. At 13,980 inches per second the bullet bored through the best part of his brain, scattering ripples of capillaries, veins, arteries, whitish-gray tissues of lore, much as a rocket makes V-shaped injuries in the upper atmosphere. Bone and blood and brain gushed with the bullet's exit from the opposite side of the man's head and Pete descended as on a garage elevator into a pit.

The man with the camera had shot, but Pete had not.

* * *

The Farm Report came on the Radio Shack clock radio and talked of gypsy moths. Pete would have to get up and find Joey Murdock.

Into the kitchen he shuffled again and was furious at the doctors. Pete was usually angry on first waking but never let anyone feel what he felt, least of all Enid.

"Why don't you, uh, d-d-do something for her instead of just prescribing all those drugs?" he had said to one doctor.

"The medicine helps her over the rough times."

"But, uh, maybe she wouldn't have such rough times if you could help her straighten things out?"

"Why don't you help her?" the doctor said.

"Jjjjesus. I-I'm trying," Pete said.

"Maybe that's the problem," the doctor said, meaning maybe you're the problem, Pete.

Well, maybe I am and maybe I'm not, Pete thought. I don't think I am. Quite the contrary. But I suppose you could make a case for it. Anything can be decided subjectively and justified objectively. And even if I am the problem, I think it would be the same with any other. Any other except Adair, which would make matters horribly worse. He wondered if she ever told the doctors about Adair. He doubted it. She had never told him, even though he knew. He couldn't help, it was written all over her. Yes, it hurt Pete a little, especially because of the innocent friendship of the three before the year of accidents came. But it was all over between Enid and Adair before she and Pete were married. Should Pete have told the doctors? No. It didn't sit right with him.

Pete started the espresso machine and hated this morning more than most—with good cause, as it turned out.

He had to go to the bathroom while the coffee was working and that meant he had to pass the stone Quetzalcoatl on the mantel.

He gave it the finger.

Thus was the gauntlet cast that would join the battle of the gods over Thomas Valley, Pennsylvania, a place where you could feel safe even from a nuclear war.

The mayor of Thomas Valley, one Warren P. Otis, went to bed on the Friday night before all this happened in the

third year of his four-year term. He resolved never to hold
public office again.

The people who had elected him were all right, mostly.
But the people who telephoned him were mostly crazy.
And the town council, well . . . Maybe he could sometimes help the people who telephoned him. But no one
could help the town council. Not even God, and certainly
not Mayor Warren P. Otis.

Then there was the latest craze, the nonsense about the
animals. For weeks people had been telling him about
their missing pets, chiefly cats. Hell, cats wander off, he
thought. His own cat did with predictable regularity. Then
just today he got a call from Old Lady Peterson. It seemed
her dachshund had dropped dead before her eyes, and she
had voted for Warren Otis and wanted to know what he
planned to do about this.

For this, for being mayor, he was paid the sum of $475
a year. Worse yet, it was all costing him business in his
pharmacy. Regular customers had taken their business
out of Otis Drugs and down to the Buy-Rite in protest of
one thing or another.

If things were disagreeable for Mayor Otis on Friday,
the coming days would be insufferable.

On Saturday morning he went out to feed the dog and
cat. The dog, a seventeen-year-old collie named Matilda, was dead. The cat, an eleven-year-old tom of indifferent breeding named Rufus, was gone. The two
animals were fond of each other and always slept together in the doghouse behind the mayor's house. They
were adept at getting up in the night to chase raccoons
away from the mayoral refuse cans. The mayor had reflected that raiding his garbage must be a status thing
in raccoon circles.

Matilda's death was no surprise to the mayor. She was,
after all, decrepit. The poor old thing's heart probably
gave out in the night. Nor did it surprise him that Rufus
wandered off. He was probably in a snit over Matilda's
passing. The mayor would spread the word with the
neighbor kids to keep an eye out for him.

By the end of Sunday Mayor Otis was beginning to
wish someone would keep an eye out for him, mainly

God. He was so unnerved he even took some of his own
product to calm himself. First, the desk called to report
the deaths of Old Lady Peterson and the Riley girl. The
substation had standing instructions to report all matters
of life and death immediately to the mayor. Not that the
mayor could do anything about it. He just wanted to know
before the newspapers did so he would not be surprised
and so he could have some kind of homily ready should
a reporter call him. Then later in the day the desk reported that Al Murdock had been found dead and little
Joey was missing. This saddened him greatly because Al
was a personal friend and they often lunched together.
Indeed, Al was one of the few people the mayor encountered who didn't pester him with politics.

Then little Tamar Caldwell knocked at his door.

"Hi, Mr. Otis," she said.

"Hi, Tamar. How are you, dear?" the mayor said.

"Fine. I found your cat, Mr. Mayor."

"Oh, terrific. Thank you, sweetie. Where is he?"

"In the woods about a mile from here. He's dead."

"Are you sure?"

"Oh, yeah. His guts was all cut out."

Then the telephone rang again. It was the desk report-
ing the discovery of Debbie Winegarden's body, and that
murder was suspected. The mayor poured himself a shot
of bourbon.

Then that evening the telephone rang yet again. A family of three passing through from Pittsburgh had been
found dead in their car parked in the SpeediBurger lot.

Something was terribly wrong, and something needed
to be done.

Charlie Sevenpines had not yet arrived at the substation
when Pete got there shortly before dawn.

Pete remembered the noise in the car on the day he
found Al Murdock's body. He would give the car a thorough going-over while he waited for Charlie. He got a
flashlight and looked underneath and found nothing. He
rocked the car up and down from each of its four corners
and looked underneath again, then under the hood, and
found nothing. He looked in the glovebox and under the
seats and found nothing.

He looked in the trunk last. It was the usual stuff.
Heavy-duty first-aid kit. Road emergency packet. Riot
gun. Tear-gas kit and gas mask. Cardio-pulmonary resuscitation unit. Geiger counter. This contraption was a
relic of the Three-Mile Island episode many years back
and a hundred miles away. Pete had never used it and he
doubted that anyone else on the force had either. He tried
to remember how it worked and how you tested it. Then
he remembered Geiger counters were sensitive enough to
react to the minute radiation of luminous watch dials.
Pete had an electronic watch, but Billy Gianotti had a big
wrist chronograph with luminous dials, and would be at
the desk.

"Hi, Pete, whatcha got there?" Billy said.

"G-g-geiger counter."

"Oh, yeah, forgot all about the damn things. Another
one of the old man's boondoggles."

"Yeah. Hey, Billy, would you, uh, mind sticking out
your arm? I want to test the thing."

"Sure."

Pete pointed the instrument at Billy's watch and was
so shocked by the sound he nearly dropped it. "J-J-
Jesus," he said. It was exactly the same clatter he had
mistaken for a bomb the day before. "Jesus."

Charlie Sevenpines pulled his Yamaha motorcycle up
to the substation and made his entrance. He was not
overly diffident.

"Hi, Charlie," Pete said.

"Hey, Charlie," Billy said, "what's the good news,
babe?"

Charlie thrust out his arms with mock theatricality,
grinned broadly, and intoned the jingle, "Maz-OOO-la,
corn gOOOOOdness! Hey, you dumb flatfeet, guess
who's the latest boob-tube star?"

They laughed and settled down to business. Pete and
Charlie would ride their motorcycles overland to the spot
where Al's body had been found. Both bikes were en-
duros built for riding on and off the road. They would
then decide whether to track Joey on foot or astride their
machines. The helicopters would be asked to stay in range
of Pete's portable radio.

Pete packed his thermos bottles and a small first-aid kit and a canteen of water, and they left.

Sergeant John Kunkel of the New Jersey State Police felt bored and grumpy this Monday morning. He sat in his Dodge tucked beneath an underpass with the radar scanning oncoming traffic. He had set the audio beeper to go off at a minimum sixty-eight miles per hour. God, was he bored! He would much rather be driving than sitting and watching digital readouts and fighting sleep. Hell, there was hardly any traffic on the interstate at this hour.

Kunkel got himself interested in a couple of birds colliding in mid-flight. He was trying to decide whether they were fighting or copulating when the audio alarm beeped.

Kunkel could scarcely believe the readout. A hundred seventeen, it said. That was higher than he had ever seen it. He wondered if there was something wrong with the radar. The goofy things were always going haywire, to the glee of attorneys. A microwave oven working in a camper would drive them crazy. Sometimes an oak tree that had stood in the same spot for a hundred years would dash by at better than seventy miles an hour.

A hundred seventeen miles an hour. Jesus, nobody in his right mind would go that fast.

Then the shock wave of the black TransAm hurtling beneath the underpass rattled the windows of Kunkel's Dodge. He quickly pulled out in pursuit, gumballs flashing and siren blaring, and got on the radio to request a backup. Kunkel didn't know if he could catch this maniac.

The beauty of the sun rising over ground fog and the scent of earth and plants and wildflowers nearly distracted Pete Bilyeux.

"This is where I, uh, lost him," Pete said when he and Charlie got to the stand of rhododendrons.

"Yeah," Charlie said, "I can see why. This ain't going to be easy." He crawled on all fours through the thicket, stopping to pick things up and scrutinize them. "Looks like he slept here, Pete, at least for a while. Night before last. Hey, man, this is going to be tough. We're gonna have to lock up the bikes and do this one on foot."

"Okay by me," Pete said.

"Jesus, this doesn't make any sense. Look. Look here, Pete. See this? He went straight through this crap," Charlie said when they reached a patch of thorny wild blackberry bushes. "Nobody, not even a little kid, is dumb enough to tear through this shit. Look, here's a piece of his shirt or something. Jesus, here's a spot of blood."

"M-maybe it was in the dark, Charlie. Maybe he couldn't see where he was going. Was he running?"

"Looks like it. Yeah. Had to be."

"This kid must've been scared to death to run through this stuff in the night of dead, uh, I mean the dead of night. What do you suppose c-could have scared him so much, Charlie? A bear?"

"Nah. Bear don't fuck around with kids. Not the little bear around here, maybe out West or up North eats 'em up. Wasn't no animal near him anyhow. No tracks that fresh."

It took the men longer to track Joey through the rough area than it took Joey to make the tracks two nights before. The sun was now well up in the sky.

Pete was always spellbound by the way Charlie could find a trail. Pete wasn't bad at it himself, but it seemed Charlie could spot eloquent details on granite that told the path of his quarry. Pete once asked Charlie how he came by this singular skill.

"Know where the name Fletcher came from, Pete?"

"No."

"Well, back in the old days in England a fletcher was a guy what made arrows. This skill was handed down from father to son and the name stuck. Well, tracking was a pretty big job back in the old days with my people. The skill was handed down likewise."

Pete opined that with Charlie's fee of two hundred dollars a day plus expenses and mileage, tracking was still a pretty big job. But at that, Charlie was cheaper than any helicopter, and most county governments in this part of the state had given their sheriffs carte blanche to call on Charlie. He never failed.

"Okay, Charlie, if a g-g-guy, uh, is named Fletcher because his, uh, ancestors made arrows, then how come your name isn't Tracker instead of Sevenpines?" Pete couldn't resist twitting Charlie. After all, Charlie would do the same to him.

"That's another story, wiseass," Charlie said.

They found the burrow where Joey had slept much of the day before. The sun was now high.

"What kind of animal lives in here, Charlie?"

"Doesn't live here, eats here. Owl. Male. Won't come near the place for a couple of weeks now that the kid's been here."

"What do you make of it?"

"Kid slept here."

"Last night?"

"No. Daytime yesterday. This morning dew wet over his marks. He stopped running by the time he got here. Tracks are straight. He stopped walking into things too."

"I thought so," Pete said. "Ready for a p-p-pattern?"

"Try me," Charlie said.

"The kid's father dies of a heart attack or some damn thing. The kid, uh, waits for help and n-n-nobody comes. It gets late and he, uh, takes refuge in the boonies. Something spooks him in the night and he runs like hell. He's tired and lost and he goes to sleep in the shade here. When he gets up he goes to look for two things—water, and a way, uh, to get home."

"I agree," Charlie said.

"B-b-but, uh, there's one thing weird."

"What's that, babe?"

"That deep footprint back where the body was."

"He stomped something."

"Yeah, but, uh, what? The same kind of print was near the, uh, girl's body too."

"Hmm," said Charlie, in the way his ancestors had learned to shrug off ambiguity.

They followed Joey's tracks into his secret jungle. It was now midday and the trackers were slowed by having to drop and crawl beneath low foliage under which Joey had walked easily.

"Jesus, look at that," Charlie said, pointing to a dead

trout on the banks of a brook and two more floating in the water.

"What do you, uh, suppose caused that?"

Charlie squatted and inspected the dead fish. "No turtle," he said, "maybe something they ate."

They found the place where Joey had waved to the helicopter.

"Look at this," Charlie said, "he was jumping up and down."

"Must have, uh, seen a chopper."

"Yeah, and it didn't see him."

"Jesus. Uh, this is nuts, Charlie. I think I see a pattern."

"Try me."

"This kid was always, uh, getting under something. It's like he was p-p-paranoid about something over his head."

"I agree," Charlie said.

"Yeah, but what?" Pete said.

"Hmm," Charlie said, Indian-style.

Later they found, in different places, the fresh bodies of several dead bats. None showed any apparent harm.

"Hmm," Charlie said again.

"The sonofabitch sees me all right," Sergeant Kunkel bawled into the radio. "It's all I can do to hang on to his tail."

"Right, Johnny," the radio said. "We're working to set up a block at the one-nine marker. Got a plate number?"

Kunkel called in the number.

"Okay, Johnny, we'll run it into the computer. How you doing?"

"Hanging in there," Kunkel said.

Sergeant Kunkel had his hands more full of Dodge automobile than he had ever desired. Every time there was a good stretch of road, the Dodge would start to catch up with the TransAm. Then it would lose ground to the more nimble car in the sharper curves. Now the Dodge was beginning to overheat. Kunkel turned on the heater to bleed some of the heat away from the engine and onto him. He began to sweat with windows closed to reduce aerodynamic drag and hoped the car would make it to the roadblock.

The man at the desk had punched the Pennsylvania license plate number into his computer, which relayed it to the New Jersey master computer in Trenton, which of course found nothing and relayed it on to a more masterful computer in Phoenix, Arizona, which found the name of the license owner and relayed this name to the National Crime Index Center (NCIC), the most masterful computer of them all, in Washington, D.C. *Mirabile dictu*, it all worked, and the most masterful computer of NCIC had a most interesting tale to relate.

"Hey, Johnny," the radio said urgently.

"Yeah?"

"Watch yourself, old buddy. This bastard is wanted for suspicion of homicide in PA."

"Holy shit," Kunkel said, and loosened his nine-millimeter semiautomatic pistol in its holster. He was glad he had worn his bullet-resistant vest this day.

Reed Hamilton saw himself being led into the chamber where the ugly chair yawned with its leather straps and electrodes dangling as tongues of a mute dragon poised to eat his life for something he did not do. He drove with this vision in his mind as much as the sight of the New Jersey trooper in his rearview mirror.

He would have to find some way to ditch this cop before he picked up more of them. He couldn't take a side road. They knew them better than he did. He would have to outmaneuver the cop.

Suddenly he saw the roadblock two miles or so ahead of him. A couple of white cars, red lights flashing, along with two carefully jackknifed tractor-trailers covered both east- and westbound lanes.

Reed would have to make his move now.

With eyes fixed on the rearview mirror, he slowed the TransAm just enough for the trooper to sit directly on his tail as he saw them do in the stock-car races on TV. There he is. Good.

Reed slammed the brake pedal down with all his might

and saw white smoke escape from the screeching surfaces of the locked tires. The police car struck him in the rear and this pushed his tail out ninety degrees to the right. That was lucky, Reed thought, and cranked the steering wheel full to the left, pointing the nose of the TransAm across the median toward the westbound lane, where he could make another run for his life.

When Reed hit the grass of the median he was sliding sideways out of control. He kept the brakes on. The tires weren't getting any bite. The grass was dewy. Reed could see out the corners of his eyes that the police car was also sliding on the grass, tenacious bastard. Suddenly with a violent jolt the TransAm struck something hard and unseen protruding from the grass of the median. The car would not steer and Reed knew it was the electric chair for him as he let the broken car wallow lazily to a stop.

He saw the trooper get out of his car with gun in hand a hundred feet or so away. Reed got out of the TransAm to surrender and absently reached toward the shirt pocket inside his jacket for a cigarette.

In an instant the trooper dropped to a crouch and pointed his pistol at Reed, using both hands to aim.

"Freeze! Don't move," the cop said.

"No!" Reed screamed, meaning, No, don't shoot me.

The time was exactly 6:43 on Monday morning.

By about one o'clock that afternoon Pete and Charlie had found where Joey slept the night before under the abandoned car.

"Still in the, uh, pattern, isn't he?" Pete said.

"I agree," Charlie said. "How about some of that espresso now, good buddy?"

Pete poured the coffee and they drank and Pete began to feel unusually anxious. He had always tried to stay dispassionate, even jocular, when searching for a lost child. It helped him abjure emotion in favor of logic, and so put himself more logically in the mind of the missing child. It had not yet failed. By now he had a circle of young friends among the formerly lost and their associates, and he liked being around children. It pained him that with each day it grew less likely he and Enid would ever have children. It grieved him that Enid was only a step or two away from some kind of institution. He wasn't sure whether he was truly sorry for her or for the family they would probably never be. As though these were not enough thoughts to feed his anxiety, he puzzled over the illogic of all the recent deaths. And the only people alive to bear witness to those deaths were a lost five-year-old and an equally lost teenage lecher who just might, despite Pete's intuitions, be a murderer.

Pete tucked these thoughts away in favor of the task at hand and sipped the last of his coffee. Then a queer sympathy with Joey, a sort of avatar, invaded and impelled him with urgency.

They had reached the end of Joey's jungle.

All day in the distance, and often overhead, the helicopters had clattered to no avail.

Pete pressed the button to key the microphone of his radio. "Portable One-One to Bird One," he said, "d-do you read me?"

"Loud and clear Portable One-One, this is Bird One, what's your twenty?"

"W-w-w-we're, uh, at the woods of a little tip, 'scuse me, I mean the tip of a little woods I m-m-make to be about three mmmmiles north of the, uh, northmost chopper. Over."

"Ten-four, Portable One-One, this is Bird Two. We're closest to you. We can see you guys now. Hey, whatsamatter, pal, cat got your tongue?"

Pete seethed and got back on the air. "This is P-portable One-One to Bird Two, and my best friends call me Deputy Sheriff P-P-Pete Bilyeux and we got a lost k-k-kid to find. Can you give us a fly-by?"

"Ten-four, Pee-pee-pete . . ."

"T-ten four," Pete said, and let his finger off the button and closed his eyes and gulped back his indignation.

Charlie's eyes looked into Pete's with a sad expression. Who ever said these people were inscrutable? "Over here, Pete, he went up this hill," Charlie said.

"We're wasting time. Time's running out." Pete's voice was distant and low and dejected.

Within a minute the helicopter was overhead.

"Portable One-One to B-Bird Two, uh, can you see us?"

"Right, Pee-pee-pete, give us a smile, sweets."

"There's, uh, a top hill, no, I m-m-mean a hilltop just over your southwest. C-can you slide over it?"

"Ten-four."

"Okay. Let me know, uh, what you see."

"What do you mean?" the radio said.

"D-Do you see anything?"

"What the fuck do you mean, see anything, Pee-pee-pete? It's just the same old shit we been looking at for two days now."

"Look, you supercilious asshole," Pete said, in wonder at the strength and coherence of his voice, "do I have to spell it out to you? Do you see a fucking kid, do you see a fucking road, do you see a fucking house, do you see a fucking anything, or are you just sitting up there in that eggbeater pounding on your dead pud?"

"Look, sister, you ain't doing us no favors," the radio of Bird Two said. "We're here to help you."

"Sorry," Pete said. "I thought you were here to do your job."

The radio was silent for a moment. "The only thing around here is an old farmhouse. No kid. No nothing."

"Thanks," Pete said. "Uh, where is the, uh, house from us?"

"About a quarter-mile up the hill to your northeast."

"Thanks. Please stand by."

"Ten-four."

Pete bolted up the hill in his boots and Charlie trotted easily after him in his worn Gucci moccasins.

"Hey, babe, what's your hurry?" Charlie said.

"I don't know," Pete panted.

They had nearly reached the top of the hill when Pete had to pause for breath.

Charlie wandered a few feet away. "Hey, Pete, you got the pattern, all right. Lookie here." Charlie pointed at the prints.

"How, uh, how long ago?" Pete said.

"Two, three hours at the most."

"Let's go," Pete said. "Merciful God."

Pete recognized the house from the descriptions he had heard as a kid. It was the old Mueller house, scene of the last homicide around Thomas Valley and its only horror story until now. Not even Adair would go near the place.

Pete took out his flashlight and ran over the porch. His face and neck and armpits were drenched with sweat. A solitary fly hovered over him.

"Hey, Pete, don't go in there," Charlie said. "He went around this way."

Pete ran to the back of the house after Charlie.

Then he saw the refrigerator.

"Oh, no," Pete said, "oh, my God, please, God, *no!*"

Pete tore the door open and reached inside.

The little body was white and limp but warm. Pete laid Joey on his back on the ground and parted his lips and blew air into his mouth and massaged his chest.

After a few minutes he paused and tossed his radio to Charlie. "Here, Charlie, call the choppers in! See if one of them has a paramedic with a CPR unit. I think I have a pulse."

"How do you work this fucking thing?" Charlie asked.

"Just press the button and talk."

"Hey, helicopter," Charlie said.

"Who is this?" the radio said. "Identify yourself."

"This is Charlie Sevenpines. I'm with Deputy Sheriff Pete Bilyeux and we found the kid. He's in bad shape. Any of you guys got a medic on board or a CP . . . something unit?"

"Nah," the radio said.

"What about oxygen?" Pete looked up and said.

"What about oxygen?" Charlie said to the radio.

"Sure, we got it," the radio said.

"Bring 'em in," Pete said. "We got to get this kid to the hospital. There's a pulse but it's feeble as hell . . ."

"Hey, helicopter, land, will you?" Charlie said. "We gotta get this kid to the hospital."

"Who in fucking hell *is* this, I said?" asked the radio. " Give me your call number."

"I got no call number, you pimpsqueak! I told you this

is Charlie Sevenpines. I'm with the sheriff's office and I'm a full-blooded Indian, and if you don't come down here and get this kid I'm going to climb up there and scalp your pink ass!''

A helicopter landed and a trooper ran out with an oxygen bottle and clamped the breathing apparatus over Joey's mouth and ran back with Joey in his arms and flew away toward the County Hospital.

Part Two

FROM MONDAY TO THURSDAY

*There are more things in heaven and earth,
    Horatio,
Than are dreamt of in your philosophy.*

6

When Sergeant Kunkel saw the kid get out of the car, he almost felt sorry for him. He thought he had been pursuing someone like Burt Reynolds in *Smokey and the Bandit,* only meaner. He hadn't known it was just a scrawny kid. But so had Billy the Kid been scrawny—scrawny and gattoothed. Kunkel had read about the Kid and seen a picture of him in *Real West* magazine in the barber shop. A homicidal maniac, the Kid was, who had killed twenty-one men before he was twenty-one years old.

Suddenly this kid on the median of the interstate reached in his jacket for a gun and Johnny Kunkel wasn't about to be number twenty-two for this little bastard. Not after his pal, Trooper Zack Carney, had been gunned down by a crazy terrorist not five miles from this spot. No, not with a son approaching Rutgers age and a daughter with braces to pay for. Besides, Johnny Kunkel just didn't think it was his time, and had always held the opinion that he who shoots first speaks last.

"Freeze! Don't move," Kunkel yelled. He crouched and flipped the safety off his pistol and took swift aim for the kid's heart. He began to squeeze the trigger.

"No," the kid yelled, and threw up his hands, scattering the better part of a pack of Marlboros to the breeze.

It was too late for Kunkel to stop the trigger but in the final millisecond he jerked the barrel to the right.

The bullet crashed into the rear of the TransAm and blew the gas tank into billows of orange flame that belched black smoke that consumed the kid.

The kid ran out. The seat of his pants was afire and the kid screamed and ran down the grass of the median.

Kunkel was afraid the kid might run into oncoming traffic and get killed, so he fired the pistol into the

75

ground. "Hey, stupid, sit down," yelled Kunkel. "Sit down, stupid, your butt's on fire!" Boom went the pistol again.

The kid dutifully sat down and brushed his burning bottom cool in the wet grass of the median.

"You okay, kid?" Sergeant Kunkel said.

The kid put his face in his hands and sobbed convulsively.

"Well, kid," Kunkel said, "stick out your hands. I'm going to put the cuffs on you and read you your rights."

Reed Hamilton put out his hands. Thus had he got the hot seat and Sergeant Kunkel an official commendation from the governor.

Pete and Charlie watched the helicopters leave and sat with their backs propped against a vintage 1947 Maytag wringer washing machine and drank the last of the espresso.

"Cheers," Pete said.

"Shalom," Charlie said.

"Quit showing off," Pete said with a chuckle. He got up and dusted off his uniform and got his flashlight and started into the house.

"Man, don't go in there," Charlie said.

"B-b-bullshit," Pete said. "I want to kid what the see saw, uh, I mean see what the kid saw."

"I disagree," Charlie said, "you won't find nothin', man, except maybe what won't do you any good. That place is spooked. Don't you believe in haunts?"

"Nnno," Pete said, thinking of the execution in Saigon and his failure to act. "No, Charlie, I'm going in."

"I disagree again, man."

Old Man Mueller had come back early and sick from a blistering day in fields now long fallow. His only child, a son of six years, had died mysteriously and Mueller wondered if he had anything left to live for. On this July day of 1948 he found his wife in bed with a hired man and knew he had nothing to live for. He tied them up and cut off their heads with a bow saw. Then he took rat poison and fell in the privy. The bodies were not discovered for ten days in the summer heat. It was said the place had a curse on it. Passersby told tales of shrieks in the night and strange lights and shapes in the windows. Even the most adventurous of local youngsters had shunned it since the killings. But Pete had a belly full of curses. They were nonsense and he would go in.

"I'm not going in there with you, man," Charlie said, and lit a cigar.

"F-f-fine," Pete said. It was his job. He was a policeman and felt a responsibility for the things that were happening, and he would do something. "Make a decision, son, make a decision," the burnt pork butt had said. What does it matter? Pete thought. My wife is going crazy and I can't express myself worth a damn and the people in my town are dropping dead all over the place. What do I have to lose?

The rotting boards of the porch felt spongy under the weight of Pete's boots and he walked as through a mine field.

The stench caught him in the doorway, nidorous eructations of human ordure from times past, as from the grave itself. Newspapers, some old and some not so old, were scattered over the remnants of a living-room rug. BROOKLYN DODGERS TAKE WORLD SERIES read one headline.

Then he heard them. They came on invisible wing audible as with vengeance. They swarmed. They hovered. They darted.

Pete dug in his utility belt and got his emergency waterproof matches. God, how the place stank of bygone crapulence now gone carious. He struck a match and foxfire phosphorescence lit the scene and gave off whiffs of smoke that drove the flies away and reflected the form of Deputy Sheriff Peter H. Bilyeux in funhouse angles from bits of broken mirror and window glass on the floor.

Tramps must have stopped here for years, Pete thought. Their signs were everywhere. So was their feces. Bums had got their temporary shelter and shit on the floor to mark the occasion.

Pete started up the staircase.

Dzzzzzzzzt went a sound at the far end of the living room. Pete had lived through bombs and this was not one of them. It was either a bug or a rattlesnake.

Cccraaaaaaaaaaaccck went a board from the staircase.

It gave way and Pete's boot was caught and he felt himself being pulled down. The stench in his face was now the hot breath of a dead beast. He felt as if he were inside a horror movie. He struggled to free his boot from the hole in the staircase. His heart beat hard in the stifling heat and he fancied Toltec gods were tearing at it.

Dzzzzzzzzt. It was a rattlesnake, Pete knew.

He tore his boot from the stair and walked up. Mindful of black widows, he shined his flashlight and gingerly parted the cobwebs at the head of the stair and walked into the Mueller bedroom.

It was the cleanest place in the house. Scarcely a mote troubled it. It even smelled all right, with a hint of perfume after some forty years. Pete fancied he could feel the presence of a female ghost. All day Pete had tried to think Joey's thoughts, and now he knew he was feeling Joey's fears.

This place is a nuthouse, Pete thought. It's been full of scumbags and dipshits and scuzzmonsters and spiders and flies and snakes and it's only a bad dream with nothing to learn from the interpretation.

Then, when he let the light shine on the upstairs bathroom mirror, he felt a shock and began to wonder whether there might be an interpretation after all.

The mirror was intact. On it were written some words in old dried blood or lipstick the color of burnt sienna, he was not sure which. These were the words:

MENE   MENE   TEKEL   UPHARSIN

It was from Daniel, V,1. You have been judged and found wanting. God has numbered your kingdom and finished it, it meant.

Pete went down the stairs knowing less than he knew before. The stink of the ground floor struck him with the ferocity of the tear gas in the training chamber they made you walk through in the school for military policemen. This place is vile, Pete thought. Vile is the only word in the English language to describe it.

The flies flew and buzzed angrily. Pete took off his hat and waved it to make a wind that pushed them away.

Dzzzzzzzzt. The rattlesnake was annoyed.

Pete shined the flashlight over the floor and spotted the

snake, about five feet long, coiled in a corner. An old curtain rod lay on the floor. Pete picked it up and hooked the snake on it and went to a window from which he could see Charlie. He held the protesting creature out the window and let it wriggle on the rod.

"Hey, Charlie, is, uh, this a f-friend of yours?"

Charlie laughed. "Tastes just like chicken neck, but I'm more in the mood for liverwurst today."

Pete laughed and let the snake drop and slither away.

He walked out of the house abashed at the gratuitous machismo of this gesture. Yet instinct told him that defiance was the appropriate defense against superstition.

The evil spell lay broken, for now.

"You guys are always making the same damn mistake, aren't you?" Charlie said.

"What's that?" Pete said.

"Never mind."

Pete and Charlie walked without saying much back to the place where they had left their motorcycles, the place where Al Murdock had been found dead.

The elation of saving Joey and braving the vile house and catching the snake wore off and Pete grew tired and depressed. He was not at all sure Joey would live.

And something had frightened Pete about the house. Yes, it had been the quotation from the Book of Daniel on the mirror. He felt it applied to him, but probably most people would feel the same way. He was only an indifferent reader of scripture and would never have known this passage had it not been for a particularly ruthless crossword puzzle. *Mene* was the answer to which the clue had been "handwriting on the wall." No doubt the handwriting on the mirror had been some tramp's idea of a joke, an immortalization of an itinerant blot of human detritus. Pete idly wondered whether tramps and crossword-puzzle writers were cut from the same cloth.

Something had also frightened Joey about the place. What could it have been? Its reputation as a haunted house? Hardly. Joey would not have known it, and on the unlikely chance that he had, he wouldn't have ventured within a mile of it. The foul smell? It was repellent but not scary enough to make you want to hide in an abandoned refrigerator. The snake? Unlikely. To a five-year-old it would only sound like a baritone cicada. What else was there? The flies, of course. But flies are nuisances, not nemeses. This lot was a nasty one and unusually aggressive, probably because the house was their breeding place. Yet Joey had been trying to stay under and inside various shelters. God, that refrigerator! Pete had forgotten to dismantle the door. He would go back and do it. Starting tomorrow he had two days off. Hadn't Joey's parents warned him about old refrigerators? But why should they have? For more than twenty years it had been illegal to discard refrigerators without removing their doors. Pete had not heard of a child refrigerator death since he was in grammar school.

Joey's pattern of seeking protection had probably been the natural childish desire to be self-contained after the trauma of witnessing the death of a parent. Poor kid. It was bad enough when Pete at the age of twelve lost his father. Pete thought how much worse it would have been had he seen it happen. God! God, that had been a cruel year. Elspeth and Enid and Adair had both parents wiped out in a single accident not two months after Pete's father was killed. Then Elspeth and the twins had been packed off to two different foster homes. Enid never got over it and Pete doubted Adair had either. Big Sister Elspeth was luckier. She got into a good home.

Yes, life was full of its ironies. What is it Shakespeare had Gertrude say? ''When sorrows come, they come not single spies but in battalions.''

Now Pete's world was trooping to chaos in battalion numbers.

It had to have been the snake. Snakes are cold-blooded and cannot tolerate temperature extremes. Probably it was crossing the porch to get in the shade of the house when Joey happened by. But Pete would rule nothing out until he found out more.

Desk duty at the Thomas Valley substation was the most cushy job a deputy could get. You sat around and answered a few phone calls, you sometimes punched into the computers with the great national memories, you dispatched the cars when necessary, you punched the button that blew the whistle for the volunteer fire department or the volunteer ambulance corps or an atomic attack, and mostly you sat around and read *Playboy* or *Penthouse* or *Popular Mechanics* or *Field & Stream* or *Road & Track* or *Real West*.

The most senior man on a shift got desk duty if he chose it. Pete Bilyeux was the second most senior man at the Thomas Valley substation and never chose desk duty. He did not like talking over electronic devices, for obvious reasons. He was a road man, a people man. He was considered by all in Thomas Valley to be the detective, as it were, detectives being in scant demand in this neck of the woods. Even the sheriff respected Pete's ability to snook things out.

To his deputies the sheriff's most admirable trait was that he did whatever he did away from them. His second most admirable trait was that he permitted no captains or lieutenants or sergeants in the Elmsford County Sheriff's Department. There were only deputies with different grades of pay, most of them tolerably fair. It was anarchy, and this was good because the deputies were highly professional and quite capable of organizing themselves.

One Joseph Sherman Cody by name, this sheriff claimed to share ancestry with William Frederick Cody, Buffalo Bill of yore; one of many claims his deputies were wont to regard as specious.

Most of the deputies were younger. They were all well-educated, and some, like Pete, held college degrees. It was universally agreed among these policemen that Joe Cody was an imbecile. Difficulties would predictably arise on the odd occasion when the old man would turn up and manifest one of his infrequent delusions of adequacy.

Sheriff Cody's grip on his office rested on the fact that he never ceased campaigning. Upon reelection to a four-year term, he began a four-year campaign for reelection to another term. He was responsible for all tax collections in the county and pursued this enterprise as diligently as he chose. His campaign vehicle was an American Motors station wagon, a very old one. Otherwise, he drove a Lincoln Town Car with deeply darkened window glass, the better to keep his luxury in privacy. There was not a back he would not slap, a baby he would not smooch, an undercooked chicken or overcooked roast beef he would not eat, nor a testimonial dinner he would fail to attend. No birthday, graduation, twenty-fifth or fiftieth wedding-anniversary celebration, party, wake, funeral, or bar mitzvah need be without the smiling presence of Joe Cody, Sheriff.

The story was told that once when on the campaign trail he was asked this question by a more liberally minded constituent, "Sir, what do you think of euthanasia?"

The sheriff did not know what the lady who questioned him meant by this big word. Had he known, he might have confided that it would be best to put the too-old, too-stupid, and the too-black to sleep like decrepit dogs.

Instead, the sheriff's eyes prayerfully besought the heavens, and he replied, "Ma'am, as an American I believe youth in Asia should have a simyular fine future as youth in our great nation."

The school that was attached to the Convent of Our Lady of Sorrows in North Philadelphia was both a school and a home. The children of the school had no other place to live. Some were orphans, some were placed by the courts as foster children, some had a parent or two who could not care for them, some had simply wandered in off the street, some had already been junkies. As all children, none was overly fond of school, and so they referred to this one as Sorry School when the nuns were out of earshot. But it was not nearly as sorry as the circumstances they had left behind.

Take Irene Byrne, for example. Burned Irene was her school nickname. She had acquired this soubriquet because her last guardians, if such you could call them, had acquired the habit of punishing any naughtiness she might commit by thrusting her hands onto the flames of a hot stove or the surface of a hot frying pan. She was at last discovered by the police with third-degree burns on the palms of her hands. She had nothing to say except that she hurt.

The judge was aghast and moved quickly to throw Irene's guardians into the clink. He then remanded Irene over to

Our Lady of Sorrows, where she had spent the last four and the happiest of her thirteen years.

Irene's story is not typical of North Philadelphia. This area is called a ghetto but considered a neighborhood by most people who live there, albeit a neighborhood far from excessive affluence. And as all poorer places, it knows how to sing its songs of the destitute few. Her story was fairly typical of the students of Our Lady of Sorrows, though, some of whom could tell you worse. One who could not was Hernán García. Hernán was one of the few nonblack children at Sorry School and the only one in the eighth grade. But he was tolerated by his classmates, who regarded him as a court jester. No doubt he came naturally to his sunny disposition as he had no sorry story to tell. That is because he had no story to tell at all. He had been found as an infant in a hallway in Our Lady of Sorrows wrapped in a towel with his name pinned to it. Hernán knew no other home and this one was quite good enough for him. He neither spoke nor cared to speak any Spanish. Nor did he even pronounce his first name correctly but referred to himself as Herman, which he shall hereafter be called.

Of matching vivacity was Sister N'Teta, math teacher, eighth-grade counselor, and the most popular nun in the place. Sister Nettie, she was called by all the nuns and children, of which she was the only fluent in Swahili by reason of it being her native language. A born African, Sister Nettie's skin was in sharp contrast to the black American nuns whose gradations of skin hue betrayed the past humiliations of an enslaved womanhood. So black was it that the merest hint of light would set it aglow with a silvery aura exalted in radiance by the merry whites of her eyes and the flash of teeth quick to bare themselves in a smile. She was deeply in love with God.

At about the same time Reed Hamilton's TransAm was caught in Sergeant Kunkel's radar, the eighth grade class of Our Lady of Sorrows was embarked in a rickety yellow school bus of 1950s vintage. Sisters Melanie and Helga would take turns driving. Sister Nettie rode with her charges, as she was not a licensed driver.

They set out west and north of Philadelphia for their long ride to their picnic in the solitude of sparsely attended and wholly untended Jacob Walz State Park—which was not at all far from Thomas Valley, though quite as near as some would ever go.

When Pete Bilyeux got back to the substation, it was obvious from the outside that something was going on inside. There were a half-dozen more cars than usual parked in front and only one was a police car. Pete said good-bye to Charlie, who rode off.

"Hi, Billy," Pete said to the harried man at the desk. "What's happening?"

"Oh, Jesus, Pete, don't ask. The fucking county prosecutor is in there, the fucking mayor's in there, the fucking board of health people are in there, the fucking old man's on his way here, and two more people conked out since you left. Jesus, people are dropping like flies around here."

"How's the M-M-Murdock kid?"

"He's in intensive care, Pete. They don't know if he's going to make it. Sorry."

"Oh, God," Pete said. He went to get a drink of water and to compose himself, and returned. "Okay if I, uh, go in there?"

"In there" meant the small windowless conference room that sat over the substation's lockup. The room was usually used to interview juvenile offenders and their parents.

"Better you than me," Billy said.

Pete took off his hat and went in and looked for a place to sit among the mélange. The prosecutor was yelling into the phone and the health people were smoking cigarettes and yelling at the mayor. They felt he had put them on the spot and were not pleased. The mayor was one of those few select politicians for whom Pete would gladly vote again. The man was pale and perspiring and happy to see Pete.

"Pete, how are you?" the mayor said. "Let me get you a chair."

"Will you people please keep it down," the prosecutor said with his hand over the mouthpiece of the phone. "Jesus Christ, I've got a terrible connection and I'm trying to get a murderer back here." He took his hand away and talked into the phone. "Sorry, Hank. Hey, Hank, look, we've known each other for a long time. What? . . . Yeah, yeah, for you I'll stipulate, fella . . . What? . . . What do you mean a writ? There's no time for a fucking writ, there are seven people dead around here and we think this kid . . ."

The mayor held up two fingers to indicate two more deaths.

"Quiet, please, will you, Mayor?" the prosecutor said. "No, no, the autopsy's not in yet, there were complications and they're still working on it . . . How? . . . How? . . . Well, for Christ's fucking sake, the little bastard buried her in a shallow grave, so help me God, fella. Our state police were out with choppers looking for a lost kid when they found the grave . . . What? . . . No, no, a little kid they were looking for, not Hamilton, a little guy with signs of sexual abuse all over him, had to be the Hamilton kid that did it. You know, Hank, fella, you and I can handle this before it hits the papers. Can you imagine what the papers will say? 'County attorney refuses to give up mad-dog sex killer,' that's what they'll say, even the Jersey papers. Now, what's that going to do to your campaign for state senate?"

"Mayor, this is wasting our time," a county board of health man said.

"Then go back and find your place in *Hustler*," the mayor said.

"You little sonofabitch, you should never have been elected," the health man said. "I happen to be a deacon of my church."

"Then act like a goddamn Christian," the mayor said.

"Oh, will you please shut up," the prosecutor bellowed. "No . . . no, Hank, sorry, I didn't mean you, fella. I'm in the middle of this crazy meeting about the sex murderer you're holding out on us. The *New York Post* is beating on our door now, you can just see the headlines if we cut a deal. Clip 'em out and stick 'em in a flyer for your campaign. 'Gallant prosecutors trap sex killer in pincer movement.' Hey, think of that, huh? . . . Hey, fella, we'll both stipulate . . . You will? Hey! . . . All right . . . Hey, great . . . See you in Sin City one of these days, huh?"

The county prosecutor bade good-bye to the phone and turned to the men in the room and smiled. "That little Hamilton bastard will be here by nightfall," he said.

A knock came at the door. "Come in," Mayor Warren Otis said.

It was Billy Gianotti from the desk. "Excuse me, Mayor, gentlemen, sorry to interrupt, but the autopsy reports on Murdock and the Winegarden girl just came in. Here they are."

"Thank you, Billy," the mayor said. "That was thoughtful."

The prosecutor snatched the reports out of the mayor's hands. He tossed one aside and quickly scanned the other. Then he caught a snort coming from the back of his throat.

"Jumping Jesus," the prosecutor said slowly. "Shit. Shit on fire, there goes the best case I ever had. Fuck! Shit! Fuck-fied shit! All this trouble for nothing!" God, why do things like this always happen to me? he thought. Why, God, why me? I could have sent the little bastard all the way to the chair. It could have made me governor. Being governor could have made me president!

The prosecutor flung the report at the mayor and stormed out.

Pete looked over the mayor's shoulder at the two reports. The key phrase in both was "cardiac arrest." Pete would read the reports more carefully later, but Debbie's clearly precluded homicide.

The health people looked over the reports. "Mayor," one of them said, "you have just wasted an accumulative total of twelve man-hours of the taxpayers' dollars."

"Gentlemen," the mayor said, rubbing his balding head, "by shirking your responsibilities, you have just signed a blank check for the deaths of nine people in my constituency, and God knows how many more to come. May you live and die knowing it."

Mayor Otis sat and shook his head after they left. "Oh, Jesus," he said, "I feel like crying. Pete, oh, Jesus, Pete, there's got to be a reason for all this, nine people don't die of heart attacks all at once. Oh, God, maybe I'm crazy, maybe it's just coincidence. Tell me, Pete, what do you think?"

"I, uh . . ."

Sheriff Joe Cody ambled into the room, clad in customary bright-yellow jacket, orange tie, and flamingo-colored golf trousers, all polyester. He also wore his artificial shrieval smile. He took the cigar out of his mouth with a flourish and offered his hand to the mayor. Why was it, Pete wondered, that he didn't mind cigars when Billy Gianotti or Charlie Sevenpines smoked them, but found them repulsive in the mouth of the sheriff?

"Hiya, Warren," the sheriff said. "Still frittering away the taxpayers' money on all those welfare cheats?"

"We don't have welfare in town, Joe," the mayor said.

"Just a manner of speaking, War, just a manner of speaking. Don't be so serious, old son. Hello, Bilyeux, still married to that crazy poet? Bilyeux, stick around, I want a word with you when this is over." The sheriff sat down at the conference table. "Okay, War, what's on your mind?"

"What's on my mind? Jesus, Joe, what do you think's on my mind? Four people, probably five more, just dropped dead of heart attacks, Joe, that's what's on my mind."

The sheriff shrugged. "What do you think you or me could do about heart attacks?"

"Joe, you know goddamn perfectly well that nine healthy people don't just keel over from heart attacks in less than forty-eight hours. Something's got to be causing it all."

"That's just like you liberals," the sheriff said, "always wanting to change the world. I suppose now you're going to tell me the President of the United States wears contact lenses and dyes his hair."

"As a matter of fact, the sonofabitch does," the mayor said.

"Now hold on!" The sheriff pounded the table with his fist. "That's treason! I'll have you know you're on county property now, Warren, not town property, and treason will not be tolerated by me or any man under my command!"

"Sorry, Joe," the mayor said, "let's not get political. I'm just all strung out. God, all those people . . ."

"War, let's not fight, old son," the sheriff said. "Tell

you what, old son, I'm going to let you in on a little
secret just between you and me and the lamppost here,"
he said, wafting a hand in the direction of Pete Bilyeux.
"I'm a step ahead of you, War, a step ahead, old son.
Now what's the best medical research thingamabob within
a hundred miles?"

"Hershey Medical Center," the mayor said.

"You got it, old son, you got it. I'm going to jerk all
three of those Pittsburgh stiffs out of the county morgue
and have them hauled down to Hershey for an A-number-
one-first-class-bull-bitch autopsy. I have the power to do
it, and the budget. How's that?"

"Good, Joe, good idea, that's a start."

"Hell, War, Rome wasn't built in a day." The sheriff
got up and put his hand on the mayor's shoulder. Every
time he did that to Pete it made him want to cringe.
"War, old son, you just go out there to those good people
and you tell 'em old Joe Cody's on the case and old Joe
never fails to get his man. Tell 'em that for me, War.
Okay, old son?"

"Okay, Joe," the mayor said. "Thanks. Let's stay in
touch."

"Will do, old son, will do. Put 'er there."

The two shook hands and the mayor shuffled ruefully
from the room to face a community in mortal danger.

The sheriff closed the door after the mayor. This made
Pete feel as though locked in a compartment of a sub-
marine with a boatswain who wanted to bugger him.

"Bilyeux?" the sheriff said in a low and conspiratorial
tone.

"Y-y-yes, Sheriff?"

"Bilyeux, I'm three steps ahead of that sniveling little
shit. You can't let bleeding hearts like that little fart of a
mayor run things. Bilyeux, I'll be brief, old son. Old son,
they're on us again just like they were before McCarthy
threw the bunch of them out."

"B-b-beg pardon?"

"Bilyeux, they've infested Niggeracqua, and now
they're right here in Elmsford County."

"Beg pardon?"

"Come a little closer, Bilyeux. Right. Now look me
dead in the eye. Bilyeux, old son, I think you're a man

that can be trusted. I'm going to tell you one word, Bilyeux, one word.''

"What's, uh, that, Sheriff?''

"Fluoride.''

"F-f-fluoride?''

"Fluoride and godless communism.''

"Fluoride and gggggggg . . . ?''

"You got it, old son,'' Sheriff Cody said. "The commies have been trying to shove fluoride down the throats of decent, God-fearing Christians for years. Years, Bilyeux! That's what the Kremlin wants. Fluoride is an acid. A deadly poison, Bilyeux, deadly! That's what caused those heart attacks, Bilyeux, you mark my words. Fluoride shipped straight from Moscow.''

Pete had his doubts. After all, he brushed with Crest. But he said nothing. Ideology is for idiots.

"Yep, old son, you mark my words. Somebody's been dumping fluoride, massive heaps of it, right into Kittelberger Reservoir. Now here's the drill, old son. I'm going to pick up the phone and get those health boys back here right now. You take 'em to Kittelberger and have them test for fluoride and report straight back to me. Not a word about this to anyone, old son, anyone. Loose lips sink ships, and I don't want those commies tipped off that we're after them. Got me?''

"Right, uh, Sheriff.''

"Good man. Old son, this may be bigger than the both of us.''

The sheriff gave Pete a hug that nearly made him sick, and left.

Pete did what he was told and knew no fluoride would be found. The voters of Elmsford County, generally a conservative lot, had thrice defeated referenda to fluoridate the water supply. They had been told the communists were behind it, possibly in cahoots with the American Dental Association and the Colgate-Palmolive Company. It is doubtful they believed this, but they took no chances.

Pete wondered what he would do. He dreaded the time wasted if the sheriff forced the department to pursue the chimera of fluoride. He dreaded what might happen if the heart attacks continued—and he thought they would. God, what could it be?

So far, the only person alive and conscious to have seen it happen was Reed Hamilton.

A meeting was arranged for an assistant prosecutor and a public defender to greet Reed's arrival at the substation by helicopter about eight o'clock that night.

Pete would have to go home for dinner and explain to Enid without alarming her why he would have to do some work that night and maybe the next day when he was supposed to be off duty.

7

"O, Lord, I fear the Evil Ones are amongst us," spoke the other.

"Even as I have taught ye, for the heart of evil is in the heart of life. Thus shall it remain unto my return to Tula upon the set of moon in full day," spoke the one.

"I know," spoke the other, "that from the truths thou speakest thou canst be none but that most greatest of gods, he of the brilliant quetzal plumage."

"Thou presumest much," spoke the one. "I am known by many names."

"Wilt thou return us with thee to Tula and the ripe fields and rich fruits, O magnificent god?" spoke the other.

"What is a god if not a god?" spoke the one. "As to the Evil Ones, I do iterate they take all forms: thine own babe that suckles at thy breast; the egg in the nest; the rodent of the land; the fishes of the seas; yea, even the insect of the air."

"And what, glorious god, may I render unto thee that mayst hasten our return to Tula?" spoke the other.

"Thou canst render up the heart of evil which is in the heart of life." So spoke Quetzalcoatl, the one.

Enid walked in the woods with her equipment and knew nothing had been working well. No sacrifice was accepted. When sacrifice is not accepted, when surrender is not accepted, something is awry.

That was the way it had been with the fat people. Nothing she or Adair could do in that foster home was right. Nothing worked. They would sacrifice their work to the fat people, they would sacrifice the Christmas gifts they got from charities to the fat people, and the fat people still shut them in the cellar to live on a musty mattress. They could hear the fat people chortle, the floorboards overhead creaking with their waddles. The sewer pipe was on Enid's side of the mattress and she could hear the flushes of the toilet and feel the rush of excrement past her elbow when the fat people would vacate the bloat surfeits of their gorges.

For five years she and Adair had lived in this place with no comfort but their two bodies become one.

Nobody helped them no matter how much they prayed and wished. Elspeth tried, but Elspeth was only two years older than they and had no influence. That was the trouble. They, none of them, had influence, not even with God. God and the United States of America and the Commonwealth of Pennsylvania had turned their backs on Enid and Adair Godwin.

Then the welfare people came one day and took them to Harrisburg to take the tests for college and to live in another place, and the fat people wept when they left. Enid and Adair wept when they left. The place had become their home. They were used to it, it was their world, and they had to leave it.

Nothing worked, now as then.

The heart of evil remained in the heart of life. The tales of the Toltec gods, both she and Adair thought, must be metaphors. Likewise was sacrifice a metaphor, even in Judeo-Christian traditions. There is virtue in ritual.

Yet not the sacrifice of the cats, the squirrels, the fox terrier seemed to avail.

Maybe she was doing it wrong. She had always hit

them with the mallet first. The hearts were no longer beating when she got them out. Maybe that was it. The hearts were dead.

She reached the little clearing where cats liked to sun themselves. Ringed by a dark, coolly scented patch of oaks, sycamores, and maples, it was their secret place to savor the sun, their daytime social place where they would greet and take siestas.

There was one now. He was a big tom with sorrel tiger stripes. The light from behind made a halo of his fur and he was still asleep. Trying not to disturb the air with sound, Enid crept upwind of him. She slipped the can opener and the tin of tuna from her kit and opened the tuna. She need not fear the noise, since she knew cats liked the sound of it. Sure enough, the big red's ears twitched at this small noise. But his eyes remained closed. She scattered some of the oil from the can over the grass and took out small bits of tuna and tossed them at the cat.

The cat awoke and began to eat his way toward the can in the shadow of an oak, where Enid waited with her statue of Quetzalcoatl. She put on heavy work gloves and took up a stainless-steel butcher knife. Then the cat stopped and looked into Enid's eyes and switched his tail. The woods were silent but for the droning of a few solitary flies.

"Kitty, kitty, sweet kitty, good boy, we got nice fishy for the kitty. Come on, kitty, kitty."

She tossed him a larger piece. He tiptoed toward it and ate it and licked over his lips and paws.

Enid pushed the can a few more inches toward him. The cat looked at the can, then back at Enid again, unable to decide.

"Sweet kitty, kitty, nice boy, come kitty, kitty."

Enid held some fish in her glove and squeezed it and let the cat smell it. Timorously, he began to advance toward her. Now, now, he's almost in range, Enid thought. Two more feet and he'll be at the can and I can get him. Good. One more foot. Nine inches. Six inches. It had to be done alive this time. Only a living heart would work. Four inches. Three. Two. One. His nose is in the can.

Enid lunged. Got him! She held him firmly by a fore-leg.

The cat tried to pull free. The fur on his back stood erect. "Kkkkhhhaaaaaahhh!" the cat hissed. "Mmmm-rrrrrrooowww!" he wailed.

Enid reached behind her for the knife and held it by the hilt in her fist and poised on her knees to stab down-ward.

Whether the cat saw or understood the knife can only be conjectured. But instinct told him he was in dire dan-ger and instinct told him what to do about it.

The blade flashed down and the cat flipped on his pli-able spine. He fought to free his foreleg but could not do so and jerked his hind legs up high toward the woman's face and kicked furiously with both legs in unison, claws distended, as to eviscerate his natural prey. Then he sank his teeth deep into the woman's wrist as his lecnine cous-ins would to sever the spine of a gazelle.

"Aaaaaaaaa," Enid screamed. The hind claws tore into biceps and sinew as a power tool. Still she stabbed and thrust with the knife and clung to the foreleg If she let go now, she knew her sanity would also let go. She must kill in the prescribed manner. But she could not manage to strike.

"Yaaaaaagh! Oh, God!" Enid cried as the cat sunk his teeth deep in her wrist and clamped down.

"Rrrrrowowrrrowowrrrr," the cat growled, fighting as he knew for his life.

"Ouch," Enid yelled as the cat kicked upward toward her eyes with claws out full. The free foreclaw dug through her jeans.

Then a hind paw raked her face. A single claw caught deep in her skin and not even the cat could free it.

"Oh, God!" Enid wept and knew she was losing. The cat's teeth grated against the bones of her wrist. Still she held the cat's foreleg. The cat struggled to free the claw from her cheek.

Enid dropped the knife and reached with her free hand and tore the claw from her cheek and felt the hot salt blood rush out. Still she clung to the cat's foreleg. She saw her blood spatter in droplets on the wild green grass.

She and the cat stopped struggling and rested, locked.

Neither woman nor cat knew what to do next. A solitary fly droned over their heads.

The cat's eyes caught hers and held in defiance.

Back and forth the fly flew, as though deciding on which head to alight.

Then it landed on the cat's nose, and bit.

"Rrrrrrrooooowwwww," the cat screeched and fought to be free of the woman.

Instinct told Enid something queer had happened. She and the cat were no longer enemies. She helped the animal loose.

Then she thought she had been deceived. The cat was free and her face and wrist and thigh were bleeding and she must get the knife and kill the cat.

The cat growled and wobbled drunkenly away. Enid raced at him with the knife. Then the cat convulsed and swooned downward.

"Kkkkkhhhh . . ." The cat tried to hiss and struggled on the ground with all four feet out straight. He got hold of his senses and struggled to get up, kicking his feet in spasms and gasping.

Enid knelt with the knife over the cat and their eyes met again. The cat's eyes were now soft, with sad dilated pupils washed with sparkling animal tears. The cat blinked as if starting to sleep.

Enid put down the knife. "Oh . . . oh, you poor dear," she said, "I'm . . . I'm sorry . . . you're a good heart . . ."

The cat stared at her drowsily and seemed to understand and forgive her. He was still gasping when the fly alit on the top of his head and bit again.

The fly, Enid thought. Oh, God, it was the fly!

The cat jerked at the bite and blinked and seemed to assent. Then he stiffened and his big yellow eyes grew weaker and he could no longer utter sound. The fly flew off.

"Oh, I'm sorry, dear," Enid said, and with her good hand stroked the cat's warm cheek. "I'm so terribly sorry, dear, it wasn't your fault . . ."

Enid's blood was still dripping on the grass. The fly that had bitten the cat flew down and wallowed in it.

"It was you, wasn't it, you wretched little vampire?"

As she spoke she leaned down to the fly feasting on blood.

Then she stood up and aimed her heel and stamped down again and again until the fly disintegrated in a pit in the ground. "Tell that to Tezcatlipoca," she said.

Enid was herself again.

She saw that the red cat was truly dead and grieved and took a circuitous route back to the house so no neighbors would see her all bloody.

The afternoon was wearing and she felt weak and sore from her cuts as she went into the house. She tore open a packet of sanitary napkins and used them to stanch the flow of her blood. Then she threw her clothes into the washer and got into the shower. The wounds opened again under the warm water and the blood dissipated in counterclockwise swirls down the drain and flowed off to become sewage. She felt physically weak, yet her mind was strong and her courage high, inspired by the red cat. The cuts were not so bad. She was a big girl and could take care of them. God, he was brave, Enid thought, brave and good and forgiving. No more cats would die. Something else would be sacrificed.

She got out of the shower and tamped her wounds with more sanitary napkins. They're sure in hell good at soaking up blood—Enid laughed to herself—you'd think they were made for it. She cleansed the wounds with hydrogen peroxide and watched it bubble all the animal nastiness out. *Pop-pop-fizz-fizz,* you can almost feel the little bubbles melt the slime away, she thought. She got out iodine and Q-tips. She screamed silently as she swabbed every gash and hole and welt of tooth and claw. She put sterile gauze soaked in antiseptic around her still-bleeding wrist and wrapped the wrist in an Ace bandage. She put Band-Aids on some of the deeper cuts in her arm, and another over the cut on her cheek. She was proud of how rationally she undertook her own first aid.

She felt faint when she put on her long-sleeved housedress and cleaned up the blood in the house. She went to the kitchen to prepare supper. Frankfurters and sauerkraut would be the easiest to make. Pete didn't like them all that much, but he never complained either. She filled the sauerkraut pot and put it on the flames. She felt enervated and anxious at once and knew she was on her second wind. She was afraid of catching a cold, so she mixed two grams of powdered Vitamin C into a tall glass of crimson V-8 juice, and added salt and pepper and a dash of Tabasco and some Worcestershire sauce and two shots of tequila and gulped it all down with a full gram of chlorpromazine.

Later that evening Louise Kavanaugh took a long breath and sliced deeply into the child's abdomen.

It was a male of about eight. The face still showed the angelic innocence of a boy soprano. Louise inwardly cursed her squeamishness, but knew she would feel it again. It would cause her to be irritable for days after. She always felt this way when she performed an autopsy on a young person.

The post-mortems she had done on the parents were unsettling enough. As Louise did with accident victims, she saved the children until last. But these were no accident victims. Worse yet, Louise had no idea what had victimized them—two young adults and a boy. Obviously a family. A damned healthy family, too.

She examined the boy's lungs. There was no visible or palpable evidence of pulmonary failure or embolism. She was sure she would find the same in the child as in the parents—nothing.

Louise felt herself succumbing to the hot, vague, depressive anxiety she had been fighting for months. She was alone with the corpses and almost envied them. She did not wish to think of the consequences of failing to discover what caused their deaths. She felt that professionally she was living on borrowed time, and Louise was nothing if not professional.

She reached in and snipped away the branches over the arch of the aorta, then the ligamentum arteriosum, then groped toward the anterior side of the heart.

Damn, but it was strange, Louise thought. Even though they had been found in a car, there was none of the pink skin coloration that indicated carbon monoxide poisoning. Opening the first of them ruled that out completely. Neither were there indications of trauma. There was no sign of the vomiting that often follows the oral ingestion of toxins. In fact, their cheeseburgers and french fries were quite identifiable, having barely begun to be digested. There was no visible indication of methemoglobinemia, only a little of cyanosis.

Of course, Louise thought, the annals of forensic medicine are chock full of anomalies. There had to be a reason for the sudden deaths. If the cause—or causes—was not apparent to the eye, then most likely it would turn up in exhaustive testing. If not . . . Well . . .

She extracted the heart, stripped away the pericardium, and placed it on the scale.

She paused to wipe her forehead, cold as the room was. Dammit, there *had* to be a cause. It could have involved the nervous system. Or perhaps it was some form of cardiac agent. There are plenty of them in the world, some occurring in nature.

Louise blew an exhalation of air out through her surgical mask. She looked at the organ on the scale. She would track down the cause laboriously, painstakingly extracting tissue and fluid samples and examining them. To be on the safe side, she would send duplicate samples to pathologists and toxicologists in New York; and, failing the success of that, all over the world if need be.

She glanced at her watch. It would be best to look into some books and mull it over a little sleep.

Besides, this family wasn't going anywhere. Their journey had ended in the parking lot of a fast-food restaurant in Thomas Valley, Pennsylvania, a place of which Dr. Louise Kavanaugh of Hershey Medical Center had never heard.

The smoke detectors were bawling klaxons when Pete got home. He could smell it even in the garage. He ran into the kitchen. A pot of food, he could not tell what it once had been, had melted aluminum and gutta-percha handle all over the stove. He shut off the fire and opened a window and turned on the exhaust fan.

"Enid? Enid?! H-h-hon. Enid?" he called.

He found her in the bedroom, fast asleep in her housedress under the covers, lying on her side. He could not see the side of her that was injured.

He touched her forehead and eyebrows tenderly and

she did not respond. He touched her chest and could feel her breathing normally. He went into the bathroom and counted her capsules of medicine. She had taken five, a strong but not dangerous dose.

Let her sleep, Pete thought, it's been a hard day for everyone.

Awesome, the kids of the eighth-grade class thought when they arrived at Jacob Walz State Park.

Awesome, Irene Byrne thought. This place is just for ourselves. Ain't a soul else here, just like Adam and Eve had before they got kicked out.

This place is wiggy, Herman García thought. It's so goddamn pretty it makes me nervous. I don't trust the air, he thought. Can't see it.

"Oh, Lord Jesus, it's like the mountains of Kenya," Sister Nettie trilled in her lilting voice. "Oh, Lord God, I so love the things You make for us to see and hear and smell and feel. Oh, children, darlings, look at that sky, look at those mountains, at that lake, those trees . . . there you see the hand of God all naked."

I don't want to see no naked God, Irene Byrne confided in herself. Just as soon the sumbitch put on his clothes and set things straight for a change. Still, it beat North Philadelphia. She went to help Sister Nettie set up the picnic tables in a place sheltered from the sun by towering elms.

Sister Melanie and some boys set up the volleyball net, and Herman went with Sister Helga and some other boys to drag the often-patched rubber raft out of the bus.

Those children not helping the nuns wandered off to explore the park, timidly at first, the wilderness being unfamiliar turf.

"What that shit growing all over that rock?" little Sue Ellen Hutton asked big, gangling Talmadge Brown.

"I dunno," Talmadge said. "Looks like some kind of grass."

"Shit. Ain't no grass grows on no rocks. Now don't you touch that, Talmadge Brown. it might be poison."

"Shit." Talmadge said, and touched the spongy moss anyway and laughed and made a mental note to ask the sisters about it.

"Hey, will you look at this action," Sue Ellen said in a cool and dark patch of woods. "Mushrooms. Growing right out of the ground. They big. Shit, just look at 'em."

"Woo, they big, all right. Pretty too. But I don't think you want to eat them muffas. I hear some of 'em is poison," Talmadge said. And he was right. They were *Amanita phalloides*, the death cup, deadliest of the deadly.

Needless to say, these children ate nothing they found in Jacob Walz Park, not even the plump wild blackberries and blueberries that abounded in the place. For that matter, they ate nothing they found lying around in North Philadelphia, either.

And so the youngsters helped the nuns organize the day's outing and poked and probed at their new world.

Wanda James had the quickest and most curious eye. She noticed two dead birds, a dead squirrel, a dead fish on the shore of the lake, and a dead thing that looked like a mouse with wings.

She went to tell Sister Nettie.

"Darling, that's just God's way," the nun said. "Things just naturally die and out here there's nobody to give them burial."

"Do they go to heaven?" Wanda asked.

Sister Nettie laughed her tinkling laugh. "Well, I suppose they do, those that are good. Why, surely they go to some animal heaven. They're God's creatures and God takes care of His own."

Herman García was last to work at pumping air into the rubber raft. Sister Helga, born in Germany, was finally satisfied the thing was properly inflated.

"This is good, Herman," she said. " For this, you get first chance to go on boat with me and one other. Do you like this?"

Herman tugged at his ear and was unsure. He had never been in a boat of any kind. "I, uh, I dunno, Sister, I can't swim."

"You don't need to swim, Herman, for this we have raft."

"Well, okay," Herman said, contrary to his judgment.

"Not worry, Herman, we stay out of deep part. Maynard, you helped too, you want ride in raft with Herman and me?"

"Oh, yeah, Sister, for sure." Maynard was dying to ride and was a little jealous that Herman had been asked first because he had worked just as hard as Herman. That damn Herman was always getting away with murder.

The raft was launched and the three jumped in it.

"Now don't sit high, boys," Sister Helga said. "You must sit low in raft, *ja?* This way it is more stable, you see."

Sister Helga taught the boys how to row with the small paddles, how to make the raft turn and reverse direction.

Herman fretted about falling off and drowning, but Sister Helga kept the raft close to shore and assured him he would be safe, and Herman grew to enjoy the bobbing of the raft and the lapping of the dark waters of the lake.

Sister Melanie prowled the periphery of the park to make certain none of her young explorers was exploring one another.

She was the first to die and no one saw or heard it happen.

Pete cleaned up the stove and made some toast and soup and coffee and ate and drank. He looked in on Enid to make sure she was all right, left a note for her, locked the house, and rode back to the substation.

The assistant prosecutor and public defender had arrived and were in the conference room when Pete walked in. Introductions were made. Reed Hamilton had not yet arrived.

The lawyers were still young enough to have some concern for justice. The assistant prosecutor wanted to charge Reed with negligent homicide and leaving the scene of an accident.

The public defender would have none of either and pointed out there had been no homicide for Reed to have been negligent about, nor an accident the scene of which he could have left.

Pete knew they were plea-bargaining. He listened until he felt the timing was right to inject himself into the conversation.

They talked, a deal was struck pending Reed's willingness to make a statement, and the scenario for Pete's

interview with Reed was laid in time for the approaching
helicopter.

Pete mustered a stern expression and went out to the
rear parking lot painted with a large O that served as an
infrequent helicopter landing pad.

A trooper brought a chastened Reed Hamilton out in
handcuffs. Pete signed for the custody and gestured for
the trooper to remove his handcuffs.

"Hello, Mr. Bilyeux," Reed said, lips aquiver, eyes
on ground.

"Hello, uh, Reed," Pete said in a solemn baritone. He
led the boy by the arm.

Gary Busch was at the desk and glared at Reed, who
averted his eyes. The lawyers had left.

"Sit down, uh, Reed," Pete said when they were in
the conference room.

"Okay . . . uh, Mr. Bilyeux, I, uh, don't mean to be
rude, but, uh, they say I, uh, don't have to make a statement without, uh, advice of c-counsel . . ."

Pete was inwardly amused to hear someone else have
trouble with his words. "You d-d-don't," he said, and
got out his citation book. "Let me drive your, uh, see
your driver's license."

Reed gave him the license. "What, uh, what are my
. . . my chances, Mr. Bilyeux?" he said, tears beginning
to well.

"You, uh, don't have to tell me anything and I don't
have to tell you anything," Pete said, copying from the
license.

"Mr. Bilyeux?"

"Yeah?"

"D-d-do they, uh, have the electric chair in Pennsylvania, sir?" He was beginning to sob.

"Yeah," Pete said, still writing.

"M-m-mind if I, uh, smoke, Mr. Bilyeux?"

"Yeah, I mmmind. I don't like smoke."

"Oh, uh, sorry. Mr. Bilyeux, uh, I mean we don't have
to t-tell each other or anything, but it's not like we were
strangers or anything. I, uh, I mean I won't hold you to
anything you say if, uh, you don't hold me to anything I
say . . ."

Pete looked up from his writing and let his expression

relax ever so slightly. "Okay, you got a deal. What's on your mind?"

"Oh, God, what are my chances, Mr. Bilyeux, oh, please?"

"Of what?"

"Of g-g-getting the chair," Reed sobbed.

Pete was beginning to feel a little cruel. "Somewhere between zero and, uh, none, Reed. Right now you're in a hell of a lot more trouble in New Jersey than here."

"What?" Reed said, suddenly less lachrymose. "Then, uh, what are you writing in that book?"

"A, uh, summons."

"For what?"

"For b-b-burial without a permit. The, uh, prosecution and defense agreed to it if you make a statement. It's a misdemeanor, not a felony, maximum fine three hundred dollars. They'll probably hit you for only a hundred."

"B-b-but why?"

"You b-b-buried her, didn't you?"

"Yes, sir." Reed looked down and wept again. "I, uh, I was afraid they'd think uh, that I mmmurdered her . . ."

"Nobody goes to the electric chair because somebody, uh, has a heart attack," Pete said.

"Oh, God, oh, thank God, you know! Oh, thank God! Oh, Mr. Bilyeux, I felt so sorry for her. I tried and tried, but there was nothing I could do. We were, well, you know . . . and, uh, then something happened and nothing I could do worked. I thought they'd blame me, oh, thank God . . ." Reed buried his face in his hands and wept again.

Pete knew it was time to spring the speech, as much as he disliked speeches. "Okay, Reed, uh, look, here's the deal. The prosecution and defense lawyers were just here, and the prosecution will throw the book at you unless you dep a makosition, excuse me, make a dddeposition to the lawyers tomorrow about what you tell me tonight. Now that deposition is only good in Pennsylvania. There's nothing we can do about New Jersey, and you'll have to go bbback there and face charges because a policeman and, uh, shooting was involved. But they'll go easy on you here—*if* you tell me right now every detail

of exactly what happened. You may not know this, but
in the last few days nine people have died in Thomas
Valley of alleged heart attacks and, uh, you're the only
one to have seen it happen who's in any shape to talk.
What you say, uh, could save a lot of lives . . ."

"Jesus Christ," Reed said, "I don't know anything
about . . ."

"Yes, you do," Pete blurted, and knew he might be
letting his own hopes be too involved. But he continued.
"You saw it happen, dammit, Reed, and I want you to
tell me everything you saw. Absolutely everything! Do
you understand?"

"Yes, sir," Reed said. He told of picking up Debbie
at her house. No, they had not used any drugs. No coke,
no grass, no aspirin-smoking, no glue-sniffing, nothing
but Marlboros and sex. Reed related the dismal details
to the best of his memory.

"Is that all?" Pete said.

"Yes, sir, Mr. Bilyeux, that's all. I swear it, sir."

It was now Pete who held his face in his hands. He
knew the boy was telling the truth, especially since there
were things he disliked hearing. The toes of Pete's boots
ground against the floor in frustration. "Okay, Reed,
thanks. Uh, one advice of word between you and me,
Reed . . ."

"Yes, sir."

"The, uh, next time you pull your pecker out of your
pants, uh, try it with someone with as much experience
as you. You, uh, you'll even find that it's more fun that
way, son."

Pete led Reed to the wooden bench in front of the desk.
He asked Gary Busch to phone for Reed's father to take
him home. No, Gary said, there was no further word on
Joey Murdock.

Pete loosened his uniform tie and started to walk out.
By now he had a headache.

"Oh," he said, and cursed himself for almost forgetting. It had been a long day and his feelings were too
involved. "Reed?"

"Yes, sir?"

"Uh, there was a d-d-deep little, uh, pit in the ground
by the tree. Did you stamp something?"

"Uh . . ." Reed tired to remember. "Well, uh, sir, I put out a couple of cigarettes, maybe three or four . . ."

"This was, uh, a deeper hole. You stamped something hard."

"Oh, yeah, uh, yes, sir, I remember. It was a fly."

Pete's heart tripped over its own beat and his skin prickled. "Ah, uh, wh-what?"

"A fly, sir."

"Why did you stamp it?" Pete said, feeling the rush that let him speak clearly.

"Well, uh, Mr. Bilyeux, I was upset after it all happened and the fly had been on Debbie—"

"Was it on Debbie before or after the heart attack?"

"Uh, before, sir, just before."

"Mother of God," Pete said. "Oh, holy Jesus!"

Reed and Gary Busch looked at Pete strangely as he turned and left.

8

Sister Nettie told Irene Byrne to take a break. The tables had been set and the nun would start the cooking with the help of others who had not yet worked.

Irene sat on an old stump in the shade and munched on a broken hamburger bun. Yes, this was a pretty place, she thought, and the air smelled fresh and clean, surprisingly cool for this time of year. Philadelphia smelled dirty and musty and humid.

A squirrel loped by and stopped and looked at Irene.

"Well, ain't you a crazy little thing, you. Did you come to say hello to Irene, or do you just want to mooch some of my bun? Here, you little turkey, here's a piece."

She tossed it to the squirrel, who picked it up in his paws, sat, sniffed, chewed, gobbled it down, and begged for more.

Irene laughed. "Well, you just a little greedy-guts, ain't you? Hey, where you get that big old bushy tail? How come you switching that thing at me? That some kind of squirrel talk? Here, come get a piece out of my hand. What's a matter, you afraid of my hands? Well, maybe they ugly but they work fine again, doctors fixed 'em right up. Don't be afraid. Come on."

The squirrel kept its distance.

"Well, you just naturally scared, ain't you? You don't trust nobody, do you? Know something, little guy, you right. Here."

A girl and a boy stopped by the scene.

"Hey, Irene, what you talking to?"

The squirrel dropped to all fours ready to run.

"Shush up," Irene said, "you'll scare him off."

Soon a small crowd gathered. More buns were brought and the squirrel put on an antic show, hopping, darting, catching morsels in midair, much to the hilarity of the spectators.

The squirrel caught a piece of bun just as a fly landed on its back. Oblivious to the fly, which it could have flicked away with its tail, the squirrel busied itself in eating.

Suddenly a shrill peep with a desperate edge came from the throat of the squirrel. Even the youngsters of asphalt vistas and fetid concrete recognized the sound as dire.

"What the hell going on?" Irene said.

"Awesome," said a boy as the squirrel palsied and died.

"Hey, nigger, what you feed that squirrel to make him do that?" Irene said to the boy who had tossed the last morsel. "You give him crack or smack?"

"I didn't give him nothing but this bread," the boy protested. "Must've been that fly."

"That's right, Irene. He didn't give it nothing but bread, I seen it," another boy said. "That muffa just up and keeled over soon as that fly landed on him. You know what I'm saying?"

"That's right. That's right." The sentiment was ech-oed among the other children, who looked at one another quizzically.

Irene suddenly felt chilly. She tried to think of what kind of squirrel would be so weak as to die from the touch of a fly, and then of what kind of fly could kill a squirrel. "Maybe he ain't dead. Maybe he just fainted or something," Irene said.

A boy went to the squirrel and touched him. "He dead all right. Deader 'n shit."

"Where is that muffa?" Irene said.

"Shit, girl, right here. I touching him," the boy said.

"No, stupid, I mean the fly," Irene said.

The boy shrugged. "Must be around here somewhere."

Sue Ellen screamed. "It's on my blouse!"

"Don't move," Irene said. "And don't touch it. Somebody get something and kill that sumbitch."

Nobody had anything to kill it so the boy by the squirrel sneaked toward Sue Ellen. None of the children moved. Suddenly the fly took off and circled Sue Ellen's head.

Then it landed on her neck.

Deftly the boy moved his hand toward the girl's neck. The fly squirmed and tried to settle itself into some kind of position.

The boy snapped his middle finger against his thumb and the fly spun down to the grass.

"Stomp that sumbitch," Irene said. "That muffa's bad news."

The boy did. The children broke into cheers, except for Sue Ellen, who broke into tears of relief.

Sister Nettie rang the familiar cowbell for lunch and everyone seemed to forget the incident as they dashed for a good place in line at the food table—everyone except Irene, who resolved to tell Sister Nettie about it.

Sister Nettie then rang the cowbell in the direction of the raft far up the shore of the lake. She saw someone wave both arms in acknowledgment. My goodness, they certainly are a long way off, the nun thought, but Sister Helga knew what she was doing. Sister Nettie would make sure to save food for her and the boys, and for Sister Melanie, wherever she had got off to.

* * *

The trouble was that Sister Helga was dead and so was Maynard. It happened so quickly Herman could scarcely comprehend.

The sister had rolled up her sleeves to help paddle. Suddenly she let out a cry and struck at a fly that had landed on her forearm. She began to thrash. The fly flew off. Maynard reached over to help the nun. Maynard was a straight-A student and would know just what to do. Then the same fly landed on Maynard and he screamed. The spasms of the boy and nun nearly capsized the raft.

Herman tried to comfort and revive them, but it was impossible, and the christawfullest sonofabitching fly in the world was buzzing around and Herman was about to be its next victim.

The fly landed on the side of the raft and Herman killed it with a paddle. He heard the lunch bell ring and waved toward it and screamed for help. But the sister on the shore turned her back and walked up the hill toward the picnic.

Herman paddled frantically toward the place where they had launched the raft. Fear and cold pulses threatened to rob him of his reason, a hunted animal in the center of a spotlight behind which sat a man with a rifle. In his panic he did not think to make for the nearest shore and run.

Then he heard them. More flies. Many more than one. Three of them landed on the raft, two on bodies. He heard more droning over his head. He thought he could feel one in his hair.

He knew there way no way he could fend them off.

Irene thought Sister Nettie would scoff when she heard of the fly and the squirrel, but she did not. Instead, she looked off.

Sister Nettie, of course, knew of the tsetse fly and Irene did not. The nun excused herself and left others in charge of the cooking and went off to gather cry wood, just in case.

Karen Franklin had sat in the shade and started into her custom-made cheeseburger with lettuce and sliced onion smothered in ketchup when the fly landed on the top of her ear and bit.

She spat out the food and screamed as if choking. Some

of the children saw and heard and ran to her help. No one noticed the fly at first.

"Sister, Sister!" one of the girls called out, "it's Karen! She's choking!"

Karen had fallen to the ground by the time Sister Nettie reached her. The nun dropped the wood she had gathered. "Somebody hold her up!" Sister Nettie barked, and when a boy did, the nun began to perform the Heimlich maneuver to dislodge the food she was sure had caught in Karen's throat. "Now, relax, Karen, darling, try to cough. That's good. You'll be all right . . ."

But it was soon apparent she was not all right. Sister Nettie tried mouth-to-mouth resuscitation and chest massage and could not restore the girl's breathing or pulse. She said prayers over her.

All the youngsters were so absorbed with this scene that only Irene Byrne noticed the several flies that had gathered.

"It was the fly, Sister, the fly!" Irene said, and for the first time saw fear pass over the face of her favorite nun. "They all over the place."

"OOooowwwOOOWWWwwwggghhh," screamed Orville Ramsey, who fell clutching his chest.

"It's the flies, Sister! They killing us!" Irene yelled.

Herman could not swim and had always panicked whenever someone tried to teach him. Yet he knew what his choice must be, and he shuddered as he yanked off his shoes and put them on the bed of the raft. He tumbled toward the black waters of the lake, saying rapidly to himself: Hail-Mary-full-of-grace-the-Lord-is-with . . .

As he went over, he clung tight with both hands to the thin rope by which the raft could be moored. The cold of the water soaking its blind fingers through his clothes shocked him. He stretched out his toes and the tips of them found the muddy bottom of the lake. The rope was at its full length and one of Herman's hands slipped from it. The other held for his life while the free hand groped. His heart beat wildly and his chest soon felt it would implode as he clutched to get both hands on the rope. He knew the clammy, pallid, eyeless blundering of the drowning. He needed air. He would die soon without it.

He felt the weeds that grow upward from the bottom to
the height of a man slither and surround and threaten to
entangle him. He jerked upward on the rope with the
hand that yet clutched it, and opened his eyes. They
burned as he saw shining as a mirror the surface that
blocked his air far above him. At last his free hand found
the rope and he pulled hand over hand upward. His body
felt seconds from its end when finally he broke the surface and expelled the bad air and gulped in the good.
Then he heard the flies and took in a rapid lungful of air
and slid on the rope to the lake bottom as a fireman in
an old-time movie slid down a pole.

He began to walk along the slimy bottom, holding the
rope, slipping toward land. He resolved to repeat his
wretched surfacing and sounding forever if need be. The
alternative was sudden death.

"Make smoke, darlings," Sister Nettie commanded.
"Make smoke with those sticks, put them in the fires
quick, the smoke will drive off the flies. Don't let them
land on you, darlings! Don't let them touch your skin!
Oh, merciful God . . ."

The children rushed to do as she said and soon the
burning faggots were waved as smudge pots against a sky
to which the children looked in horror.

Sister Nettie ran to Orville's corpse and could do nothing but pray over it and return to protect the rest of her
flock.

"All right, darlings," the nun said. Her calm was now
restored and her voice again melodic. "Everyone gather
together. Come on, now, quickly. Good. Now stay in a
bunch and keep those sticks smoking up high and keep
your eyes open and go to the bus."

Sister Nettie walked behind them and kept a wary eye
out for the flies, which seemed to be gone. When the
terrified procession reached the bus, the nun halted them
and carefully inspected the interior and made sure the
windows were shut tight and went out and told the dejected children to file in.

The nun doused the torches and got in the bus and
closed the door and stood in the aisle to speak as the
youngsters found seats. The sun was at her back and

shone on the faces of children now looking drawn and older. All they could see of her was a dark specter limned in backlight.

She spoke in the voice of a matriarch to survivors of a community desolated by war.

"All right, darlings, we're safe for now. God works His will in ways we can't always understand. Let's pray that the Lord Jesus has taken Karen and Orville to his bosom to dwell in the house of the Lord, where there are many, many rooms."

"Amen," said the children, and prayed silently.

"Amen," Sister Nettie said. "Now, let's see. Who's missing? I count Sister Melanie, Sister Helga, uh, Maynard, let's see . . ."

"Herman," Irene said.

"Yes, Herman," the nun said. "Is there anyone else missing?" The children shook their heads. "Well, we'll wait a few minutes and if they don't turn up, I'll go look for them."

"No, Sister," Talmadge Brown said. "I'll go."

"No, Talmadge, you will not . . ."

Suddenly there was a crash at the door of the bus. Sister Nettie started and some of the children screamed.

The nun went to the door. "Oh, dear Lord," she said.

She opened the door. Covered cap-a-pie with slimy black ooze and festooned with water weeds as a creature in a monster movie, Herman García stumbled into the bus with his shoes in his hands.

"Oh, thank God, thank God," he babbled, with tears in his eyes. "Don't anybody go outside! Nobody! There are crazy flies around killing people all over the place. . . ."

"You ain't telling us nothing new," Irene said.

"You don't understand!" Herman screamed on the verge of hysteria. "There are flies out there killing people! Flies! So help me God! In the air! They killed Sister Helga! They killed Maynard! They must have killed Sister Melanie! She was in the woods on my way back. She was dead!"

The nun and the children crossed themselves on hearing of the dead and of a new death.

"Nobody's listening to me!" Herman ranted. "I'm telling you flies are killing people! It's fucking crazy!"

"Herman," Sister Nettie snapped. It was an unwritten rule at Sorry School that students did not employ the same kind of adjectives in the presence of nuns that they used in privacy. Herman's faux pas drew titters that broke some of the tension.

Afternoon came slowly and with it the mood of terror evolved to one of dull dread. Sister Nettie announced her decision. "Children, I'm going to have to go out and get help."

"No!" "No, sister." "Don't go out there, Sister." Her statement drew a chorus of protest.

"Well, darlings, someone has to go. We can't just sit around waiting for help, can we? The Lord helps those who help themselves, they say. We can't blame all our problems on God. Perhaps He's testing our faith as He did with Job. Remember what Jesus said of the sick who were healed? 'Thy faith has made thee whole.' And if faith was good enough for Jesus, it's good enough for us, isn't it? Oh, don't look so sorry downcast. We'll be all right. I'll pray for you and you'll pray for me and we'll have faith and it'll be all right. We haven't come this far to lose the entire thing, you know, darlings. Now I don't think I'll be that long, but however long it takes, the rules are the same. Windows closed in the bus. Nobody goes out except to the bathroom and then you've got to completely cover up. Here, watch me, darlings."

She rummaged in a bag and got a kerchief and arranged it over her face like a bandit in a cowboy movie. Only her eyes and a thin band of forehead skin showed between her wimple and her stagecoach-robber mask. She tucked her hands inside the long floppy sleeves of her habit and held the sleeves closed from inside.

"See, darlings, no hands. This is how we do it."

She showed Irene Byrne and Talmadge Brown how to open and shut the door of the bus with the lever by the driver's seat. She hugged each youngster in turn. "God bless you," she said to each. Then she went out. The door was shut behind her and she waved gaily to the children gawking and waving at the windows.

There were no flies nearby.

The children gathered at the rear of the bus and watched the lonely raven figure set out, and most of them remembered to pray for her. Many of them leaked tears.

They could see the nun turn several times and wave to them on the dirt road that led from the county road that led from the highway that led from the interstate. The children waved in return. Then the nun rounded a bend and disappeared.

Sister Nettie, N'Teta, often thought of other things while praying and always felt guilty for this. She now prayed constantly and thought at the same time as she trudged through the afternoon heat and knew this was her nature and hoped God would understand.

This place was truly not like Africa at all. The trees were too tall and the land too shadowy. But in its wildness and purity of air she felt of it as she had of her native land, where she had discovered God invested in each molecule of plain. There was God in the clear air with horizon white in day, carmine at dawn and dusk. There was God in the yellow stalks of midsummer grass that might conceal *simba*, the lion, or *chui*, the leopard; creatures, too, of God. There was God in the vast milling herds of gnu and *punda milia* with their babies who could run with the herd nearly from birth. So, too, was there God in the elms and oaks and maples and sycamores of this place, in the bluejays, sparrows, crows, squirrels, and in the rocks themselves. And if there was God in the strike of the deadly mamba of her land, so was there God in the queer deadly flies of this one. It was all a part of a plan forever unknowable to man, who is forever jealous of God.

Sister Nettie walked for several miles on the dirt road, praying and thinking and growing a headache in the heat.

Flies troubled her now and again, but she easily frightened them away with the waving of her great sleeves. You don't grow up in Africa without knowing how to cope with flies. She noticed some of these flies seemed to be averse to the sun, so she stayed out of the shade whenever she could.

She came to a place where a brook of limpid water, a *kijito-angavu*, ran among tall trees in a defile by the side of the road. She walked on the sunny side opposite it and

prayed for the children and reckoned she was nearly halfway to the paved road.

She had not been so physically exercised in years, and
never so emotionally exercised. When she prayed and
called on her faith to relieve the throbbing in her head,
it was relieved. When her concentration lapsed her headache returned. She was feeling weak and desiccated in
the heat of the sunny side of the road. She was corporeal
and the flesh was threatening to betray the spirit as it had
done even to saints. Perhaps she should go to the *kijito-
angavu* and cool herself and drink of the waters. This
would sustain her mission and help her find a road with
cars by nightfall.

The cool of the shade near the brook refreshed her.
She murmured a prayer of thanksgiving and was better
able to concentrate on it. She looked and listened carefully for flies and there were none. She withdrew her
hands and dropped her bandanna. She bathed hands and
face in the cool water and wet her wimple and kerchief
and was reminded of the people who had bathed the feet
of Jesus after a day's journeying. She cupped her hands
and drank of the cool sweet water and let it fill her mouth
and slake her parched throat.

She stood in the shade and replaced the cooling wet
bandanna over her face.

On her left middle finger she wore the silver ring that
symbolized her marriage to God.

Suddenly on the finger next to it she felt an electric
shock of agony. Hideous pain coursed through her body
as quickly as if it had been struck by lightning. Sister
Nettie's heart felt gripped in cold and pain. She knew it
would not start again and she had not even seen the fly.

"G-G-God!" she cried through the pain, "love . . .
children. Please . . . *mwanangu* . . . *Mungu* . . . help
children . . ."

Sister N'Teta knew she was already dead as she sensed
her body falling backward into the brook. The pain was
gone and with it her concentration. The world became
dark purple on the edges of a circle in her mind's vision.
She was drowsy in the shining center of the circle and
began to feel immaculate relief from a long and cruel
burden. She stood over the brook now and looked down

at her body and saw her eyes open under the water and
the current making billows of her garments. The purple
circle closed and in its place came a dazzling brilliance
from which emerged a hand wearing a ring identical to
hers, beckoning to her . . .

Now the children of Our Lady of Sorrows were sor-
rowful and alone in the wilderness with the flies.

9

A few weeks after she left Roger, Louise Kavanaugh was
so untutored in the use of latter-day conveniences that
she did not know which size vibrator to buy. So she tried
small, medium, large, even ribbed, and didn't like any
all that much.

For years off and on, Cynthia had tried to seduce Louise. So Louise thought she'd try that. She went out to
Cynthia's place in the Hamptons for a cozy brunch, a
friendly afternoon, and dinner. The dinner got on prom-
isingly with a wicked leer in Cynthia's eye, lots of double
entendres, hints of new and transcendent ecstasies to
come, followed by a nude dual dip in the pool. The rest
was ignominious. Louise felt embarrassed and foolish
and could not relax and not only failed to enjoy it but
nearly vomited. She pleaded headache and departed for
New York.

Louise was furious to realize that she needed men, the
slobs. She was healthy, newly single after years, more
than occasionally randy, and gimcracks and lesbians
would not suffice. Oh, did this vex her.

This was because she was very angry with Roger,
which she had every right to be. Roger was a rat. She
had an affair with him that lasted through the better part
of a year in medical school. It was a beautiful thing.
Roger was a beautiful man. They had almost married

then, but each had been too devoted to beginning a career. So they drifted apart and worked hard and had other affairs and wrote each other occasional and frank letters and finally lost touch when Roger went overseas. Louise had been working at the New York medical examiner's office for nearly two years when, lo, who should turn up as a new staff member right out of the pages of a romantic novel but, of course, Roger, Mr. Right. They fell in love all over again. They married and stayed that way long enough for Louise to realize she wanted a child or two, though she still wanted to pursue a career that had gone from promising to brilliant. There was little doubt that she was the most highly regarded young pathologist at the center, which is a highly regarded institution. Her desire for a child was fine with Roger, who also found himself wanting children, he said. They planned the first one to arrive about the time Louise turned thirty-four.

But the bubble burst about the time she turned thirty-three. She was never sure how much of it was due to Roger's skullduggery. It had to do with slides getting transposed and there being two Dr. Kavanaughs at the examiner's office. Louise got called on the carpet for a mistake she knew she didn't make. It was not a bad-enough mistake to get her fired, but it resulted in a confused autopsy report in an important criminal case and it meant her career had lost its sheen. Whether Roger had made a genuine mistake and she got blamed for it or whether Roger had deliberately set her up, Louise would never know. She suspected the latter. Scarcely had she left her dressing-down than she was confronted by that cute little assistant, Miriam. Miriam disclosed she was having an affair with Roger and demanded that Louise release him for her to marry. Suddenly the romantic novel had turned into a sordid soap opera.

Louise did not even confront Roger. Miriam had told her enough of the little secrets of their love life that Louise knew she wasn't lying.

Louise resigned forthwith, moved into a hotel for the nonce, and hired a lawyer.

Louise had always been a natural feminist. That is, she had never taken the equality of the sexes for anything less than granted. Her father was a successful neurosurgeon and her mother a respected professional architect and amateur painter. Both parents were devoted to each other and to their children, of whom Louise was the oldest. Nobody ever made Louise play with dolls. If she played with dolls as a kid, it was because she damned well felt like it. If she whacked away with a hammer as a kid, it was also because she damned well felt like it. When she first menstruated, both parents canceled all appointments to take her out to dinner at a posh restaurant to lavish affection on her and assuage the intimidating transition from childhood to adolescence.

Growing up, she had been annoyed a few times with blatant sexual discrimination but was too emotionally secure and had been too carefully prepared by her parents to let it get under her skin.

That was before Roger happened. That got under her skin. It was a dirty trick. It followed a priori that romance and sentiment were dirty tricks played on exploited females by unctuous males.

Louise's consciousness suddenly ascended to an apogee somewhere on the far side of the planet Pluto.

The vibrators and the female lover had taught her that she needed men in bed. So she set about creating an elaborate complex of defensive salients based on the time-honored premise that the best defense is a good offense. Louise Kavanaugh became, at least for this painful part of her life, a sexual great white shark. She would seduce men and love them and leave them.

Louise had never cursed much until the divorce. Now she went out of her way to outcurse a deckhand on a Brooklyn tugboat.

Her secret ambition was to pick some unsuspecting guy who was a perfect stranger and walk up to him and say, "Hey, shithead, you think you have the balls to pound my pudding?"

The very thought of this outrage and the look she knew it would bring to the guy's face always made Louise laugh to herself. She had not, of course, done it. But she reserved the right to . . . someday . . . if the timing were perfect. After all, wasn't it the kind of stunt construction workers in New York would pull on secretaries during lunch hour?

But events like this were more than rare in Hershey, Pennsylvania. And she did not think much about sex on the night after the autopsies. She fell into a fitful sleep through which fretted Latin conundrums and snippets from medical journals.

Her sleep would be even less restful the following night.

10

Pete Bilyeux awoke before dawn again and made espresso again, this time only one thermos-full. He went out to the garage and found a couple of old mayonnaise jars and dusted them off and punched holes in the lids. He stowed them in the saddlebags of his Suzuki motorcycle and wondered whether he should take his service revolver along. Unlike many policemen, he disliked being armed when off duty. But today he would be alone doing police-work at a strange time, so he decided it would be prudent to take it.

Enid was still asleep when Pete tiptoed through the bedroom and went to the closet to get his Colt Python with six-inch barrel, his shoulder holster, and .357 Magnum hollow-nosed cartridges.

The Elmsford county deputies were required to use this particularly potent ammunition, albeit they had little need for it. In fact, the hollow-nosed bullet—called a dum-dum in the vernacular—so ravages flesh that it is banned worldwide in military use. It is permitted, however, for policework and for hunting; criminals and animals presumably not being signatories to the Geneva Convention on civilized warfare. But the Elmsford deputies were allowed to choose their own sidearms and were reimbursed for them up to $150 every five years. This gun had cost Pete more than twice that, used. It was a vintage piece, far less a service revolver than a target gun that was compact enough and tough enough for daily wear. With a low serial number, 2975, it was prized by collectors. This was just as well, as it was the only gun Pete owned.

In the kitchen, Pete left a note for Enid and loaded five cartridges in the six-shot revolver so the firing pin would rest on an empty chamber, a precaution dating from cowboy days.

This Tuesday he would begin gathering flies at the Mueller house, and then go to the places where Al and Debbie had died.

He took a shorter route to the vile house puttering astride his Suzuki on what had once been a dirt road but was now two traces of bare earth. The wild grasses had even begun to encroach on these and would have overcome them but for an occasional car that traveled the road. This still happened, and recently too, Pete surmised from the bent grasses in the center.

Birds gamboled and sang their morning songs at scented hills that swelled to hail the arrival of a warm and ruby sun. A family of cottontail rabbits romped across a meadow.

Pete wondered at how sharply this pastoral contrasted with the violent deaths of recent days. If God had willed such scenes, which Pete did not doubt, had God also willed the recent human events? Pete did doubt this. He had long reached the ineluctable conclusion that the deity was not much of an interventionist in human affairs, and Pete saw too much poetry in that which was not human to believe man to be the apple of God's eye.

When finally he topped the hill from which he could see the Mueller house, the sight raised the hairs on the back of his neck.

The house was gone. It had burned to the foundation and all that remained were ashes and cinders and wisps of smoke. Not a fly flew anywhere near it.

Pete thought it was all too much. It could not be coincidence. He stopped the bike and got off and wandered around the yard. Yes, there were fresh tire marks that had not been there yesterday. Yes, there were some empty gallon jugs. And, yes, the jugs smelled of gasoline.

He took pliers to the old refrigerator and worried the

hinge pins off and put them in his pocket. This refrigerator would not suffocate another child. He pulled off the
door and threw it aside. Then he saw what had not been
in the refrigerator the day before. It was a note, words
cut from magazines and newspapers and pasted down. It
read: mind YOUR OWN business and LIVE LONGER.

Now, that is interesting, he thought. Maybe we're getting somewhere. He was a little surprised by it, since he
had no reason to suspect criminality in all this business.
Of course, it could well have been a prank. No doubt
word of Joey's discovery here had spread, tempting adventurous youths to join in the fun. Yes, most likely it
was that. After all, criminals do not leave such evidence
as empty gasoline jugs lying around—not unless they do
it to make a statement.

He tucked the note in his pocket and started up the
Suzuki. He looked cautiously about and knew no one
could be watching him from a distance close enough to
be harmful, and he twisted the handle of the throttle and
rode toward the scene of Al's death.

It took him an hour of riding on easy ground overlooking the path Joey and Charlie Sevenpines and he had
taken. There were no marks of people or vehicles of any
kind and Pete took care not to leave any: not for fear of
being followed but because he disliked disturbing ground
nature had laid. He noticed desultory dead animals here
and there. He put on his gloves and picked up a dead
baby rabbit, then later a dead bat, both of which he stuffed
in his saddlebags.

He came to the place where Al died and parked the
machine and dismounted and got out the mayonnaise jars.

After catching some dozen flies in one jar, he sat in
the shade by the dark pool feeling like a retarded man
who had summoned all his resources to construct a child's
firefly lantern. He poured some adult espresso from his
thermos.

Then the fly came.

He could not hear it but he saw it in the corner of his
eye as his right arm raised the cup to his lips.

Slowly, as you would approach a grizzly bear in hiber-
nation, Pete let the cup down and held the rest of his
body still and wriggled his right glove back on to his

hand. He waited with a patience he thought would be the envy of Charlie Sevenpines.

Borne on eddies of air known only to the fly, the insect performed queer aerobatics. It dived, climbed, whirled, whorled in corkscrew patterns.

Pete sat still. It was hard to focus on this fly. Yet it seemed bigger than most and its color brighter, an iridescent emerald nacreous as the inside of an abalone shell.

The fly alit on the left arm of his windbreaker, which Pete had nearly removed because of the heat. The position was a stroke of luck. It wiggled its body and batted its wings and seemed to be trying to work into some kind of attitude. Then the fly shook itself and began to crawl down his sleeve toward his naked wrist.

Come on, baby, Pete thought. Let's see what you want.

The fly walked down to the hillock of sleeve just above the elastic wristband. Pete held his breath, fearful that this impediment might cause it to take to the air.

The fly stumbled over the sleeve toward the sweating flesh.

Pete slowly moved his right hand into position.

The fly stopped on his wrist. Its posterior wiggled and its wings flapped. It probed with its spindly front feet. Its head went down to bite.

Pete's gloved right hand caught it between thumb and forefinger. "Gotcha, you sonofabitch," he said.

Pete tried not to squeeze so hard as to kill it. But the fly was a corpse when it tumbled to the bottom of the captive jar, and the other flies avoided it.

Suddenly behind him Pete heard the unmistakable successive clicks of a gun being loaded and cocked.

He reached casually inside his windbreaker as though for a pack of cigarettes. Then he pulled the Python from the shoulder holster, spun around, and threw himself prone with his feet stretched into the water of the pool. With his thumb he cocked the hammer of the pistol and prepared to pull the trigger on a figure carrying a shotgun in the shade of the wild rhododendrons.

"Freeze!" Pete said. "Police officer! Don't make a move!"

The shadowy figure paused. "I wasn't gonna shoot

you, you dang fool," the man said. "Prove to me you're a policeman."

Pete held out his badge and ID with his free hand.

Three doves that had been foraging on the bank of the brook flew away from the commotion.

"Aw, shit, now look what you went and done," the man said.

"Uh, what?" Pete said.

"You scared away my game."

Pete told the man to open his shotgun and unload it and he did. Pete eased the hammer down on the Python and put it away. He got up and went to the man and checked his identification and hunting license and everything was in order. He made a note of the man's name and address.

"What the hell's this all about?" the man said.

"Jjust, uh, checking. The next time you, uh, start to shoot around someone, I, uh, suggest you give some warning."

"Why, hell, that'd scare the dove off."

"Beats getting shot, doesn't it?"

The man grudgingly conceded the point, but Pete doubted it would change his ways. From his appearance and his address Pete judged him to be an old farmer who would see little reason for doing things contrary to the way he had always done them. Pete brooded at how quickly a misunderstanding could end a life.

"What's all this ruckus about?" the man said. "What in hell you ketchin' them flies for?"

"Just, uh, tttesting. Uh, try and stay away from flies for a while. They might be dangerous. Don't let any land on you."

"Do I look like I draw flies, Officer?" the man said, chuckling to himself. "Damnedest thing I ever heard tell. Damnedest thing. Fella not far from here said the same damn thing yesterday. Aketchin' flies and telling me to stay away from them. Said he was from the board of health, but I say no."

"What?" Pete said.

"Do I have to repeat myself all the time to you, Officer? I said fella ketchin' flies yesterday said the same damn thing."

"What did he look like?"

"Younger fella. 'Bout your age, 'bout your size, but with black curly hair, all thick. Black eyebrows thick too. Wore a suit with a tie. Business fella, he was, city fella. Talked through his nose like he come from Philly or New York."

"W-w-what, uh, what time was it?"

"Late. Gettin' along toward dusk. Good time for dove."

Pete questioned the hunter some more. He had been alone. The incident had occurred about a mile downstream and half-mile or so from the Elmsford Road. The hunter had seen no car. He hadn't known the Mueller house burned down but thought it salutary.

"High time that dump caught fire," the man said, and spat upon the ground and stepped on the spit. "It was downright insanitary."

"Okay," Pete said. "Uh, thanks. Happy hunting."

"Oh, the same to you, Officer, the same to you." The man looked at Pete's flies and laughed.

Pete rode to the place where Debbie died and caught more flies and saw nothing unusual.

On his way home for lunch he would stop at the substation. Billy Gianotti would be at the desk and Pete knew the question would not be if more people had died from the mysterious seizures but how many.

But Billy was not there. In his place was Vince Egert, who looked tired and sad.

"Hi, Pete," he said. "I guess you heard."

"Heard what?" Pete said.

"About Billy. Didn't you know? I phoned your wife this morning and told her to tell you."

"W-w-w-, uh, what about him?"

"About three this morning. Apparent heart attack. The missus tried to help but Billy never woke up. He was DOA at County."

"Oh, Jesus," Pete said, and crossed himself. Poor Billy. Saturnine, laconic, funny Billy with his cigar clenched in his teeth trying to look tough when he'd drive a drunk home rather than run him in if the guy's story was a sad one. Billy was thirty-four years old. Pete had helped break him in and they had been friends ever since.

"The times of the wake and the funeral are posted on the board. Everyone's kicking in five bucks for flowers," Vince said.

Pete gave him five dollars. "Who else?"

"Just a farm kid near Elmsford. Not in our district . . . Pete?"

"Yeah?"

"Just what the hell's going on around here?"

"Uh, if I tttold you what I think, you'd think I was crazy."

"Tell me anyhow." Vinnie's long lean face looked anything but what a cop's should look like. Pete thought he saw tears in it and knew he felt them in himself and fought the feeling.

"Vinnie, I, uh, I think its f-f-flies. Poisonous flies."

"Flies?"

"F-f-flies."

"You gotta be out of your fucking mind."

"Told you so. I'm, uh, I'm going to look into it more."

"Jesus H. Christ, you've got to be kidding."

"I'm not, Vinnie. Stay away from flies."

Pete made a note of the times of the viewing and the funeral and looked up a phone number and went to the conference room to use the phone. The name of the pathologist to see at Hershey Medical Center was Dr. Kavanaugh. Pete told the doctor's secretary who he was and how urgent it was, and the secretary said the doctor might be able to squeeze time in for him around three that afternoon.

It was now nearly twelve. Hershey was a good two hours away and he would have to grab a quick lunch and leave. He wondered whether he should even go home for lunch but thought he should spend some time with Enid, and it would be better if he took their old Volvo station wagon to Hershey instead of riding his bike. He stopped at the farm stand and bought fresh cucumbers and tomatoes. He would make a salad for lunch. Enid always liked his salads. He would find some way to warn her of the flies.

Enid was not there when he got home. He searched the house and yard and then rang the big brass ship's bell

on the porch that they used to signal each other when out
of sight.

He washed the vegetables and took out lettuce and
opened a can of anchovies with the key that came on the
can. He took out a can of tuna and looked for the can
opener and couldn't find it. He looked for the big butcher
knife with the stainless-steel handle and blade and
couldn't find it either. He was not surprised, as he had
never been able to persuade Enid to put the same thing
in the same place twice. So he cut the vegetables with a
steak knife and worried the tuna can open with a bottle
opener and nicked his finger and cursed and sucked the
blood and made the salad.

The phone had rung early that morning to tell Enid
that Billy Gianotti had died. She cried when she heard of
Billy. She thought he was very nice even if she did de-
spise his cigars and his wife. Then she took a pill and
went back to sleep.

When she finally got up, she realized she had left everything, even Quetzalcoatl, in the place where she had
tried to kill the cat. She dressed quickly and ran back to
the place. She found all but the can opener and cried
again as she desperately probed for it. She felt voltages
in her nerves and a tight inner grip on the back of her
neck.

She found the can opener just as the ship's bell rang.

When Pete saw Enid run in looking anxious with bandages on her face and wrist, he was shocked. He was still
sucking on his finger from the small cut.

"Hi, hon, uh, what happened?"

She did not kiss him and he did not force the ritual.

"Billy died. Did you hear?"

"Yeah . . . I mean, uh, what happened to you?"

"Oh, I fell out of a tree. It happened yesterday. I was
trying to prune it. What happened to you?" she said,
indicating his finger. Could he know? Oh, God, could he
have noticed the missing utensils? Maybe he even followed the trail of blood and saw her things and the dead
cat. She knew he was keeping something from her.

"Oh, I, uh, c-cut my finger opening the damned tuna can. What'd you do with the can opener?"

He knew something. "Oh, I lent it to Mrs. Foxx. Hers broke."

"Oh. Uh, ready for some poor boy's Niçoise?"

"Yeah, terrific," Enid said with little conviction, and knew she must be on her guard. He didn't belong snooping in her world. "Why are you wearing your gun?" she said as they sat to eat.

"Uh, I've been helping case an out—I mean, helping out on a case, and, uh, well, you know . . ."

"Anything to do with Billy's death?"

"Oh, no, Jesus, no, hon, B-B-Billy died of a heart attack."

She was sure he way lying. He wasn't good at it.

"Hon," he said, "d-d-do you, uh—I mean, did you have any plans for this afternoon?"

"Take me to New York?" she said, smiling her ingenue smile.

"Uh, sorry, uh . . ." Pete reached across the table to pat her hand and she pulled it away. "I've, uh, gggot a three-day coming up next week, maybe then. N-no, I'd like to use the Volvo . . ."

"Oh, Pete, really, dammit, what for?"

"Were, uh, were you planning to use it?"

"No, goddammit, I was hoping we could go somewhere together for a change. We never go anywhere except to those goddamn doctors!"

"Enid, please . . ."

"Really, Peter! Really!"

"Hon, uh, please, you know I'm on a case. You know p-p-police work, you sometimes have to make sacrifices."

Sacrifices! Damned right he knows, Enid thought. The bastard's smarter than he sounds. This, my husband with whom I have shared my body, is playing a cat-and-mouse game with me. He's playing the inspector to my Raskolnikov. I know that game, and two can play it. "I guess we both have to make our sacrifices," she said, mischievously tossing her head.

"I'm sorry, Enid, I'm sorry."

God, he's a good actor when he wants to be. Just look

at those mooncalf eyes, she thought. But what can he really do to me? What have I done? Just kill some stupid animals, just trying to work things out. If anyone other than Adair tried to understand me, they'd know it was just good old-fashioned trying, that's all. Enid felt like breaking down and telling him everything and asking him to understand and help, but she knew that's what he wanted. To break her down, yes. Maybe to rebuild her in the image of the perfect wife that he and the doctors had in mind, or maybe just dump her with a clear conscience. She finished her salad in silence. Again Pete tried to touch her hand and again she pulled it away.

"Hon," Pete said, "uh, there's something you should bbbe careful about . . ."

"About sacrifices?" Enid said, sarcastically.

"No, uh, hon, please, I'm sorry about today . . ."

I'll bet you're sorry, you sonofabitch, Enid thought. Sorry you didn't catch me, you subtle Iago, you, but you're not subtle enough for Enid. "What should I be careful about?" Out with it, *shtum,* out with it. I know my Miranda rights. I'm not a cop's wife for nothing.

"Well, uh, well, j-j-just for safety's sake, uh, try not to expose yourself to any flies. Uh, I mean, not to worry, but there's a chance something nasty might be going around from f-f-flies . . ."

Oh, that was devious, she thought. Very, very devious. My hat's off to you for that one, mister. Damned right he knew about the cat and the fly. Did he also know that Tezcatlipoca uses flies as his evil agents? Anyhow, Pete's implication was clear. The bastard's trying to tell Enid to quit exploring the meaning of things or he might claim Enid's mind is diseased.

"Okay," Enid said, and smiled sweetly. That'll fake him out. "Where are you going?"

"To, uh, Hershey," he said. "I'll be back seven or eight. Uh, why don't I pick us up something for supper?"

"Yeah," Enid said, "get us a bigass candy bar, sweets."

"Okay." Pete smiled weakly and tried to kiss her and she rebuffed him and gave him the finger.

"Hit the road, prick," she said.

11

Were you ever afraid to walk in the shade?

In trying times it often happens that, wanting organization on the departure of a leader, another will quietly emerge to assume the mantle. And it will be acknowledged by the led, if unspoken.

So it happened that as Irene Byrne saw Sister Nettie depart around the last bend, she found herself sitting in the seat of the driver of the bus without giving it a thought.

She did nothing. She simply sat and gripped the steering wheel with her scarred hands and looked down and prayed fiercely for the life and the soul of the African nun.

No one on the bus said a word for more than an hour. Some drooped with somnolence brought on by exhausting emotions and the stale air of the bus.

Irene's eye was caught by a rabbit browsing for choice forage in a small meadow outside the bus. The plants the rabbit seemed to favor grew in a patch that now lay in shade. Yet whenever the rabbit ventured into this patch it was set upon by flies. The rabbit would then twitch its big ears violently and bound into sunlight. The flies would pursue it a few feet into the sun and then grow bewildered and fly in circles and retreat to the shade. But other flies abounded in the sunlight. Some of these showed an interest in the rabbit, alit on it occasionally, and flew casually away, leaving the rabbit unmolested. These sunshine flies, however, seemed less interested in the rabbit than in objects on the ground. The rabbit appeared oblivious to these flies. And while the flies that Irene watched emerging from the shade disdained the sun, the sunshine flies—the ones that did not frighten the rabbit—would often vanish into the shadowy habitat of the other flies with no apparent fear. Irene observed all this and resolved to think about it.

The shadows grew longer until they finally covered the tiny portion of the world in which the bus was parked.

At last someone broke the silence. "I think it's getting dark," Herman García said.

"That's one thing we love so much about you, Herman," Irene said, "you so quick to pick up on things."

Some of the other children laughed nervously.

"Looks like Sister Nettie's not coming back," Herman said.

"That's what it looks like, don't it?" Irene said, and crossed herself.

"What we gonna do, Irene?" Talmadge Brown said.

"We gonna do just like Sister told us to do," Irene said. "We gonna wait. We gonna pray. We gonna think. And we gonna win. Ain't no more of them dirtyass flies gonna kill no more of us or my name ain't Irene Byrne."

"What we gonna do tonight, Irene?" Wanda James asked.

"We gonna do just like we do every night," Irene said. "We gonna sleep. Then we gonna get up in the morning and figure out what we gonna do next."

"I'm hungry," Herman said.

"So's everybody," Irene said. "Why don't you just sashay you ass outside and gobble yourself up a nice fly or two?"

The children laughed.

"That's not funny," Herman said.

"Hell, Herman," Irene said, "you always say that, and the more you say it, the funnier it gets."

The children laughed some more and even Herman joined in the laughter. This helped more relax sufficiently to sleep.

Irene rummaged in a box near the driver's seat and found a flashlight, some extra batteries, emergency reflectors and flares, a tool kit, a first-aid kit, and a grease-smudged operator's manual. She fashioned a flyswatter from a church magazine left behind by a nun, devised a regimen for those who needed to relieve themselves in the night, and settled back. Her watchful night was not

as difficult as it might have been because few children
had much in their bodies left to excrete. Irene knew that
food and water would be an important topic of morning
discussion.

"Damn," said Sue Ellen Hutton, "look at that moon
and them stars . . . pretty. I never slept under moon and
stars before."

"Well," Irene said drowsily, "just like Sister Nettie
say, ain't nothin' so bad you can't find no good in it."

The children of Our Lady of Sorrows slept and sometimes waked to the calls and hoots of strange creatures
in a strange night in a foreign landscape.

Irene woke at first light and watched for a long time
and saw no flies or anything notable except a clear and
dry Tuesday morning. She spent the time waiting for
other children to awake by poring over the unfamiliar
terms and illustrations and diagrams in the bus operator's
manual.

By rote and by association, she began to commit the
various instruments and devices to memory. The speedometer, well, that was okay. But the odometer was something else. All those little numbers adding up, she
couldn't understand why the hell anyone would want to
know how far the damned bus had traveled in its lifetime.
This odometer read 87943.2. What she didn't know was
that it had already logged a hundred thousand miles before that and had returned to zero to start the process all
over again. The ammeter and temperature gauges were
likewise superfluous. Who cares whether electricity is
charging or how warm the motor is? The bus either works
or it doesn't.

The steering wheel, of course, Irene understood even
if she didn't understand why this one lay in a flat plane
when most of them lay in an up-and-down plane. But
what the hell, it was easy. So was the horn. Now that
was useful. It would make people get the hell out of the
way. The lights would be useful at night. The flashing
lights could come in very handy. Irene knew the rules.
You can't pass a school bus with its lights flashing. The
windshield wipers would be good if it rained, any fool
knows that. As for the gearshift handle, she memorized
the H-pattern of the four forward gears, and how to shift

into reverse. But the whole notion was ridiculous. Why have all those gears? The bus could only travel in two directions: forward and backward. Why the hell do you need four gears to go forward and only one to go backward? It was extravagant, impractical. Irene concluded that the three extra forward gears were luxuries, frills thrown in by the factory to titillate bus aficionados. The hand brake was easy enough to understand, but likewise a redundancy. Why should you need one brake for the foot and another for the hand? Silly. She understood the brake pedal and the accelerator pedal, of course. They were as simple as stop and go. But the clutch pedal, now there was a humdinger.

"To shift from a lower to a higher gear, or a higher to a lower, disengage the clutch, move the gearshift lever to the next selected gear, and reengage the clutch." That was what the manual said and it was as full of shit as a Christmas goose. First, they don't tell you which gears are higher and which lower, or why you want more than one in the first place. They don't tell you what the clutch is for. You'd think it was made to clutch things but they don't say anything about that or, for that matter, why a school bus would want to clutch anything. And what's all this disengage and reengage bullshit? To engage meant to get ready to be married. To disengage meant to call the thing off and tell the bum to take a walk. What is this crap in this book? If you know how to drive the damn thing, you don't need a manual. And if you don't know how to drive it, the manual should tell you. Disengage and reengage indeed. This jargon was a jive.

Irene also opined that you'd have to be one hell of a long-legged paperhanger to do all the things this book told you to do.

The sun was now full and warm in the eastern sky. One by one the youngsters awoke and complained of thirst and hunger.

"What's happening, Irene?" Herman said, disengaging cobwebs from his mind.

"Nothing," Irene said.

"Hey, Irene, I'm thirsty," Talmadge said. "We gonna just sit here on our ass and roast all day?"

"No."

"Well, what we gonna do, girl?" Talmadge said.

"Yeah, Irene, what the hell we gonna do?" Herman said.

"Thanks for volunteering," Irene said.

"What?" Herman said.

Irene fixed Herman with a stern eye. "Herman, you think you're pretty smart, don't you?"

"Well . . ." Herman said, "my grades are okay."

"Okay," Irene said. "Now, you tell me who got more brains—you or a stinking fly?"

"Guess I do," Herman said.

"Riiiiiight," Irene said.

"But them damn flies are poisonous. You know what I'm saying?" Herman said.

"Right again," Irene said. "That's the only thing them muffas got over us. They're poisonous and we ain't. But we smarter and we bigger and we ain't going to let no bunch of nasty flies shove us around."

"Well," Talmadge said, "what we gonna do about it, girl?"

"We gonna find out how them muffas organize and we gonna organize the otherwise," Irene said, "then we gonna beat their little asses. Now, Talmadge, you and Herman here get something and cover up and come on outside with me."

"What!" Herman said. "I ain't gonna go out with those fucking poison flies running around loose."

"Herman," Irene said, "you act like you got a broom in your case. You volunteered for this mission, you and brother Talmadge here, and you gonna get your ass in gear or answer to me. You know what I'm saying?"

"I didn't volunteer for nothing," Talmadge said.

"You said you was hot and thirsty, didn't you?"

"Guess so . . ." Talmadge looked at his gangly legs.

"Well," Irene said, "you the one with the mouth to drink."

"Oh, all right," Talmadge said.

"Shit," Herman said. But he borrowed a jacket and began to cover his head with it.

Talmadge did the same and so did Irene. Irene showed Sue Ellen and one of the boys how to work the bus door and where the driver's implements were. Then for the first time human beings ventured willingly among the venomous, mysterious flies.

"Now, Talmadge and Herman," Irene said, tasting the fresh morning breeze, "I got an idea. I think those poison flies like the shade, so let's stay in the sun."

"Right," Talmadge said.

"Right," Herman echoed.

Garbed as medieval friars confronting plague with prayer, the three walked stealthily into a sunny meadow.

"Look out," Irene said. "Flies!" She pointed to the ground at a heap of dung over which flies swarmed. Herman and Talmadge jumped back. Irene stood her ground.

"What them muffas doing?" Irene said.

"Well . . ." Talmadge said, studying the nauseating scene. "Looks to me like they eating shit, girl."

"Okay," Irene said. "Now if a fly eats shit, what the hell he want to bite into people for? Huh? Unless they two different kinds of flies. Maybe there's your shit-eating fly and your people-biting fly . . ."

"Hmmm," Herman said.

"See, Herman, I told you that you was more intelligent than a fly," Irene said. "Even you."

"You gonna trust them flies just 'cause they eats shit, girl?" Talmadge said.

"Hell, no," Irene said. "We gonna do a experiment. Let's go down where the picnic was."

Part of the picnic area lay in shade and part in sun. The children carefully shooed flies and squirrels away from the food and gathered all that was good and put it in coolers in the sun. Irene noticed that the bodies of Karen and Orville lay in the shade where they had fallen the day before. She tried not to look at the young corpses, sprawling as someone's forgotten laundry. She knew if she looked it would upset her and her duty was to the living.

With their sleeves covering their hands, Irene and the boys gathered all the garbage in a pile in the sun.

"Okay," Irene said, "we wait for them muffas to come."

"Shit," Herman said.

"Shit," Talmadge echoed.

"Shut up," Irene said. "You get yourselfs some rolled-up papers or sticks or something to swat them muffas."

Herman discovered a particularly juicy excerpt from a contraband *Playboy* magazine and rolled it up. Talmadge got a flat stick.

Two flies buzzed in diminishing circles downward toward the garbage.

"Oooooo . . ." Herman sighed. "Hail-Mary-full-of-grace—"

"Shut up," Irene said. "That's just the advance party."

One of the flies alit on the garbage heap and flitted over the offal and lingered to savor morsels delectable to its kind. Then it took off and flew to rendezvous with its airborne confrere. The two flies flew off together.

"Watch," Irene said, "they gone to get the rest of the tribe."

"Ooooooooooo . . ." Herman moaned. ". . . the-Lord-is-with-you-blessed-is-the-fruit-of-your . . ."

"Shut up, Herman, you be all right," Irene said. "You just be ready to swat 'em."

They came singly, in pairs, in threes, many from the shade, and landed on the garbage and began to gorge themselves.

"Stand by to attack," Irene whispered. "Try not to mash 'em too much. We gotta examine the bodies . . ."

"What are you talking about, girl?" Talmadge said.

"Listen, Talmadge, you want to live or you want to die? If we gonna beat them muffas, we got to figure them out. You know what I'm saying?"

"Shit, girl, we just stay on that bus and by and by the man come and rescue our ass out of here," Talmadge said.

"That's right," Herman echoed.

"Shee-it," Irene said. "You think the man give a damn about a bunch of poor niggers? The man working for the other side, the supply side. Us niggers too short on supply and too long on demand, so we got to wait for the good shit to trickle down on us. The man working to make sure us poor folks don't exploit the rich folks, so don't look for no man to help us out. You better be ready to kill them muffa flies before they kill you."

"Ooooo . . ." Herman murmured. ". . . the-fruit-of-your-womb . . ."

"Shut up," Irene said. "Pray later."

As they watched, more than a dozen flies gathered to feast. Others darted in the air and prepared to land.

"Stand by," Irene said. "Attack!"

Whack! went Talmadge's stick.

Splat! went Herman's *Playboy* excerpt. "Ow! Ow! Ow!" Herman howled as if it were he being killed.

"Kill 'em!" Irene barked.

The boys beat and swatted and beat some more until the enemy was thoroughly discomfited and his survivors took to the air in disordered ranks.

"Ha! Ha!" Irene hooted. "I said you was smarter than a bunch of flies, now, didn't I? Ha! Ha!"

The boys began to laugh along with Irene.

"Herman, gimme that magazine," Irene said. "I'll keep them muffas away. Now you and Talmadge pick up the corpses—use paper plates or something, don't touch 'em with your hands—and set 'em up on that table over there."

The boys did as they were bade, gingerly gathering up what was left from the attack.

"Hey, that wasn't so tough," Talmadge said.

"Nah, it wasn't," Herman echoed.

Irene surveyed the line of fly corpses, now a proud general taking a body count after a successful engagement. "Well," she smiled from beneath her hood at her troops, "you gentlemen know how to kill flies. All right."

"All right," Herman said.

"All right," Talmadge echoed.

"Trouble is, I don't think these flies the poison kind," Irene said.

"Oh, shit," Talmadge said.

"Damn," Herman echoed.

"What we gonna do now, Irene?" Talmadge said.

"Well, let's gather up some of the buns from the garbage."

They did, and Irene found a place in the sun about twenty feet from the shade of a large grove of trees. The boys held their weapons at the ready. Irene scattered bits of bun and they waited for an animal to wander by.

They did not wait long. Soon a squirrel ventured toward the bread and commenced eating. Soon after that the children had trained the squirrel to beg tidbits from them. Irene took some bread and walked slowly toward the line of shade.

"Hey, where you going, girl?" Talmadge said. "I thought you said those poison muffas like the shade."

Irene carefully adjusted the covers protecting her skin and moved on toward the canopy of shadow. "Shush now," she said. "I'm doing a experiment and you two be ready to charge in and kill flies."

"Shit," Herman said.

"Damn," Talmadge echoed.

Irene coaxed the squirrel into the shade. A few flies followed her from the sun, evincing more interest in the bits of food than in the squirrel. Then a fly emerged from the shade, and then another. These flies began to circle the squirrel.

The shade flies had nearly landed on the squirrel when Irene tossed some bread into the sun and the squirrel chased after it. The flies from the sun remained in the shade to alight on the morsels the squirrel had left.

The shade flies pursued the squirrel to the demarcation between shadow and sun, a few feet beyond, then reversed direction and retreated to their cool dim habitat.

Herman and Talmadge looked at each other in wonder and not a little fear.

Irene repeated this experiment until she was satisfied it was a success. The time came for the next experiment. Irene squeamed at the thought of sacrificing the squirrel but knew it would be necessary to prevent the sacrifice of more humans. Besides, it might not work. Irene paused and prayed for the soul of the squirrel and asked God to forgive her if she caused its death. Then she turned resolutely to the boys and said, "Okay, gentlemen, cover up good and stand by to attack."

"Damn," said Talmadge.

"Hell," said Herman, tightening his grip on *Playboy*.

Irene threw a large portion of bun a few feet into the shade and the squirrel scampered for it. The flies that had followed the food from the sun paid little heed to the squirrel. Then other flies emerged from the shade, and bit it.

The animal had barely begun its death throes when Irene called the attack.

All three children charged into the shade. More flies burrowed into the fur of the squirrel and killing them was easy.

Herman batted away with his *Playboy*. Talmadge beat down with his stick. Irene stamped with her foot, hard enough to kill but not so hard as to mangle.

"Hey, look out, Herman!" Talmadge yelled. "One of them muffas is on top of your head!"

"Oooooo," Herman moaned, and batted his head with the magazine pages.

The fly flew off and landed on Irene's shoulder. Talmadge saw it and lashed out with his stick, hitting Irene a glancing blow.

"Ow!" Irene bawled. "What the hell coming down, nigger? You supposed to be killing flies, not me!"

"Sorry," Talmadge said, and could not restrain his laughter.

The children looked cautiously around and could see no more flies. The enemy had been routed from the field.

"Okay, gentlemen," Irene said, "let's scrawnch up the bodies onto Herman's magazine here and get our ass back into the sun real quick. Don't touch them muffas, you know what I'm saying?"

The gentlemen did not need to be reminded and carefully gathered the dead flies onto the *Playboy* centerfold, now a funerary van for defunct insects.

They laid them on the table in the sun next to the dead flies from the garbage heap.

"Well, I be dipped in shit," Herman said. "This is two kinds of flies. Look. Here's your sunshine flies. Now here's your shadyside flies. They're a little bigger and their bellies are sort of green-like."

"That's right," Irene said.

"That's right," Talmadge echoed. "I think these greenbelly flies are the badass muffas. I think the sun-shine flies is just plain old shit-eating flies what don't give a damn where they go and the greenbelly kind is bloodsuckers what hate the sun.''

Irene took the cover from her head and removed her windbreaker and stood in her short-sleeved jumper with face and arms fully exposed to the danger.

"Hey, what the hell you doing, girl?'' Talmadge said.

"Cut that shit out, Irene,'' Herman said.

Irene raised her hand for order and could feel it trembling. The sweat from her stifling hood had soaked her face and ruined her hair and lay in glistening droplets on her skin. The cool of the exposure of perspiring skin to the lake breeze penetrated her to the heart along with a cold wash of adrenaline.

"This is . . .'' She started to speak and could feel her voice choking on the terror she felt. She cleared her throat and swallowed and forced at least her speech to regain its show of courage. "Follow me, gentlemen, and keep covered up. This is the last experiment.''

"No, Irene, no!'' Herman said.

"No, girl!'' Talmadge said.

She advanced slowly, so not to disturb the newly gathered flies at the garbage pile from which they supped in the sun.

"Gentlemen,'' she said, "Sister Nettie says the Lord He helps those what help themselves. Now God, maybe He wants all this crap coming down on us and maybe He don't. But if we don't help ourselves, we can't blame nobody but ourselves. Now if anything happens to me . . . Well, uh, well, you just get you ass back to the bus and read that book and figure out how to drive that turkey out of here . . .''

"No!'' "No!'' the boys said.

"Shush,'' Irene said.

She advanced on the garbage pile with her throat refusing to swallow and her heart pounding viciously in her breast as had leaders among her ancestors risked impossible chance in circumstances menacing intolerable inflictions for nearly four hundred years. Feeling like a shuffling lynch-mob victim being led to the noose, she said a Hail Mary and an Our Father in her mind.

The flies at the garbage stirred at her arrival.

She knelt and thrust quivering naked arms over the garbage and bowed her head and continued to pray.

The first fly landed on her arm and dipped its head onto a bead of sweat. Irene could feel its feet pawing. So heightened were her senses that time elapsed as an auto accident filmed in slow motion. She could feel the fly's head dip onto her skin to ingest. She forced herself to restrain a shudder and to pray and to ask God to forgive her should this be suicide.

Then she felt another fly land on her other arm. Another still alit inside her ear. More flies came and walked and dipped and wriggled and squirmed over her flesh.

She grimaced and closed her eyes hard and prayed hard.

She sensed herself aswarm with flies drinking the sweat of her body. They crept. They wallowed. They itched. They tickled.

Irene's face began to relax. Her eyes opened to behold the odious scene of a score of flies creeping over her thirteen-year-old skin. They were everywhere but on the scarred palms of her hands, which exuded no perspiration. Daintily, as if recovering from a curtsy to an emperor, Irene got to her feet. Her arms stretched out, cruciform, with her insect charges as though they were the birds of Saint Francis of Assisi.

And still the flies tickled.

"Okay, gentlemen," she said, with smiling tears in her eyes. "You may uncover. Please go to the bus and tell the brothers and sisters we're going to finish our picnic in the sun."

The boys looked at each other and at Irene. They all smiled. Then they laughed, and laughed, and laughed. The battle, and the day, belonged to the children of the Convent of Our Lady of Sorrows.

12

The mustachioed rotund wraith of Milton S. Hershey weeps over his paradise lost. The last of the great American entrepreneurs and philanthropists, his passage is no longer mourned.

He built the town of Hershey from a cornfield near his place of birth with two overriding principles in mind: how to make a good candy bar for a nickel, and the quaint and forgotten notion that if you build a great business and are loyal to the workers who helped you build it, they will be loyal to you in return. Fabled for his generosity if not his reticence, he built the Milton Hershey School, an orphanage. He founded the Hershey Hotel and the Hershey Bears Hockey Club. He parceled out land to employees or those who had lived in the town for two years or more. By their property he built streets with such names as Chocolate and Cocoa, lit by streetlamps shaped as Hershey Candy Kisses. He built a trolley, a huge free public rose garden, a free public golf course, more schools, a public library, an amusement park with a band shell for public Sunday concerts, an excellent community center, an experimental bakery, and an experimental dairy where he concocted such delicacies as carrot and beet ice cream in the belief that children should eat more of vegetables.

Things have gone downhill in Hershey, Pennsylvania, since the demise of Milton Hershey, but not that badly. Long-time residents may grumble, but they are still better off than residents of most small towns. While company largess has been curtailed and many amenities are no longer free, the company still supports the theater and schools. Hershey is still a pleasant place to visit, a factory town that actually delights children. One of the company's key executives is a fellow who graduated from the orphanage school to which Milton Hershey, who was without children, left most of his estate. And the trust created to run this school so prospered that eighteen years after the founder's death it donated the money to establish the Hershey Medical Center, which is also the medical school of Pennsylvania State University.

In an age when nothing seems to work well for long, Hershey Medical Center works very well indeed.

It was into a parking lot at this institution that Pete Bilyeux eased his humble Volvo a little after two-thirty on this Tuesday afternoon. He had prudently brought a large grocery bag into which he placed the jar of flies and the dead animals.

He found his way to Dr. Kavanaugh's office and introduced himself and was told the doctor was on coffee break in the lounge.

He went to the lounge and asked someone to point out Dr. Kavanaugh. He was directed to a table near a window where sat a well-groomed, good-looking man with a well-groomed, good-looking woman who wore aviatrix glasses.

"Uh, excuse me," Pete said to the man. "Doctor Kavanaugh?"

"No, I'm Doctor Knox," the man said, and gestured toward the woman. "This is Doctor Kavanaugh."

"Oh," Pete said to the woman, "I'm, uh, sssorry."

"That's all right," she said, "some of my best friends mistake me for a woman."

Pete felt he could not have made a more inauspicious introduction. Dr. Knox was obviously homosexual and Dr. Kavanaugh obviously one of that intense new breed of career person as yet unwary of the miseries that befall such ambition with a fine disregard for sex.

"What can I do for you?" Dr. Kavanaugh asked Pete.

"Well, uh, D-Doctor, my secretary phoned, I mmmmmean I phoned your secretary about coming to see you for a few minutes. My n-n-name's Pete Bilyeux, I'm a deputy sheriff in Elmsford County . . ."

"Oh, yes." She extended her hand for Pete to shake, "I thought perhaps you were here to fix the plumbing. Sit down, please. Do you mind showing me some iden-

tification?'' Pete showed her his ID and badge. "Well,"
she said, "you're certainly better-looking than your picture, Deputy. Does it bother you if I smoke?''

Pete shook his head no.

"Cigarette?'' she said, offering him one from a gold
combination case and lighter with her initials on it. "I'll
even light it for you. I adore lighting cigarettes for men.
It's a form of obverse chivalry, you see.''

Pete shook his head in the negative and tried to
chuckle.

"Well, at least you've got a sense of humor,'' Dr. Kavanaugh said. "How unusual for a policeman.''

"Oh, cut it out, Louise,'' Dr. Knox said at his col-
league's needling of Pete.

"Don't mind Freddie, here, Mr., uh, Milieu, is it?''

"B-Bilyeux.''

"Bilyeux, of course. Sorry. Well, I suppose you're here
to see me about those friends of yours I cut up last
night,'' she said.

"Uh, well, partly.''

"No pun intended, of course, parts being the state
they're in now.''

Pete did not know how to respond and said nothing.

"Very strange,'' she continued, exhaling from her cigarette, "weird. In layman's language the only thing I
could find is their hearts stopped. Click. Just like that.
We're running all kinds of tests, but we don't have anything yet. There are millions of things that didn't do it,
but so far I have no idea what did.''

"Uh, I, uh, think I know,'' Pete said.

"You're not the shithead that wanted them checked for
fluoride, are you?''

Pete shook his head no.

"Jesus,'' Dr. Kavanaugh said, "I would hope not.
That's the silliest thing I ever heard and you don't look
that dumb. Sorry, that was gratuitous. In fact, I suspect
you're a rather bright guy. Jesus! Fluoride! Christ, they
would have had to drink it damned near straight and it
would have eaten out their alimentary canals, not stopped
their hearts. Fluoride indeed. Okay, what's your idea,
Mr. Milieu?''

"B-Bilyeux,'' Pete said.

"What the hell's that?" Dr. Kavanaugh said. "I don't know what you're talking about."

"Bilyeux. It's, uh, my name, doctor. Not Milieu."

Dr. Knox, of course, was accustomed to the staccato bursts of Dr. Kavanaugh's machine-gun mind. He stifled a laugh.

"Right," Dr. Kavanaugh said. "Sorry, Mr. Bilyeux. Cigarette?"

Pete shook his head and smiled and the doctor lit another and he thought she looked a little sheepish for a moment. But only for a moment. She was a good-looking woman, not beautiful like Enid, but good-looking.

"Okay," she said, "what's your idea, Mr. Bilyeux?"

Pete thought it best to start from the beginning and try to involve the two doctors in the anomalous heart-seizures case by case. They listened intently. He told of Al Murdock, of old Mrs. Peterson, of little Stacey Riley, of Debbie, of the Pittsburgh family, of the two more, of Billy, and of the kid near Elmsford. He stammered and stumbled and rambled and inverted his phrases, but he got it all out and, looking the doctors directly in the eyes, could tell he was registering his points.

"Hmm," Dr. Kavanaugh said. "Okay, what's your idea?"

Pete told of Joey Murdock's frantic efforts to get inside or under something. Then he told them of Reed Hamilton's account of Debbie's death, and of the fly.

"Uh, I, uh, know it sounds hell as crazy, excuse me, I m-m-mean crazy as hell, b-b-but I've got to investigate the possibility that, uh, at least some of the flies around my district are toxic."

Dr. Kavanaugh looked at Dr. Knox. Dr. Knox's eyes said nothing.

"Well, Mr. Bilyeux," Dr. Kavanaugh said, exhaling smoke. "Let's go back to the fluoride idea. I mean, flies, really. Flies are nasty and give you diseases, but they don't give you cardiac arrest, Mr. Bilyeux, I trust you know that."

"Yes, uh, ma'am, I know . . ."

"Don't call me ma'am. I hate the expression. It's sexist."

"Yes, D-Doctor. I, uh, I know flies don't cause cardiac

arrest, but, uh, I'm a pppolice officer and this is, uh, the strongest lead I have, and, uh, eleven people are dead suddenly in a small town and something's wrong and a lot more people may die unless we do something. Look, Doctor, please understand me, it's only a hypothesis but, uh, I have to do everything I can, everything! I guess I could go to the New York medical examiner, but you have the bodies, Doctor Kavanaugh. Do you understand?''

"You're talking about my alma mater," Dr. Kavanaugh said.

"What?" Pete said.

"The New York medical examiner. I used to work there and so does my ex still, may the bastard partake formaldehyde in his potato salad. Okay, Mr. Bilyeux, what do you want me to do? I'll try to help, but you've got to understand my time is limited and so is my patience. What do you want?''

"Well, uh . . ." Pete said, and dug in his grocery bag and pulled out the jar full of flies and set them on the table. The flies buzzed, indignant in their imprisonment. Pete noticed both doctors looked a little shocked. Good. They were involved. "C-c-can you check these things out?''

"But what do you want us to do?" Dr. Kavanaugh said.

"Well, uh, number one, I'd like you to check them out for radioactivity, and, uh, number two, I'd like you to check them out for t-t-toxicity.''

"Radioactivity?" Dr. Knox asked, and started to laugh. Dr. Kavanaugh pointed her finger at him and wagged it and lit another cigarette.

"Uh, yeah," Pete said.

"Well, you came to the wrong place," Dr. Kavanaugh said. "Freddie's a radiologist. He doesn't know a blessed thing about radioactivity. He's not a nuclear physicist. He just fusses over pictures and fiddles with machines.''

"Officer Bilyeux," Dr. Knox said, "I hope you understand we're not laughing at you. It's just our way. We're a little cabal of two here, you see. We're both a bit mad and neither of us knows whether we'll be here this time next year and we don't much care. We'll be glad to help you, within certain limits. Your case is in-

teresting, in fact, and it happens that we're both looking
for subjects for papers to write. It also happens that Louise here is right in that radiologists work mostly with X
radiation. But with the Three-Mile Island incident years
back we got some new equipment and boned up a bit. In
fact, we're probably ready for a nuclear war. It'll take
me a few minutes to check them. Stay here and have a
cup of coffee with this madwoman and I'll run your
friends through a test." Dr. Knox started to unscrew the
lid of the mayonnaise jar.

"I wouldn't do that if I were you, Doctor," Pete said.

"Well," Dr. Knox said, "I was just thinking about
transferring them to a sterile jar."

"They, uh, they're not sterile flies, Doctor."

"Okay, I hear you," Dr. Knox said, and left.

"Would you like a cup of coffee?" Dr. Kavanaugh
asked Pete.

"Well, uh, I'm off duty, uh, yes please. Do they have
Italian coffee?" Score one for Pete. Let her be defensive.

"What?"

"Uh, espresso."

"Hell, no."

"Well, then, uh, black, please."

She ordered the coffee. "Uh, Mr. Bilyeux," she said,
"do you mind if I ask you a personal question?"

"No. Go ahead."

"I don't mean to be rude. But I'm a medical person
and I like to know these things."

"Yes?"

"Well, uh, do you have a speech impediment or are
you just nervous?" Dr. Kavanaugh said.

"Yes," Pete said.

"No, I mean which? A speech impediment or nervous?"

"Uh, yes," Pete said.

Dr. Kavanaugh chuckled and brushed her hair from her
forehead and took off her glasses and wiped them and
blinked at Pete and put the glasses back on. The score
was a tie.

"How do you like police work, Mr. . . . May I call
you by your first name?"

"Yeah, sure, it's, uh, Pete."

"Well, you can call me Louise, Pete. Let's shake on it."

They shook hands. Dr. Knox came to the doorway of the lounge and beckoned to Louise. He seemed more serious than before he had left the room. Louise got up and the two doctors held a hurried sotto-voce conference replete with the animated gestures of two people who know each other well.

Louise signaled for Pete to join them. He did, and the three walked down a corridor. From snatches of their conversation he understood them to be going to some laboratory.

"Well, Pete," Louise said, "it looks as if you might be onto something. The jar with your friends in it is hot. Not dangerously so, about the same as some radioisotopes we use in testing people, live ones. But it's a hell of a lot hotter than normal background radiation, and that's unusual. Freddie's got an assistant checking each bug individually . . ."

"I, uh, hope that assistant is c-c-careful, Doctor Knox."

"He knows," Dr. Knox said.

"There's, uh, one fled die—I m-m-mean, one dead fly that I killed accidentally when I caught it. It looked, uh, to be a different kind from the rest, with, uh, a greenish cast to its body, and it seemed to want to suck my blood like a mosquito . . ."

"They'll each be tested individually," Dr. Knox said.

They got on an elevator and got off and walked down another corridor and came to a door that Louise opened with a key. "Welcome to my house," she said.

The room had a chemical smell to it. The place was colorful, with vials and microscopes and electronic gadgetry and cages with small animals and a computer terminal and large clear jars containing odd shapes of many pastel hues.

"If you have to leave, Pete, go out the way we came in. Not through that door." She pointed to the far end of the room.

"Uh, what's in there?" Pete said.

"The morgue," Louise said.

Then Pete understood what the pastel contents of some of the jars were.

Louise took off her suit jacket and hung it on a hat stand and put on a lab jacket and Pete noticed that she was well put-together and felt a little ashamed for noticing.

An assistant came in with Pete's fly jar. Two more flies from the jar were now dead. The assistant reported that only the dead fly with the greenish cast was radioactive.

One by one, the living flies were placed in a glass case where they alit on a white mouse painted with a sucrose solution. The mouse suffered only from the loss to its dignity.

The procedure was tedious. Pete could sense the patience of the doctors wane, and with it his own spirits. He wondered where he would go with the case if this avenue ended.

The last living fly was put in with the mouse. Nothing happened.

The two doctors looked at each other and shrugged.

"Well, Pete," Louise said, "it was a good idea while it lasted. Look, I hope you won't think me rude, but I've got a long day ahead of me and this has been a freebie . . ."

"Look, uh, Doctor, uh, Louise, I, uh, I appreciate your t-t-time, I really do. I mean, we try our best, don't we? I just wondered if, uh, there's some way you could test the dead radioactive fly for any toxin, if that's p-p-possible."

Louise looked at Pete and then at Dr. Knox.

"Try a serum?" Dr. Knox said.

Louise tapped her foot and looked at Pete. "How many people died in your town?"

"Eleven," Pete said.

Louise tapped her foot some more and looked around the room. She went to a desk and sat down and looked at some papers. "What the hell," she said, "I didn't have a date tonight anyway."

She made serums from each of the dead flies, labeling each solution. On the vial that held the serum of the greenish fly she placed a red sticker. "We'll test the others first as a control."

She injected two mice with the sera of the first two flies, resulting in nothing but irritated mice.

Then came the turn of the third mouse to be injected with the red-stickered serum. Louise picked it up and put the needle into the fleshy part of a haunch and pressed the fluid into its body.

The mouse let out a screeching sound.

"Ouch!" Louise said as the mouse jerked itself free from the needle and squirmed out of her hand. Louise nearly dropped the syringe. "The little bastard bit me!" she said.

The mouse writhed across the lab table and tumbled to the clean tile floor. It got up and began to scamper to the opposite side of the room, its tiny paws kicking for traction. Suddenly it stopped as if it saw a cat. Its flanks heaved for air. Slowly it wiggled backward along the floor as if the imaginary cat were advancing on it. Then it sprang nearly a foot in the air and fell to its side, gasping. It stopped gasping, stiffened, and went limp.

Pete and the doctors looked on transfixed.

"Holy molasses," Louise said. "That fly must have been dunking in one hell of a shitpile."

13

"And so I come to know of thee, dread god, if there by aught sacrifice that can be made to thee to keep thy minions from destroying my kind?" spoke the other.

"But thou art my minion. Thou destroyest thyself lest thou sacrifice folly," spoke the one.

"But Quetzalcoatl demandeth hearts, O god, and thou demandest so little," spoke the other.

"Speak not of the meretricious," spoke the one. "Know that what is demanded is not little. Fulfill *not the law and thou and all thy kind shall be the sacrifice."*

"But what is this law, most dreadful god, that it may be fulfilled?" spoke the other.

"Fool," spoke the one, "thou dost welter in thine own excrement. No thing could be more apparent than the law. The very stones of time know and obey and cry out the law. Art thou less sentient than stones? Thou thyself wert created of the law. The law is immutable."

"What if we remain ignorant of this law, awesome Lord," spoke the other. "Wilt thou then destroy the race of man?"

"I will," spoke Tezcatlipoca, the one, "in due course."

Adair Godwin no longer cared much about anything but the puzzle. He knew as he lay on the cheap mattress in the cheap hotel in the shadows of the Pyramid of the Sun, the Pyramid of the Moon, the Temple of Tlaloc, the rain god, the Temple of Quetzalcoatl, an arrow's shot from the Street of the Dead in Teotihuacán, that the days of his life had been measured.

But he was in no pain save for that of the mind and the spirit. The thing was merciful in its want of infliction.

Indeed, it had been the absence of pain the night in the jungle in Yucatán that had caused him to discover it.

On the bed, sipping Waterfill and Frazier Mexican whiskey—(¡El Mejor de América!)—through a straw because it was the only way he could drink, he thought on the irony.

The jungles of Yucatán had become his spiritual home. With all his soul he had come to love the pungent dank demiparadise smell of dark earth rich with the mulch of millennia. He loved the strata of tree growths conjoined in botanical conspiracy to proscribe penetration by the sun. He loved the vines dangling drowsily downward from limbs so distant upward they skulked from sight. He loved the chatter of arboreal creatures who in their lives might never stand upon ground, and the call and flash of the rare brilliant quetzal birds. More than all else, he loved the jungle for nurturing within its womb the vestiges of the vanished.

This civilization had followed an exiled god upon a pathway to oblivion and it was not the first to do so. Thrice, at least, did this banished deity lead cultures to the other side of something. And great societies they had been, too. The first, the Toltec, were engineers of accomplishment while the English ran naked and painted themselves blue.

What happened to the Toltec? No one knows for sure. What happened to the Maya? They had been thought the best, but recent discoveries point to them as the worst: a culture that lasted for a thousand years on the intoxication of mutilation. But no one is sure what happened to them either. What happened to the Aztec? That is one event of which we can be sure. The Spanish happened to them, that's what. Yet how could *that* have happened? How could a beleaguered band of greedy ruffians who fought one another as bitterly as their enemies have overcome a vastly superior number of disciplined and war-hardy enemy fighting on that enemy's own soil?

Adair was certain this question was central to the solution of the puzzle. Here somewhere lay the nerve of reason why great civilizations fell at the onslaught of upstarts.

They were spooked. Yes, Adair was sure the Aztec had been badly spooked. Had not Moctezuma feared that Hernán Cortez embodied the return of Quetzalcoatl? Cortez had arrived from the direction of the god's home on vast and unimaginable vessels that he ordered consumed by flames when he departed them.

Yet why should the Aztec have feared the return of the god they revered highest?

The answer demanded disquisition into the logic of myth and a journey into madness that Adair was ill-equipped to undertake.

He would get Enid to do it for him.

The concept of sacrifice was also a central symptom of the malady of these civilizations. Yet it could not have been sacrifice alone. We all sacrifice something. It had to be some perversion of the concept. After all, the notion of sacrifice permeates many if not all of the world's religions. It is said the precedent was set by the Almighty Himself. Did He not sacrifice His only begotten son to atone for the sins of man? So say the Christians, many of whom were themselves sacrificed by persecutors.

Adair sought precedent in synoptic scriptures for the concept of God's sacrifice to man and could not discover it. It was surely not to be found in the words of Jesus, which were passionately and consistently directed toward the advent of the Kingdom of God, and which pointedly eschewed mysticism. No, the idea of God's sacrifice to man followed the death of Jesus.

Yet even man's sacrifice to God in most religions requires the rendering of something dear, be it real or symbolic.

Here was a radical departure in the ancient Mexican Indian celebrations of sacrifice. There is no evidence they had sacrificed anything dear, human or not. They may have sacrificed nothing to a god they would not have sacrificed without a god. The records are ambiguous. But it is known there were wholesale slaughters in which victims were dragged up the steps to the tops of temples where they were held by strong men while their living hearts were ripped from their breasts by priests wielding obsidian knives, the hearts then cast into deep wells in the temple centers, presumably for the scrutiny of Quetzalcoatl.

It is certain that tens of thousands of prisoners captured in war were thus sacrificed by the Aztec. But what kind of sacrifice is that? Was the slaughter of six million Jews and some half-million gypsies in the late Hitler war a devotion to a god? It is easy to sacrifice enemies and easy to create enemies to sacrifice.

Evidence is strong that the corpses of those sacrificed by the Aztec were dismembered and bounced down the sides of the temples, thus tenderized, for waiting throngs on the streets below. Evidence also exists that wars were often levied for the sole purpose of obtaining victims to sacrifice and that such sacrifices occurred most often in times when meat was scarce. The three great Indian civilizations were known for their skills in botanical agriculture, not in animal husbandry.

Adair's writings had been among the few to advocate

the hypothesis that human sacrifice as practiced by Toltec
and Maya and Aztec had been less directed toward the
gain of divine grace than the gain of protein. This had
all but got Adair declared persona non grata by the United
States of Mexico.

Perhaps, Adair reasoned, vacuous worship is at least
one moral equation latent in the destruction of civilizations. Adair knew the psychological equation could not
be his to resolve. Leave that to Enid.

He could not physically love her again, for reasons obvious to those who attended on him. This was just as
well for reasons obvious to those who attend on social
codes. But he still loved her. No one could stand athwart
that love, not even his good friend Peter.

He would express himself to her in letters. She would
never see him again.

14

"God Almighty," said Dr. Louise Kavanaugh. "Jesus
Christ." She lit a cigarette heedless of the NO SMOKING
signs all over the laboratory. She inhaled and exhaled
several deep drags and drummed with her fingers on the
table. She regarded the dead mouse on the floor as if a
genie had emerged from a Bunsen burner. She looked at
Dr. Knox as if for succor and got none from the radiologist, whose face was a study in impassivity. She looked
down again at the mouse, then looked at her fingers tap-
ping, then looked at the tip of her cigarette and inspected
the ash.

After the death of the mouse she looked anywhere except in the eyes of Deputy Sheriff Peter Bilyeux. He could
not be permitted access to her befuddlement.

"Jesus," she said, and took a final drag from her cigarette and stubbed it out. "What do you do when medicine encounters the medically impossible?"

Dr. Knox said nothing.

Pete Bilyeux said nothing.

"All right," Louise said. "Fuck it. I'm going to have to go to work. Freddie, what do you say we consult on professional matters for a change. Let's see, strychnine, curare, an OD of digitalis, botanical stuff," Louise said, thinking aloud, "something that works the instant it hits the bloodstream. Toxicology's not my specialty, but I've had some experience with it. I suppose curare's a possibility. In the right dosage—and it has to be about the same amount as strychnine—I've heard it can be pretty quick. There was a case involving it in a New Jersey hospital where murder was suspected. New York knows how to test for curare and I can get the information from them on the phone, but Jesus, there's no goddamn fly that could deliver that much curare, not even to a mouse . . ."

Dr. Knox filled and lit his pipe and nodded in agreement.

"Then there's always good old cyanide," Louise said. "Cute stuff. That's the trick they use in the gas chamber. Cyanide eggs, normally used for hardening metals, are dropped into a vat of sulfuric acid over which the patient is strapped in a chair. Hydrogen cyanide gas swirls up while the poor sonofabitch tries to hold his breath. Then he finally breaks down and inhales and screams with a sound only he can hear, and starts to turn blue. He's dead for sure in ten minutes. The mandatory autopsy is performed and gives you all the classic residuals of cyanide poisoning. There was no indication of anything like that in the people I cut up last night. I wish there had been. I know that sounds awful, but it's nice to know your enemy. We don't know anything now. Of course, I'll test for it and everything else. Now, let's see . . . Freddie, what do you know about nerve agents?"

"Nothing," Dr. Knox said.

"The only reason nerve agents popped into my heard is that I read somewhere that they're non-persistent. As soon as a few minutes after they've done their work, there's no trace of them . . ." She paused and went to a

desk and picked up a phone and pressed the intercom
button and asked someone to bring data on nerve agents.

"Uh, Doctor K-K-Kavanaugh?" Pete said.

"I told you to call me Louise," she said.

When at last she looked at him he saw in her face a
contrived look of tough nonchalance. "Uh, okay, Louise
. . . uh, it means to see—I mean, it seems to me there's
not much more for me to do here. Uh, this is your department. M-m-my job is to find out how to flop those
sties—I mean, stop those flies from killing more people."

"I understand," Louise said.

"Uh, okay for a few questions?"

"Sure."

"Uh, the dead fly you made the serum from. Is it a
different species from the others?"

"I don't know," Louise said. "It looks like it, but I'm
not an entomologist and we don't have one on staff here.
What do you think, Freddie?"

"I feel the same way," Dr. Knox said.

"Do, uh, do you d-d-doctors, uh, know any entomol-
ogists?"

Dr. Knox puffed on his pipe. "Yeah," he said, "yes,
I do. Doctor Applebaum, Abraham Applebaum, works
for USDA in Maryland just outside D.C. He's a dear
friend of mine."

"Was he the one at that dinner in Gettysburg?" Louise
asked. "The guy they call Anteater Abe?"

"Yeah," Dr. Knox said, chuckling across the stem of
his pipe.

"He's funny," Louise said.

"Yes, but he's damned good," Dr. Knox said, and
looked at his watch, "one of the best in the field. He'd
love to sink his teeth into something like this. He could
go on the lecture circuit with it. Let me see if I can get
him on the phone." He left to make the call.

Louise looked at Pete and with her hand brushed the
hair away from her forehead. "What else, Pete?"

"Well, uh, it seems to me that my jjjob is to track
down the flies, and, uh, your job is to track down the
toxin. How, uh, long do you think it might take you?"

"Who knows? Maybe an hour, maybe never. All we

can do is make educated guesses and run one test a time until we either find it or run out of tests.'' She held up the vial of serum that killed the mouse. ''I'm going to send some of this stuff by courier to the medical examiner's office in New York, along with tissue samples from the corpses in there, and ask them to help out. From a practical point of view—that is, from the way you have to look at it—it's a pretty safe bet that flies killed those people. Off the record, in fact, it's a sure thing. But I can't work off the record. My discipline has to be etiological. Besides, whatever the flies have got may tell us a lot about where they got it and how to get rid of it. Understand?''

''Sure. Oh, uh, you might want to have a look at these.'' Pete opened the bag with the dead baby rabbit and dead bat.

''Hmm,'' Louise said when she looked inside. ''All right.''

Louise looked at her watch and filled a syringe. She explained she was injecting atropine sulfate into some mice at five-minute intervals. Atropine is itself a poison, Louise explained, an alkaloid extract from the belladonna plant—also called the deadly nightshade—used in doses of about $1/120$ gram as a circulatory respiratory stimulant. Overdoses make the patient extremely excitable, sometimes feverish and delirious, and can kill. But atropine was known to be an antidote to nerve agents, at least the kinds she knew of, and the search for an antidote had to start somewhere.

Dr. Knox returned. He had been unable to reach Dr. Applebaum at the U.S. Department of Agriculture and would try him at home later. He assisted Louise as they began injecting mice.

The first mouse was given the toxic serum by Louise and simultaneously injected with atropine by Dr. Knox. It died anyhow, peeping piteously, but it seemed to Pete to take longer to die than the original one injected only with the serum. A second mouse that had been injected with atropine five minutes before was then injected with serum. It, too, screeched and convulsed. But it continued to breathe for several minutes before it died. A mouse that had been injected with atropine ten minutes before was then injected with the serum. It squeaked loudly, ran in circles, trembled, vomited, settled into a sickly lassitude, and lived.

For the first time since the first mouse died, Louise Kavanaugh smiled. "Well, boys, it looks like we lucked into something. The question is how the hell a fly could be a carrier of a nerve agent."

An assistant came in and left a manila folder with some photocopied papers in it for Louise, and left.

Louise began to scan the papers the nurse had brought. "Shit," she said after a few minutes.

"What's wrong?" Dr. Knox asked.

"The symptoms of nerve agents," Louise said, "all wrong."

She scanned more papers. Then she lingered over one. "Wait a minute," she said. "Here's another entry under nerve agents: 'VX, several times more toxic than sarin but less volatile . . . kills within minutes if inhaled or deposited on skin . . . accidental release in Utah in 1968 caused the deaths of thousands of sheep, some as far as sixty-four kilometers from where the gas escaped . . .' "

Louise looked at Dr. Knox as if she had just opened a fortune cookie that told her she would be Empress of China.

"Now listen to this, Freddie and Pete," she said. " 'The formula of VX is classified Top Secret by the United States government.' " She grinned broadly. "Uh, Pete, what kind of military or CIA or government installations are there within, say, fifty miles of your town?"

"Uh, there aren't any, Louise," Pete said

"Not any?" she said. "Are you sure?"

"Yes, uh, I mean, no. I mean, yes, I'm sure there aren't any."

Dr. Knox used a silver tool to clean out the bowl of his pipe and emptied the ashes in a plastic-lined garbage can and said, "What else does it say about VX, Louise?"

Louise read: " 'First prepared in the 1950s as an insecticide' . . . oh, hell . . . 'effects are residual even in soil for several days' . . . damn. An insecticide would have killed the flies and there's nothing even faintly residual about what killed the people. So much for intuition.''

"But atropine seems to work if it's in the system long enough," Dr. Knox said.

"Sure in hell does, doesn't it?" Louise said.

"Uh, Louise, what are the atropines—I mean, the chances of getting atropine sent to Thomas Valley?" Pete said.

Louise shook her head in the negative. "I can tell what you're thinking, Pete. No good. It would take days to get much of the stuff there, and were the population to be inoculated with it as a preventive, forget it. Children or older people could die from it. You might end up killing more people from atropine than the flies would kill. We'll get you some. In fact, I think the army or the civil-defense people actually manufacture it in kits for self-administration. We'll try to get some of them sent up to you, but there's no point in going beyond that. In return, how about sending me some more of your flies, if you're up to it?"

"Okay," Pete said. "Uh, one more favor? Would you mind calling Sheriff Cody at Elmsford about the flies?"

"Is he the asshole who suspected fluoride?" Louise said.

"Yeah," Pete said, "he's my b-boss."

"With the greatest pleasure," Louise said, and smiled at Pete and put out her hand. "Good job, Pete."

They exchanged home telephone numbers.

"Good job, Officer, good thinking," Dr. Knox said.

"Thank you," Pete said, "thank you both, uh, v-very much. You certainly did a good job." He left feeling as if he had been seated between two bright and pleasant conversationalists in the first-class section of an airplane just before it crashed.

15

"O magnificent god, why wert thou cast out from Tula?" spoke the other.

"For wisdom and knowledge of good, from which thou dost yet partake," spoke the one.

"But what can cast out a god, O Lord?" spoke the other.

"Another god," spoke the one. "Thus are the gods of good and evil forever locked in contest."

"And my kind were likewise driven forth with thee, great god, for the same reason?" spoke the other.

"Even so. Those who gave me their hearts for knowledge and wisdom must thence taste of barren earth and bitter fruits unto the time of my return when the full moon shall set in full day," spoke the one.

"And what of the minions of Tezcatlipoca?" spoke the other.

"Be not jealous of their kind," spoke the one. "For they are as dwellers in hell. They toil and from this travail know naught of surcease," spoke the one.

"I know again from thy words that thou art truly that greatest of gods, emerald Lord, feathered serpent, Quetzalcoatl by name," spoke the other.

"I am called by many names," spoke the one.

"What mayest I render unto thee, great Lord, that will hasten the day of thy return?" spoke the other.

"Render unto me the heart of one that is most and least known to thee." So spoke Quetzalcoatl, the one.

What do you do when a god tells you to kill your husband?

Enid was sure that was what was meant. Adair's letters had been filled with cryptic references to it. Adair never said it, but the moral conclusions of his letters were inevitable, or so she thought. Peter must die or Enid's soul must die. She saw this as she lay depressed late on Tuesday afternoon listening to the telephone ring and ignoring it.

But that's ridiculous, Enid thought. She laughed aloud at this folly. The Toltec gods were fables, legends, ancient superstitions.

Then, why did you kill the animals, Enid? What were you trying to do or discover?

I was just trying to explore the substance of the myths, she replied to herself. I'm a poet. Who was it that said poetry is emotion reflected in tranquillity? I wanted to experience the emotion and tranquilly reflect on it.

Is it morally justifiable to kill helpless creatures in the name of poetry? The one side of her mind asked.

Is it morally justifiable to kill helpless creatures in the name of science? The other side of her mind responded.

It was getting hot in the house. Of course, it's summer, it's supposed to be hot.

She got up and turned on the air conditioners. That would make her feel less sweaty. She turned the fans to HIGH and the thermostats to COLDEST.

She spent a few minutes trying to remember what she had been thinking about so she could catch up with it. Then she wondered why it got so cold in the house. God, here it was the middle of summer and you'd think it was January.

Did Pete really know about the animals? She felt her skin flush against the cold at this thought. Of course he knew. He mentioned flies and told her to stay away from them, a veiled reference to the Evil One and the red cat. He made snide innuendos about sacrifices. He thought she was crazy. He had no right to think such things of her, no right whatever. He knew she was going through a difficult time and common courtesy demanded that even a total stranger show a little consideration for it, let alone

your husband. That was terribly inconsiderate. It was un-
forgivable. It was infuriating.

She felt her skin grow hot from the rage of these
thoughts. It was frightfully hot in the house. She went to
the air conditioners to check them. Yes, the thermostats
were set all the way to COLDEST. Yes, it was hot as hell
in spite of this. The damned things must be on the fritz.

16

Deer flies, Pete's father had called them. Deer flies. The
story had been told to him when he was very young and
even then he knew enough to wonder if it was apocry-
phal. It sneaked past the decades back into his mind in
the parking lot now half-emptied at the Hershey Medical
Center. They weren't like houseflies, his father had said.
They live in dark and woodsy places where deer live.
They're a little bigger than ordinary flies and prettier, if
you can call a fly pretty. They bite you and drink minuscule amounts of your blood as do mosquitoes and fleas
and ticks and sand flies at the beach. Nature's tiny vampires, they have even bigger brothers called horse flies
that also bite and drink blood.

That the greenish fly that nearly bit him was capable
of killing could no longer be doubted. But how? Pete
would rule out nothing but the supernatural, in which he
stoutly disbelieved. As yet unexplained was the fly's radioactivity, the burning of the Mueller house, the note in
the refrigerator, and the dove hunter's story. If that story
was true, and it could well have been an old farmer's way
of pulling his leg, then someone else was also interested
in the flies. Perhaps they would meet. Such a meeting
would explain much.

The Volvo was five miles from Hershey when Pete realized he had forgotten something. He turned around in mid-highway, tires screeching, and raced back.

He was relieved to find the Hershey Visitors Center still open. He bought mammoth Hershey bars of various kinds and two large bags of chocolate kisses. He knew Enid was being sarcastic about the candy but also knew she would probably be amused to get it. He paid for the candy and thought it curious to be charged full price. You'd think you'd get a discount in a factory town.

He went to a public phone to call Enid to tell her he would be a little late and was required to deposit nearly a dollar in coins. No one answered and the money clanked into the coin-return chute.

It was about a hundred miles to Thomas Valley. In the northwest militant clouds formed a weather front that was moving toward Pete's destination as a dark curtain drawn by the hand of a malevolent god.

When Pete was about halfway home he stopped to phone Enid again and again there was no answer. Droplets of rain fell now and then on the Volvo's windshield and Pete thought of Enid and wondered where she could be and what was happening to them, and blinked away tears.

He tried to clear his thoughts and took comfort in the memory of a book he had read recently. The context, quantum physics, he found unusual. But the concept he found unutterably real.

Microcosms enfolded within macrocosms as an infinity of mirrors of ever increasing and ever diminishing sizes, he remembered reading. The microcosms divide into ever smaller particles until just when the tiniest particle seems to have been identified, the traces of infinitudes of smaller particles are discovered. The macrocosms are seen to expand into quasars, black holes, and beyond, the mirror image of subatomic electrons, quarks, and hadrons. At least macrocosms are comforting. Who is there who walks among us who steals no comfort in the belief that the universe is infinite and that time is eternal?

It is all so random, so horribly random, Pete thought. And so the scheme of God abjures logic, the theme defies music, the mind evades match, and the passion is emulated by bathetic bleats from an upright animal cursed as no other with the dread knowledge of its own finitude.

The author of the book had called the doughty Einstein "the last of the classical physicists," and averred the great thinker's disquietude at the thought of "a God who plays with dice."

Well, Pete thought, one man's anxiety can be another's peace. With all respect to the shade of Dr. Einstein, a deity who diced honestly with fates was preferable in Pete's mind to one who rigged the game.

Pete turned on the radio to search for a weather report, and the crackle of electronic static caused by distant lightning told him all he needed to know.

He looked at his watch and saw he would reach Thomas Valley in time for the first viewing of Billy Gianotti at the Waldwick Funeral Home. He thought it best to go there before going home.

He pulled into the parking lot of Ed & Edna's Diner to phone Enid, and thought it odd that no light showed inside. But then the dusk was premature under a sky metallic with impending violence.

Eddies of storm-borne breezes caught the screen door of the diner and rhythmically opened and shut it. On Saturday afternoon Pete had chuckled to himself at the domestic fracas over holes in the screen. Now a piece of screen peeled back by the wind was flopping and it was Tuesday and it was no longer funny. He saw what looked like a dog sleeping on its belly just inside the screen door. Then he remembered that Ed and Edna had no dog.

The first peal of thunder echoed over wooded western hills.

He knew he was truly afraid but did not know why. He had been anxious in the Mueller house but not terribly fearful. Now he was. He remembered how he felt when as a boy he had gone to see Alfred Hitchcock's *Psycho*. He remembered how he felt when the detective climbed the steps inside the old house. Don't go up there, he thought to the detective, don't do it. Something awful is up there, something with the breath of hell.

Rain began to fall in heavy drops and the thunder growled again. Foolish or not, he took out the Python and held it, a child's talisman to ward off the teeth of Satan. He forced his feet to step toward the door.

He opened the door, and all that was missing from *Psycho* was the banshee wail of scream and the sting of soundtrack music.

The sleeping dog inside was what remained of Ed and Edna. Edna's body lay atop Ed's, flyswatter in hand. A lone customer lay sprawled in death on his back where he had fallen from his seat at the counter. It was the dove hunter Pete had met that morning. The corpses were covered with flies, most of them the large greenish flies, the deer flies. He could hear them buzzing in macabre chorus. Some flew up from the dead toward him. Vampires.

"Oh!" The sound volunteered itself from his throat.

He slammed the screen shut and ran to the car and got in and shut its door and rolled up its windows. He holstered the gun and turned on the interior light and rummaged for debris. It was Enid's car and Enid would not be Enid if she did not leave debris trailing in her wake as Isadora Duncan's fatal scarf. He found a couple of empty Frito corn-chip bags. Enid adored Frito corn chips. The bags would do for his hands. Under the driver's seat he found one of Enid's long-lost ski caps. It smelled of dampness and grease, but it fit over Pete's head and neck, and he could see tolerably well through the chinks between the knits.

The thunder was coming closer. Pete could see the glow of lightning through the tiny holes in the cap.

He fumbled on the back seat for the mayonnaise jar the doctors had returned to him, sterilized. He zipped and buttoned and closed everything that could be zipped and buttoned and closed and was satisfied his skin would be protected if he did not linger.

He got out of the car again and walked through the rain into the diner and stepped over the bodies. He scooped flies into the jar and worried that he might vomit. The bodies of Ed and Edna were still limp and warm and jiggled as he went about his task.

Flies hummed around him trying to find a piece of skin to bite, and when he had a free hand inside a Frito bag, he shooed them off.

Once when Pete did this, he lost his footing and tripped

and fell backward over the dead people who had been his
friends. The flies were irate and buzzed furiously around
him. Pete's fall had flipped Edna's body onto its back.
Dilated eyes had rolled upward toward the lids and
showed a ghastly white. The mouth of the old woman lay
agape and its saliva still shone on the dentures. The flopping arm hit the floor on the disturbance and bounced
upward as that of the drowned Captain Ahab pinioned to
the white whale beckoning his shipmates to duel with a
Satanic deity.

Pete scrambled to his feet, careful not to expose skin
to the flies that angrily droned in droves, seeking to drink
and destroy his blood.

No mind is immune from the disease called paranoia.
When you wake in the morning and stub your toe in the
dark, then turn on the light to have it blow out, then make
coffee and burn up the pot because there is no water in
it, then slip in the shower and bash your head, then dress
and realize a zipper is broken, you get the feeling it is
not your day and that maybe something is working against
you.

This feeling gets worse when something wants to kill
you.

Pete screwed down the perforated lid on the jar now
filled with more than a dozen killer flies. He listened and
felt the airborne vampires around him, and wondered if
indeed some government experiment in biological warfare had gone haywire.

In his queer costume Pete tucked the jarful of flies
under his arm and went into the kitchen looking for a
phone that would not require him to use coins and thus
bare his skin.

The flies followed and he twitched and writhed and
slapped at them. He found the phone. Next to it was Ed's
quart of rye from which the old man had taken his peri-
odic pulls. Impulsively, Pete opened the bottle and swallowed a large gulp through the porous wool of the ski
mask. The whiskey fought its way down his esophagus
with a violent chemical action that was hot and cold at
once. He belched and the aftertaste was olid with the
sweet-sour scent you get when you walk out of the fresh
air into a bar around closing time.

It occurred to him the rye might act as a repellent to the flies, so he poured the rest of the bottle over his head and over as much of his clothing as he could.

It worked. The bloodsuckers disliked rye whiskey. He dialed the substation. A strange voice answered and did not give his name in the usual manner of the Thomas Valley deputies.

"Uh, who's this?" Pete said.

"This is Deputy Albano," the voice answered. "Who's this?"

Albano was from the Mount Ivy substation and Pete did not know him well. "This is, uh, B-B-Bilyeux, Albano, I . . ."

"Bilyeux, for chrissakes, where the hell are you? We been looking for you all afternoon . . ." It seemed to Pete that some of the flies were venturing closer to him despite the rye. He swatted at them. "Listen, Albano, this is, uh, an emergency, we have a code nine."

"The old man changed the schedule on everybody," Albano said.

"Albano, goddammit, this is an emergency," Pete said. "We got a code nine, three dead people at Ed and Edna's Diner on the Elmsford Road. No survivors . . ."

"Where?" *Ccccccchhhhhh* went the static on the telephone line. *Booooommmmm* went the thunder.

"Ed and Edna's. The Elmsford Road. Now, uh, listen, Albano, this is important. Extremely important. Whoever comes *must* cover up completely. This place is full of poisonous flies that kill people instantly."

"What?"

"I told you, dammit. P-p-poisonous flies. They killed the people here. They're killing people everywhere around! Watch out . . ." *Ccccchhhhh* went the phone line again.

"Where the hell are you, Bilyeux? You been drinking or smoking something?"

"Look. Albano. I'm not kidding. The c-c-county is full of poisonous flies. You can, uh, confirm that with Doctor Kavanaugh or Doctor Knox at Hershey Med Center, they just ran some tests. Now look. Listen. I've got to get my butt out of here before I get killed. Where can I reach the old man?"

"Just went over to the funeral parlor," Albano said.

"G-good. I'm on my way there . . ."

Pete hung up and dashed for the Volvo with his captives.

Thomas Valley, Pennsylvania, was embattled, besieged in the stormy night.

Pete pulled in and parked in front of the phone booth at the Gulf station just outside of town. Again he tried to call Enid and again no one answered. He went into the station men's room and there tried to wash the stench of rye from his clothing.

Not until he reached the center of town did he realize the extent of the pandemonium. Some kind of meeting was apparently breaking up at Town Hall. Cars full of people picked and probed and puttered their way toward the narrow exit of the parking lot as if leaving a hit movie at a drive-in on a Saturday night.

Pete worked his way through what must have been Thomas Valley's worst traffic jam ever. He could not drive, let alone park, within three blocks of the funeral home. He finally left the Volvo in the post-office lot in defiance of the POSTAL EMPLOYEES ONLY sign. There would be no postal employees until morning, if then. He walked toward the funeral home, listening for flies between thunderclaps and looking for them by flashes of lightning.

The people gathered at the front door of the funeral home were anything but funereal. Some held umbrellas, some simply soaked in the rain, all talked and gestured feverishly. Some wailed and screamed and cursed and were comforted by others. Pete could not hear what the ruction was about, but he had his suspicions.

He did not wish to be recognized and have anyone talk to him because he would not know how to respond. He remembered a back door that led to a room that was used as a spare coat room for overflow crowds at large funerals. He walked around the building to it. A bolt of lightning struck a tree on the hill a quarter-mile above and behind the funeral parlor. The thunder was nearly immediate and fell on Pete as a dump truck spilling a cargo of bowling balls. He turned toward the flash and saw the ghost of the bolt's spark. The tree burst into blue flame along some twenty feet of its trunk and glowed as with fluorescent light. Then it began to spout orange flame against the rain.

From hundreds of routine nightly door-checks, Pete knew that the back door, even if locked, had a beveled contact bolt that could easily be slipped with a pen knife or credit card. Nobody worried much about burglaries in Thomas Valley, least of all the proprietor of the funeral parlor.

The porch light over the rear door was unlit, nor did any light show in the room within. Pete had no flashlight with him and so felt along the length of the door with his VISA card. The card caught the latch and the handle turned and the door opened and Pete went in and closed the door behind him. He paused for a few moments to let his eyes grow accustomed to the dark. There were two doors leading from the room: one led to a viewing room and the other led to the basement that contained the embalming room and crematorium. Light leaked from beneath each.

Pete walked gingerly in the dark toward the light of the viewing room. Suddenly the light was blanked out. Something struck Pete in the chest and he lost his footing. He grabbed the thing that hit him and it moved as if on wheels. Pete stumbled along with it. One hand held what felt like a bar of cold steel. The other touched a hard object under cloth. The moving thing was rolling. It caromed off a wall with a crash and Pete lost his grip and slid to the floor. Another thing hit Pete on the back of his neck so hard it made him see meteorites behind his eyes.

Pete reached up to grab it to regain his footing and felt his hand on a small cold face. He heard footsteps running up from the cellar.

A lightning flash illuminated the room and Pete realized he was in the company of four corpses on wheeled stretchers.

The basement door flew open and a powerful flashlight held by a figure in silhouette against room light shone in Pete's eyes. "Who's there? Put your hands up or I'll shoot!"

"Uh, Ernie?" Pete said.

"Yeah. Who are you? I can't see, my glasses fell off! Careful or I'll shoot!"

Ernie Waldwick, son of the founder and now proprietor of Waldwick Funeral Home, who couldn't see much out of one eye and saw astigmatically as the artist El Greco out the other eye, pointed a superb Browning twelve-gauge semi-automatic shotgun toward the abdomen of Pete Bilyeux. At this range, a single shot from the gun would blast Pete virtually in half.

"Uh, Ernie," Pete said, "uh, uh, it's see, Meat, uh— I mean, it's me, P-P-P-P-Pete B-B-Bilyeux . . ."

"Oh, Pete, thank God! Where the hell have you been all day?"

Booooommmmm! went the shotgun.

The muzzle blast lit the room with a miniver tint. The smell of exploded nitrate and fulminate of mercury drenched it. The shotgun automatically loaded another cartridge in its chamber.

"Pete! Pete?" Ernie howled. "Sorry! Sorry! That was a mistake! It was an accident! You all right?"

"Uh, I hope so," Pete said, buckled in a small heap on the floor under a corpse wagon, head tucked beneath knees clutched by his arms. Pete was unsure whether he had been hit or not. He knew gunshot victims often felt this way at first. The blast of 00 buckshot had struck the floor next to his left foot and bored through vinyl tile, oak flooring, and pine subflooring. His left foot felt numb near where the shot had hit. He wriggled his toes and they worked, though they were cool. He had put on light suede desert boots that morning. He reached down to his left foot with his right hand and could feel that the toes of the boot were gone. But the stocking and his own toes were intact and no fluid came from them. "I'm, uh, okay," he said. "Ernie, for God's sake, ppplease put that damn gun on the floor."

Ernie did. "I'm sorry, Pete," he said. "Oh, my God, I'm sorry. Oh, Pete, my God, what's happening to us all? It's terrible. It's horrible. Oh, God, please, what's happening?"

Pete stood up. He was surprised the shotgun noise had not attracted people from the other room and assumed they thought it was thunder. "I, uh, was jjjust going to ask you the same question, Ernie."

"Jesus, Pete, don't you know? Seven more people died this afternoon alone! That's eighteen people. Eighteen in seventy-two hours! Count 'em, eighteen! Count 'em for Pete's sake . . . No, no, I'm sorry, Pete—I mean for God's sake! I had to tell County Hospital to stop sending any more. I said the next-of-kin should send them to parlors in Elmsford or other towns or have them cremated. That's what . . . what one of these people is waiting here for, cremation. The others I have to work up for funeral and burial. I mean, I have to do it for the Murdocks and Webster . . ."

"What?" Pete said. The lightning had lit the room too quickly for Pete to recognize the face of the dead child he had touched.

Ernie Waldwick turned on the room light and replaced the cover over Joey Murdock and straightened the covers over the others.

Pete was shocked to see Joey's face. He had hoped and prayed it would not come to this and now that it had he felt as if he had been dropped down a well. He crossed himself.

"Yeah," Ernie said, "poor little guy, went out this afternoon. Poor little guy . . ." He clucked mournfully and not at all professionally. Perhaps it was Ernie's lack of detachment that made his stewardship of the old family business even more successful than that of his father. He was genuinely sorry for the dead in his care, and their families knew it. Pete didn't know how Ernie could stand it, and the truth was that he didn't stand it all that well. Years before, he had acquired a permanent facial tic.

"That's his mother over there and Jack Webster from the bank over there, Pete. They, uh, found them this morning on the terrace of the, uh, the same room at the Sunset Motel. That's just between you and me, Pete. The remains just came in from the autopsy and I, well, I had to take them. Al's still out in a viewing room. He was due for burial this afternoon, but now, with the two others and their families all here, it's all going to be done together. God, to think of it. A husband dead and a little kid in a coma and she's shacked up with her boyfriend. Jesus! Of course, nobody's saying anything about it . . ."

Pete was privately irked but not much surprised. Police work often exposes you to ignobilities in the human soul.

"What's, uh, the c-crowd outside, Ernie?" Pete said.

"Oh, them, oh, God Almighty. Some of them followed the mayor and the sheriff here and they're mad as hell because nothing's being done about the deaths. Some of them are mad at me because I took the Murdocks and Webster in and didn't take their deceased. But, hell, I had to take the Murdocks, and Webster was manager of the bank, after all. But I'm not taking any more, Pete, I'm not! I just don't have the facilities. God, when is this going to be over? It's all like a nightmare."

Pete asked to use a phone. He dialed home and again there was no answer. Then he asked where the mayor and the sheriff were and Ernie led him the back way into the viewing room where Billy Gianotti lay in his casket.

Of all the deputies there, Pete was the only one not in uniform. He had planned to go home and change but there had been no time for it and what he had been doing was more important than protocols. He did not think Billy would mind and knelt before the casket and crossed himself and prayed.

Pete abhorred the overpowering sickly sweet florid odor of funeral parlors. There was something dishonest about it. Dishonest, too, was the appearance of Billy. Dead people are supposed to look peacefully asleep, but they all looked like characters in a second-rate wax museum to Pete, and Billy was no exception with all his blemishes covered with mortician's makeup and no cigar in his mouth.

Pete nerved himself to console Maggie Gianotti, not the easiest person to cope with in normal circumstances.

"Oh, Pete, oh, Pete, oh, why?" she said as she turned her cheek for Pete to kiss and clutched his arms with the talons of a raptor. "Pete, oh, Pete, thank you for coming, thank you so much. Billy would have thanked you, too, Pete. He thought the world of you, Pete, and now he's gone. Gone! I can't believe it, I just can't. He was so good, Pete, so good and so rugged and healthy. He was almost never sick. Pete, I just can't believe what happened. I can't! Oh, God, why did it have to happen to him? You've got to tell me that, Pete, you've got to explain it to me and to Billy and the kids. Tell us why!''

Pete muttered the platitudes you say to a youngish widow and let Maggie keep repeating herself and keep digging her fingernails into his arms until some relative came along and distracted her. Pete introduced himself to Billy's ashen parents and to Maggie's and stumbled over more platitudes.

He hated all this. It all seemed barbaric to him. It was bad enough for people to lose a loved one. It seemed to Pete the thought of spending hours cooped up with the corpse only exacerbated the grief of a loss that would be felt the rest of their lives. Enid felt the same way and even more strongly. They had both agreed that when they died they would donate their organs for transplant and be cremated immediately after. Of wakes and funerals, Enid had got off one of her better lines: ''Anyone who wants to see me dead is no friend of mine.''

Pete drifted away from the relatives and toward the sheriff and the mayor, who were holding a subdued if animated conversation.

''Hello, Pete.'' The mayor saw him first and offered his hand. The man looked as if he had not slept in a week.

''Bilyeux, where the hell have you been?'' Sheriff Joe Cody blurted in a loud stage whisper. ''Why aren't you in uniform, man? Don't you have any respect for the dead?''

''Uh, sorry, Sheriff, I was, uh, working on the case. Uh, did Koctor Davanaugh, uh—I mean, did Doctor Kavanaugh call you?''

''No doctor called me,'' the sheriff said. ''What case are you talking about?''

''Uh, this one, Sheriff,'' Pete said, indicating Billy.

''This is no case, Bilyeux,'' the sheriff said. ''The wop died of a heart attack. There's no case.''

''The hell there isn't, Joe,'' the mayor shot back.

''Uh, Sheriff, I have to t-t-talk with you,'' Pete said. ''It's, uh, urgent. Can we go someplace?''

''What for?'' the sheriff said.

''Uh, I found out what's doing it,'' Pete said.

"You found out?" the mayor said "What is it, Pete?"

"Now hold on, War, old son," the sheriff told the mayor. "This man reports to *me*, not you."

"You both report to me, you sonofabitch," Mayor Otis snapped. "You're on town land now and as chief executive officer of this community I am *directing* the both of you to come with me and give me a full report. If I don't get it immediately, I'm going to make two telephone calls. The first is going to be to the state attorney general and the second is going to be to the press. Now what do you say, Joe?"

The little mayor suddenly grew taller in Pete's eyes.

The sheriff glared at Pete and at the mayor. "Have it your way, War, we don't want reporters swarming around here," he said with an air of lèse-majesté.

The mayor went to find his umbrella.

"Bilyeux, you mush-mouthed sonofabitch, don't you ever pull that stunt on me again," the sheriff hissed to Pete.

"What, Sheriff?" Pete said, somewhat ingenuously.

"You know, you pup, you. You tried to show me up in front of a civilian."

"Uh, what, Sheriff?" Pete said.

"Tell me something, Bilyeux. Those big medical bills your dipshit wife has been running up, how do you think you'd pay for them without medical insurance or a salary?"

Pete looked at him and wanted to hit him and tried to conceal this feeling and did not know what to say.

The mayor returned with his umbrella. "Let's go to my store," he said.

The three went out the back. The mayor held the umbrella for the three as they walked the two blocks to Otis Drugs. Between thunderclaps, the mayor explained to Pete that he had just finished with an emergency council meeting to try to quell public panic over the mysterious deaths. But it had quite the opposite effect because there were no explanations. Immediately after the meeting he tracked down the sheriff and demanded some.

The mayor opened the darkened store and the three went in. They went behind the pharmaceutical counter and the mayor turned on a small light explaining he wanted to attract no attention. He had been getting plenty of it lately.

The mayor told Pete to make his report.

Pete looked at the sheriff. Naive as Pete was in political matters, he thought it prudent to report directly to his boss. "It's, uh, f-f-flies, Sheriff, p-p-poisonous flies."

"Flies?" the sheriff said. "Bilyeux, is that booze I smell on you? You mean to tell me that old Joe Cody and this honorable mayor here have to tell those good people out there that their loved ones had heart attacks because of a bug that eats shit?"

"Wait a minute, Joe," the mayor said. "This isn't the first I've heard that. A rumor like that was spreading at the meeting. It seems some farmer saw some of his stock die after being bitten by some kind of fly. I forget what they called it."

"Uh," Pete said, "uh, deer flies, Mayor?"

"Dear flies," the sheriff snorted. "Who in goddamn hell would call a fly dear? Now I know you've been drinking, Bilyeux."

"No, Joe," the mayor said. "D-e-e-r flies," he spelled it out to the sheriff. "And, yes, that was what the farmer called them."

"Who in hell was this farmer, War?" the sheriff said.

"I forget. We can look it up in the minutes of the meeting."

"Uh, I, uh, don't think that'll be necessary, Mayor," Pete said. "Uh, Sheriff, the Hershey Medical Center people ran tests, and a deer fly carried some kind of poison that causes nearly instant death."

"How the hell do you know, Bilyeux?" the sheriff said.

"I, uh, was there, Sheriff. With the doctors."

"What the hell were you doing there? Who the hell authorized you?" the sheriff said.

"I, uh, was on mmmy own, Sheriff. It was my off day—I mean, my day off."

"What were those doctors' names, Bilyeux?"

"Uh, Knox and K-Kavanaugh, Sheriff. Doctor, uh, Kavanaugh is the one who knows the most about it."

"I'll call him right now," the sheriff said.

"Uh, he's a she, Sheriff," Pete said.

"Now that's enough out of you, buster! I've had enough

of your smartass stunts and wisecracks, Bilyeux," the sheriff yelled.

Pete had not meant to be snide or funny, only to spare the sheriff his own embarrassment on meeting Louise Kavanaugh. He had not meant in any of the exchanges of the past half-hour to irritate the sheriff at all, yet had certainly succeeded in doing so. Then the situation dawned on him. He had read somewhere in a book on management that when your boss behaves angrily at you for no apparent reason, it is likely that he fears you are out to get his job. The idea was ludicrous, Pete thought. He didn't want Sheriff Cody's job. But he wouldn't put it past the sheriff to suspect that he did. The man was, after all, a politician, with only this dubious skill to commend him.

"I'll call Doctor Kavanaugh," the mayor said, and seemed to Pete to be much less the politician and much more the statesman. "What's the phone number, Pete?"

Pete gave him both phone numbers and the mayor dialed the hospital first and verified who she was and found she had gone home a half-hour or so before. The mayor dialed her home number and Pete could hear the phone being answered. From the mayor's half of the conversation Pete could tell Louise was corroborating, in medical language that the mayor understood, Pete's story of the poisonous flies.

"Well, thank you very much, Doctor," Mayor Otis said. "What? . . . He's right here, as a matter of fact. Want to talk to him? . . . Hang on. Pete, she wants to talk to you . . ."

"Hi, Louise," Pete said.

"Hi, Pete. Jesus, what a shitty day you put me through. Listen, I just want to bring you up to date. I tried calling you at home but you weren't there. I also tried calling your friend the sheriff. Twice, in fact, but I couldn't track him down. So far all the human tissue and fluid testing we've done has been negative. Now here's an interesting thing. The dead bat's radiation dosage was internal. I cut him open and found one of your greenish flies in the upper section of his digestive tract. It was nearly perfectly preserved, which tells us two things: A, the bat died almost instantly because digestion didn't even start and, B, the bat and the fly probably killed each other simultaneously. Freddie finally got a hold of Abe Applebaum, the entomologist. He's going to try to come up and meet you in a couple of days or so, when he can get the time. I gave him your phone numbers. He was stupefied when he heard about the flies and said he never read or heard anything like it. We described the bat's fly to him and he said it sounded like the family Tabanidae, genus Chrysops maybe, whatever that is. Anyhow, they're called deer flies. Now, Pete, listen to this. There are two important distinctions between flies, from your point of view: the kinds that bite and the kinds that don't. *Musca domestica*, the common housefly, doesn't bite. Deer flies and their relatives do. The females, like mosquitoes, are quite literally vampires. They'll settle for any blood, animal or human. Their usual habitat is wooded and shady places. They almost never go out in the sun.''

"Good, uh, thanks," Pete said.

"Have any more people in your area died with the same symptoms?" Louise asked.

"Yeah, uh, the total is up to eighteen. No, t-t-twenty-one." Pete added Ed and Edna and the dove hunter to the latest tally.

"Twenty-one people?" Louise said. "That's goddamn incredible! Listen, Pete, you've got to get me some more of those flies ASAP, okay?"

"Yeah, uh, I have them already," Pete said.

"Good. Talk to you later. So long."

Louise hung up and Pete related what she had said to the sheriff and the mayor.

"Well, Joe?" the mayor said to the sheriff.

"Okay, War, old son, I'll buy the fly story."

"Yeah, but what are you going to do about it, Joe?"

"Well . . ." the sheriff said, "I guess until this etiologist fella shows up, we're just going to have to tell the good people to stay away from flies, old son."

"What about the press?" the mayor said. "They've been ringing my phone off the hook."

"Tell 'em it's under investigation." the sheriff said. "For God's sakes, don't let those bastards know about the flies. The last thing we need is a bunch of snot-nosed reporters running around getting in the way."

"If we tell the people, the reporters are going to find out anyhow," the mayor said.

"Yeah, old son, but finding out is one thing and getting in the hair of public officials in an emergency is another."

"I agree," the mayor said. "So it's under investigation, then. I mean you *are* investigating, right, Joe?"

"Goddammit, War, I've been just patient as hell with you. Now you listen to me! Nobody, not even the County Board of Supervisors, tells old Joe Cody how to do his job. You got that straight, old son? You're fucking-a-john right I'm going to investigate. Joe Cody is taking personal charge of this case, old son, you can bet your life on it."

"Okay, Joe. Good. Thanks. Let's stay in touch. Just so you know, I'm going to call the fire chief right now. If he's not too drunk, I'm going to ask him to have the men go door-to-door to warn people about the flies."

"Good thinking, War, old son. I'll get in touch with the other volunteer fire departments in the county and ask 'em to do the same."

"Okay," the mayor said. "Good. Now I've got some work to do, if you gentlemen will excuse me . . ."

The thunderstorm continued to wage war on the landscape as Pete and the sheriff walked toward the front door of the drugstore. The sheriff stopped Pete just before they went out.

"Bilyeux, I'm making shift changes and putting everyone on overtime for the duration. Everyone gets time-and-a-half, not comp time. You're going on the four-to-midnight starting tomorrow night. And, Bilyeux, I *am* taking personal charge of this case. You're not to report to anyone but me. Understand?"

Pete could not see the sheriff's face in the darkened store, but the tone of the man's voice told him he did not want to. "Okay, Sheriff, I, uh, I understand."

"You damn well better," the sheriff said.

Pete walked through the storm to the Volvo.

He bought some pizza to take home and stopped at the substation and briefed Deputy Albano on the situation and gave him the jar of flies and asked him to get the state police to relay them to Hershey by morning, very carefully.

The sheriff's belligerence worried Pete on the drive home. But he was much more worried about Enid.

Louise Kavanaugh was puzzled and worried and exhausted. She was appalled to hear that a total of twenty-one people had died in less than seventy-two hours in that rinky-dink little hamlet. Her instincts as a medical person were much aroused.

She poured herself a stiff scotch-and-soda and tried to relax for bed and realized some other instincts had also been aroused.

It was the cop. Pete. Once you got beyond what seemed to be some form of motor dysphasia, he was a pretty smart cookie. Pretty tough, too, in a human sort of way. She had fired off some of her best barbs at him and he had taken it well. A dogged sonofabitch he was and in his own way just as professional about his work as she about hers. She wondered if there was something that he, too, was trying to prove or live down. Perhaps the speech impediment. She had laid cops before and they were as mushy behind the macho as most guys, if not more so. God, but men are weak, Louise Kavanaugh thought. It's mind-boggling how their muscles and their penises can get so hard and their souls be so soft. Make love with one on a winter weekend afternoon and the first thing the guy will do when it's over is switch on the football game he had been missing. Louise reckoned there was something epicene in grown men who watched other grown men play games. So it was a relief to meet one now and then who seemed to have some inner strength. This cop might be an interesting challenge.

God, but that ninny who finally answered his phone sounded flaky as all get-out. Louise wondered if it could have been his wife, but nobody with what that guy had going for him would stick around a nut like that. Besides, he didn't wear a wedding ring. Even Roger had worn one. No, she was probably some cute little junkie he'd picked up for a night or two. Cops are always getting laid by weird women.

17

Enid Bilyeux began to surrender to the peace of defeat.
The phone had been ringing constantly, but it stopped
jangling her nerves. The storm rampaged outside and she
found it restful. Let it have passions; she wouldn't. She
would ignore it. Likewise she would also ignore the telephone.

She had answered one persistent call early in the evening. It had stripped the defenses from her nerves as in-
sulation from tiny wires. It was when she answered this
call that Enid knew why Pete was behaving so strangely
with her lately. There was another woman. She had a
husky voice and sounded sexy and sure of herself. She
said she was a doctor. What a laugh. Only one of the
doctors Enid had seen was a woman and she had a Vi-
ennese accent. Pete himself had not been to a doctor
since they were married. He had probably spent the afternoon with that woman. He had probably forgot and
left something behind at her place and she was calling
him about it and made up the doctor story when Enid
answered the phone.

At first this realization charged the cells of Enid's
central nervous system with frenzied messages and counter-
messages as though she had taken both a powerful stimulant and depressant. The muscles at the back of her neck
compacted with cruel claws and gave her that sensation
that tells you that you are about to get a cold or at least
a three-aspirin headache. The tips of her ears burned.
Her life was a strigil scraped across a blistered back. She
trembled and wanted to tremble even harder, as if the act
would quake away the demons that dwelt within her.

Oh, that bastard, that dirty bastard, Enid thought. How
could he do it to her just when she most needed help? I

really should kill him, she thought—yes, do it. He betrayed me. Both my loves betrayed me. Adair went away
to chase ghosts in Mexico and Peter went to another
woman.

She went to the kitchen and got out the big stainless-
steel knife she had used on the animals and was going to
use on the red cat. She would kill Peter Bilyeux with it.

Then she thought of the incident with the red cat again
and twitched violently as you do when you are falling
asleep when you shouldn't and something inside sets off
an alarm.

A fly had killed that cat. It had happened before her
eyes. The fly could have but two meanings: it was either
hallucination or it was the servant of an evil Toltec god.

It was the choice Enid made between the two meanings
that let the peace descend upon her. The gods were metaphors, myths, allegories dreamed by ancient people who
needed some ratiocination for events and phenomena they
could not understand. If you were lucky one day and then
did exactly the same things the next day and were un-
lucky, there had to be some extrinsic reason for it—a
spirit, a numen, a god that made the difference. It followed that if you appeased or propitiated or sacrificed to
the numen, the good luck would come back. When it
didn't, that simply meant you had to try harder at such
appeasement, ad infinitum. This was the hold that gods
held on humankind.

No, it was hallucination. Enid sobbed briefly when she
knew her combat against madness had been lost. Then
she felt relieved. People like to know the answers, good
or bad.

She sat down on the couch in the dark and took off her
shoes and rested barefoot with the knife in her hand and
listened to the storm and waited. She felt as she had after
spending her passions with Adair. Enid was in her strange
little Eden again, she thought. The telephone rang and
she disregarded it again.

Where do you go to go crazy? she wondered. Just what
do you do? What's expected of you? Do you have to fill
out some form and put your Social Security number on
it?

She laughed at these ironies.

She felt as though she had been swimming for years against floodwaters. She would now stop struggling and let herself be borne along by the boiling current where it would. Would she kill Pete when he came home? Would she kill herself? Would she just take a nap? She didn't know. She would simply wait and let insanity supply the answer.

Between beats of rain lashing against house and gutter and window, between gusts of wind screaming through elms and sycamores and oaks and maples and evergreens, between flashes of lightning and blasts of thunder rolling as avalanches across the lawn, Enid thought she could hear something whispering.

She went to the window and looked out. Clouds tumbled and erupted over treetops. Boughs whipped as fingers of seaweed in the waters of a whirlpool.

Art thou the one that criest from before? spoke the one.

"Are you Tezcatlipoca?" asked Enid as she searched through the window for epiphany in the storm.

I am that I am, spoke the one.

"Am I now given over to you, terrible god?" Enid said.

Thou art a creature of the law. I give the law. In that wise do all creatures of the law belong to me, spoke the one.

"Now that my mind is no longer my own, must I call you my god?"

Canst thou possess a god? spoke the one. Was thy mind ever thine own?

Enid scanned the storm-swept night sky for sight of manifestation of the god of darkness who spoke to her. She saw only a riven landscape punctuated by flashes of brilliant blue illumination that left spectral images to burn on. So this was insanity, she thought. This was what it was to be. She was to be drawn, spellbound, a living thing in hypnotic trance in a horrid dream venturing toward home, the bosom of the god of darkness.

"May I, now that I am given over to you, see your face, O Lord?" she said.

You may see my face only in the law, spoke the one, and the law is everywhere to be seen. Were I to say that

I were like unto any thing, then thou and thy kind would say I was like unto ye.

"May I then see no likeness of you, God?" she said.

Law is likeness, spoke the one, and likeness is law.

"Your words are ambiguous, O God," Enid said.

I am god, spoke the one.

"And what of Quetzalcoatl, O God?" Enid asked.

The bird doth moult and the serpent doth slough his skin, spoke the one.

"When you cast out Quetzalcoatl from Tula, Lord, from the rich fields and ripe fruits, why did you also cast out my kind?"

I cast nothing from nothing, spoke the one. I give law.

"Is it your wish that I renounce Quetzalcoatl, God?"

Renounce folly. You and all ye must follow law ere it be too late. So spoke Tezcatlipoca, the one.

"Tell me how, O Lord," Enid said.

There was no reply.

There was nothing but rain and wind and thunder and amorphous clouds spitting the power that lit the sky.

Suddenly in the afterglow of a stroke, a wisp of cloud billowed and began to form the formless.

Lightning struck again, and Enid knew she was witness to metamorphosis, and the duel of gods.

"It's you, isn't it?" she said.

From the zenith of night to faraway troubled foothills the form coiled downward and radiated aureate and refulgent green.

Enid could feel the hot blood surging and dilating the arteries at the sides of her neck.

"It was you all along, wasn't it?" she snarled.

At last Enid knew what truly had betrayed her. It was not Peter. It was not Adair. It was not even her mind. It was myth. It was the genesis of the metaphor, the allegory, the legend, that had seduced her and her kind into unending circles of awe, unanswerable riddles of promise and sacrifice, insoluble alchemies of anguish and superstition. She had been deceived by myth and she was enraged and so help her God she would destroy it.

Without bothering to use the door, she flung open the window and jumped through it. Knife in hand, she ran across the grass to the base of the epiphany of the feath-

ered serpent, the emerald lord, the great god Quetzalcoatl.

"What do you want of me?" she screamed upward at
the plumed gargoyle head.

Give me your heart, dear one, spoke the one. *When I
have thine hearts, yea, all of them, then shall we return
to Tula on that moonlit day. For the heart of evil is in
the heart of life, and evil must be given over for Tula to
come . . .*

Enid interrupted the god. "Fuck off," she spat. "I
give you my curse!" She presented the god with the finger.

The rain had drenched her clothing and her feet sank
into turf of sponge and her toes felt cool and alive.

Enid shivered as much from fury as from chill rain.
Lightning struck a tree close by and the thunder slammed
into her ears with concussive force as she stood at the
base of the godhead, defiant and haggard as a mad king
on a barren heath.

Enid did not wait for the god's reply. "You beguiled
me, you damned myth of a nasty snake. You sonofabitch,
you tormented me with your stories of paradise gained
and lost and fruits and sacrifices. And the worst of it was
that I believed it. I believed it, I believed it, I believed
it! It was deceit. It was guile! It was nowhere but in my
imagination, nowhere but in my mind and millions of
other minds for thousands of years. We were innocent
and you made us guilty. You made us believe the natural
was unnatural and made us conceal ourselves from ourselves and from the truth. We were frightened of what
was real and you made us think it was something that
was never real. *You* are not real . . ."

With each utterance Enid felt stronger. Her mind was
her own again. Her skin tingled and she felt enwrapped
in a peculiar power that made her feel strong and calm
at once, isolated on a tiny pinnacle buffeted by unseen
waves.

The power made the hair on the nape of her neck rise.

Everything was still and yet charged with power as she
raised the knife blade to point the tip at the godhead. "I
renounce you! I renounce you! I renounce you," she said.

The next sound to escape her throat was involuntary and it is doubtful that she was aware of it.

The earth, too, was charged with power. As she raised the knife, the power crept up through her body to the dense and frantic molecules in the steel. On the point of this phenomenon, electrons in the air became dislodged from their atoms and made a positive charge and an ion path leading thousands of feet in the sky.

Fretted molecules contesting in the air above sensed in the ion path rupture and relief from their agonies. This power needed a home.

In the space of eight-millionths of a second the power gathered itself for its journey. When the power could gather and engorge no more of itself, it plunged downward at a speed that could girdle the earth more than seven times in a single second.

Along a core some one and a half centimeters in diameter surrounded by a corona several meters wide, more than a hundred million volts of negatively charged naked static electricity coursed in a current of ninety thousand amperes onto the tip of Enid's knife and vaulted through her body home to earth.

In its journey of nanoseconds the power caused the muscles of the body to stiffen, expelling air from its sacs. It set the blood aboil, darkened it, and prevented its coagulation. It melted steel and caused it to burn through flesh and fuse with bone as though arc-welded. It melded bone joint to bone joint. It set small sparks adance from head to arm, arm to ground, finger to finger. It burned clothing and hair. It raised the temperature of skin to a hundred fifty degrees Fahrenheit. It steamed the neurons of the brain cells that had so troubled Enid Bilyeux.

The electricity liberated enough energy in the body of Enid Bilyeux to propel an automobile; then when it had found its way home it released the body and let it tumble as a sawn board to the ground.

All the tissues through which the power had passed were destroyed utterly. The lovely, unhappy woman was ugly and dead.

And she had begun to understand. Now it would be up to the other twin to do the same.

18

Irene Byrne privately thought it curious that no one else
had arrived at the park and that no one had come looking
for them. By the fall of evening this Tuesday the nuns
and youngsters of Our Lady of Sorrows would be twenty-
four hours overdue at home. Surely the mother superior
or someone would report them missing. Irene could not
have known that someone had.

Her bravado in having told Talmadge that they were on
their own had been just that. All along she secretly believed someone would help but thought it best the others
not count on it. As the day wore on their solitude began
to haunt them and Irene too. She began to wonder if what
she had told Talmadge might prove true.

Enough food was still unspoiled for each person to
have something, and the waters of the lake quenched their
thirst. Irene hoped it wasn't polluted. Herman and Talmadge had spread the word about the greenbelly flies and
Irene's experiment, and that the kids should stay in the
sun on pain of death. They needed little persuasion.

The picnic and a rest finished, Irene organized some
of the survivors into teams to retrieve the bodies of Sister
Helga, Maynard, and Sister Melanie. This done, the bodies of Karen and Orville were dragged from the shade
and laid beside the other three. Irene improvised a funeral service from a Bible left on the bus, and read from
the passages she knew and loved best; the twenty-third
Psalm, the Lord's Prayer, and the Sermon on the Mount.
Their respects to their dead duly rendered and deeply
felt, Irene asked that the bodies and some debris be arranged in a manner that might yet benefit the living.

During this time Irene felt a mounting anxiety from a
source she could not identify. Senses not yet attuned to

the wilderness, she knew something was wrong. Then she realized her shadow was growing fainter. The lake breeze had changed to a steady west wind. Irene looked up at a sky growing quickly cloudy.

"Okay, brothers and sisters," she said. "Pretty soon even the sun's going to be in the shade. Let's head for the bus. Slow now, real slow. We don't want to attract attention from the wrong parties, do we?"

As a band of weary guerrillas approaching their stronghold after a successful raid, the children made their way to the safety of the bus just as the first fat gouts of rain began to fall.

The day had been theirs but the night was yet to be won.

The children had all been in electrical storms before. But in the city, not in the countryside. You seem safe from such storms in the city even when you are not. In the country, you know you are not safe. The storm rolled in from the west with the roar of the Metroliner through the North Philadelphia Amtrak station. Blue distant flashes became mighty sparks hurled by angry gods. The thunder rattled the windows of the bus.

"Let's get our ass out of here, Irene," Sue Ellen said.

"Yeah, girl, let's shag ass," a boy said.

"Quiet, please, ladies and gentlemen," Irene said. "We safe where we is. The bus here is insulated what with rubber tires. Ain't no lightning gonna hurt nothing on rubber tires. Go to sleep. What the hell's that noise?"

"That's Albert Tipton," Sue Ellen said.

"What the hell wrong with him?" Irene asked.

"Nothing, girl," Sue Ellen said. "He's snoring."

The storm brewed electricity that leapt from cloud to cloud and from cloud to tree. The rain whipped against grass and leaf and window.

Many of the boys had their noses pressed against the steamy glass of the windows, which they occasionally wiped with their sleeves. "Woooo . . ." they murmured as if watching fireworks. "Shit alive, lookie that . . ."

The thunder was amplified by the natural amphitheater of the park and vaunted toward the bus and shook it as with drumfire.

"You sure those tires gonna protect us, Irene?" Herman said. "I mean, tires aren't made out of real rubber anymore. You know what I'm saying?"

"You want to take your chances outside?" Irene said.

Herman did not reply.

The elm tree that hovered over the bus waved its ancient boughs in eddies of gale.

This elm had been a sapling in the days of the earliest French explorations of this part of America. It may have seen skirmishes in the French and Indian War. It was older than many elms when Abraham Lincoln took his first oath of office. It had developed small caverns in the base of its great trunk that sheltered generations of wolf pups now extinct from the region. Raccoon and opossum and squirrel had been nurtured in its arms. Wild bees hived in its crevices. It had seen coal and oil and mineral explorers come and go in defeat. Now it was late to bud in the spring and early to drop leaves in the fall. Many of its branches stretched barren, waiting for the next fierce wind to snap them away. The young male deer still stripped their woolly antlers to shining on its bark, but this bark was becoming ever more brittle. Its roots had extended to the girth of its massive head of limb and leaf. Then, as such things go, some roots were washed bare by rain and ice and time and now the roots of younger trees competed for the juices that nourished the elm.

This elm, with its taproots touching the water table, caused negative charges and paths of ions to rise toward the clouds.

This night a positively charged cloud accepted the ion message and gathered a few hundred thousand volts to send to the elm.

The children felt their hair stand at the charge and jumped up startled to see blue sparks playing down the large tree. The thunder bellowed and with its blast burning twigs and dead limbs were hurled from the tree, throwing fire onto the bus as cigarettes tossed at night from a speeding automobile.

"I don't like the looks of that tree, Irene," Herman said.

"Lightning never strikes in the same place twice," said Irene.

But it does. As long as it has something to strike at.

Two more positive bolts hit the old tree in rapid succession. It glowed nearly red. It burned orange along its trunk. Something tore at its base. The dehydrated roots could no longer bear the strain of its bulk. It began to topple toward the bus.

"Hail, Mary, full of . . ." Irene said, and covered her face with her arms and swung in the driver's seat away from the windshield. "Duck, everybody, cover up! Get ready to get out the windows!"

The bus shuddered under the fall of the tree. The double rear wheels lifted under the force of a large limb striking the hood. The limb was aflame and for an instant covered the bus with fire. Children screamed at the smoke. Sue Ellen thought she smelled gasoline. Windows were opened and youngsters tumbled into puddles illuminated by fire and lightning. Irene opened the door but remained in the driver's seat to make sure everyone got out. The hood of the bus was burning.

Suddenly a head of steam appeared and blew into the flames and, together with the rain, extinguished them.

Little Albert Tipton had made his way out the rear emergency exit with a large fire extinguisher. After putting out the fire, he clambered up the steps of the bus, dragging the device that was nearly as large as he. He took off his glasses and wiped them with his sleeve. Then he rubbed his eyes and put his glasses back on and blinked and looked up at Irene. "Can I go back to sleep now?" he said.

"Sure, honey," Irene said. "You do that."

Adair Godwin awoke on this night with a start. He knew something terrible had happened but not what. There was no phone nearby, and for him to prepare himself to go into town to use one would attract the kind of attention he wished to shun. In any event, if something had happened—and it might not have—there would be nothing he could do for now. Word would reach him soon enough.

For now he would drink some more whiskey and try to sleep.

He wondered what he would do if something truly had happened.

* * *

Pete's dread began to take the form of inner tremors as he drove toward the house. The night stormed on. A bolt of lightning struck so near the house that Pete thought it might have hit the place. He fancied for a moment that he heard a human cry but put this down to the jitters. He wondered what Enid would say to him. He knew all he could say was that he loved her and would work hard to help her and make things right. He supposed he would have to tell her in detail about the flies. It might spook her badly and send her into one of her states, but she would find out soon enough from the neighbors. It would be better if he was there when she learned of the terrible events.

He parked the Volvo in the garage and the fact that Enid did not meet him at the doorway between kitchen and garage spoke eloquently to his fears. He got out the still-warm pizza and the candy from Hershey and went into the kitchen knowing the first thing Enid said to him would likely telegraph the course their marriage would take. He prayed that she would be glad to see him and would think the candy was funny.

"Hi, hon," he called out. "Enid? Enid!"

She was not in the kitchen. She was not in the bedroom. Pete rapped gently on the bathroom door and opened it and she was not in there either.

He went into the living room. The wind that blew through the open window chilled at his heart. The curtains billowed inward and rain spattered the carpet.

From the amount of rain that had collected Pete could tell that the window had been open for only a few minutes, he hoped a short-enough time not to tempt any deer flies in.

"Enid," he shouted. "Hon, where *are* you?"

He ran to the front door and to his surprise found it locked and bolted from the inside.

"Enid," he bellowed. "Enid!"

My God, the window, he thought. But why? Maybe she had got into one of her states and gone out through it.

He ran into the kitchen to get the big flashlight. He unlocked the front door and went to the window on the outside and closed it and prayed he would find Enid before a deer fly did.

"Enid," he called through the storm. "Eeeeniiiid!"

Lightning flashed and thunder growled and barked. Pete found the imprints of Enid's bare feet in the garden beneath the window and was now certain she had climbed out into the storm. He tried with his flashlight to pick up her tracks from there but lost them in the grass.

He searched the riven night with the powerful flashlight and could see nothing. Then a lightning bolt struck a quarter-mile away and he saw it.

"Eniiiiiiid," he screamed, and dashed for the fallen figure.

Wisps of steam rose from the body lying on its face. Pete flipped it over on its back and shone the light in the face. The eyelids were wide apart and the eyes bulged unnaturally as if a goiter were forcing them near bursting from sockets. The mouth hung agape and Enid's features were contorted as those of a truck driver he had once tended after the man was crushed dead when the jack slipped while he was changing a tire.

"Enid," he bawled. "Eniiiid!"

He had never known such horror in his life. He felt for a pulse and her skin burned his fingers and parts of her flesh were crisp and the pungent scent of overcooked meat and burned hair filled his nose. My God, third-degree burns, he thought. She was no fly victim. Oh, God, no, she'd been struck by lightning! Oh, God, my God, how could you have let it happen to her? he thought. How could you?

Pete's mind raced backward to his first-aid training. What do you do for electrocution? Remove the wire. Don't touch it or the body. Use a stick or some nonconductor. But, dammit, this electricity came from the sky. Administer cardio-pulmonary resuscitation. Yes, he would give her CPR, like Joey.

For the second time in two days Pete found himself blowing into dormant lungs and pumping on a heart that would not do this work for itself. Her lips and the skin of her breast were hot. Her body was stiff, but from some other cause than rigor mortis, he did not know what. He

would work, by God, he would work. He would bring
her around. This was Enid, his wife. He loved her.

He pumped and blew air and worked for what seemed
hours to him and could not persuade himself that he felt
the faintest pulse. But neither could he persuade himself
that she was gone, that it was irrevocable.

He was swept in the cruel riptide of despair and forlorn
hope that flouts reality, the perfervid passion to correct
the uncorrectable; the illogic of rejoining a head severed
from its body; patching together the skull and brains of
a loved one apart by a rifle bullet; washing and
salving the molten flesh of a napalmed child.

Finally he forced himself to take times from his watch.
Five minutes went by and still he worked and nothing
happened and he could not accept it. He worked for another half-hour and nothing happened, and he slowly realized he never would accept it.

A keening wail escaped his throat and he threw his
cheek on hers and sobbed and stroked her hair, all matted
and scorched.

"Oh, Enid, oh, Enid, oh, I love you so much . . . Oh,
no . . . oh, no . . . oh, God, no . . ."

He stayed with her and grieved long into the night until
at last the storm began to abate. Later he would wonder
what kind of fate had preserved him from his own electrocution.

He started to pick Enid up and take her into the house,
then logic resumed control of his mind. An accidental
death would have to be properly reported. He would also
have to notify Elspeth and Adair.

He forced himself to stand and walk to the house without turning to look back at Enid. He telephoned the desk
and Gary Busch answered and Pete stumbled through the
report.

"Oh, no, oh, God, Pete," Gary said. "Oh, Jesus, guy,
I'm sorry. What can I tell you, Pete, I'm so sorry . . ."

"Thanks," Pete said, and remembered how it had been
when the other kids found out his father had died. Everyone had to say he was sorry. Now they would do it again.
He wondered if he could take it.

"Was it a fly?" Gary asked. "Two more people got it
tonight, if that's any comfort."

"Uh, no . . . nnno, it wasn't a fly. She, uh, she was, uh, she was apparently ssstruck by l-l-lightning . . ."

"Oh, Jesus, Pete, oh, God, I'm so sorry. I'll get the ambulance corps out. I'll leave a message for the old man too. You know, uh, Pete, you know I'll have to send Ron out to take some pictures. It's the law, you know."

"I know. That's, uh, why I c-called. Tell Ron and the ambulance people to stop by the house first."

"Right, Pete. Jesus, guy, I'm sorry."

"Thanks."

Pete hung up the phone and dialed Elspeth's number in Scranton and was surprised when Elspeth herself answered. He sensed his voice cracking. "Hi, Elspeth. It's, uh, me, P-Pete . . ."

"Pete? What on earth's happening? Why are you calling at this hour? Oh, my God, there's something wrong, isn't there? It's Enid, isn't it?"

"Uh, yeah. I'm, uh, I'm s-s-sorry, Elspeth."

"She finally went off the deep end, didn't she? Oh, the poor kid. Oh, God, the poor baby. I tried. Pete, oh, God, how I tried. Oh, the poor kid . . ."

"Uh, Elspeth, it's, uh, it's w-w-worse than that. She's . . ." The back of his palate gagged as he swallowed back a sob. "She's dead, Elspeth."

"Oh, no. Oh, my God. How did it happen?"

"She, uh, she was s-s-struck by lightning. She was out in the yard in a storm. She was holding on to something, uh, mmmetal. It bbburned through her hand. Oh . . . oh . . . I tried to help her, Elspeth. I, uh, got there right after it happened. I gave her CPR for a long time, but . . . but I tried . . . I tried . . ." The words echoed in Pete's ears as the pronunciation of his damnation. He broke down and sobbed over the phone.

Elspeth let him go on until he got control of himself again. "I know you did your best, Pete," she said, "and I know Enid knows it too. You did what you could. We all did what we could for her, even Adair. Nobody's blaming it on you, Pete, except . . . Well, do you need help in making the arrangements?"

"Uh, arrangements?" Pete said, gathering himself. "Oh, uh, no, thanks, uh, we agreed to be c-cremated, each of us . . ." Not until later was the irony to strike

Pete that Enid had already been cremated once. "Uh, that's what she wanted, Elspeth."

"I understand," Elspeth said, "I understand. Listen, Pete, honey, I can't make it over there, you know. You see, I'm not so well myself these days."

"Yeah," Pete said, "I'm, uh, I'm sorry."

"Not to worry, Pete. It happens to us all. It just hurts and keeps me awake nights. Don't ever get cancer, hon."

Pete had heard Elspeth was suffering from arthritis and he knew she was a tough bird. But he hadn't any idea she had cancer. "Uh, is there anything I c-c-can do, Elspeth?"

"No, hon, thanks. Just look after our little girl, what's left of her, and look after yourself and try to remember the times that were better. You may soon be the only one left to remember them. Uh, Pete?"

"Yeah?"

"I don't know how Adair's going to take this, hon," Elspeth said. "There are some, well, some indications all is not well with him down in Mexico. I have to tell him, don't I, Pete?" It was not a question.

"That's, uh, all right, Elspeth, I'll t-t-tell him. What's his phone number?"

"He doesn't have a phone and you shouldn't be the one to tell him, Pete. I'll cable him. I don't know what he'll do. Look out for yourself, Pete. Enid would have wanted it that way. She loved you, honey. I know it. Take care of yourself."

"Yeah, thanks."

They said good-bye and Pete's senses were too dulled to know it would be the last time.

He saw the emergency lights of the patrol car in the driveway. He went to the door and opened it for Ron Hausmann and saw the ambulance come, blazing red lights not far behind.

Ron was holding the big camera with the Polaroid back and an electronic flash. "I'm sorry, Pete," he said.

The ambulance corps volunteers, a woman and a man dressed in white, wheeled a stretcher out of the van and rolled it to the door. Pete knew he knew their names but he could not remember the names. They looked overworked.

"Is the, uh,—I mean, is she inside, Pete?" the ambulance corps man said.

"No," Pete said, and gestured for them to follow him. The procession trudged and squelched in the sodden grass across the back lawn to the body.

Ron Hausmann took pictures from various angles. As he did so, Pete could hear the ambulance people suck air through their teeth and murmur. He was angry at this. He knew she looked to them like a burnt pork butt. To Pete she looked like Enid, badly hurt.

The strobe light from the camera lit the wet ground with the same intense quick blue hue of the lightning bolts now gone. In the afterglow of one camera burst Pete suddenly recognized the chipped and partly molten metal object in Enid's hand.

He felt faint at this sight and wobbled and would have fallen but for the alertness of the ambulance people. This enigma, on top of all the others and the pain of losing Enid, was too shocking. What, he thought, in the name of God had she been doing in the peak of an electrical storm holding a butcher knife of solid steel? He took some deep breaths and wondered if it was a question he truly wanted answered.

The pictures were done. Ron took Pete's official statement and was merciful in the brevity of his inquiry. Pete brushed the ambulance people aside and lifted Enid's body onto the stretcher and laid it down. He tucked the blanket around her and left her face uncovered and bent down and kissed her on the forehead.

A shadowless sun began to suffuse a dreary damp morning as Pete tugged the stretcher across the grass. He tried to get in the ambulance with Enid, but it was against the rules. They drove off to have her autopsied. It was formal.

Ron Hausmann stayed in the house trying to comfort Pete until he sensed he was no longer needed or wanted. Then he left Pete alone with his thoughts.

Pete was exhausted but did not know it. He went to the kitchen and made espresso. Absently, he began to get out vitamins for the two of them and then realized what he was doing and put Enid's vitamins back in the bottle and took his own. He threw the pizza in the garbage and

put the Hershey candy up on a shelf and made a mental
note to give it to some kids.

He sat on the couch feeling pain in his heart and his
bones and his head and forced his muscles and his mind
to relax. They would phone him when the autopsy was
done. He would wait until then.

Troubled bits of conversation came to him and he did
not know if he was truly asleep. Enid was fine and they
had decided it was time for them to have children. Then
the man was led into the square in Saigon again. Pete
stood by and did nothing as the gun went off against the
man's temple and the fellow cringed and brains and blood
gushed out the other side of his head.

Pete jerked awake and remembered something Enid
had said to him. It was something Burke had said, according to Enid: "The only thing necessary for the triumph of evil is for good men to do nothing."

What should I do, Enid? he thought. What should I
do?

Forget me. Forget me for now, she seemed to be whispering. Oh, Peter, darling, forget me for now. For just a
little while.

But I can't, he thought.

You must, darling, she whispered.

He stood up and shook his head free of dusty sensa-
tions. He went into the kitchen and made espresso again.
He ran the cold-water tap into the sink and bathed his
head and the stubble of beard on his face until the dust
in his mind washed away. He drank coffee and looked at
his watch. It was 7:36 on Wednesday morning. The autopsy would not be over at least until noon. He took the
phone off the hook so he would not be disturbed for the
time being.

Then, plodding, he began to do his duty, what Enid
had in the full of life told him she expected in death.

He got the stepladder and stood on it to reach the empty
suitcases in the garage attic. He cleaned them and took
them in and put them on the bed. There he packed all of
Enid's belongings. He carefully folded her clothes. He
packed her shoes and boots in plastic bags. He packed
all His-and-Hers wedding-gift towels. He packed her
jewelry, her cosmetics, her medicines, her unused bubble

baths. He left no trace of her but in the burgeoning suitcases, or so he thought. The last things he packed were
their two wedding rings, each hung on a yellow silken
ribbon. They had worn them for the ceremony to save the
priest embarrassment.

"Goddamn medieval." Enid disdained wedding rings.
"Asinine. They're like slave bracelets. They're anti-
feminine, anti-masculine, anti-everyone. Might as well
wear them through your noses like pigs."

They had decided to wear these rings for the ceremony
and then take them off forever and put the silk ribbons
on them and tuck them away in a drawer with a cachet,
souvenirs.

By nine o'clock Pete had filled the suitcases with everything and put them in the house attic. Then he changed
the sheets and did all the washing, including the dishes,
and dusted and vacuumed the house.

As he dusted the mantelpiece he looked at the statue
of Quetzalcoatl and wondered if he should pack it away
too. He had always resented it, but for some reason he
no longer cared about it. It was merely a pre-Columbian
artifact of chipped and carved stone created by hands
returned to earth half a world and a hundred centuries
away. It was an antiquity. He let it be.

Irene Byrne had wheedled and threatened the children
of Our Lady of Sorrows back into the bus the night before.

In the cloudy morning that followed, Irene covered up
against the greenbelly flies and got out to survey the damage. A large limb of the old tree lay across the hood of
the bus and had caved in some of the metal. There were
signs and scents of rain-purged fire but little other damage to the bus. Irene beckoned the youngsters to cover
and come out. She chose the four frailest to stand watch
against the flies. To the others she said, "Okay, brothers
and sisters, let's move this damn tree."

When Pete finished cleaning the house, he put the
phone back on the hook and waited for the call of the
autopsy report.

Then he thought he had better call Ernie Waldwick first to make sure he could handle the cremation.

"Oh, no, Pete," Ernie said when informed of Enid. "Oh, Pete, oh, Pete, I'm so sorry. Was it a fly?" Pete grimaced and explained and wondered how often he would have to do this and became angry at the thought. He took some comfort in the thought that word of the poisonous flies had spread rapidly.

Ernie assured him he would do his best and offered, despite his own troubles, to provide a full funeral and burial for Enid, at cost. Pete thanked him and said that cremation was Enid's wish.

A half-hour later the County Hospital called.

"Is Mrs. Bilyux there?" a cheery female voice inquired.

"Uh, no, this is Mr. Bilyeux. M-m-mrs. Bilyeux p-p-passed away."

"Oh," the voice said, "I'm sorry to hear it. Sir, we have a preliminary autopsy report of an Enid Bilyux . . ."

"Bil-yoo," Pete said, correcting her pronunciation as he had with others all his life.

"Oh, all right, Bilyeux, then," the voice said. "We have a preliminary autopsy report on an Enid Bilyeux. Do you wish to hear it, sir?"

The voice went on to demand identification and other answers from Pete and did not seem to understand a word he said and made him repeat himself often and was obviously writing down what he said and getting little of it right.

"Sir," the voice said as if reading from a prescribed form, "pending further pathological examination of tissue samples, preliminary findings are that the deceased suffered deceasement by accidental electrocution. Please accept my condolences and those of the staff of Elmsford County Hospital on the deceasement of your daughter, Mr. Bilyux."

"Thank you," Pete said.

"Was it your wish, Mr. Bilyux," the voice said, "to authorize donation of any bodily tissues or organs for transplant, sir?"

"Uh," Pete said, "yes, okay," knowing Enid had wanted it.

"Well, I'm terribly sorry, Mr. Bilyux," the voice said, "but the report indicates that due to the nature and extent of the trauma, no tissues are transplantable. Have you chosen a funeral home yet, Mr. Bilyux?"

Pete told the voice he had, and gave instructions and grew exasperated and at last got rid of the voice.

He started to make more espresso when the phone rang again and he answered it again.

"Bilyeux, oh, Bilyeux, old son," the sheriff's voice sang in sepulchral tones. "Bilyeux, I'm terribly sorry, old son, I'm just torn apart. Son, I want you to know at a time like this that I share your sorrow deeply, may God bless you, old son."

"Uh, thanks, Sheriff." Pete felt like hitting something.

"Bilyeux, as you know, county regulations entitle you to four days' bereavement but, Bilyeux, as God is my witness, old Joe Cody says you have my oath that you can take all the time you want at full pay, within reason. Old Joe Cody swears this to you on a stack of Bibles. Do you hear me, old son?"

"Uh, thanks, Sheriff," Pete said. "B-but, uh, with respect, uh, I was p-planning to work the four-to-midnight tonight."

The sheriff paused on the phone. "You're a great officer, Bilyeux, a great officer, and old Joe Cody hardly ever says that. Son, that's going down in my book as the whitest mark I ever gave to any man on the force. You're a Christian martyr, Bilyeux, old son, a real Christian martyr. By God, man, you're an example to us all! But, no, may the good Lord look down on you, I have to deny your request. I already have a replacement for you from the Walker's Hollow branch, old son. You've got to rest and straighten things out, but I admire your spirit. You've got guts, boy, just like I did when I was your age. You're the kind of man I want to be my chosen successor when old Joe hangs up the old badge, old son. This is just between you and me, old son, I never said that to anyone else in my life."

Pete thought about what Enid had said about what Burke had said, and thought about the summary execution in Saigon and about all the people the flies had killed and would kill, and he made his final decision. "Uh, Sheriff, I'm, uh, w-w-working tonight, sir. If you want my badge, take it, but, uh, sir I m-m-must work tonight. Uh, thank you very much for your call, Sheriff."

"God, what a man!" Pete heard the sheriff say as he hung up the phone. Pete wanted to vomit. He was sad and sick and alone and he was forcing himself to do what something said was right.

He would go to work as if nothing had happened to Enid. He would so avenge Enid's death, and so pretend he did not miss her life. He was not the only one to feel this way.

19

The *señora* went up the steps to the room of the *señor* and hoped he would not be there. But apparently the *señor* had been expecting her knock. Words were exchanged in Spanish. The message was slipped under the door with the signature receipt. The receipt was signed and slipped back under the door for the *señora* with a tip of a thousand devalued pesos; five-hundred for the *señora* and the same for the *muchacho* who had ridden the bicycle to bring the message.

Adair tore open the envelope. The message read: VERY SORRY INFORM YOU ENID PASSED AWAY BY ACCIDENT LAST NIGHT. WAS HOLDING SOMETHING METAL ON LAWN IN THUNDERSTORM AND STRUCK BY LIGHTING AND WENT INSTANTLY. PETE FOUND AND TRIED TO REVIVE FOR LONG TIME BUT INJURY TOO SEVERE. PRIVATE CREMATION TO TAKE PLACE SOON PER ENID WISHES. PETE TRYING TO BEAR UP AS ARE WE ALL BUT SUFFERING MUCH INSIDE. YOU TRY BEAR UP TOO HONEY. IT ALL HAS TO END SOMETIME. LETS PRAY. MUCH LOVE—ELSPETH.

Adair had been expecting something bad but neither

his mind nor his feelings were prepared for anything quite this grotesque. He re-read the cable several times. If you were to have asked him how he felt he would not have been able to tell you. It was as if he were some kind of organism purged of its fluids and preserved in a hermetic jar.

What in hell had Enid been doing out in a thunderstorm? She was always terrified of thunderstorms. Of course, it could have taken her by surprise, but that would have been uncharacteristic of Enid. Where in hell had Peter been if he was close enough to try to revive her but had not kept her from the storm? Had they been having a fight? She was holding something metal. Jesus! Enid may have developed her own special brand of flakiness but she was never stupid. What in hell could the metal have been?

Oh, Enid, oh, Enid, oh, my God, Adair thought, losing you before I die is like having to die twice.

Drained and desolate, he sat staring at the cracks in the paint on the opposite wall. He projected himself beyond the cracks and tried to meld his spirit with that of Enid, to be one again.

Since the wedding, he had felt a queer contempt for Peter Bilyeux that he had always been at pains to conceal. They had been close friends until Peter began seeing Enid months after she and Adair had decided that convention demanded the end of their physical love.

Adair knew Pete admired him for his aplomb, for the easy way he carried his former good looks, and for his agility and courage. Adair had admired Pete for his refusal to be daunted by his speech problem, for his ability to comprehend almost anything, his almost mystic worship of beauty, his canniness and subtle flashes of wry wit. Adair knew in his mind Peter would be the ideal husband for Enid. But in his secret heart he could not bear the thought of them being lovers. It repelled him. It aroused a feeling in him to which he was not accustomed: jealousy. It was not that Peter had done anything wrong. When he first started seeing Enid, he told Adair of his interest and offered to keep his feelings to himself if they would interfere with the old childhood friendships. Adair advised him to the contrary if Enid reciprocated his feelings. What else could he have done? Still, he hated the feeling it gave him, but came to understand it as natural and never betrayed it to Enid or Peter. Now he felt liberated from maintaining his secrecy and allowed his mind to be angry with Peter Bilyeux for never being for Enid what he, Adair, had been.

What in hell was she doing holding metal in an electrical storm? Suddenly he felt a part of Enid again and began to understand. The feeling ravaged him with the force of a maelstrom that whirled him in savage vortex and sucked him through the cracks in the paint on the walls. The stench of death rode an evil wind and Adair sensed he was seeing implacable yellow eyes slit with thin black vertical pupils—reptilian eyes that spoke of no hope for those who beheld them. Adair's debilitated body filled afresh with hot blood. His heart raged and he knew he must wreak some terrible vengeance. He did not quite know how to accomplish this but knew he must get to Peter Bilyeux.

Pete was having enough trouble coping with himself on this worst day of his life. It was as if he clung to form and appearance and routine until his knuckles were white. His head ached and he took liberal doses of aspirin. The telephone was the worst thing. Too many people were calling him to say they were sorry too many times and he was forced too often to thank them.

As he was just going out the door to the funeral parlor, the phone rang again. He wondered whether he should just let it ring but decided he must do the expected thing.

"Uh, hello," Pete said.

"Hello, Pete? Louise Kavanaugh here. How are you today?"

"Uh, f-f-fine," Pete said.

At least here was a person not offering sympathies. He wondered if he should tell her and decided against it. It would only be self-pity and irrelevant. Louise didn't know Enid.

"You don't sound so great," Louise said. "I didn't get you out of bed, did I?"

"Uh, no, Louise, I jjjust have a bit of a headache. Might be c-catching a cold."

"Drink lots of liquids and try to get some rest if you can," Louise rattled off. "Listen, Pete, I thought you should know that nothing positive has turned up yet, so we'd better get used to the idea. When do you think I can expect those flies to get here?"

"Uh, they're not there yet?" Pete asked. They should have been, he thought.

"No," Louise said. "Reception knows I'm waiting for them."

"Uh, well," Pete said, "they should be sere thoon—I mean, there soon. Uh, let me know if they're not there by three and I'll, uh, get some more for you. I've, uh, g-g-got a d-d-dental appointment now, b-b-but I should be back by three or so . . ."

"Got a toothache?" Louise said.

Pete's headache, dulled by the aspirin, returned with vigor. He wished she would say good-bye and let him go. "No, I, uh, it's jjjust a dental checkup."

"You probably shouldn't go to the dentist if you've got a cold, you know," Louise said. "You might spread it."

Pete fought the temptation to become annoyed with her. He knew she was simply trying to be friendly and helpful, but he hoped she would get the hell off the line so he could do what he had to.

At last, for want of propulsion the conversation rolled to a stop. They said good-bye and Pete rushed out of the house.

That morning Mayor Warren P. Otis elicited an agreement from the school superintendent, who was not under his jurisdiction, to use the air-conditioned school buildings for emergency shelters for those people who could not adequately protect themselves from the flies. The mayor stayed away from his store and worked by telephone from his home.

He called all his suppliers and ordered massive and urgent deliveries of insect repellents, insecticides, flyswatters, even flypaper. He called farm-store jobbers and ordered beekeepers' masks. He called hardware distributors and ordered fine mesh screen. He called fabric wholesalers and ordered great quantities of mosquito netting, gauze, tulle, any material of fine mesh, damn the cost. They would all be delivered to Town Hall and let the council worry about raising the money.

During one of these conversations he noticed a patrol car pull into his driveway. When he finished talking he went to greet Vince Egert at the door.

"Hi, Mayor," Vince said. "Sorry to bother you at home but the council president has been trying to get you on the phone and he says the line has been constantly busy."

"Well, think of that," Mayor Otis said. "What does he want?"

"He wants you to call him, Mayor," Vince said.

"I'll call him when I have a minute. Thanks for stopping by, Vince. Good to see you. Have a nice day."

The mayor went back to his desk and got back on the phone about important matters. Finally, satisfied that his emergency orders were going into effect, he dialed the council president, one Rupert R. Chandler, a member of the not-so-loyal opposition, proprietor of Thomas Valley's sole used-car lot. "Hi, Rupe, Warren Otis here. Got a message you wanted to talk to me."

Rupert R. Chandler, one of four aspirants to the mayoralty on the five-member town council, did his best to feign civility. "Thanks for returning my call, Warren. I left the message for you nearly three hours ago. Did you just now get it?"

"No, Rupe, I've been busy."

"I noticed," Chandler said. "Now, look, Warren, let's not fight. Let's not get political about this. But just what in the goddamn hell do you think you're doing, man?"

"I'm trying to save people's lives," the mayor said.

"But is it necessary to scare the shit out of everybody by sending the fire department around telling people about flies? I mean, really, Warren. And what's this I hear about the expenditure of taxpayers' money without authorization from the council? Is that *true*, Warren?"

"It's an emergency, Rupe. I'm using my emergency powers under the law. If the council doesn't want to pay the bills, that's up to you."

The mayor could hear Chandler take a deep breath as though counting to ten. "Warren, who declared this emergency? In what form was it authorized?"

"I did," the mayor said. " 'I declare an emergency. There. That's the form."

"But who gave you that right, Warren? Why should you get all the credit—I mean, take all the responsibility? You're not the only one in town government, you know, goddammit!"

"No, but until I leave office I am the only mayor. The charter gives me the right to declare emergencies, Rupe, you can look it up if you like."

"Warren," Chandler said. "You've got to stop these personal political attacks on me. Now, Warren, the charter works both ways. Now you listen to me for a change, you bleeding-heart secular humanist, you. The charter says that the legislative branch may demand—that's *demand*, Warren—a full report of the activities of the executive branch. Now, Warren, I'll swear to you I didn't lift a finger against you, but every single solitary councilman has called me at least three times today *demanding* to know what you've been up to. I stuck by you as best I could, Warren, I swear to you on my mother's grave that I did. But I can't stand against a tide of outraged public opinion, Warren, that's too much for you to ask of me! Four council members called me, Warren, four, Republican and Democrat members alike. That's unanimous public opinion, Warren, even you can see that. Now, as a result, Warren, I was restrained to call a special council meeting at four-thirty this afternoon to investigate your actions, and I'm serving you notice right now. You'll be there, won't you?"

"If I'm not too busy I'll try to come," the mayor said, and hung up and poured himself a shot of bourbon and went back to work.

As it happened, he didn't make the meeting. He did his best, but at 4:37 on a Wednesday afternoon now turned sunny, Mayor Warren P. Otis was walking up the Town Hall steps in the shade of sycamore trees when he was bitten in the back of the neck and became the twenty-eighth victim of the flies.

Pete Bilyeux arrived at the Waldwick Funeral Home a few minutes before the hearse arrived with Enid's body. Ernie grabbed him by the shoulders and hugged him and his eyes were genuinely moist. "Don't watch, Pete," he said as the hearse pulled up. "It won't be good for you."

Pete remembered what Enid had said about no friend wanting to see her dead. He nodded and saw the body roll in, encased in a black zippered bag that looked for all the world like a cover for a large guitar. "I, uh, I . . . Ernie, I j-j-just want to be near her for the last time, you see," he said.

"It takes a while, Pete," Ernie said.

"I understand," Pete said.

Ernie led him to a seat behind his own desk in an office that Pete thankfully noticed was not filled with funereal flowers. He sat in Ernie's comfortable antique leather chair and looked around the oak-paneled room with family pictures, some new, some musty and spotted with age. On the desk was a Tiffany-type lamp and Pete turned it on and stared into its jauntily colored cascades of grapes. There was an ancient inkwell with a quill in it. There was a 1920s vintage bronze Chinese knickknack of see-no-evil-hear-no-evil-speak-no-evil monkey. There was a turn-of-the-century pen holder with a burnished marble base and an ornate brass top. And everywhere were pictures of children.

Pete could hear sounds, creaking and thumping sounds, coming from the basement and lost tears with each such sound. He prayed to God for Enid's soul, for renewal of his faith, for forgiveness in violating the Church's strictures against cremation, and for the strength he would need. His prayers did not seem to go anywhere and his headache returned.

At last Ernie came into the room. He was perspiring and his skin looked unusually gray and his face seemed to have grown purplish bags under the eyes and puffy wattles on cheeks and neck.

"Okay, Pete, it's okay now," he said. "Why don't you go home and get some rest. The ashes will be ready for you in an urn in the morning. You can come get them if you like, or I'll hold them here as long as you want."

"Thanks, Ernie. Uh, dddo you mind, ah, k-keeping them here for a while until I, uh, fffigure out what's right?"

Ernie's facial tic seemed even more pronounced and

rapid. He did not look at all well to Pete, but then nothing looked well. "Sure, Pete, sure," Ernie said. Then he seemed to react to something he was hearing.

Pete was silent and listened with Ernie. Ernie pointed his finger in the air as if asking for quiet and slumped into a chair opposite Pete. "Wait a minute," Ernie said, "wait . . ."

Ernie cocked his head to one side. Pete held his breath and listened with him and could hear nothing unusual.

Ernie's hands went to the sides of his head. "Oh, God," he said, "oh . . . oh . . . oh . . . I have a terrible headache . . ."

He pitched forward onto the floor.

Again Pete tried CPR to no avail. Between breaths and massages he quickly used Ernie's phone and called the desk to send an ambulance.

Ernie Waldwick was dead on arrival at Elmsford County Hospital. Later, the autopsy would reveal Ernie had suffered a massive cerebral accident; a fatal stroke. When Pete phoned in his report to the resident pathologist and told of what had happened and the last thing Ernie said, the doctor said, "Funny. Those were Franklin Roosevelt's last words too."

And who will undertake to essay the role of the departed undertaker?

Pete had spent more time at the funeral home than he thought he would when he got there.

At last done, he walked quickly to the Volvo and got in and started it. In its side-view mirror he noticed a man in a business suit rush into a maroon Cadillac Eldorado. Pete thought little of it at first. He was in a hurry to get home and change into his uniform and get to work. But at every turn he made, he could see the maroon Eldorado follow behind. He took three unnecessary turns and still it followed. He drove home and the car followed him until the last turnoff onto his own street, then drove away.

Adair Godwin had not yet departed Mexico City.

When he recovered from the shock, Adair donned gloves to cover his hands and walked the back alleys to the clinic of Dr. Huerta, conscious of the evil-eye-go-away signs being made at him by the local mothers hanging up laundry and hiding their children behind their skirts. Typically of Adair, he thought several steps ahead and paid the clinic triple his usual fee to bind his face and certify him as a burn victim. He returned to his room, packed everything, and put his statue of Quetzalcoatl, the twin of Enid's, in a small canvas carry-on bag with some of his papers and notes.

He paid all his rent and sent for a cab. It sped him into the city once spooked by Hernán Cortez-cum-Quetzalcoatl and Adair wondered again at the myth. He walked up to the Pan American Airlines ticket counter and wrangled for the first available flight to New York, pleading the necessity of burn treatments.

He had not set foot in his own country in some six years.

On this afternoon, a penitent Reed Hamilton paid a hundred-dollar fine plus court costs for the misdemeanor of burial without a permit, and was extradited to New Jersey.

At 5:17 Council President Rupert R. Chandler gaveled the governing body to order with a moment of silence for the beloved, departed mayor. The agenda was now changed to select someone to fill the unexpired term of Mayor Otis. A councilman who happened to be an employee of Chandler's Used Cars, a Republican, placed Mr. Chandler's name in nomination. Mr. Chandler himself, also a Republican, seconded the nomination. The two Democrats on the council took issue with this and nominated one of their own, just for the fun of it. The third Republican councilman, Saul Glickstein, had made the mistake of buying an auto from Chandler's Used Cars, and demurred when it came to selecting Rupert Chandler to be mayor. The wrangling continued until 10:43 that night, with Mr. Glickstein saying little, mostly gazing at the floor as though contemplating cockroaches playing volleyball. At last compromise candidates began to be discussed. At three minutes past midnight, with a twinkle in his eye and a Gioconda smile on his lips, Mr. Glickstein let it drop that perhaps Father Fierro might make a good interim mayor. The issue was settled. Father Fierro was summoned from his bed and sworn in. The priest made three announcements: that his political affiliation was Jesuit, that the policies of the late Mayor Otis would remain in full force and effect, and that, as far as he was concerned, the meeting might as well be adjourned.

A sense of unalterable change struck Pete Bilyeux as he unlocked the house and went in and slipped into his uniform. No trace of Enid existed in the little place and yet she was everywhere. He felt tears come and forced his mind to change the subject and knew as he did so that the house had become a tomb for memories and he must one day live elsewhere.

He went into the garage and stabbed more holes in jar lids and packed the jars into the saddlebags of his Suzuki and rushed to the substation. The phone rang again on his way out and this time he did not answer it. He was late for work.

To Pete's surprise the sheriff's Lincoln Town Car was parked in front and both patrol cars were gone. The sheriff stood talking to Gary Busch at the desk. "Bilyeux," he said, "oh, dear Lord, old son, you did it, didn't you?"

"I, uh, I wwant to work, Sheriff," Pete said.

"Oh, son, oh, old son . . ." The sheriff walked up to Pete and removed his cigar and took Pete's shoulders in his hands and embraced him. "Son, I want you to know that something very similar happened to me when I was about your age. I . . . I . . . guess I still haven't got over it. But . . . but that's all done with now, isn't it? I felt the same way then as you do now. I wanted to lose myself in work. Now, Bilyeux, I want you to have the benefit of my experience. Don't overdo it, son." He released Pete and turned toward his audience, Gary Busch at the desk. "By God," the sheriff announced to the world, "this man is a shining example to us all!"

He turned back to Pete. "All right, old son, all right. But I'm keeping you on light duty for a week or so. I have men for both cars, so you can use your own vehicle and put in for mileage reimbursal. Tell you what, I've got a special assignment for you. Some mackerel-snapping nun keeps calling my office from Philly. Seems a bunch of nigger kids from an orphanage went on a picnic in a school bus day before yesterday up to Jacob Walz Park and never came back. Hell, between you and me, they're probably full of dope and screwing their little brains out. But we have to check it out, don't we? Equal justice under the law, eksetera, that's the ticket, isn't it? Never let it be said that old Joe Cody doesn't uphold the law, even for a pack of coons.''

The thought of children missing and uninvestigated for two days appalled Pete, but he said nothing

"Now, Bilyeux, why don't you take a portable radio and get your butt up there and check it out." The sheriff slapped Pete on the behind as a Little League coach confiding in his young pitcher that he should walk the next batter.

"Uh, okay, Sheriff," Pete said.

"That's the spirit, Bilyeux, old son. Oh . . ." the sheriff said, and went to a box at the desk and withdrew a strange mesh object. "Almost forgot. We're issuing these to the force. Wear it whenever you're outside. It's a beekeeper's mask to cover up from those damned flies."

Pete thought it a good idea and took it and thanked the sheriff and put it in his pocket and left.

On the motorcycle, he set the emergency flasher on and tugged the throttle back. He cranked it through the gears and raced under a late-afternoon sun at top speed toward Jacob Walz State Park.

Several times he took curves at ninety miles an hour with the bike at a forty-five-degree angle to the horizontal and used his inside foot to skid along the pavement for stability. At that, the park was so remote it took him a long time to reach it.

The place lay completely in shade with no sign of life when he arrived. He put on his gloves and the beekeeper's mask and made sure no skin would be exposed to the flies. "Hello," he called. "H-e-l-l-ooooo! *Hellooooooooo!*"

No sound replied in the natural amphitheater but the echo of his voice and the droning of the ubiquitous flies.

He found the tracks of a large vehicle. They were overlaid by one another and confused and went in all directions and, once, in a full circle. The vehicle was double-wheeled in the rear and single-wheeled in the front. There were ruts, and spatterings of mud on vegetation. Around the spot where the vehicle had been parked the damp earth was pocked with scores of small footprints. Buried deep in one of them Pete found a girl's shoe. A large elm tree had recently been uprooted near this spot. Part of it was scorched and blackened and Pete surmised it had been struck by lightning. One limb was bent and its branches gone. These branches had not fallen off or been sawn but, ends splintered, looked to have been ripped by main force from the limb. The peculiar methodism of vandals was lacking here. The scene reeked of controlled terror. Pete walked toward the picnic area and beyond the stupor of his grief began to feel the indefinable dread he felt at Ed & Edna's Diner.

The shadows lay long and dusk was coming and brought with it a cool breeze laden with dampness. Pete did not recognize the bodies as such at first. He saw the yellow inflatable raft near a large pattern of cloth and plastic and junk held to the ground by stones. He began to wonder if it was a cryptogram laid to convey some meaning, a Stonehenge of fabric and polystyrene. The legs of the pattern were laid out to point to the sky. The sky, of course! It was a signal. He ran to the base of the legs and backed toward the edge of the lake and felt his flesh creep. H-E-L-P, it spelled. The plaintive cry of the endangered. And now it lay in darkness.

Parts of the word, the H and the L, were raised from the ground in a uniform way. Pete went to the left leg of the H and was pierced by the stare of the wide eyes of a dead nun. He knelt toward the body, then backed away as he realized the eyes were full of ants and flies and the corpse was beginning to stink.

He discovered another dead nun, a dead girl, and two dead boys. He covered his mouth with his hand and staggered upwind of the horror and gasped. Half-collapsing, half-sitting, he went to the ground and searched the sky and sought God and knew this part of the world was now clutched in the grip of hell.

He struggled with his portable radio and called and hoped vainly that the signal would bounce from the evening atmosphere in a skip wave back to the substation, much as in the deep dark dead of night the radio in your car will pick up Salt Lake City while you are driving through Georgia. All he heard was static.

His mind fought itself and nerve flensed nerve. He forced himself to get up and go back to his motorcycle, and he was growing tired of forcing himself to do things.

Flies buzzed. He tarried to catch some with his jars, using his body as bait.

He tucked the jars into his saddlebags and sped into the night, trying to follow the tracks of the school bus.

This part of the county was interlaced with small roads; some paved, some merely graveled, some dirt.

Pete searched for hours after the tracks of the bus had long vanished on a paved road. He had little fuel left in the tank of the Suzuki and knew that further search would be futile. As he sorted in his mind the HELP sign, the tearing of the tree, the footprints, and the methodology of survival, he came to find a shrewd grace to it all, hurled into the teeth of the demon. He longed to find and meet these young people and hear their story.

But it was not to be. Ghosts in the night, they were gone.

He stopped at a phone booth and reported to the desk what he had found in the park. Then he went on.

He realized he was in a place where he could short-cut overland past the Mueller ruins toward the place where Al Murdock died, thence back to the Elmsford Road. He followed this course.

He stopped at the burnt house. The smell of smoke had been washed away. He took out his flashlight and searched the ground for more tracks or signs and expected to find none.

When he had looked into the eyes of the dead nun he had been astonished and horrified. Now he was astonished and puzzled. The place was crisscrossed with the fresh tracks of motorcycles. For minutes he forgot his sorrow, and the instincts of a hound after quarry raced in his veins. The tracks came from overland and departed overland. He looked in the refrigerator, wondering if there would be another note. There was none.

Then he decided to play a trick of his own. He got out his citation book. In the blank space for the defendant's name, he wrote: To Whom It May Concern. In the blank space for the charge, he wrote: Arson. In the blank space for officer issuing citation, he wrote his signature and badge number. He left the citation in the refrigerator.

He caught more flies and kicked down in the darkness on the starter of the Suzuki. The engine coughed to a start. Then, far in the distance, he thought he heard an echo of the same thing. Yet it could not have been an echo. He was on a hilltop, not in a hollow. With the speed of a striking snake, he struck the master kill switch of the bike to OFF. The engine stopped dead without a sputter. For the merest seconds, he heard another motorcycle engine roar in the night and then stop.

He knew now he was not simply spooked. Something was out there. Be it the local teens, be it the government, be it a Toltec god or the devil incarnate, Pete's blood was up and he would snook the thing out with the best bait he had—himself.

He started the Suzuki again and turned on the headlight and rode overland toward the Elmsford Road. Several times he could hear the other motorcycle keeping about the same distance from him. He saw no light, nor did he expect to.

He rode to the place where he had found Al's body and cut the engine quickly again. Now not one, but at least three other engines were simultaneously cut in the hills beyond.

Well, he thought, so much for disbelief in conspiracies. There was something orchestrated behind all this.

He casually gathered more flies by flashlight and waited for something to happen. Nothing did.

He started the Suzuki again and turned on the light and rode slowly for the Elmsford Road. He could hear the sputterings of other engines behind and above.

He reached the road and jammed the bike through its gears and watched the speedometer needle climb to its peg. He could hear their engines do the same behind him, but he could see no lights. He slowed the bike to a stop beside a clump of trees and killed the light and the engine and set the bike on its kickstand and strolled into the trees to feign urination and listen. He could hear the other motors idling in the distance.

He cruised in second gear in the direction of the sub-station. He cut the kill switch off and on to simulate engine trouble, a sick and thrashing fish inviting shark attack. But these sharks kept their distance.

He pulled into the substation. Gary assured him that the ambulance corps had gone to Jacob Walz Park for the bodies. No one had seen a trace of the school bus. Only one person had died of fly bite since Mayor Otis was killed. This was the first Pete heard of the mayor's death and he was nearly too confounded to feel sorry for the small man he had so respected. He rode home and listened for the following riders and heard but did not see them. They passed after he turned off on the road to his house.

Pete parked the Suzuki in the garage next to the Volvo. He poured the big plastic container of two-stroke motorcycle fuel into the bike's tank, topping it off.

He double-locked the doors and put the vacation-time burglar locks in the windows and turned the air conditioners to Low.

He took the phone off the hook and heard the tocsins and the amplified metallic voice squawking for him to replace the receiver.

Pete disdained this electronic advice and dug in a kitchen cabinet for the gift bottle of Glenfiddich single-malt Scot's Whiskey. He dumped ice cubes into a tumbler and filled it full of the Scotch. He gulped and shuddered against the unaccustomed potency of the drink. He took off his uniform and hung it up. He sipped some more whiskey and turned on a bedroom light and draped his gun belt and pistol over a bedpost on his side of the bed.

He drank more whiskey and felt it fight his internal organs. The phone stopped warning him and went dead. He searched the house again for unlocked doors and windows and unwanted fires on the stove, and for flies.

He drank more whiskey yet, washing down extra vitamin doses and three aspirin tablets with it, and readied his Italian coffee and more vitamins for a morning he would rather not see.

Once or twice he thought he heard motorcycles rumble in the distance.

He got more whiskey and lurched toward the bed in which he would sleep for the first time a widower.

At last he was sure he was truly being hunted.

And Adair Godwin had yet to leave Mexico City.

20

Nobody actually saw the accident happen that night but many were witness to the carnage that followed.

The waybill indicated the truck was en route from Indiana to New Jersey with a cargo of hogs. Something went wrong on a long downhill curve on the interstate near the Sunset Motel.

It was apparent from the skid marks that the trailer jackknifed when the rig lost adhesion to the road. The driver obviously had his wits about him and managed to skid it along the shoulder of the road. The first living witness said she saw the trailer lying on its side with its wheels still rolling lazily in the air. The driver had turned on the emergency flashers. Investigation later revealed he had also cut the ignition to obviate the danger of fire. Other witnesses corroborated that he did not appear at all harmed, and walked deliberately from cab to trailer with flashlight in hand. Some witnesses say this was when the pigs started to break loose, but others disagreed and said they thought the driver let them out. All agreed that through the open slats of the trailer they heard some of the hogs start to shriek violently. All witnesses agreed that at some point a number of the pigs got loose and ran onto the highway. Accounts differed widely on the precise sequence of what happened next. All that was certain was that a number of hogs screeched piteously and dropped dead. The driver had been trying to herd them when suddenly he screamed and clutched his breast as though he had been shot, and pitched forward convulsing on the asphalt. A man in a Dodge pickup truck in the same lane as the tractor-trailer ran to help the driver. Several more pigs shrieked and died. The man from the Dodge pickup suddenly bawled and fell.

The witnesses who remained said many other bystanders got back in their cars and sped from the scene. The opinion began to form that a sniper with a silencer was firing randomly.

The first state police car drove up with lights blazing and siren blaring. The trooper ran out and lit flares behind the stopped traffic. Suddenly someone screamed in one of the cars. The trooper ran to this car and shone his flashlight inside. Then he ran back to the patrol car and barked something into its radio. Then he went back and opened the door of the car from which the person screamed and seemed to be trying to administer first aid. Then he cried out and tumbled onto the front seat.

Within a half-hour, six state police cars, four ambulances, and two helicopters, with a third hovering overhead, had arrived at the disaster. Curiously, no human or animal died after the arrival of the helicopters. In all, five persons died on the interstate that night, including the trooper. Twenty-three pigs lay dead and the others fled into the countryside.

Adair Godwin sat stewing a rage in the airport at Mexico City. He would not be able to fly out until early Thursday morning. He had tried to book anything, even flights via other Latin American countries, but everything was a loss due to a down computer. As the hours lazed by, Adair's anger subsided, if not his grief. He cast around for something to divert emotions he could not control. He knew he could not sleep.

He wandered to a row of empty waiting-room chairs. He was not good at waiting. He found an issue of *The New York Times* left on a chair. He had not read the *Times* since he was last in the country, and had always liked it. This issue was datelined Wednesday and marked "Late

City Edition." It was not the usual abbreviated edition you find outside New York. Someone had brought it in fresh on a plane that day. Adair started to read and found little in the newspaper to interest an anthropologist. He scanned the "Around the Nation" sidebar and paused over the following article:

TOWN EXPERIENCES EPIDEMIC
OF HEART SEIZURES.

Thomas Valley, Penna (UPI)   Local health officials report 11 deaths by heart attacks within or near this community in the last 48 hours. Autopsy reports confirm the causes to have been cardiac arrest.

"This is highly abnormal in a town in which the last census measured the population at 3,493," reported Mayor Warren P. Otis, who spoke of his sorrow for the families of the victims and his concern that the trend may continue. The mayor reported having asked local health officials and the Elmsford County, Pennsylvania, Sheriff's Department to conduct a thorough investigation. County Board of Health officials confirm only the autopsy reports and the fact of the investigation.

Adair thought this news curious but irrelevant to Enid's death. He read on into the night, as a marooned commuter. He scanned the duller parts of the paper hoping they would bring sleep. Surely the weather report on page A25 would make for reading that would evoke emotion in none but farmers and sailors. A weather front was working its way eastward toward the Atlantic. The prediction was for showers and possible thunderstorms in the city until late Thursday, followed by a clearing trend through the weekend. Adair was nearly asleep. Then he realized Thursday's storm in New York was probably Tuesday night's in Pennsylvania that killed Enid. He began to examine the small section inside the weather report. He paused at the quadruple diagram of the phases of the moon, beginning to dread what he might see.

The full moon was to set next Saturday, a day that would be cloudless in midsummer, at 11:59 A.M.

The arteries in Adair's neck pounded. He felt as if he were growing horns. He stood to his full height.

A Pan Am woman walked up to him. "Mr. Godwin?" she asked.

"Uh, yes," Adair said, in a voice grown progressively hoarse.

"Mr. Godwin, Pan American is very sorry for the inconvenience of our flight arrangements for you. Our management wishes to inform you that we're upgrading your ticket to first class, if you're agreeable. We'd like to invite you to our first-class lounge now, sir."

Adair looked at the tired young woman and tucked his fury away as if in an inside jacket pocket. He donned his courtly personality.

"Thank you," he said. "And please thank your management for me. That's very thoughtful."

With the help of the Scotch, Pete Bilyeux slept a long and mostly dreamless sleep. A part of his mind had been alert for sounds in the night, and there were no unusual ones, only cicadas, crickets, the tickle of wind in the branches of trees, and the nightly routine of raccoons tumbling over garbage cans to forage among their contents. He then let himself sleep more deeply.

Roosters crowed at first light. Birds tittered. His sleep was troubled by the passage of dawn and he started to snuggle next to Enid. Then he remembered Enid was dead. Soon the crows came and screeched their morning discoveries to one another.

Pete awoke slowly. His slumbering mind enumerated each event in its turn and the synapses in his brain shot messages in circuits and counter-circuits. What should he do now?

The legislative aide to the Governor of Pennsylvania was sorely annoyed early this Thursday morning. What bothered him most was that he had not got to go to Japan with the gubernatorial trade-mission party. The governor and lieutenant governor went, as did the governor's administrative aide. So did just about everyone but the governor's legislative aide, and the legislature was not even in session. "Somebody has to mind the store," the governor had told him, gripping him on the shoulders and smiling his campaign smile and clearly implying his confidence in his legislative aide and his mistrust of anyone else. That was a consolation prize, of course. What it meant was the governor had left him with all his responsibility and none of his authority. But, then, it was an election year. The polls showed the governor in a close reelection race against that energetic young Democrat from Radnor. Radnor? Jesus! The aide had thought when this challenger copped his party's nomination. He didn't even think there *were* any Democrats in Radnor. Now one was out to put him out of a job.

All right, that was bad enough. Then this mother superior kept calling about some nuns and kids from North Philly who were missing on a picnic out in the boonies. The aide referred her to the state police, who referred her to the Elmsford County sheriff's department, who referred her back to the state police, who referred her back to the governor's office. The aide put pressure on the state police to do something. But this pressure was only moral suasion and vague threats, as the aide did not have the power to tell the state police to do a thing. The state police assured him they would put pressure on the Elmsford sheriff, such pressure being only moral suasion and vague threats, as the area was in the sheriff's jurisdiction.

Then in the middle of the night the aide had got a call from the state police. A trooper and four people had been killed on an interstate highway, not by any accident, but by some mysterious cause. It was an advisory call, of course, there being nothing the legislative aide could do except share a general anxiety that made it difficult for him to get back to sleep. When toward dawn he finally nodded off, his private phone rang him out of peace of mind for a long time to come. It was some priest who said that he was the new mayor of some rinky-dink town, and that flies had bitten and killed more than thirty people and just what was the Commonwealth of Pennsylvania going to do about it? Flies? The aide paused and tried to grapple with his mind. He had tried LSD twice in his student days at Penn, and had occasionally snorted coke until he got involved with politics, at which point he swore off all such excesses. He wondered if he was having a drug flashback. He wondered how a backwoods priest had got hold of his carefully guarded private phone number. He asked the priest to repeat himself and started to worry about the Catholic vote in November, not to mention the black vote from North Philly. Then the force of the number of deaths washed the mud from his mind, and the aide was wide awake, his heart throbbing and his ears alert and his shoulders sagging with compassion for the story he heard.

Still he could not quite believe it. He asked the priest for his phone number and promised to call back. Without bothering to shower or shave, he threw on his clothes and drove to his office.

He flipped through his Rolodex and got the Elmsford County sheriff's private number and dialed it and woke the man.

The sheriff had phlegm in his voice, but congeniality in his tone. Yes, the sheriff said, all hell was breaking loose. Yes, people had been killed by some new kind of poisonous fly. Yes, Mayor Otis suddenly died and was replaced by a Father Fierro, a good fellow, even if he was a Catholic. No, the sheriff would probably not need outside help unless the situation got worse. He would be in touch should that happen.

"Sheriff," the aide said, "uh, just how many people have died from this cause?"

"Oh, I dismember, I don't know for sure. Heaps."

"Sheriff, can you describe the action you're taking?"

"Sure, old son. Thanks for asking. All our deputies are on overtime. Our board of health people are out pounding the pavement trying to track this business down. We've got all the volunteer fire departments out warning people to be careful. This morning the police auxiliary and the boy scouts will set up roadblocks to warn people away from the area, eksetera."

"Good, Sheriff, thanks," the aide said. "I'll be checking with you from time to time. Don't hesitate to let me know if I can help."

"Old son, old son," the sheriff sounded unprofessionally emotional, "old son, you and old Joe Cody here, that's me, the sheriff, we don't know one another, but old Joe asks God to bless you and looks forward to the day I can shake your hand. I can't tell you how grateful I am for your calling all the way from Harrisburg to help us out here. That's real white of you, old son, real Christian, yes, sir, real Christian.''

As it happened, the legislative aide to the Governor of Pennsylvania was a Jew, Joshua Rosen by name. A conservative of deep conviction whose philosophy was rooted in passionate devotion to integrity, he was also a pragmatic political operative and quite sympathetic to the problems of black people. Alone early on this Thursday morning he set his personal hot-water pot to heat for his personal freeze-dried black coffee and rummaged through papers and worried with the sinking heart of a prominent but powerless person.

Josh Rosen shuffled through his IN basket to see if he had got the cable due him with the governor's final itinerary.

He found it. It was dated the twentieth of the month: HIYA, JOSH, WHAT'S HAPPENING? BIG DEALS OVER TOKYO WAY. NOVEMBER ELECTION SEWED UP IN A BIG PLASTIC BAG. CLEAR MOUNTAINS AND KICK OUT BEARS WE COPPED A DEAL TO SUBASSEMBLE MINI-TRUCK TRANSMISSIONS AND DO FINAL ASSEMBLY ON 10-SPEED BIKES AND THERE'S MORE TO COME, THANKS TO YOURS TRULY. SEE YOU DAY AFTER TOMORROW. LANDING PHILLY INTERNATIONAL 8:57 AM. PLS ARRANGE PRESS CONFERENCE AT AIRPORT AND CHOPPER TO HARRISBURG. HANG IN THERE, JOSH—GOV.

Josh rubbed his eyes and looked at his wall calendar. Since the cable was dated the twentieth and the governor would be back the day after tomorrow that meant he would not arrive until Sunday morning, the twenty-second. He made a note to contact the press and have them at the airport. Then he knew he must act. He picked up the phone and dictated a cable to the governor's hotel in Tokyo urgently requesting that either the governor declare a state of emergency in Elmsford County or that the governor delegate him the authority to do so.

When Alma Pickett went to feed the chickens, Bob-John was on the cultivator more than a mile away. Alma

was shocked at what she saw. She had been dumbfounded
to hear about the poisonous flies when a man came around
from the fire department away on over into town. But she
knew the man and knew Mayor Otis from church and
knew they wouldn't lie to her. So she and Bob-John were
careful. It was a good thing, too, because they didn't
have a telephone. Bob-John had finally caved in on getting a TV just like his old daddy had caved in on getting
electricity time back. But Bob-John couldn't see any need
for a phone as the good Lord had never seen fit to bless
them with children. And nothing had prepared Alma for
what she saw this Thursday morning.

She had never seen so many colored in all her life. The
only people she was used to seeing were at church on
Sunday or at choir practice on Tuesday nights. None of
them were colored. Mr. Riley who owned the OK Garage
away on over into town was colored, but he was a Meth-
odist, and Alma saw him maybe once in a blue moon
because Bob-John did all his own mechanical work. Mr.
Riley was a nice man, though. Now here was a whole
passel of colored trooping out of a beat-up, sooty old
school bus across the road in a patch of sunlight by the
pond where the stock drank and did other things Alma
didn't want to talk about. They all looked so young. One
of them even looked white.

"This water looks like somebody pissed in it, Irene,"
Herman García said. "Smells like it too. You know what
I'm saying?"

"That's right," Talmadge Brown echoed.

"Then go dig a well," Irene said.

"Shit-fire, girl, we shouldn't have never took these
damn back roads," Talmadge said.

"You want to go on the highway and get catched by
the man?" Irene said. "Shee-it, them hillbillies around
here, they don't think nothing of clapping you in the damn
jail and popping out your eyes just for old times' sake.
If you don't like the water, don't drink it. And if you
don't drink it, don't complain about being thirsty."

"Uh-oh." Herman was first to catch sight of the
woman, face shaded by a bonnet, hands on hips, legs

kicking through her long skirt as she strode purposefully toward them. "I knew we should have took the fucking highway."

"Now you stop that right now!" the woman hollered to them.

"Oh, shit," Talmadge muttered.

"Shush," Irene whispered. "You let me handle this." She walked modestly toward the woman and tried to adopt the attitude of the sweet inferior Negro girl talking to the massa's wife, the great white lady—a pose just a little short of Muhammad Ali with tongue in cheek doing the Zip Coon shuffle.

" 'Scuse me, ma'am," Irene said, "we don't mean to make any trouble, ma'am. I mean, we don't mean to be trespassing or anything. We're just as thirsty as—I mean, we're very thirsty."

"Well, land's sakes," Alma Pickett said. "Goodness gracious, if you children are thirsty, you shouldn't be drinking out of that place. Animals drop things in it. Land's sake, if you're thirsty—I mean to say, just come to our well. All you have to do is ask and you can have all the water you want."

The dark-brown eyes of the young city girl searched up into the gray sunburned eyes of the lank farm woman. The woman began to smile and, as she did, showed she did not have all her teeth. Some instinct told Irene the signs were good. She smiled at the farm woman and made a body gesture that was a sort of latter-day curtsy.

"Well," Irene said, "we thank you, ma'am. That's real nice of you. We'd like some of your water, if it's all the same with you."

"Well, of course it is," Alma said. "Didn't I say so?"

Alma took the kids to the old pump in front of the house. They were shy at first. Then when she started the pump the kids seemed fascinated as if she were a sorceress seducing cool fresh water from the ground to gush from the nozzle of the pump she worked with her arm. Alma stood back and let them work the pump and was thrilled at the delight they got from this simple act.

Alma offered them food, and the girl who was apparently their leader demurred thankfully. But Alma could tell from the way she did so that the children were hungry. Alma thought all these children had very good breeding and she was a little taken aback at this. From what she had heard of the colored, she hadn't known them to set such high store by good breeding, but when she thought about it, she saw no reason why they shouldn't.

At last Alma persuaded them to eat. This was, after all, as she explained to Irene, a farm. Farms have nothing if not plenty of food. They went inside and Alma got a newly cured ham and plenty of milk and the girls helped make large sandwiches for all.

Alma made two huge sandwiches and a large bowl of strawberries smothered with honey and cream and put them in the refrigerator. She explained that this was for Mr. Pickett, who would soon be home for his lunch.

When Alma saw Bob-John approaching, she went out to meet him and tell him of all the new things. Bob-John nodded and wiped the sweat from his face with a big red cotton handkerchief.

When the youngsters saw Bob-John they were agog. He was huge, taller even than Talmadge Brown and about twice as wide. He nodded to each child without a word. He wore a baseball cap with the name of a diesel tractor company on the peak. He took off his hat going into the house, and the young people saw the sharp contrast between the burned reddish-brown of his face and neck and the albino white of his scalp. It reminded the children of hands that were black on the backs and pale on the palms, and what a strange state of affairs all this natural business was. Mr. Picket sat down and ate leisurely, chewing his food as a cow her cud. When he finished, he belched audibly and wiped his mouth with his kerchief, nodded to Alma and the children, and went back out to work without uttering a word.

Alma explained to the children that Mr. Pickett was not an overly loquacious man. He used each word as though he had to pay tax on it. The children were amazed.

Alma was equally amazed at the children and their story, when she finally got it out of them. They gave her much useful information about the toxic flies and she would pass this on to Bob-John and the people at the church. She agreed not to report the children and their bus to anyone, as the children were intent to the degree of fanaticism on fending for themselves. In return, she exacted a promise from the children to stay for supper. The children agreed to this on condition they be given some work to do around the farm. Alma put them to work at various chores and worked with them and was amused at their responses to things that to her were common-place. Only little Albert Tipton seemed at home right away, which is to say he was at home or at sea wherever he turned up. The ranking class brain after the late May-nard, Albert was the wizard who had discovered how to hot-wire the bus. He sat around the farm and fixed things that had wires in them.

Herman García came under attack by the beak and spurs of Corkie, a truculent old rooster. Herman ran as this ap-parition cackled and flapped its wings and kicked at him until Alma explained that old Corkie just wanted attention. The rooster was a natural bully and a coward at heart, and Alma demonstrated how to face him down and make him retreat.

Extra tables were improvised and set and a dinner was laid of roast beef, chicken, ham, home-made noodles, potatoes plain and sweet, turnips, tomatoes, corn on the cob, beets, succotash, plenty of milk, and strawberries and tapioca for dessert.

At table, Bob-John Pickett tucked his red kerchief into his shirt as a bib. He let fall both fists, each clutching a utensil, with a portentous thump on the table, giving sign he would speak.

The children fell still. Mr. Pickett gazed toward the heavens for a moment and then thrust his chin onto his chest and spoke into his plate in a monotone so deep it rumbled as a cyclone across plains, saying: "Almighty-God-we-thank-Thee-heartily-for-Thy-bounties-and-the-food-Thou-preparest-for-our-harvest-in-the-name-of-the-Father-Son-and-Holy-Ghost-Amen."

"Amen," the children said, and crossed themselves. The Picketts looked upon this gesture strangely.

Dinner was done and the long shadows began to lie

across the farm and the children helped Mrs. Pickett clean up. Then they filed toward the bus. Alma gave them the most rudimentary indication of the direction of Philadelphia as she had never been there herself. She kissed and hugged each youngster in turn and bade them Godspeed. The children were surprised when Mr. Pickett thrust out a huge, horny, calloused hand for each to shake.

The Picketts, hand in hand, followed the young people to the bus. They heard Irene protest a few times at the little stings of electricity that shocked her as she hot-wired the starter. The engine kicked over and soon the bus began to lurch down the dirt road. The children waved and called their thank-yous and good-byes, and the Pickets waved in return.

Bob-John Pickett noticed his wife smiling and weeping at once. He put his arm around her.

"They'll be all right," he said.

Alma wasn't so sure. They would both pray for the children on this Thursday night.

That morning Adair's jet sped down the runway and in an agony of screeching engines thrust its nose upward and pierced the sky.

Adair had always loved the sight of Mexico City from the air and he looked down on it until it receded in the distance and knew he would never see it again.

He tried to sleep on the flight to New York but he could not bring drowsiness on, not even after sipping Jack Daniels Black Label on the rocks through a straw. The rich whiskey was a vast improvement over Waterfill and Frazier, but it did little to improve his mood. He tried to think as a juror and give benefit of doubt to the defense, but the facts were uncontrovertible and spoke eloquently. The deaths by accident of both parents. The long durance in the dungeon of the fat people. The sweetness and passion of his love for Enid and its bitter loss. Elspeth's inability to help; her suffering from arthritis and as Adair had come to infer from her letters, probably something worse. The thing that was destroying him. And now Enid's death by lightning. It could not possibly have all been random.

He took the statue of Quetzalcoatl from his bag and looked at it for a long time but learned nothing from it. Not yet. No, he was not quite sure what it was. But he would find out. Then he would do something about it.

Pete forced himself through his morning and forced Enid from his mind. Yes, he would grieve later. Clean and shaved, he dressed in a pair of jeans and a shirt. His left desert boot had been ruined and he did not wish to put on his dress shoes, the ones he had worn to the funeral parlor the day before, so he put on an unseasonal pair of high-topped laced hunting boots, supposedly waterproof.

He phoned the substation and Vince Egert answered and told him about the roadblocks. Nobody had died that night. No shifts were changed. Pete was still considered on bereavement leave and would be so until Sunday, that being official policy. He was welcome back but not expected back.

Pete decided he would personally take the flies he had caught the night before to Hershey. He would ride there on his Suzuki. He did not feel like driving the Volvo just now.

He pushed the motorcycle into the driveway. Then he went up to double-check the lock on the front door. On the porch was a large dead red cat. It was stiff and maggots were sporting in its nose. Muddy footprints led up and down the porch to the tracks of a single motorcycle that had come from the woods on the far side of the place where Enid died. There had been no effort to disguise the tracks. Quite the contrary, they were a message.

Careful not to disturb the prints, Pete went back in the house and dug out his old camera and took pictures of everything. He hastily buried the cat and went in and hid the camera inside an intake shaft of the forced-air heating system. He got his Colt Python .357 Magnum and checked the bullets in the cylinder and added the untrustworthy number six. He put on a belt that held extra cartridges, a flashlight, handcuffs, and other emergency items. He put on his shoulder holster, got his badge and ID, and put on his windbreaker and went out again.

He lost the motorcycle tracks on the graveled road in front of his house, then picked them up again in a large barren expanse near the paved road. The grooves in the ground were deep. This motorcycle had been ridden by a heavy man. Its tracks led to other tracks where more motorcycles had milled around. Here he found an empty mayonnaise jar with holes punched in the lid. Pete recognized it as his. There was a piece of paper inside it. He opened it and read (this time in handwriting) "Told you so, pig."

A copse to the west suddenly erupted in rifle fire. Pete could see the flashes of the muzzles and dived for the ground. He also saw a brief sparkle in the sun, as if someone had held up a mirror for an instant. The guns barked and the bullets cracked over his head. As nearly as he could tell, there were two rifles shooting at him, maybe three. He lay in a swale sheltered from direct line of fire. He took out the Python and cocked it and set it on the ground in front of him. It might be useful if they got closer, but at this range it was no match for the rifles.

He knew he must do something unexpected as the rifle shots ripped desultorily over him. He found a long twig and reached in his pocket for his white handkerchief and tied this to the stick and waved it over his head as a flag of truce and waited to see what would happen. It was the kind of thing described by Washington pundits as a trial balloon. The rifle fire stopped and the morning fell silent for a few moments. Then out of the woods came first a cackle followed by giggles followed by bawdy laughter. The laughing continued until it was drowned by motorcycle engines starting in rapid succession.

The cycles rode away out the far side of the woods and Pete never saw the riders. He uncocked the Python and replaced it in its shoulder holster and rode into the woods. He parked the Suzuki near where the other bikes had been parked. There had been three of them. The tire marks were similar to his own, enduro tires for combined street and dirt riding. Pete looked at the vantage point from which they had fired, and realized he had been a superb target. He found the impressions where three men had lain on the ground. One of these was especially deep. To the right of the impressions, Pete rummaged and found empty brass shell casings. He picked them up with his handkerchief and held them up to the light and was surprised at what he read at their bases. Each rifleman had used a .300 Weatherby Magnum. It was exotic stuff, and expensive too. Pete never heard of a Weatherby without a telescopic sight and a very good one at that. They are extremely powerful rifles, made to stop big game. Pete looked again toward the place where he had been the target: There was no way these guys could have missed him with Weatherbys. They were playing with him. They hadn't meant to kill him. Not yet.

It was a psych, Pete knew. A cop gets close to things and you burn down a house and leave a note in an old refrigerator that had been a deathtrap. A cop goes on duty the night after his wife dies and a motorcycle crowd toys with him. A cop wakes up the next morning and finds a dead cat on his porch and footprints and motorcycle tracks, and the motorcycle people shoot over his head with rifles that could damned near blow him in half. And what about the man the old dove hunter had spoken with and the man who followed Pete in the maroon Eldorado? Might they have been the same man? But perhaps the latter was stretching things a little. Perhaps it was only the prejudice Pete shared with many policemen that Cadillac drivers were the most obnoxious on the road. Anyhow, somebody was obviously trying to spook him.

Experience had taught Pete that in belligerency the other side is always at least as worried as yours. If they were trying to psych him, then he must be onto something important. He only wished he knew what it was.

He packed everything into the saddlebags and followed the cycle tracks through the woods and lost them on the main roads. Then he rode toward Hershey. He had not traveled six miles before he ran into the roadblock.

It was a pathetic thing. A Thomas Valley police auxiliary wagon, lights flashing, straddled the crown of the road, leaving a path for traffic to pass on either side. Boy scouts in uniform and wearing bee masks and gloves

flagged down traffic with sticks with crudely painted
signs. "Sir," he heard a scout say, "excuse us, sir, but
we got a bad epidemic and we have to warn you to take
a detour or travel at your own risk." Most drivers acknowledged and continued at their own risk.

Pete heard the name "Bilyeux" crackle over the auxiliary wagon's radio as he walked up to say hello. A boy
scout had stopped a large refrigerator truck. The truck
driver and his passenger were wearing bee masks. They
nodded to the boy and said something Pete couldn't hear.
The boy waved them on, and the truck skirted the shoulder of the road and crept in first gear toward Thomas
Valley. Pete stood at the side of the road as the truck
passed, and as it did, it seemed to him that the passenger
was scrutinizing Pete from behind his mask. Pete made
a note of the plate number of the truck.

He went over to the auxiliary policeman. The man was
giving up a day's wages to do this volunteer duty.

"Uh, somebody after me on the radio?" Pete said.

"Caught you, didn't we? What did you do, Pete?" the
man said, smiling.

Pete smiled back and keyed the microphone of the radio. "Bilyeux here, what's happening?"

"Pete, Jesus, glad we got you," Vince Egert said.
"The old man's here and he's hot to talk to you ASAP.
Hang on."

"Bilyeux!" the sheriff said. "Oh, thank God I got you,
old son. Son, man, listen to me. The world is just coming
apart on me. TV people are here raising hell and there's
a big fat hairy Jew in here and he's got a big fat hairy
spider on his shoulder!"

The sheriff sounded terrible and Pete could sense his
strength waning. The man was really too old and too
untrained to cope with calamity.

"Man, Bilyeux, I've got to tell you I think that Jew is
a queer and crazy too. He's got a couple of people with
him. One's another queer and one's a broad with big
glasses and big tits. They say they're doctors and the Jew
claims to work for the feds. They're all driving foreign
cars like you'd give a speeding ticket to even if they were
standing still. They claim to know you and want to speak

to you and they're driving me bananas and otherwise getting on my nerves!''

"Uh, ten-four, Sheriff,'' Pete said. "B-be right there.''

By the time Adair's plane landed at John F. Kennedy
International Airport he had been asleep for about two
hours, the longest he could ever sleep at a time anymore.
He woke to the *bump-bump* of the wheels hitting the runway and looked out the window at his native land. It was
late afternoon and the runway was wet from rains and
the air gray and he couldn't see the city.

The flight crew got Adair off the airplane first and
wished him good luck. He thanked them for their excellent service. The customs officials whisked him through
without bothering to look into his luggage. He went to a
Borough of Queens Yellow Pages and looked under
"Autos—Rental" for a Rent-A-Wreck company. He
called one in Jamaica and reserved the fastest car they
had, a 1967 Ford Galaxie with a monstrous engine and
few smog controls.

He went out of the terminal to get a taxi.

A cabbie not in the regular line ran up to Adair.
"Where you going, pal?" the cabbie asked.

"Jamaica," Adair said.

"No, pal, that's where you been. Where you going? I
give good breaks to foreigners, only ninety bucks for you
to any hospital in the city. Get you there in fifteen minutes.''

"Thanks just the same," Adair told the cabbie, and
walked toward the proper line of cabs.

The cabbie tagged along behind him.

"Okay, pal, for you only sixty bucks, including tip.
Where you going?''

"To Sutphin Boulevard in the neighborhood of Jamaica
in the Borough of Queens in the City of New York, and
I wasn't born yesterday," Adair said.

"Pal, just for you it's only forty bucks, plus tip, how's
that? You look like you're in a bad way. What's wrong?''

"Not much," Adair said, "just a touch of AIDS.''

The cabbie left quickly and Adair stifled a spasm of
laughter. He got a black cabbie who would go by the

meter and went to Jamaica and rented the Galaxie on his American Express card.

Down the Van Wyck Expressway he sped, down the Grand Central Parkway, over the Triborough Bridge, up the Major Deegan Expressway past Yankee Stadium, and across the George Washington Bridge into New Jersey, watching his mirrors for police cars. He looked at his watch. The sun was setting—what could be seen of it beyond the clouds—and if he really pushed it he could be in Thomas Valley in six hours, five maybe.

He was in central New Jersey when he saw a familiar sign. He had nearly passed the turnoff. He locked up the brakes and could hear the tires squeal and smell the smoke as he brought the Galaxie down from ninety-three miles per hour to forty-six to make the twenty-five-mile-per-hour exit ramp. He pulled into the shopping center in front of the well-lit Herman's Sporting Goods store. He went into the store and looked around. He stopped at a glass case that displayed some Buck knives. This was a good brand, Adair remembered, from a suburb of San Diego, of all places. His eyes fixed on a knife with a long blade with superb shaping, almost like blood grooves on a bayonet. He bought it. He walked to a nearby Burger King, bought food and six cups of black coffee to go, and sped westward into the night.

The idea had begun to plant itself in Pete's mind the day before. It occurred to him again just before he was shot at. It now occupied all his mind on the ride to the substation.

He could keep his job and take some time off to properly mourn for Enid and then go back to work until the pain went away years later. Or he could risk his job and perhaps his life and perhaps drift in pain for a long time by doing what he knew was right.

"The only thing necessary for the triumph of evil is for good men to do nothing." The putative Burke quotation came back to him again, as did the shooting in Saigon. The defiance of his boss the day before came back to him again. He made the decision again, for the last time, he thought. It would mean a confrontation with the sheriff, if need be. It would mean turning in his badge, if need

be. It would mean getting killed, if need be. No, the
decision was not hard, but he feared the execution of it
would task him terribly. Yet he would do it. He would
regain control of this case and solve it, and if it cost him
dearly . . . Well, so be it.

The parking lot at the substation was full of strange
cars. Among others, there was a BMW 535i, a Mercedes
Turbodiesel, and a red Porsche 944 Turbo. There were
cars with press stickers on them and a camera truck. On
the porch, the sheriff was holding forth to television and
newspaper reporters.

The matter of the flies was under investigation, he
could hear the sheriff say, and the suicide of the chairman
of the board of health was entirely unrelated, the fellow
having been in failing health for a long time.

Since Pete was emotionally primed to face the sheriff,
news of this death set off an alert in his mind. He had
not known the health chairman to be in bad health. Of
course, he could be wrong. But he had been wrong too
often in this case already, erring on behalf of deductive
logic. There had simply been too many anomalies in the
case, chiefest of them the poisonous flies themselves. Yet
this much was certain: they were poisonous, and some
people were somehow involved, people who didn't want
Pete involved. Enough, he thought, from now on no one
is above suspicion. In truth, that web of suspicion also
began to include himself, suspect for being a fool. It was
a suspicion to which he had been prey since the taunts of
his adolescence. He reminded himself that he was no
longer an adolescent. He was a professional with a dread
duty. Fool or not, from now on he would lay a network
of verbal trap lines, one of which might conceal the jaws
to snap on an unwary guilty, if Pete was lucky.

Pete took the saddlebags off his bike and went in the
back way. On chairs in the glass-walled interview room
sat Louise Kavanaugh, smoking nervously, with Dr. Knox
and a big hairy man who did indeed have a big hairy
spider perched on his shoulder. The three of them were
wearing Ralph Lauren casual attire. The large hirsute man
wore a necklace. Its pendant contained the body of a
scorpion entombed for eternity in amber. A string was
tied from the necklace chain at one end around the ab-

domen of the spider at the other end. The spider, which
measured about six inches across, looked distressingly
comfortable.

"Oh, Pete . . ." Louise jumped up to shake his hand.
"Thank God you're here. Is there some place where we
can talk?"

Pete gestured them into the privacy of the conference
room.

"Deputy Bilyeux," Dr. Knox said, "I'd like you to
meet Doctor Abraham Applebaum."

"Uh, g-good to meet you, Doctor." Pete shook the
man's large hand, an appendage that seemed to grow hair
on its knuckles.

"Delighted to meet you, dear boy," Dr. Applebaum
said. He, too, had a speech impediment of sorts. He
lisped rather like Sylvester the Cat in the Looney Tunes
cartoons. Thus was a sort of kinship established with
Pete. "Don't mind Dolores here, she doesn't bite," he
said, gently stroking the hideous spider. "Even if she
did, she's not poisonous. Not to humans, anyhow. She's
of the phylum Arthropoda and eats mostly other arthro-
pods but will not disdain occasional diversity. Flies she
regards as a delicacy much on the order of caviar—that
is, tasty, but not filling. She's more popularly known as
a Mexican red tarantula, which is somewhat misleading.
She's not Mexican, as I found her under a fig tree in
Phoenix. Neither is she precisely red, as you can see,
dear boy." Dolores arched her long hairy legs and
stretched them and responded to Dr. Applebaum's speech
like a cat returning affection. "Even though I'm also an
MD, dear boy, as you see, bugs are my kind of people."

Pete took this to have been a show put on for his benefit, and was amused and smiled at the eccentric fellow
called Anteater Abe. Under other circumstances Pete
would have laughed.

"Can't we take you anywhere, Abe?" Louise said.
"God, bugs are killing people around here."

"Now that is very, very interesting," Entomologist
Applebaum said. "Unprecedented, in fact. I don't suppose you have any of those little devils around. Dear boy,
what's your first name?"

"Pete."

232 STANLEY R. MOORE

"Please call me Abe, Pete."

"I've, uh, g-got some right here," Pete said, and took the jar of flies out of a saddlebag.

"Oh, nummie-num! Will you look at that, Dolores?" Dr. Applebaum clucked. "Four-and-twenty blackbirds baked in a pie."

The entomologist went on to scrutinize the flies, living and dead, and to ask Pete where and under what circumstances he had caught them.

Suddenly Dolores the tarantula, who had been wiggling her long legs and gazing wistfully on the jar full of flies, took it into her head that it was time for a snack. She hopped swiftly onto the fly jar and tried to poke her legs into the air holes.

Dr. Applebaum caught her before a poisonous fly did and picked her up by the abdomen and admonished her. He untied the end of the string from his necklace and, clucking, took the great spider over to the water cooler and tied the string to its spigot.

"As I was saying"—Dr. Applebaum took out a magnifying glass and resumed his inspection of the flies— "you've got at least five species in there. All the dead ones are *Musca domestica,* the common housefly, the species of the feces. I suspect they didn't die of old age."

He explained that most of the rest were of the family Tabanidae. Some were of the genus Tabanus, horse flies. The others were of the genus Chrysops, deer flies. He counted at least two species of these, there being some thirty-five species of Chrysops flies in this part of the country. Of the two, one species was darker and lacked the greenish iridescence of the other. Dr. Applebaum confirmed with all that it had been a greenish fly from which the virulent serum had been brewed. "Good," he lisped, "we've got more females than males."

"How can you tell?" Louise asked.

"By examining their equipment, dear girl, how else?" Abe Applebaum fixed her with a wicked twinkle. "You see, like mosquitoes, the females are the bloodsuckers. The males sup only on nectar."

The entomologist went on to tell everyone a great deal more than anyone wanted to know about the life cycle of

Chrysops flies, about how their habitat is the shade, how the females lay eggs in dank, swampy places, often in pools, where the eggs metamorphose through larval and pupal stages to adulthood. He told of how, once the adult female lays eggs, she has exhausted her bodily proteins. If she is to bear again, she needs the nourishment of more protein. Blood, in a word, about forty milligrams of it, and it matters little where it comes from. She alights on her donor. A pair of razor-sharp minuscule mandibles slice the surface of the skin. A pair of maxillae grind up and down the mandible incision, stimulating the flow of blood. Tiny secretions of a substance like saliva are deposited, with an anticoagulating agent to ensure a continued blood supply. A labium laps it all up. This goes on until the fly is engorged or until the donor shoos it away. Later the donor will have an itchy welt or, as in this event, will lie supine in a coffin.

Abe asked his colleagues if they could get him a Geiger counter and some mice. They went out to the cars to do it.

"Uh, Abe," Pete said, "uh, as I see it there are t-two ways these flies could have become pppoisonous. One, that a species suddenly developed with a powerful toxin, or, two, that they were contaminated by some sssource."

"Two, dear boy," Abe said. "The tabanids have had about two hundred million years, give or take a couple of hundred millennia, to evolve a toxic species. Why should they suddenly do it in one summer?"

Louise and Dr. Knox returned during this. "Do you suppose the source could have been deliberate, Abe?" Louise said. "Like the CIA?" Pete had wondered when she was going to bring up the CIA.

"Not impossible. If any flies could survive a violently toxic agent, it would be the tabanids. To poison them in their habitat you'd have to poison damned near everything else too, humans included. About the only practical way of killing them, other than bashing their little brains out, is to trap and burn them or drown them. Get me a mouse, will you, Louise?"

Abe took out a pair of tweezers and gingerly opened the jar and caught a greenish Chrysops fly and replaced the lid.

Suddenly the fly escaped and flew down toward the carpet.

"Oh, shit," Abe lisped.

"Jesus Christ!" Dr. Knox barked.

Louise gasped.

Pete jumped aside.

The hairy legs of Dolores wriggled gleefully.

Pete was glad, after all, that he had worn his boots. He found a copy of *Sports Illustrated* and rolled it up and got down on his hands and knees to look for the fly. Dr. Knox took off a shoe and did the same. Soon Dr. Applebaum joined them and the three males were crawling on all fours.

Louise gave a shout. "There's the sonofabitch! On the ceiling!" She flourished an expensive shoe in its direction.

At this moment, the sheriff, sweating and rattled from his press conference, opened the door and looked in. " 'Scuse me, folks, everything all right in here?"

Everyone yelled at him to shut the door. He did, behind him.

He was treated to the spectacle of four otherwise dignified people ganging up on a solitary fly, albeit one that might kill everyone in the room. The sheriff's mind did not work rapidly enough to grasp his own danger.

At last the fly was cornered between Pete's magazine and Dr. Knox's shoe. Abe Applebaum made the capture with his tweezers, muttering assurances to the fly that it would be all right. Dolores settled quietly. The sheriff mopped his brow and did not notice her ensconced on the water cooler. But he did feel thirsty.

"Sheriff," Louise said, "are there any CIA or army or government facilities in the county?"

"What?" the sheriff said. Louise repeated the question. "No, ma'am," said Sheriff Cody, looking puzzled.

"Uh, Sheriff, w-w-watch this," Pete said as Abe put the fly in a plastic cage with the mouse. The fly made a beeline for the mouse's rump and settled in. The mouse peeped shrilly and went into the agonies of death.

"Dear Lord," the sheriff said.

"Jesus Christ," said Abe Applebaum, who had never encountered anything like this. Pete idly wondered why some Jewish people invoke the name of the Christian Savior when surprised. "Jesus Christ," Abe repeated, "score one for the Chrysops flies."

"Dear Lord," the sheriff repeated. "I hope you doctors know there's a whole epidermis of that going around."

The doctors looked at one another quizzically.

The sheriff reached without looking in the direction of the water cooler. He felt something tickly on his hand. He looked down and screamed.

His face contorted and he froze in terror as Dolores began to explore his arm.

It was a moment tailor-made for Pete Bilyeux. He had never touched a tarantula before. In fact, he had never seen one except in movies, where they are always deadly poisonous. But, as boys will often do, he had played with daddy longlegs and other spiders as a kid. He took Abe's statement on faith and picked her up gently and untied her from the spigot and returned her to her owner. He poured two cups of water, kept one, and gave the other to the sheriff. "Can I, uh, have a w-w-word with you, Sheriff?"

They went into the hallway and drank their water.

"Land of Goshen," the sheriff said, still recovering. "I don't know what kind of crazy kike homo would keep a pet spider."

"Uh, I w-want to finish this case, Sheriff," Pete said firmly but gently.

The sheriff looked into his eyes for a long time. The old fellow was still perspiring and seemed badly shaken by much more than the tarantula. The skin of his face showed more gray than before and more purple under the eyelid puffs. Pete remembered Ernie Waldwick and worried that the sheriff might be approaching the same kind of thing. But he had to press for the end of the case and cover himself in the process.

"I admire you for it, son," he said at last, "I really do, but after all you've been through . . ." The sheriff shook his head.

Pete wondered if now would be the right time to offer his badge again and started to speak. But the sheriff spoke first and something in his tone told Pete the older man knew he must this time defer to the younger one.

"Son, if it means that much to you, well . . . well, I guess at that you've probably got more poop left in you than I do."

"Thanks, Sheriff. Uh, I'd l-l-like your okay to c-call Charlie Sevenpines in on the case. I'll need him. Uh, uh, according to D-Doctor Applebaum, there's a source, and I'm going straight for it."

"Sure. Sure, go ahead, old son." He took Pete by the shoulders and this time seemed to be using them for support. Pete worried that the sheriff might fall. "Bilyeux," he said, his eyes growing misty, "Bilyeux, all those flies, it could be dangerous, I have to tell you that. It would be a terrible thing if man and wife were both lost."

"I understand, Sheriff," Pete said, and felt a pang for Enid.

"Okay, Bilyeux, old son, go to it. Go anywhere you want. Do anything you want. Take anyone you want. The case is yours, you're in charge. I'm behind you a thousand percent. Go to it. Go get 'em. There are only two things I ask of you."

"Yes, sir?"

"First, be sure to keep me informed. Second, get those goddamm doctors and their filthy bugs out of here as quick as you can."

"Yes, sir."

The sheriff shuffled back toward the desk. Pete felt relieved. He also felt a little guilty and foolish for baiting the sheriff, unwarranted as it now seemed. The confrontation he had mentally rehearsed was anti-climactic, and he discovered a dimension of pity for the older man that he had never felt. But feeling anything made him feel more for Enid. Sensibility betrayed his vulnerability, so he reset his mind as you might the hands of a watch, and returned to the conference room.

"Jesus," Louise said in the direction of the departed sheriff, "talk about dead wood, that guy's a petrified forest."

Pete tactfully invited the doctors to his house, where they were welcome—urged—to spend the duration. The doctors at first insisted they did not wish to impose on his hospitality, but Pete was more insistent that their help was critical to finishing the case and explained he now had carte blanche from the sheriff to do so, and the doctors' visit would be a great convenience. He could sense the doctors felt it would be an outing for them, a welcome break from the routine, a picnic. Anyhow, the doctors insisted on buying the food and wine and earning their keep if they were to be Pete's guests, and Pete agreed to this. For the first time in five days Pete began to feel better about things. The only thing wrong was that Enid was dead. He would not think about her for now.

He got some large-scale Army Corps of Engineers maps and some push-pins from the substation. He made a quick phone call to Charlie Sevenpines in private to advise him to be reachable if he had to call him for a search. Pete explained the business of the flies to Charlie, who lived nearly fifty miles away. Charlie was a bit drunk and thought he was kidding at first. Pete also cautioned Charlie that two of the doctors were male homosexuals and one was a woman, so he knew what to expect. He told Charlie about the tarantula.

"Hey, man," Charlie said, "how about that? Shit, I had a tomatula, tormentula, whaddiyoucallit fall out of a mesquite tree into my coffee cup when I was on location for Mazola in Arizona. Hey, that rhymes, doesn't it? Scared shit out of me, it did. Fished him out with my spoon and put him on the ground. Sonofabitch shook himself like a wet dog and took off hell-bent for election across the desert. But it turns out tomatulas don't bite. Don't like coffee, either. Hey, man, how's our kid doing? The one from the refrigerator?"

It dawned on Pete that nobody had thought to tell Charlie. "He d-d-died, Charlie," Pete said.

There was a pause on the phone. Charlie sounded more sober when he came back on. "Jesus, Pete, I'm sorry, really sorry."

"Right, uh, thanks, Charlie. Mmmmaybe, uh, maybe we can save someone this time around," Pete said.

"Sure, man, sure," Charlie said.

Pete was depressed again as he got on his Suzuki and led the caravan to his house. Louise followed in her

Porsche 944 Turbo. Pete found ironies in how cars reflected personalities. Dr. Knox followed Louise in his staid, impeccable Mercedes Turbodiesel. Dr. Applebaum took up the rear in his eminently roadable BMW, with which he seemed to have difficulty hewing a straight path on the road.

Pete showed them around the house. They murmured the appropriate blandishments for what Pete was sure was the smallest house in which they had ever set foot.

Louise noticed the statue of Quetzalcoatl on the mantelpiece. "What's that?" she said. "It looks positively pre-Columbian."

"Uh, it is," Pete said.

"Yeah, but what is it, Pete? Do you know its story?"

"Uh, yeah, uh, that's Q-Quetzalcoatl, the feathered serpent, a, uh, T-T-Toltec and Aztec g-g-god."

"Oh, really," Louise said, "that's interesting."

"Don't get interested." Pete could not help but say it.

Drs. Knox and Applebaum would conduct experiments in the kitchen. Pete and Louise would shop and gather supplies.

Abe Applebaum enquired of a suitable perch for Dolores, out of sight of the flies on which they would experiment. Pete thought Quetzalcoatl might provide a sturdy anchor and offered to give Dolores a lunch of cheese.

"She disdains dairy products, dear boy," Abe said. "However if have any hamburger, she's fond of steak tartare."

Pete broke up some hamburger and took it with her to the mantel and also took an impish pleasure in tying her to Quetzalcoatl. He was amazed at how docile the ghastly insect was. She ate daintily out of his hand like a parakeet.

Pete asked the doctors if they had any objection to camping out for a night or two if need be, starting tomorrow night.

They looked a little startled.

"Well, dear boy," Abe said, "all three of us have lots of experience in *camping*, if you get my drift."

Pete went to the bedroom phone extension to call Father Fierro in private and asked if his honor the new mayor was still in the business of hearing confession and, if so, could Pete make an appointment with him for later that afternoon?

Mayor Father Fierro avowed that his avocation in no way interfered with his vocation, which was business-as-usual.

Before he left, Pete went over some of his checklist with Dr. Knox. Pete would not need to get Geiger counters. Dr. Knox had brought plenty of them, all hypersensitive ones that gave visual readings. Dr. Kavanaugh had brought many emergency sodium-atropine kits and Dr. Applebaum had brought the best insect repellents. Medical supplies were abundant. Pete would get the other supplies.

Louise drove Pete in her red Porsche Turbo 944, and by the time they reached Elmsford, he had counted seven moving violations against her and was glad they encountered none of his colleagues.

Several times she had tried to manipulate the conversation as she did the car. Each time, he would steer the conversation back to the car. He seemed morose, and her inability to reach him made her all the more interested.

They stopped first at the Elmsford County Sheriff's Headquarters and Pete went in and signed out three snub-nosed .38 Special revolvers, with appropriate dum-dum ammunition. Next they went to a local radio store, where Pete signed vouchers for five of their best multi-channel Citizens' Band walkie-talkies. Pete next guided Louise to a sporting-goods store, where they requisitioned camping supplies. He then directed Louise to the best supermarket.

Louise had prevailed on Pete to ride in her Porsche while she drove, because not entirely by coincidence it showed the profile of her upper body to good advantage. Pete not having risen to the lure, she now prowled the supermarket aisles and gave vent to frustration by grumbling in deprecation of the store's wares. She stalked the meat section and examined the flesh arrayed before her. "Hell," she said, "I've cut better-looking livers than that out of drunks who died of cirrhosis."

Last year's homecoming queen wandered by, pitching free samples of the latest ersatz fruit juice in small Dixie cups. Louise took a cup and sniffed the juice and returned it to the young woman. "Thank you, dear," she said, "but it is my painful duty to inform you that your dog is suffering from kidney necrosis."

She asked a boy with acne if the store had a butcher who would make cuts to order. The boy said they did but it would cost a little more. That would be fine, Louise said, and ordered four cuts of the best filet mignon.

The last stop was a state liquor store, where Louise selected a few bottles of the finest.

Pete had been struggling with himself to be more hospitable. "Uh, Louise," he asked on the way back. "Have you ever been to Jjjoe's restaurant in Reading?"

Louise had nearly given him up for moribund. She pounced on the opportunity. "No. What's it like?"

"Uh, wwwell, it's like expensive. But it's run by mmmmycologists."

"Professional fungi specialists?"

"Uh, more like professional m-mushroom cooks."

"Oh," Louise said, "that's fascinating."

"Uh, are you really interested?"

"Yes," she said, and she really was.

A mile or so down the road, Pete suddenly raised his hand and asked her to stop.

"What's wrong?" she said.

"Nothing," Pete said. "Uh, look over there." He pointed to a dead tree on which grew bulbous lumps of white. "Oyster mushrooms, *Pleurotus ostreatus*," Pete said. "Dddelicious. Are you game?"

Louise said she was and they got out of the car. Pete plucked the mushrooms, more than enough for supper.

Louise was interested. Here was yet more lore owned by the moody policeman whom she found so intriguing.

They arrived back at Pete's house. Pete called through the kitchen door. Drs. Applebaum and Knox had not yet concluded their experiments. They would be another hour or so. Pete and Louise unloaded the Porsche through the front door, and Pete asked her to excuse him while he rode his Suzuki into town for confession. Louise asked to go along, not to confession but to town. She would take in the sights of the embattled hamlet until he was done. She won her point by offering to let Pete drive the Porsche.

Pete had never driven a Porsche and had always wanted to. He quickly fell in love with the nimble little car. It managed to give him the feeling of flying in a fighter plane. It quickened his pulse and, though he would never know it, kept his heart beating.

Part Three

FROM THURSDAY TO THE SECOND SATURDAY

*If it be now, 'tis not to come; if it be not to come,
it will be now; if it be not now, yet it will come:
the readiness is all.*

21

Butterball cursed the discomfort.

They didn't know how much the stuttering cop knew or how much he had set in motion or how many other people knew anything, but he was just too damned persistent and getting too damned close, and the word had come down to buy time no matter what. The cop hadn't heeded Butterball's fair warnings. He had been given all he would get.

They would not kill him in uniform. They would do it when he was off duty and deposit a waterproof canister of heroin in his motorcycle fuel tank so people would know what it was about.

Butterball's belly itched as he lay on it and took off his sunglasses and wiped them and blinked at the bright afternoon light that hurt his eyes. Butterball congratulated himself on the discovery made years before of such sunglasses, the kind that look like mirrors to the fretful seen, but shield the sensitive eyes of the unseen viewer. They made Butterball enigmatic and he liked the feeling this gave him.

He congratulated himself, too, on having chosen another and even better patch of woods, impassable except on foot. The stuttering cop would be less likely to be wary of it. They would wait there until hell froze if need be.

He heard the rapping of a small engine coming from the direction of the cop's house.

"Off safe," Butterball told the team, and heard the safety catches of the Weatherbys clicking. "Fire on command."

The marksmen peered through the telescopic sights.

Butterball sensed something wrong. The sound was too

throaty. Still, he waited at the ready. Then a red Porsche swept into view. He could see a pair in silhouette behind tinted glass. Probably yuppies who had got lost. "On safe," he said. "Shit."

Pete made a confession more riven by violent emotion than he thought he had. He was given a token penance.

"You're going after them, aren't you?" said Father Fierro. "Any idea who they might be?"

"They?" Pete said. "You, uh, you're assuming this was, uh, c-caused by people, Father."

"My business isn't that much different from yours, Pete. You see a lot of things you don't want to," the priest said. "It had to be caused by people. It's not God's way. The world's problems are more often due to rotten people than rotten luck. We often make the mistake of believing God and His gifts are the servants of man, a little like a postman bearing goods that are chronically late. But you haven't answered my question. You're going after them, right?"

"Yes," Pete said.

"And you're afraid you might be killed?"

"I'm, uh, afraid, yes. Bbbut I don't think it's all that, uh, likely. I'm careful."

"I'm doing my part, you know, Pete." The priest's chest swelled a little. "As mayor."

The confession had bled Pete of some of the ugliness of his melancholy and he was able to get in a friendly joke with a hint of twinkle in his eye. "What does the, uh, Pope think of that?"

"Well, it's purely an emergency thing, you know. I have no intention of being political or running for election. You could call that a conflict of interest. Besides, what the Pope doesn't know won't hurt him."

Louise Kavanaugh was not nearly the snob she pretended to be when in a snit. She found the little town charming, if mostly deserted. It had a restful quality to it, a feeling of continuity and the preservation of human stability. It was quite turn-of-the-century, with quarried facades and cornerstones marked 1887, 1893, 1904, and Victorian houses with transoms and bathroom windows of stained glass. It was not the least pretentious, having lain undiscovered by the chic, who would have made it as insufferable as New Hope. Thomas Valley was the kind of place for which people yearned when they thought of how life was lived when things were normal. But on this day, Louise was careful to stay in the sun.

Pete seemed much more himself to her when he came back to the car. She suspected his confession was a kind of emotional catharsis. She wondered what could have been troubling him.

Dr. Abraham Applebaum was all adither poring over the notes he had taken and a couple of large volumes he had brought along. Dr. Knox looked tired as he sat at the kitchen table drinking a Scotch-and-soda.

"I put all the dead mice in the garbage, Pete, dear boy," the entomologist said. "I hope that's all right?"

"Sure," Pete said, and made a mental note to take the garbage out to the street soon.

"Well," Abe said, "there's no question about it. Many, but not all, of the female greenish Chrysops are toxic. And that's the extent of what we know."

Louise and Dr. Knox began to make supper. Abe went into the garage with Pete, where they taped on a wall conjoining maps from the Army Corps of Engineers, which were highly detailed.

Pete scanned the maps to refresh his memory of marshes or places where moisture might collect in the shade, where Abe had said the Chrysops flies bred. He began to jab push-pins into death spots on the maps. "Uh, how fly do they far—excuse me, how fffar do they fly, Abe?"

"Depends on how far they have to look for blood, Pete, and how long they live. The best extrapolation of a female Chrysops' life in the wild is about six weeks . . . Jesus Christ, some of those pins are nearly fifty kilometers apart."

"Yeah," Pete said. "Uh, but how far do C-Chrysops fly?"

"Jesus," Abe said, and there was no longer anything funny about his demeanor. "Jesus Christ! My God, nobody thinks they go more than ten kilometers—fifteen on the outside, depending on winds. Oh, my God, they can't be laying eggs in different places and breeding the poison into succeeding generations. My God, at that rate they could be in Pittsburgh and Columbus and Philadelphia and even New York by autumn. Jesus! No, it's impossible. But then so's the whole damned thing, isn't it?''

Dr. Knox came into the garage puffing his pipe and wearing a stern expression. "Excuse me, gentlemen," he said. "Doctor Kavanaugh has asked me to invite you to a sumptuous repast that she insists is growing cold to the point of rigor even as we speak. And if you tarry further, the good doctor threatens to fly either into a rage or a deluge of tears."

"Well," Abe said, putting on his funny face again, "we can't let that happen, dear boy. We must be chivalrous."

Nobody was very hungry.

Pete felt a little sorry for Louise, surrounded and harried by three men, even if two were homosexual and one newly asexual.

But Louise bullied them in return and everyone had as pleasant a dinner as possible. Pete liked the wine and thought the oyster mushrooms went well with the steaks. So did Drs. Applebaum and Knox until they learned the mushrooms had been picked wild. Pete could see their minds trying to forecast the toxic possibilities. Louise suggested that Pete mention Joe's wonderful mushroom restaurant in Reading. Drs. Knox and Applebaum had both been to Joe's and had been impressed and now were reassured, mostly. They still left the remainder of the oyster mushrooms to Pete and Louise, which was fine with them.

"Mmmm," Louise said of them, "they even taste a little like oysters. More chewy, though. Delicious."

Louise broke out a bottle of Grand Marnier and all sipped the expensive potation while Pete explained his plans. They would have breakfast and pack and leave at first light.

Pete phoned Charlie Sevenpines and asked Charlie to meet them at his house at dawn or at the ruins of the Mueller house a little after if Charlie wanted to sleep in. The Mueller house lay near the geographical center of the fly killings marked on the maps in the garage. They would park the cars there and then walk. The house was on high ground and afforded a good view.

Each of the five, including Charlie Sevenpines, would be assigned a single map adjoining another. Each would have a walkie-talkie and a plan was devised for rotating channels on a random basis. Each would relay radio messages so they could cover a lateral swath of some thirty miles if need be. Channel 9 was to be used for emergencies only. The breaker call for emergency would be the traditional "Mayday." Each would carry a Geiger counter. They would probe the western sectors first, where most of the deaths had occurred. Each would walk by breadth the north-south salients of the sectors to determine the places of highest background radiation. They would follow the radiation—on a zigzag course, if need be—until it grew more intense or petered out. The western segment should be finished no later than Saturday night, when they would meet near the end of it at the Sunset Motel if unsuccessful. They would then take a cab to Pete's house and start on the eastern segment Sunday morning. No attempt would be made to destroy the source or sources, as they lacked the means. Once discovered, Dr. Applebaum would advise the sheriff's department how to do it. No provision was made for a plan that failed.

Dr. Knox advised them of Geiger readings that would be significant. Pete offered a pistol to each of them, with an extra ten rounds of ammunition to carry in their pockets. He himself would walk the center, where the most push-pins showed. He would carry his Python .357 Magnum.

The doctors, to a person, objected only to the pistols.

Pete told them of the motorcycles and the maroon Cadillac that had followed him, and of the shots fired at him that morning.

The male doctors agreed to carry the revolvers. Louise despised guns and required more persuasion. She might be raped, the men told her. The man had not been born who could rape Louise without losing his rapier, she retorted. No one disputed her. She might get shot, all alone and powerless to help herself in the wilderness. She might be humiliated as well as debilitated. She agreed to carry the pistol, tucked away and unloaded.

Pete gave them a short lesson in how to use the guns and how to avoid shooting themselves accidentally.

The Grand Marnier was finished and most were drowsy and ready for bed on this wearying Thursday night. Dr. Knox would use the small guest room with the small single bed. Dr. Applebaum would stretch his ample form on the commodious living-room couch, close to Dolores, perched on Quetzalcoatl on the mantel. Pete would sleep on a cot close to the kitchen phone.

Louise poured herself a nightcap and went into the main bedroom, where she was assigned to sleep, and shut the door and unpacked her personal things. She undressed and changed into a nightgown that showed her to good advantage, just in case. She looked for places to put her things. By mistake, she opened Pete's chest of drawers first, instead of the other, empty one. One compartment held socks and handkerchiefs. The other had mementos and pictures. The picture lying on top was of Pete posing in swim trunks with a girlish woman of stunning beauty wearing a bikini. Mmm, Louise thought, this guy has good taste. Either that or this knockout was his sister. The hair coloring was much alike. On the bottom of the photo was written "Enid and Pete at Cape May." It was dated four years before.

Pete called the desk. Nobody had been killed by the flies all day. The defenses were working. Pete prayed they would continue to work until the source was destroyed. He lay on the cot and thought for a long time and finally slept.

Louise did not sleep well. Lying in this man's bed only reawakened the feeling she was developing for him. She felt aroused and toyed with the idea of waiting until late in the night and finding some pretext to go into the kitchen. This made her heart beat harder as she calculated and abandoned sundry ploys. At last sleep came.

Later she awoke to a soft knocking on a door. Was it him? Maybe she didn't need a reason to go into the kitchen. Maybe he felt something for her.

As sleep will often do, it came first on a tide that engulfed Peter Bilyeux and bore him along its currents. The

wave receded, leaving him as on a beach of wet sand
waiting for the next wave to come, conscious of scurrying
crabs. Then he heard a small noise and wondered if Enid
had got up in the night. But, no, Enid was dead. The
noise was someone knocking on a bedroom door.

Small sounds carried far in the little house. Through
the louvered kitchen door, Pete could hear them.

Through the bedroom wall, Louise could hear them
too.

Someone got up to answer the knock. A door was
opened.

"Hi, Freddie," Dr. Applebaum whispered. "I've been
thinking about you."

"Jesus Christ," Dr. Knox whispered, "you're incor-
rigible."

"Everybody's asleep," Dr. Applebaum whispered.
"Everybody. And I can't sleep for thinking about you."

"Goddammit, Abe," Dr. Knox whispered. "We're
guests here. This isn't a motel."

"Don't be such a prude, Freddie. Louise and Pete are
probably at it right now. God, not even straights have
your inhibitions."

"I thought you said everybody was asleep," Dr. Knox
hissed.

"Ooooh, Freddie . . ." Abe said. "I can't sleep."

"Oh, for heaven's sake, be quiet and at least let *me*
sleep. Some time when we're alone, maybe." Dr. Knox
clicked the door closed and trudged back to his bed.

"Promises, promises," Abe muttered through the
closed door, and stumbled back to the couch, the springs
of which protested his bulk being cast dejectedly upon
them.

Pete was amused and relieved it was not something
terrible.

Louise doubled up in the fetal position and clutched
her waist with one hand and bit the thumbnail of the other
to keep from laughing, the proverbial fly on the wall.
Freddie was right, of course. It would be best to wait
until they were alone.

Adair Godwin pulled into the Sunset Motel feeling
tired, and was surprised to see few cars in the lot and no

activity outside the bar that was the local upmarket hang-out. He wondered if the place was closed. He locked the Galaxie and picked up a few things and strode into the lobby.

Some people were in the lobby holding drinks from the bar and talking excitedly. Adair worried about their reaction to his bandages.

One man noticed him immediately and raised his index finger and pointed at Adair. "Now *there's* a guy with the right idea," the man said to his companions. The man got up and walked to Adair and put out his hand. "Friend," the fellow said to him, "we been wearing bee masks, mosquito netting, all kinds of insect repellents, and every other fucking thing, but nobody—I mean, *no-body*—has had the smarts to do it your way."

Adair would not have been Adair had he not been adroit. He was puzzled, but heard the man out and asked questions in such a way to get information without ex-posing his ignorance.

Adair was so aghast to hear it that he felt faint. Flies! God, he thought, flies! How perfect. How satanic.

He knew it had to be true. The other people in the lobby were all talking about it. So was the clerk when he checked into the motel and paid in advance. He went to his room and brooded. Through the window he saw the moon peep 'round in a gap in the foliage of trees. He thought about the flies and the timing and felt a chill. The full moon would set at 11:59 on Saturday. That gave him fewer than thirty-six hours.

He walked to the terrace. The ends of the sliding glass door were covered with duct tape. Taped to the glass was a hastily photocopied sign, reading *(sic):* "Danger. Do not remove tape or open door until emergensy is done. The Management."

Adair tore off the tape and opened the door and walked out on the terrace and looked down at the lights of the traffic on the interstate far below. Several flies landed on him. He brushed them away and others took their places. They were aggressive. He went back inside and shut the door. Three flies came in with him. He went into the bathroom and turned on the fluorescent light and looked in the mirror. One fly was burrowing on the bandage on

his face. Lots of luck, fly, he thought. Another was on his
chest. Deftly, he caught this fly with a gloved hand and
held it up to the light. It was bigger than most flies and its
body had a greenish cast. He went into the room and dug
the Gideon Bible out of a drawer and with a loud slapping
crushed the fly between the pages of the Book of Reve-
lations. Then he killed the other two.

Oh, God, it's true, he thought. There could be nothing
happenstance about all this. The flies were proof, colored
as they were like quetzals. Hell was afoot. Adair must
root out the heart of evil in the heart of life.

22

Pete woke well before dawn and made plenty of espresso
and poured much of it into thermos jugs. He refreshed
himself and dressed as he had the morning before and
woke the doctors.

They ate hastily and drank espresso. They washed up,
then packed everything into Dr. Applebaum's BMW. As
an afterthought, Pete ran to a closet and got the pair of
Japanese binoculars he had won in a poker game in
Vietnam. Likewise, Abe decided to bring Dolores. "She
hasn't been out in the country for a long time," he said.
"Besides, who'll be around to feed her?"

Charlie didn't arrive, so they left. Pete sat next to Abe,
the better to help keep him on the road.

Uncharacteristically, Charlie Sevenpines overslept.
When he sensed the first signs of light come into the
room, he cursed aloud through his hangover. His wife
swatted at him and rolled over in her sleep. He gathered
his equipment and dashed for his motorcycle. On the
highway, he shifted at the peak of the tachometer into

fifth gear and raced toward Pete's house with the accelerator full on.

Adair Godwin also overslept. Jet lag, his health, and angry grief had turned a nap into sleep. He was furious with himself, but it was longer than he had slept in years and he could feel some of the old strength returning. He got up and got his things and stole a sheet from the bed and rushed to the Rent-A-Wreck car.

He gunned the Galaxie at top speed toward the turnoff to the house where Enid had lived with Peter. He could not bear to go to the house itself. He would lie on the sheet and wait in a woods until he saw Peter come out.

Charlie Sevenpines took a shortcut and went overland the back way to Pete's house. Noticing a Porsche and Mercedes in front, he stopped the bike and knocked loudly on the door and called inside. There was no response. Charlie walked around and noticed the fresh tire marks of a foreign car driving away from the house. Pete and his friends must have left in it. Charlie jumped back on the cycle and kicked the engine to life and followed the tracks.

Butterball was first to hear the sound of the two-stroke motorcycle rapping down the road from the stuttering cop's house. He had lain with his belly pressed against the bugs and the worms and such crap on the cold ground all night. That was long enough.

"Hey, guys," he said. "Wake up. Off safe. Let's nail the mother. Here he comes."

Charlie's motorcycle sped into view.

"Fire," Butterball said.

Charlie disdained the corner and its stop sign and cut the corner short, going overland to the paved road.

Crack-crack!

The .300 Weatherby Magnum bullets bored into the place where Charlie should have been but was not.

This did not escape Charlie's notice. Sioux-fashion, he took a foot off the peg and threw himself to the far side of his motorcycle and raced the thing, wobbling wildly, as a warrior of old protecting himself with the body of his pony.

The men in the woods frantically pulled the bolts of their rifles back to eject the empty cartridges and slam fresh ones into the chambers. The cheek rests of the expensive rifles found their homes. The cross hairs of the telescopic sights danced and sought for the hit that would not give them more than a second before vanishing behind an embankment.

"Good morning, gentlemen," a hoarse voice behind them said.

The men turned to confront the voice. They saw nothing but a couple of flashes of startling white through the dim green jungle of woods. "Think fast," the voice said as a white object hurtled toward them.

Butterball jerked the muzzle of his submachine gun toward it. This gun, a 9-millimeter Uzi, was an Israeli model and a paragon of gunsmithery. It is quite small, considering the number of bullets it can spew forth in the bat of an eye. It is a machine pistol, actually, easily secreted on the person and used by the U.S. Secret Service. "Hey, you!" Butterball called. "You're under arrest! Put your fucking hands up or I'll shoot!"

The woods echoed with hoarse laughter.

Butterball started to squeeze down on the trigger, then thought better of it. There was no target. He and the men began to trot toward where the voice had been.

The white thing was a sheet that lay rolled in a cylinder.

"Open it," Butterball said.

A man unrolled it and out flew a swarm of green Chrysops flies. "Get back, goddammit!" Butterball yelled.

The flies flitted around them and would have attacked but for the insect repellent they wore.

Butterball and the men ran for the clearing where they had left their motorcycles strapped on the bed of a pickup truck. In the distance, Butterball saw a man with white over his head run from the truck into the woods where he vanished out of sight.

Butterball started the engine of the truck to drive out. The engine caught but the steering wheel was too hard to turn. He let the truck idle and set the brake and got out. The valves of all four tires had been slashed off, flattening them. Okay, Butterball thought, they'd get the bikes off the truck and ride this bastard down for it. But the motorcycle tires were also flat. This displeased Butterball greatly. He would have to walk.

"Hey, whitey!" Butterball yelled toward the vanished white head. "I'm going to cut your fucking heart out for this!"

From the depth of the woods came peals of laughter that built to a pitch even Butterball thought demonic.

Adair was sweating in the morning chill when he reached the Galaxie. He sped for the road and glimpsed a motorcycle miles ahead of him. Surely Peter must be on it. Soon it disappeared from view. It could only have turned off on a dirt road but there were many of these and Adair spent wasteful hours searching them until he found one with newly laid motorcycle tracks. Following these tracks to their destination took hours more, desperate hours.

The BMW pulled up to the ruins of the Mueller house and its inhabitants got out and prepared for their trek.

Pete pointed out the various landmarks and strategy was discussed and maps distributed and CB radio handles assigned. The handle for Abe Applebaum came naturally. Abe nominated Hot Paws to be the handle for Dr. Knox, who dealt with things radioactive. Dr. Knox went along with this as a lark. In keeping with her profession and her good looks, Abe suggested for Louise the handle of Dream Ghoul.

"That's demeaning," Louise shot back at him.

After some badinage, forced hard in face of a natural dread felt by all, the handle chosen for Louise was Muffet—short for Little Miss Muffet, who shared her aversion to such as Dolores.

As the handle was being chosen for Pete, they heard the sound of a two-stroke motorcycle rushing up the dirt road.

A harried-looking Charlie Sevenpines arrived. Introductions were made. Charlie drew Pete aside. "Hey, man," he said, "somebody took some shots at me when

I was leaving your place. I think they thought I was you. Is somebody after your ass, man?''

"Uh, I-looks like it, doesn't it?'' Pete said.

"Who? Why?''

"Uh, beats me,'' Pete said. "But I think we may find out soon. Do you have a gggun, Charlie?''

Charlie pulled a Walther PPK out of his pocket. "Just like James Bond,'' he said.

They went back to the group. Dr. Knox showed Charlie how to use his Geiger counter. Pete's handle would be Bloodhound and Charlie's would be Mazola.

Geiger readings from the hilltop showed only normal background radiation, with minuscule variations depending on direction. It was time to set out.

Each walked separate ways down the hill and soon all were lost from sight of one another. The morning passed and Pete began to have difficulty receiving Dr. Applebaum on his extreme left and Charlie on his extreme right.

Suddenly a call came in from Louise, who had last reported being about three miles to Pete's right. "Breaker, breaker, Muffet to Bloodhound, I've got a reading!''

She said she had been following a stream bed in the shade and suddenly the Geiger needle jumped. It turned out the source was no fixed location but a solitary fly. It started to land on Louise but was rebuffed by her insect repellent. As the fly left, so did the Geiger reading.

Pete relayed her report up and down the line and cautioned all to renew their insect repellents more often as they became sweaty. It was not long before all reported similar experiences.

When Adair got to the Mueller house, he was surprised to see it gone and even more surprised to see an expensive piece of new automotive hardware parked and locked with a motorcycle nearby. He tried to remember what kind of motorcycle Peter rode, but surely this must be it.

A party of several people—Adair could not tell precisely how many—had spread itself fanwise in a general westerly direction.

His heart sank at the bleak prospect of finding Peter in time. He ran to the edge of the hilltop and looked out, shielding his eyes from the sun. At last he picked out two small figures on foot miles to the west. He trotted along the highest ground.

"Breaker, breaker, Hot Paws to Bloodhound. Anteater reports a big nest of Chrysops in a swamp but Geiger readings negative. Dolores ate one before he could stop her and nothing happened."

"Bloodhound to Hot P-Paws, ten-four. Ask, uh, Anteater to mark the find on his map. We'll, uh, get back to it if we have to. The same goes for you and, uh, M-M-Muffet. Uh, Muffet, copy?"

"Ten-four," Louise said. "I'll call Mazola and tell him."

Dr. Knox relayed the word to Abe.

"Uh, Muffet to Bloodhound. Mazola says he's already found two nests. Negative radiation. He's marked the spots."

"Uh, ten-four," Pete said. "Uh, that's vvvery good, everybody. Please tell 'em to keep up the good work."

The ominous solitude of the day worked differently on each of the searchers.

Dr. Abraham Applebaum, professional entomologist, could not let the others see that the zoological anomaly of flies that could kill distressed him deeply—as, he thought, postal people must have felt on the discovery of the first letter bomb. Typically, he fought his uneasiness with folly, singing to Dolores such songs as "La Cucaracha" and holding forth to her in monologue.

"Dolores," he said, "have I ever told you of my distaste for euphemisms, dear girl? For example, take the word 'gay.' Being gay, I'm supposed to salute the word when it's run up the flagpole, so to speak. Well, it's certainly a term preferable to 'homosexual,' which sounds frightfully clinical. Yet gay is a corruption of a perfectly fine word, a word that used to mean happy, joyous, a sentiment everyone could own. I suggest in the alternative the coinage of a term that is neither clinical nor does it steal. How does that strike you, Dolores?"

It did not strike Dolores at all.

Dr. Frederick Knox was uneasy too. He carried two pipes and plenty of tobacco in his backpack. As soon as he finished one pipe, he would stoke and light the other.

It was wrong. It was ridiculous that flies could be radio-active and kill. It was unscientific. But, damm it, it was fact, and Fred Knox was a man who respected facts above all else. This fact made him anxious to a high degree, although he was careful not to show it to the others. He was a moderate man. And there was nothing moderate about skulking around swamps looking for hot flies and ruining his two-hundred-dollar Church's shoes. He knew he was jumpy and irritation at this knowledge made him more so. He would as soon be ambling through Central Park in New York late at night.

Charlie Sevenpines was irked, but it could not be said he was the jumpy sort. The doctors annoyed him. Their cars annoyed him. Their fancy-pants Ralph Lauren clothes annoyed him. They didn't even carry wallets in their back pockets, the better to show off their butts, as if anyone cared. The only redeeming thing about any of them was that ludicrous bigass spider hopping around the ugly doctor's head. But he tried to be tolerant. He had generations of tolerating such weirdos behind him. Mazola Corn Oil, indeed. But what the hell, they paid their bills. These people don't believe the earth has a soul. Pete came the closest to it of any of his kind. But then look at the damned fool, traipsing into that old house infested with the echoes of all sorts of nightmarish do-ings, just asking for trouble. Now the chickens of all these jokers were coming home to roost. The spirit of the earth was outraged. Charlie knew that could be the only cause and knew he would be honor-bound to help tidy up the mess.

Louise was downright scared and had the good sense to know it. The whole thing was crazy. The thing with Roger was crazy. The things that happened after Roger were crazy. Flies causing cardiac arrest were crazy. Un-identifiable toxins were crazy. Radioactive bugs were crazy. And the shady places in this demiworld were crazy as living hell. The place was alive with big mean birds that shrieked at you out of the tenebrosity. Other animals dashed from bush to bush before your eye, surprising you no less than a leopard that jumped out of a tree onto your neck. She didn't know what half these damned animals were. There was a thing that wobbled in the weeds like a huge furry rat. At least it wasn't a snake. Then there was this other big rat kind of thing that plopped into the water and paddled off like a crocodile when you didn't even know it was around. Then there was this huge cat with no tail that streaked from out of nowhere and paused to hiss at her. She even thought of pulling out the gun and brandishing it at this obnoxious cat. But the thing slunk away. And then there were the growls and crashing of fat feet on leaves and twigs. Louise did not even wish to contemplate the creature that might make such a ruckus. Whenever she saw a rabbit or a squirrel, she blessed God and thought of returning to the Church. But she would keep on. If the men could do it, she could do it.

With much relief, she noticed a sylvan hollow she had been following begin to peter out up a hill that she had no choice but to climb. She reminded herself of her mission and looked down at the Geiger counter. The needle, too, had begun to climb. There were no flies around. She had got the first faint blip from the source.

Pete's mood was dark enough without needing exacerbation. He too knew he was a little frightened. But he also knew the value of being a plodder. Prepare for the worst and hope for the best, he always thought. If it be not now, yet it will come, Shakespeare had written. Now the worst had come. Enid was dead. But now, too, he was in the business of saving the living, not grieving the dead. Let the dead bury the dead, Jesus had said. Oh, Enid, Enid, you can't really be dead, it has to be some mistake. Stop it, Peter, he thought, stop it. His head ached again and he found he was developing a nervous tic in his right eye. This comes from internal conflict, he had read, and did not doubt it.

He let himself feel the beauty that struck his senses. As Friday's shadows grew longer, he drank in the glory of subfusc sights and the tintinnabulation of tiny sounds: the warning cries of animals, the blur of pristine beasts dashing from the intrusion into their homes, the droning of insects, the leaping of trout, the woodchuck's drudging gait, the muskrat's splashing, the chittering of raccoons, the throaty gasps and crashing feet of frightened black bears, even the dartings of flying Chrsyops and the writhing of their young, the pupae, in turbid waters. He came

to pity their venomous cousins, benighted creatures who
continued to do the work assigned to them by nature,
now perverted by the hand of something.

Pete was forced to walk to higher ground on a hillside
covered with day lilies, sunflowers, and Queen Anne's
lace. The natural fought the unnatural in his mind, and
so he brooded climbing the hill and failed to discover
two new things: one was the new reading on his Geiger
counter; the other was that he had been at last discovered
by Adair Godwin.

"Breaker, breaker, Muffet to Bloodhound, I've got a
humongous new meter reading on a ridge, coordinates
seventy-nine north and thirty-six west."

Pete looked at his Geiger counter. God, he thought,
we're about a mile away and my meter's climbing too.
By direct call and relay he reported this news to all. None
of the other men had got any significant variations in
reading. "Uh, g-gentlemen," Pete said, "I suggest you
move to higher ground while you can still see, then take
readings toward the center. Muffet, we'd better meet."

Night fell as Pete and Louise and Adair groped their
way toward one another.

23

The two silhouettes on the ridge saw each other by the
indigo afterglow of a dead sun in a night yet moonless.
They waved.

"Hi, Pete," Louise said, trying to sound casual as
they came together. "We've got to stop meeting like this.
Remember to renew your insect repellent?"

"Uh, yeah," Pete said. "How are you ddoing?"

"Oh," Louise said, not quite knowing what to say,
"oh, as well as can be expected. A little weary." She
brushed her hair from her eyes and felt her face strained

and was glad he could not see it in the dark. "How are you?"

"I'm, uh, fine, thanks. Uh, I think we ought to get off this ridge, though." He pointed out that if the people who had shot at him were around, they would make fine targets on the ridge, especially when they cooked.

This was all right with Louise.

They agreed to descend into a dense woods on the far side of the ridge to make camp. This woods lay in the extreme southern tip of Jacob Walz State Park. They found their way in the dark rather than display any kind of light until they were well into thick cover. Pete held Louise's hand and led the way. He radioed the others to report their positions. Dr. Applebaum was closing toward Dr. Knox's position and the two would camp together for the night. Charlie reported that he was neither tired nor hungry nor lonely. He would snoop around with his Geiger counter and flashlight and go to sleep in a tree when he got tired. He would not stray out of radio range but asked not to be called until morning unless there was an emergency, as he was getting sick of radio conversations.

Louise gripped Pete's hand tightly and they made their way deep into the bosom of the woods without incident. Pete discreetly inquired if she wished to pitch adjacent tents or create a single adjoining one. It did not really matter, as the tents were rudimentary ones of heavy clear plastic with provisions to permit the passage of air but not rain or insects. Louise said she did not mind a single large tent. It seemed more practical. She got out her tent for him to use. Pete strung a short rope between trees to act as a roof beam and created one large tent from his and hers as Louise bathed her feet in a nearby brook.

Pete set up his tiny cook stove to prepare supper in a place where the glow would be so sheltered it could not be detected beyond a few yards. He opened a large collapsible water drum and gathered brook water that he set to boil. He gathered leaves and evergreen needles to sit on while they ate. "Louise, uh, the mmmenu is simple. Uh, Sky-Lab Salisbury steak with mushroom sauce or, uh, Sky-Lab sweet-and-sour pork. What's your choice?"

"I'll take the sweet-and-sour pork if you let me have a bite of your steak," she said.

"And vice versa?" Pete said.

"Why not?" Louise said. "Do you want to open the wine?"

Pete chuckled courteously, thinking she was kidding. She was not. Under her feet in the brook she was cooling a bottle of chablis, a Bougros Grand Cru 1984, to serve as an aperitif. Still in her pack was a bottle of bordeaux, a Château Liversan Haut-Médoc, vintage 1982, a fine year. They would drink it later. She had a corkscrew too.

Pete dropped the plastic packets of food into the boiling water and looked at his watch. He opened the Bougros and poured and they clinked collapsible cups to good health.

They chatted and told stories and drank the good chablis. The food was cooked and Pete served it on camp plates. They finished the chablis and Pete opened the bordeaux while the food was cooling. Louise tasted her sweet-and-sour pork and pronounced it better than airline food and offered Pete a bite to nibble from her fork. He gave her a piece of Salisbury steak from his own fork. She sipped some wine and licked her lips and reached out for the steak with her tongue thrust between parted moist lips and teeth that glistened in the soft light of the camp stove. It began to dawn on Pete that he was being seduced. He did not know what to do about it. He had not been with another woman since he and Enid had first made love, and had not wanted to. He drank more wine and ate and tried to think. He could cut off Louise and make her feel foolish. He could explain what had happened and be treated to the pity he dreaded. He supposed it was inevitable that he would have to do it some time. And he liked her. But he was confused. When they finished eating, he took the plastic food containers and the metal utensils to the brook to wash.

"You don't have to do the dishes," she said, chuckling.

Pete explained it was best to clean away food odors and residues because of curious animals.

She had been lying on her side, relaxing on a clump

of leaves and needles, the smell of which she professed to like. "Animals?" she said, and sat up.

Pete explained the animals were not dangerous but pesky. If they smelled food, they sometimes tore things up or soiled them while you were asleep. He omitted mention of bears.

Suddenly a chirping, clattering sound pierced the darkness. Louise clutched her shoulders with her opposite hands as if she were bare-breasted. "What's that?" she said. The noise sounded to her like a doorman's shrill taxi whistle played on a tape recorder with the batteries run down.

"Oh, uh, that's jjust a mother raccoon. It's, uh, the way they call their babies or warn them of danger."

"Are there raccoons around?" Louise asked.

"Yeah, sure."

"Do they bite?"

"Uh, n-n-not unless you try to grab them."

"Oh. Don't go far away, please," Louise said—meaning, Come here with me, please.

Pete sat down next to her and poured more bordeaux for both.

A screech startled the night and Louise jumped up and spilled wine on herself. Pete blotted it up with his handkerchief.

"What was that?" Louise said.

"Uh, an owl. That's likely to go on all night."

"Oh. How do you know all these things?" she said.

"Uh, I, uh, imagine there are lllots of things you know about that I don't," Pete said. "B-but the animals are simple. In a way I'm, uh, lucky to have lived most of my life in a sort of island where things are pretty simple in a w-world that's not so simple anymore. How about you?"

Louise tossed her mane of hair. "Join the club, pal," she said. She touched his arm as she lay on her side. They sipped wine. "I'm sorry," she said. "I didn't mean to be flippant. I guess you must have thought I was a bitch when we first met."

"I've, uh, met worse. I'm a cop."

Louise slapped his face playfully. "I'll choose to take that as a compliment," she said. They sipped more wine in the glow of the tiny stove as they lay on the leaves. She tossed her head again. "What do you really think of me, Pete?"

"I like you, L-Louise. I like you . . . I, uh, I, uh . . . It's j-j-just, uh, well, my uh . . . Well, I hope I haven't been bbbitchy with you." It all had trouble getting out, as usual.

"Just a little, but that's all right," she said, and reached to his face with her hand and stroked his eyebrows. He seemed shy at first, but he let her keep it up. Louise knew she had the bout won, and at the same time she began to think of it as more than a simple contest. Then she remembered Roger and her better judgment prevailed. She held Pete by the back of the head and pulled him toward her to kiss.

Pete dutifully did his best to kiss her well, since he knew it was expected of him. He felt a strong feeling, strong enough, but his other feelings raveled in his mind. His emotions were all ajumble. And he knew she could count a score of lovers for each of his, which made him a little frightened in addition to all else. And he was not of her social rank, which made him feel stupid. But, then, everything made Pete feel stupid. Yes, this was a thing that was expected of him and Pete knew he was a fool for what was expected of him and it would probably kill him someday. Yet he liked her regardless of her bluster and knew the doing of it would not be nearly as painful with her as with some honky-tonk angel he might pick up to slake some future lonely craving.

They undressed and murmured soft things to each other and scented the fecund damp earth and fragrant leaves. They made love.

Louise stroked his hair and moved sensuously. "Mmmmm, you're a pretty good lover . . . for a cop," she said, and laughed and nibbled his ear. Soon the lovemaking grew more intense and they both broke out in small beads of sweat against the cool of the naked dark night. Pete sensed Louise arriving at her moment and gently brought it on.

She held his back and drew it toward her. Her voice gave modest notice of a moment such as she had not had since last she was in love.

Finished for now, she rolled the two on their sides and kissed him long and deeply. A little embarrassed and fearful of being a fool again, she slapped him gently on the buttocks. "Hey, you're really all right, pal. My turn to get on top. Okay?"

"Uh, have you ever met Reed Hamilton?" Pete said.

"Who?" Louise said.

Pete didn't really know what to say or do. It was just a notion that flitted into his head, that two such expert seducers should someday shake hands, as it were. Then he felt guilty for the sarcasm. "You're wonderful," he said to assuage any possible insult. Loving her was good but it sickened him because of Enid. "Uh, sure, get on t-top. I d-did the dishes, you do the work."

Louise laughed and slapped him on the behind again.

They rolled over locked together. One more time, she thought, one more and then my friend down here is going to spend himself silly on my expense account. He's okay, though, really okay. Doesn't grunt, doesn't hurt, doesn't say filthy things. He's gentle and thoughtful, not bad at all.

She let her hair fall over his face and the tips of her breasts caress his chest and soon came to another moment. He invigorated her. Rarely had she felt less inhibited. Yet another moment came to Louise, and another after that, until she felt as if she were swimming in a warm spa. Enough, Louise thought, enough. Too much and it's emotional blackmail—Roger's trick. You're a woman, not a girl, Louise, bring this bastard on or he wins. She used all her wiles to make his moment arrive. Then at least the contest would be a draw.

"Wow," he said, "where d-d-did you study acrobatics?" He laughed so she would know it was a love joke.

She laughed too. "Who do you think you are," she said, "Porfirio Rubirosa?"

But he was priapic. He would have no moment. If Louise could not forget Roger, neither could Pete forget Enid. Perhaps in time the meaning of the thing would come back to him. But not now. Louise sensed this too. Still locked together, they lay on their sides and held each other against the cold of the night, strangers who had almost met.

She knew she was beaten. He knew he was beaten.

She thought someone else might be on his mind. "Who's Enid?" she said.

"What?" Pete said, and started as if shot.

"Who's Enid?" she repeated. "Your sister?"

"No," he said, and backed away.

"Did you love her?"

"Yes."

"Who is she?"

"Uh, w-what, uh—I mean, how did you know about Enid?"

"I couldn't help it," Louise said. "You put me in your room last night. There was a picture with your name and hers."

Pete cursed himself and got up and dressed. His hands shook and his right eye twitched again. "She was my wife," he said.

"Oh," Louise said, "I know how it is. I split up with Roger, too. He was my husband. How long since you broke up?"

The stammer left Pete again. "We didn't break up," he said.

Louise snapped on her bra and began to dress. Suspicion scampered in passion's wake. "Okay," she said. "Then why am I here and where is little Enid?"

Pete felt like slapping her.

She looked at his eyes in the dying glow of the camp stove and saw those of an animal injured in the forest. It warned her to stay back.

"Enid's dead," Pete said.

Louise wondered for a moment if this were male perfidy plotted to perfection, but his eyes spoke honestly. She would find out more. "Oh, I'm sorry, Pete. I'm really sorry, I didn't know." She reached up and held him by the back of the head as a big sister would. "I'm sorry, Pete. It must have been hurting you for a long time. When did it happen, if you don't mind my asking?"

"Last Tuesday night," Pete said.

"What?" Louise said. *"When?"*

"Last Tuesday night. The night before the night before last. She was, uh, sssssstruck by lightning," Pete said as if sedated.

Louise was still holding him by the back of the head. Using this grip as leverage, she clutched his hair, then aimed a haymaker with her other fist and struck his jaw as hard as she could with a splattering sound that drew blood from his face.

"You sonofabitch," she said, and fixed him with a gimlet stare and shook both fists in his bloody face. "You blood-curdling swinish macho ghoul. You callous, deceiving, sneaking, rotten sonofabitch! You're a *monster!* You stay away from me! Don't you touch me, you slime! You're a disease! So help me God, I ought to take that gun out of my pack and blow your sap-sucking head off with it. How could you do that to *her?* How could you do that to *me?!*"

She aimed another blow at Pete and this time he ducked.

He knew she was right.

She ran inside the plastic tent and zipped herself up in her sleeping bag.

It seemed to Pete that those who have suffered pain themselves, contrary to common belief, often lack the capacity to see pain in others.

But that was just Pete's opinion.

When Adair arrived at the ridge on which he thought he had seen Pete stand, it was pitch dark and all trace of him was lost. His only choice until the moon came out would be to sit on the ridge and scan the distance for some light.

He waited for hours and saw nothing but the shining of stars. He wondered if his eyes deceived him when once he looked in the valleys below and saw a pinpoint of light twinkle briefly.

He waited to see it again and it was no illusion. A small light was switched on in the distance and held for about the time it would take to look at a watch, then turned off. In a few minutes he saw it again. It was far to his right. Adair walked swiftly along the ridge, trying to keep the intermittent light in sight and closing the distance between them.

Late in the night a yellow glow began to appear in the east. Soon the moon, gibbous at twice its usual size and

aureate as emerging from a gilding vat, ventured its top
above the eastern hills. It shed enough illumination to
reveal to Adair that the little twinkling light was now on
a ridge to his west.

Charlie Sevenpines had taken some Geiger readings by
flashlight when he went up the ridge and was surprised
to see the needle move. The flies were supposed to breed
in swamps, which are rare on ridges. Pointed to the
southwest, the needle climbed again as a photographic
exposure meter when aimed from shade to sun. He
walked swiftly in a sort of shuffle that required minimum
energy. He stopped and took a long reading, panning the
Geiger counter left and right as a movie camera. The
needle reached its peak when it pointed toward a place
that Charlie reckoned to be Jacob Walz State Park, which
lay in black forest in a valley to the west.

Charlie shut off the flashlight and ambled by the light
of the moon down the west side of the ridge. He heard
animals scurry over twigs and leaves, but it seemed to
Charlie there were fewer of them than there should be.
He walked for a long time and neither did he hear the
flapping and howling of owls, which would surely come
out to hunt at the first light of the moon. Something was
wrong. He moved now with stealth, choosing his footing
with care and using his toes to make no sound on the
ground. He was glad he had worn insect repellent, one
of his concessions to the new culture.

Then he heard the sounds behind him. He stopped and
strained his ears. They came from about a quarter-mile
away. The thing moved quietly. Not as quietly as Charlie,
but it moved in a rush with some skill in the night. And
it moved on two feet.

Charlie looked for a tree with boughs that would give
him good cover, and where, if all was well, he might
sleep for a while. He found one and climbed it and nes-
tled in a large branch some fifteen feet from the ground.
He took off his jacket and got out his James Bond pistol
and cocked it noiselessly inside the jacket.

Soon he heard the man come closer. Now he was less
than a hundred feet away. Then he saw the man pass near
the tree. The man did not look for tracks, but for bent

branches or more visible signs of someone's passing. This
fellow knew what he was doing. Charlie let his breath
come and go in light animal pants that could not be heard.
The man looked up near Charlie's branch. His head was
covered with white and Charlie did not like the looks of
that.

Pete put out the cook stove and lay back on the mattress of leaves on which they had made love. He understood how foolish he had made her feel and it made him
feel even more foolish. He knew it was a failing to do all
that was expected of him, as though to do otherwise
would breach some contract with God. He knew he had
taken on as much as his emotions could tolerate. He
looked through the trees up to the stars and thought of
the end of the twenty-third Psalm, the part about dwelling
in the house of the Lord forever, and Pete was sure it
meant something like spirit among spirit among stars,
where even the random was divine plan. The thought gave
him rest and he fell asleep.

The moon was full and sparkling a pale yellow through
treetops when he awoke to the rustling behind him.

"I'm sorry," she said. "It . . . shocked me. I felt foolish."

"You, uh, couldn't have known b-b-because I didn't
tell you. So it's, uh, it's my fault. I'm the fool."

"You loved her very much, didn't you?"

Pete did not answer.

"Well, she was a lucky woman. I'm sorry. That's it.
Let's talk about something else."

They lay side by side and kept each other warm. Louise
talked about the beauty of the night and of this strange
new world and of how, as adults, they never seemed to
see the wonder in such nights as they had as children.
This got them talking about their worlds as children until
they talked it out and dozed off.

Pete was the first to hear the sound.

It was faint but fell on his ears as incongruously in this
place as a drugstore alarm clock. It came from neither
animal nor man. It was the distant creaking and growling
of machinery.

Then Louise woke to it.

Pete listened. The sounds grew louder. He groped for his map. He took from his belt a tiny but powerful flashlight and decided to risk using it for a few minutes.

The map showed a dirt road that circumnavigated the southern section of the park. Pete's skin prickled as he remembered this road, for many years now scarcely a cow path. This one led to the old mine, also long abandoned. Pete's heart skipped. Then the adrenaline squeezed it, forcing frigid blood to wash beneath his skin. He felt like hitting himself on the head for not thinking of it. Fool. "Oh . . ." he said, slowly. He sensed his stammer leave him again. He exhaled a long breath as if he had been holding it under water. "Oh . . . my . . . God!" He shut off the flashlight.

"What's wrong?" Louise said. "What's that noise?"

Pete took a deep breath. "Stay here, please. Pack your emergency things, gun, radio, not much more. Get ready to leave everything else behind. How many atropine kits do you have?"

"Six," she said.

"Keep three and please give me three. And for God's sake, stay off the radio even if it's one of us, unless it's a life-and-death emergency. Keep the pistol handy and be ready to shoot anyone who doesn't identify himself." He dug out his binoculars and stood up.

"Where are you going?" she said.

"I'll be back soon," he said.

"I'm going with you," she said.

"I'd, uh, rather you stayed here and met the others if I don't come back. Then you can use the radio."

"Like hell I will," she said. "I'm going with you."

"Have it your way." He admired her spunk but had no idea how she would respond in extremis.

Pete gathered only what he could wear on his belt or in his pockets or around his neck; Louise only what fit in her pockets, which included neither gun nor radio. Both wore light windbreakers. Hand in hand, they ran through the woods toward the sound.

Charlie let the wraith-like figure pass beneath him and steal off toward the southwest. He set the pistol on safe and lay back for a nap that would be shorter than he planned.

He, too, heard the machinery clattering up the road in his sleep. The road was several miles to the south. Instinct told him the sound was important and helped him overcome his other instinct's loathing of the radio. "Breaker, breaker, Mazola to Bloodhound. Do you copy?"

Pete heard the call as they ran toward the road. "Damn. I'm turning the thing off. Too much danger of interception."

Adair had not seen Charlie in the tree. Had he known he was trailing him, he would not have bothered. He had to find Peter.

Then he heard the sounds on the road. The moon had climbed higher into the night sky and was now her usual size and white. He looked up and saw the ghostly features clearly and for an instant felt the wonder of a primitive and a shiver of fear for what it portended.

He broke into a trot toward the road. He, too, knew where the road led, but it was less important to him than finding Peter. Only moondown was important to Adair. He knew somehow that things were breaking and he would make them break his way.

Charlie gave up calling Pete. "Breaker, breaker, Mazola to Hot Paws or Anteater, do you copy?"

"Ten-four, dear boy," came a weak answer from Abe, "and the old clock on the wall says it's about four-ten in the morning. To what boon of providence do we owe your communication?"

Charlie was annoyed but explained what he could. The three agreed to meet at first light at a wooded ridge near the road.

"Holy molasses," Louise said. They lay watching with their bellies on the cold damp ground of the woods overlooking the road. They saw that the machinery was a convoy led by two motorcycles followed by a luxury car. The car was followed by five large refrigerator trucks.

The trucks were followed by two more motorcycles in the lee of the procession. The machines moved very slowly and as quietly as such machines could. All lights were off, but for tiny red battery-operated bicycle tail-lights that hung from the rear of each truck.

"Jesus, is it the CIA?" Louise said.

Somehow Pete knew she was going to ask something like that. He opined that such CIA people he had known were incapable of standing upright at such a time of night, let alone operating motor vehicles in the boondocks with-out benefit of illumination. No, he feared worse.

"Not the Russians?" she said.

"J-Jesus, you're a piece of work, aren't you, Louise? D-Do you see any red stars on those trucks? Will you, uh, for chrissakes give up your international conspiracy theories?"

"All right, wiseass," she said. "But it's some kind of conspiracy, isn't it?"

"Shh, you're talking too loud," Pete said. "Uh, yeah. It, uh, looks like sssome kind of violation."

"Oh, I love it," Louise said. "Oh, God, don't you just love it? The macho he-man cop suspects the perpe-trators of perpetrating something suspicious. The in-trepid officer knows they are up to no good, but just what good they are not up to he does not know."

"Shhhh," Pete said. "*Touché.*"

The procession rumbled off into the night.

Louise kissed Pete lightly on the lips when it was gone. "Someday I'll tell you my sad story if you tell me yours."

"I, uh, can hardly wait," Pete said.

He taught her in low whispers how to slink through the woods, keeping down and making the least possible noise. The moon lit their way as it rose higher. They held each other's hands.

"Shit-fire, girl," Talmadge Brown said, "we been whupping this bus's ass from here to Christmas. I can't even count the nights now. We been damned near killed by crazy flies and damn near runned over by trucks and trains and we ain't nowhere near Philly. Shit, girl, we going in circles. We ready to settle for Pittsburgh now. You know what I'm saying?''

"That's right," Herman García echoed.

Irene stopped the bus with a jolt and jerked the hand brake on. "Okay. You want to drive this turkey and get us to Philly or Pittsburgh, that's fine with Irene Byrne. Irene Byrne has had it up to her eyeballs with you jiveass niggers. You so goddamn smart, you get your ass behind this wheel and motate this turkey!''

Light came to the entrance of the old mine and Pete and Louise took turns with the binoculars.

A second wind called upon several times in as many days made Pete a little giddy at the beauty of this dawn: the sun limned with ocher over eastern ridges, the hectic concatenations of morning meetings among birds and droning insects.

The Geiger counter needle had steadily risen.

Louise peered through the binoculars while Pete coached her. "Uh, see how those trees hang over that b-bare spot in front of the hillside?'' he said.

"Yeah," Louise said.

"That's, uh, not n-natural. Those trees have been cut down and moved there.''

"Right."

"Now look, uh, at the w-woods to the left. About thirty meters away.''

"Yeah?" Louise asked.

"Uh, in the shade you'll sssee a couple of sets of wheels.''

"Oh, yeah, right, it's a truck. Well, I'll be damned, there's a car there too, a maroon Cadillac. Hey, wait a minute, here comes one of those little whatdoyoucallits, you know, one of those little tractors with a couple of prongs in front for lifting things . . .''

"A, uh, forklift. I see it.''

"Oh, God, this can't be real. That forklift is carrying those big shitcans, what do you call them, something-something-gallon drums. They're all messed up with red and white corrosion, it looks like. Jesus, Pete! You're not going to believe this!''

"What?" Pete said.

"Some of those drums have the radiation symbol on them."

Pete exhaled a long breath. "Damn. Yeah, I believe it. I should have thought of it before. Damn! Fool!"

"Look at this," Louise said. "The guy driving the forklift is wearing some kind of decontamination suit with a big hood on it. He's driving into those fake trees with the bare spot on the ground. Wait a minute. Here comes another forklift, and another! Jesus, those guys are in a hurry to get rid of that stuff. I can't see where they're going. It's too dark."

"Uh, into the mine," Pete said.

"There's a mine in there?"

"Yeah, uh, it's huge. It's been abandoned for t-twenty years or so. As kids, my, uh, my brother-in-law—I m-m-mean, the guy who became my brother-in-law—and I used to ride out on our bicycles and, uh, explore it. There were no trees in front of it then. That, and the trucks in the woods, what does it tell you?"

"They don't want to be seen from the air," Louise said.

"My guess too," Pete said.

"Where's your brother-in-law now that we need him?" Louise said jokingly, handing the binoculars to Pete.

"Uh, in Mexico. Jesus!" Pete looked through the binoculars and reported what he saw. Several men came out of the wood where the trucks were parked. Some carried rifles slung on their shoulders and others carried what looked like big pistols or small machine guns. Most wore black leather jackets or vests and some wore Nazi-style helmets. Pete strained to see something painted on the backs of their jackets. Two of these men had large cylinders strapped to their backs and nozzles in their hands with which they laid down a fog near the mine entrance.

"Probably DDT," Louise quipped.

Pete tried to read the backs of the jackets of the others. There was a big curling symbol with a large head and red mouth. It looked like a snake. "Damn," Pete said. "King Cobras."

"What's that?" Louise asked.

"A, uh, motorcycle gang," Pete said. "They're, uh, responsible for a lot of the drug traffic east of here and in South Jersey. They're supposed to be connected with high-end organized crime. They've been involved in shootings with the p-p-police in both states and they crippled a Jersey state trooper.''

"This is just one big illicit toxic waste dump, right, Pete?''

"Uh, sssure looks like it. Uh, is it possible, Louise, that the Chrysops flies got their poison in there?''

"Nothing about those goddamn flies is possible," Louise said. "Besides, Abe says they breed in swamps.''

"Uh, Louise . . .''

"Yeah?''

"There's a, uh, sort of swamp in there," Pete said.

"Holy shit," Louise said.

Pete shifted to his side and handed the binoculars to Louise, who moved to where he had been lying so she could see better.

"Yaaaaaaaaagh," she suddenly screamed.

Her body jerked as the report of the rifle blasted a miniature sonic boom through the morning air. Pete flipped onto his back and pulled out his pistol and sat up. Out of the corner of his eye he could see Louise writhing on the ground. In the target sights of Pete's Python was the chest of the rifleman, a King Cobra in a Nazi helmet, standing in the clear on a hillock above them not twenty meters away. Silly, Pete thought, he's too complacent. Pete yelled, "Freeze! Police officer! One move and you're a dead man! Drop the gun!''

The man did not drop the gun. Pete watched him hastily eject the spent cartridge with the bolt of his rifle and propel a fresh one into the chamber.

"Oh, God, it hurts! Ouch, goddamnit," Louise said. "Oh, God!''

With his right thumb, Pete pulled the hammer back to its click stop, cocking the Python. The fleshy padding of the first joint of his right index finger took up the slack of the revolver's gentle trigger. His left hand clutched his right wrist and both arms lay on his knees to steady the aim. Pete looked at nothing but his target. From what he could tell of Louise, she was injured in a lower leg and her life was in less danger from lack of attention by Pete than from the rifleman. Neither did he look at the eyes

of the man, one of which now began to focus down his
telescopic sight at Pete. Curiously, a robin foraging in
the grass between Pete and the rifleman chose this moment to chirp notes of song. As the final microseconds
of at least one life counted down, Pete knew he had been
right in not shooting the executioner in Saigon. But this
was different. He would regret it, but there was now no
time. The gunman's face snuggled against the rifle's cheek
rest. His breast was a black dot of paper on a pistol range.
With the flesh of Pete's forefinger, he pulled rearward
with no more effort than it takes to tickle a cat. The
Python's hammer fell. The pistol bellowed and jumped
in Pete's hand. Tiny shavings of white-hot lead sparked
out the sides of its cylinder.

The force of the .357 hollow-nosed Magnum bullet hit
the man full in the chest and knocked him back with his
feet thrust forward as though he had been stricken by a
wrecking ball. The rifle discharged into the ground as it
fell from the man's hands and from its own recoil went
flying as a boomerang.

Pete cocked the pistol again and ran up to the King
Cobra, who was now sitting on the ground holding his
chest. "Hands over your head. Hands over your head,"
Pete yelled.

The man looked up into Pete's eyes like a beggar who
had been swindled out of his last possession by a rich
merchant. His hands probed his chest and he began to
cough. The bullet had ripped out his pulmonary artery.
The man yet looked at Pete, frightened and reproachful.
He started to speak, then crimson internal blood cas-
caded from his mouth and nose and his head bobbed
forward as though to gulp it back. The throat made mutilated gurgling sounds and the man pitched forward with
his head on his knees. Then the body relaxed, twitched,
and tumbled to its side, still.

"I'm sorry," Pete said to it. It had a mother once too.
"Uh, I'm, uh, really very ssorry."

Louise moaned on the ground. Pete grabbed the man's
rifle and ran to her. "Where are you hit?" he said.

"In the leg, in the fucking leg," she said. "Owwwww
. . . damn!"

"Let me see," Pete said.

"What do you mean, let you see. Dammit, I'm the doctor!"

Pete cut her bloodied slacks open with his penknife. He daubed the wound with his handkerchief. Louise sucked breath between her teeth. The bullet had gouged a nasty bleeding gash across the surface of her calf, as though she had been using a saw that slipped. It was a tangential strike and she would soon be all right. Pete knew a little about such things from his army and highway experience. It was most important to stop the bleeding.

"Ow!" she said. "What the hell are you doing?"

"I'm, uh, making a bandage with my handkerchief."

"Who the hell licensed you to practice medicine, dammit?"

Pete heard motorcycles starting in the distance. He got the gunman's Weatherby rifle and for a moment admired a piece of equipment he could not afford, then handed it to Louise. "Here," he said, "I want you to have this."

"I don't want to touch it," she said.

"A, uh, hair of the dddog that bit you," Pete said.

"Smartass," she said. She felt for her leg. She, too, heard the motorcycles coming toward them in a phalanx from the mine.

Pete gave her a brief lesson on the use of the rifle and explained to her that with so superb a piece it was difficult even for the untrained to miss, which was why it was made for the likes of affluent Porsche owners such as Louise.

"I'm a doctor," she protested, "a healer."

"Bbbullshit," he said. "You operate on corpses. There must be twenty of those bastards out there. If you don't want you and me to be corpses, you'd better be ready to make corpses out of them." He gestured toward the motorcycle gang charging in full panoply, replete with Nazi helmets, less than a mile away. He showed Louise how to fire from behind the right side of a rock and told her of his plans to steal a motorcycle.

"Macho, macho, macho-man," Louise parodied the old song. "I'm the one who got hurt, prick. I'm just as tough as you."

"I, uh, don't doubt it," Pete said. Then he walked up

a slope toward their attackers. He stopped and called into the radio, "Mayday, Mayday, Mayday . . ."

Dr. Knox, Dr. Applebaum, and Charlie Sevenpines trundled up the road for all the world like the Tin Woodsman, the Cowardly Lion, and the Scarecrow in *The Wizard of Oz*.

But this was no yellow brick road. To everyone's astonishment, Geiger readings read higher as they went farther.

Abe Applebaum, with Dolores the tarantula perched on his head, felt snubbed by Charlie. So the doctor did his best to twit the standoffish Indian.

Abe discoursed at length on the virtues of homosexuality and, especially, on the thrifty aspects of this mode of love. You didn't have to buy clothes for kids or put them through college or subject yourself to twenty years of hearing their noise. Barring the bizarre, there was no alimony on splitting up. And, both lovers being of the same sex, there were no misunderstandings that can arise between those of heterotypical anatomies.

Whenever he heeded Dr. Applebaum, which was as seldom as he could, Charlie cogitated over the good old days of taking hairy scalps. At such times he fixed the hirsute entomologist with a visage that betokened the frailty of human existence.

Abe Applebaum often burst into song, such as: "Shoofly pie and apple-pan dowdy/Makes your eyes light up, your tummy say howdy . . ."

Crackle, crackle went the radios. "Mayday, Mayday, Mayday," croaked a voice miles away, "does anybody copy me?"

"Oh, that sounds like Pete," Abe said.

"Shut up, Doctor!" Charlie said.

"Shut up, Abe," Dr. Knox said.

"We copy," Charlie said into his radio. "Come on back."

"We're under fire, uh, gggunfire," Pete's voice said. "Uh, coordinates about eighty-one west, fifty-four north. Uh, Muffet's been hit but she's okay . . . can't wa . . . radio . . . sheriff's office . . . be sure . . . State . . . too . . ."

"Come back, Bloodhound!" Charlie yelled into the radio, "come back!" The transmission had begun to break up. Then it stopped abruptly without so much as static. Charlie quickly changed his radio to Channel 9, the universal emergency channel, to call a report to the sheriff's office.

Josh Rosen, legislative aide to the Governor of Pennsylvania, was nauseous with worry and grief.

He would have felt worse had he known that his cable to the governor arrived at the governor's Tokyo hotel after the gubernatorial party had left for Nikko. The cable arrived at Nikko as the governor was enroute to Kyoto. The cable arrived at Kyoto as the governor was riding to Osaka. The cable arrived at Osaka as the governor was flying to Sapporo on the island of Hokkaido. The cable arrived at Sapporo as the governor was enroute by U.S. Marine Corps aircraft to the U.S. Air Force base at Tachikawa. There, despite the diligence of the Japanese foreign ministry, the cable was lost to the void.

The machine gun burst ripped the radio from Pete's hands. He threw himself on the ground and wallowed to make an imperfect target for the gunman he had not seen.

Boom! went a high-powered rifle.

Another King Cobra had taken the place of the man Pete had shot. Pete discovered him in time to see his uncovered skull explode. The submachine gun tumbled down the hill toward Louise, who was holding the smoking rifle. He motioned for her to get the machine gun.

Machine-gun fire now came toward them from the charging riders. Watching them, Pete realized he had been wrong. There were not at least twenty of them. There were at least forty. Now they were less than a half-mile away and the dust trailing behind their cycles and the wisps of gray gunsmoke and flashes of muzzles reminded Pete of every film cliché of a cavalry charge he had ever seen. The sounds of their gunfire mixed with the increasing roar of their angry engines.

Pete could see that one rider had pulled far ahead of the pack. Pete picked up a heavy dead tree branch and hid behind a slight rise and waited for this first motor-

cyclist to top it. He could smell arid dust mingle with the
sweat of his body. He looked at Louise crouching prone
with the rifle beside the rock some thirty meters to his
rear. He gave her the OK sign, as much reassuring himself as her. Pete noticed the same robin pecking and singing a merry air on the hillside behind her, oblivious to
the carnage above it and that which was about to take
place below. He wondered how long it would take for
help to arrive. Too long, he thought, unless they were
lucky enough to have a state-police helicopter in the vi-
cinity.

He ejected the single spent cartridge from the Python
and loaded a new one into it. That would make six rounds
in the gun, plus an extra eleven in the cartridge loops in
his belt. Louise could have only one round, possibly
none, left in the Weatherby. It could only accommodate
three rounds in the clip, plus one more in the chamber,
before needing to be reloaded. He tried to remember how
many rounds came in the magazine of the Uzi that Louise
had retrieved from the man who shot his radio. It probably had few left. He heard the engine sounds grow
louder, and especially the bleating of one engine, which
was now very close.

Pete would have to use himself as bait for this rider.
He stood up quickly, long enough to be seen but, he
judged, not long enough to make a good target. The rider
was scarcely thirty meters away, and Pete noticed as he
ducked down again that the man was making a small turn
to veer directly for him. He waited, trying not to count
his heartbeats, as the engine wailed louder.

The bike crested near Pete with its front wheel in the
air. Pete jammed the branch into the rear spokes and saw
the bike pitch forward and its rider somersault over the
handlebars. Pete ran to the man and scissored his legs
around his body and tore off his Nazi helmet and clubbed
him senseless with the heavy barrel of the Python. He
took his machine gun.

The sun was full in the sky and the moon twinkled
wanly west of its zenith.

The other riders were nearing. Pete fumbled with the
Uzi machine pistol. He had never shot an Uzi, but had
held one and dry-fired it at an FBI course. He lay down,

using the supine King Cobra and his motorcycle for cover. This bike was a Husqvarana, a motorcyclist's dream of a dirt bike. Israeli submachine guns, Swedish motorcycles, fancy California sporting rifles. These guys go first-class, Pete thought. They had money behind them.

Motorcycles topped the rise on both sides of him. Pete fired short bursts from the Uzi. Two riders fell to his left. He spun to his right and exhausted the Uzi, killing another rider.

For all their brio, Pete realized the King Cobras were merely professional brutes who were not ready for a true fight. He rated them high on enthusiasm, but somewhat deficient in skill and intelligence. On the other hand, had they any skill or intelligence, they would not have been King Cobras. He found it curious that he was so coldly rational as he watched most of the riders turn away from him toward woods on either side. Some seemed already to be retreating back to the mine.

Three who had penetrated Pete's barrage rode down the slope toward Louise. Pete aimed his Python and shot one of them off his bike. The man got to his knees, wobbling, and aimed his Uzi at Pete and fired the entire magazine at him. Pete could hear and feel the bullets cracking around him. He took deliberate aim with the pistol again and fired, and the man fell again and did not rise.

The unfamiliar stench of nitrate smoke filled Louise Kavanaugh's nostrils. She saw one rider shot down by Pete and another turn back. The last sped on directly toward her. She was still shaking and appalled at having killed the man who tried to kill Pete. She took aim at the man who rode toward her. She could see his unshaven face grinning in her telescopic sight. Two of his front teeth were missing. Stupid bastard had probably got them knocked out in some barroom hullabaloo. I'd better shoot him, she thought. She was disgusted but thought it better to be disgusted than dead. She pulled the trigger. Nothing happened.

Oh, shit, she thought, I forget to pull this little handle back and push it in again. Just like shifting gears in the Porsche, you have to remember to do it. Damn, but that leg hurts. Here he comes. There is still time. Just.

She pulled the rifle bolt up and back and pushed it down and in again as Pete had showed her. She aimed the cross hairs up at the man and braced herself and started to pull the trigger. She knew the big gun would hurt her shoulder again. She hadn't been hit that hard since she was last in a fight at the age of eleven.

The bullet tore through the fuel tank of the motorcycle and through the spinal column of the man. The cycle slid to a stop on top of the man and the fuel burst into flames as it spread over his chest, naked but for a black leather vest. He would have kicked his way free but he could no longer move his legs. The flames spread up his belly and a miasma of foul black smoke belched into the air and Louise could feel the heat of the fire on her face from where she lay.

"Aaaaaaa," the man screamed, at first in frustration and anger as much as pain. "You dirty bitch!" he yelled at Louise, "you filthy fucking cunt, look what you did! Owwwww! Owwwwwww! Oh, Momma, look what she did to me. Aaaaaaaaaaaaaaaaa! I'm burning, Momma. Oh, God, oh, Momma, somebody please help me! Please . . ."

The man's torso was afire. Hair and leather and skin erupted and sizzled and stank acrid and reasty. The man flailed and beat at the pain. Louise knew she must do something. The man might live for minutes like this. She pulled the bolt of the rifle back and forward again. She aimed at his head and pulled the trigger. Nothing happened but a clicking noise inside the gun. My God, the damned thing is empty! Louise thought

"Rrrrraaaaaggghhh! Gooooodddddd! Oh, I'm burrrrrrrrning! Oh, please help, help, help, heeeeeellllllp!" The man stopped beating at his breast and thrust his fists, each now flaming faggots, deep into his eye sockets in futile despair to protect the eyes from the ineluctable. His roast chest heaved and sizzled with his screams.

Louise remembered the machine gun and crawled to where she had laid it and pointed it and jerked the trigger. It leapt and clattered and breathed chemical smoke and Louise hated it with visions of innocent children of Nazi atrocities. The man stopped moving. Louise threw down the Uzi and closed her eyes and thrust her fist into her mouth and sobbed bitterly and vomited onto the ground. When she finished, she looked up and tried to clear her mind and remember where she was and what this was all about.

Pete rode a motorcycle to her with its saddlebags stuffed with captured Uzis. "Can you walk?" he said.

Louise struggled to her feet and stumbled to Pete using the expensive rifle as a crutch. He helped her onto the jump seat behind him and told her to hang on to his belly with one hand for dear life. "Here," he said, giving her one of the Uzi machine pistols for her other hand. "Try not to shoot me with it."

"Stop bossing me around," she heard herself rejoin.

"Jesus," Pete growled under his breath as he gunned the motorcycle down the road.

The rapping of the engine was so loud neither of them heard the burst of machine-gun fire. Not until Pete noticed the trails of dust puffs where the bullets struck the dirt road did he realize they were being shot at again. The shots came from woods behind and above.

"Hold on!" Pete yelled to Louise, and twisted the handlebars, sending the motorcycle careening downhill overland.

Minutes were all they needed, Pete thought, thirty or even fewer complete sweeps of a second hand around the face of a clock, mere little minutes. But with all senses now heightened, with all the danger surrounding them, each flit of a nanosecond could measure both their lives and seemed to occupy an hour and render vain whimsies any thoughts of escape.

They bounced across a shallow stream and toward a large stand of woods. He raced the motorcycle through the woods, zigzagging around trees, toward the general direction of the road they left.

Louise saw at least six riders chasing them and exhausted the magazine of an Uzi at them. Two went down. The cycle of another skidded on its side, dragging the rider until both collided with a tree. The remaining riders stayed with them and fired until their ammunition was exhausted too. Then two turned deeper into the woods on both sides of them. The last stuffed the gun in his

black jacket and tried to outmaneuver and ram Pete's
bike. They broke out of the woods. Pete could see the
dirt road beyond a wide steep defile separating it from
them. Louise saw this ditch gaping ahead, while she saw
the King Cobra, with less weight on his bike, pull almost
alongside them.

"Louise, drop the gun and grab tight with both
hands," Pete yelled.

Instead of dropping it, she flung the gun at the pursuing
King Cobra, then held Pete tightly with both hands. Pete
drove at full power perpendicular to the defile.

Louise gasped as the wheels shot into the sky. Pete
stood up on the pegs and leaned and pulled back and the
motorcycle seemed suspended at a forty-five-degree angle. Eyes and mouth agape, she gripped Pete's waist with
all her strength and lay her face against his back and
looked down into the boulder-strewn bottom five times
the height of a man below. Airborne, this was scarcely
her idea of a pleasure flight. She could feel and hear their
bike's rear wheel, the power wheel, spinning at the speed
of a rotary saw against the air beneath. From her bottom
vision, she was aware of a shadow, then the pursuing
motorcycle itself, just below and behind them. Then she
felt a multiple jarring crash that tore at the wound on her
leg. Had she time, she would have closed her eyes and
tried to remember a prayer. Instead, she saw the pursuing
motorcycle strike short of the lip of the ravine and dis-
integrate into disparate parts that, with the rider, seemed
to float in slow motion downward to the boulders. Lacking time even to abandon herself for dead, she felt her
own rear wheel strike something, spin, and burrow deep
furrows of flying dirt, pebbles, and dust. Then the front
wheel bounced against earth and they were speeding
along the road again.

The road curved and parts of it were visible ahead.
Suddenly Pete saw the flash of a car driving in their direction. His heart sprang as he saw it was the sheriff's
personal Lincoln Town Car. His Mayday call had been
relayed.

They nearly collided with the car. Pete stopped the
bike and the heavily tinted window rolled down and Pete
saw the face of Sheriff Joe Cody, replete with cigar.

"I don't ever want to ride on a motorcycle with you again," Louise told Pete.

The sheriff gesticulated for them to get in the front seat. Pete hesitated. His instincts now tuned near paranormal, there was something about the timing of this rescue that seemed awry.

Then from the hills above the road came rapid bursts of several machine guns, pocking the dirt with puffs of dust.

"What hell are you waiting for, Bilyeux?" the sheriff called. "Get in!"

Pete helped Louise onto the front seat and sat next to her and with some reluctance closed the door.

"What are you up to, Bilyeux?" the sheriff said. "Hi, little lady. Get yourself hurt?"

"I'm not a little lady," Louise said.

"Nope," the sheriff said, "no, dear, I guess not." He put the car in gear and drove toward the mine.

"Get your fucking hands over your head, pig," a voice said from behind Pete.

Pete could feel the muzzle of a gun pressed against the back of his skull. He put up his hands. The sheriff reached inside Pete's windbreaker and pulled out his Python and handed it to the man in the rear seat. Pete looked over his shoulder and saw Council President Rupert R. Chandler drag himself up off the floor of the far side and brush away dust and look sheepishly at Pete. Pete turned farther and saw the man directly behind him pointing an Uzi at his head. With his knee, Pete nudged Louise in the shin of her good leg as if telling her to be quiet. The man holding the Uzi on him was a King Cobra. He was fat and blond, with a stubble of yellow beard. He wore a black vest with no shirt under it, a crude neck chain with an Iron Cross, a single earring in a pierced ear, heavy rings shaped as skulls on his fingers, and sentimental tattoos on his arms. He also wore mirrored sunglasses and Pete looked into them and understood the eyes beyond. They would be dull eyes, impassive, criminal, too cowardly to admit fear. Pete's criminology professors in college would have called the man a sociopath—a void of human empathy. Pete had seen such eyes before. They came alive only in their natural habitat, prison. "Uh, hi," Pete said to the man. "What's your name?"

The man with the gun broke into giggles that made the fat on his belly jiggle. His body and breath stank as though he had not bathed or brushed his teeth since puberty. Rupert Chandler gestured for him to be careful.

"They call me Butterball," the King Cobra said.

"Ohhhhh . . ." Pete said, "ohhhh, that's a n-n-nice name."

Louise bit her lip.

Butterball laughed appreciatively. He nodded toward Chandler.

"Bilyeux, we're in business here," Chandler said, "real honest-to-goodness business. Our partners and us, we're just doing a service for other businesses that a lot of stupid red tape won't let them do for themselves."

"Uh, sssounds okay to me, Mr. Chandler. How about you, Louise?"

Louise nodded, trying to keep a straight face despite the pain in her leg.

It occurred to Pete that illicit toxic-waste dumping had become a lucrative sideline for a number of picaresque local officials. It also occurred to him that they lacked the financing to do it alone.

"So, uh, Sheriff, what's the b-big deal?" Pete said, and stared intently at the sheriff's face. The man showed no emotion, but Pete was determined he would in due course.

"Bilyeux," the sheriff said, "you and the little, uh, this woman here are in a heap of trouble. A heap, Bilyeux."

"Oh, no, Sheriff," Pete said. Now he felt himself the fool for thinking himself a fool when he had waylaid the sheriff outside the conference room. Well, they would soon find out which was the greater fool. "How come?"

"Bilyeux," the sheriff said, "it has not ekscaped your attention that you and the, uh, woman are under arrest."

"Nooooo," Pete said. "Uh, sssorry, Sheriff, but we thought we were being kidnapped."

Butterball giggled.

"Bilyeux," the sheriff said. "Butterball and his men are private detectives in charge of private property. You are charged with homicide, with trespassing, with vehicular theft, with abuse of police powers by searching without a warrant—''

Pete interrupted him. ''Oh, no, that's awful. Then, uh, how c-come you didn't read us our rights, Sheriff? Besides, you said we should do it. You, uh, put me in charge of the case, didn't you? You said, G-g-go to it. Go get 'em. I did and here we are.''

Butterball stopped giggling and listened. Chandler sat up straight and listened. Louise stopped biting her lip. Her leg felt much better.

The sheriff began to look uneasy. ''You violated private property,'' he said.

''Well, uh, maybe so, Sheriff,'' Pete said. ''But d-d-didn't I tell you I was going straight here? Huh, d-d-didn't I?''

''Bilyeux, you're twisting things around,'' the sheriff said.

''T-T-Twisting? Sheriff, now be fair. I think it's you who's twisting. Didn't I tell you I wanted to bring Charlie Sevenpines in and come right here? Didn't I? C-C-Come on, Sheriff, be fair. Didn't I? Yes or no?''

''Bilyeux, come on, man! I didn't mean for you to come right here on private property without a warrant . . .''

''That's right, uh, Sheriff, I think that's right. You mmmeant for me to come here *without* a warrant. Isn't that right? Yes or no?''

''Goddamnit, Bilyeux, that's not why I wanted you to come here. Wait, I mean—''

''There, you just said it, Sheriff,'' Pete interrupted. ''So you wanted me to come here but you didn't want me to get a warrant, right?''

''Bilyeux, that's not what I meant and you know—''

''No, that's right,'' Pete interrupted again, his voice starting to build in righteous if feigned anger. ''Gggggo to it, you said, go get 'em, you're behind me a thousand percent, that's what you said, Sheriff, isn't it? You're putting me in charge of the case, that's what you said. And you didn't say anything about a gggggggggoddamn warrant, did you? You wanted my coming here to be a surprise, didn't you, Sheriff? Just who the hell are you trying to screw, Sheriff? Me? These guys here? Who are you trying to screw? Both sides, so your ass will be clean and green no matter what happens? You were playing both sides of the street, weren't you? You hedged your bets, didn't you, Sheriff, so no matter what happened you'd come out okay? Didn't you? That's why you wanted me to jump these guys by surprise, isn't it? And that's why they *were* surprised, isn't it? Isn't it? Yes or no?''

"Bilyeux, that's not why I told you to come here and you know it!''

"There, you s-s-said it again,'' Pete said, adopting a quieter tone in a show of victory. He'd watched plenty of prosecuting attorneys bulldoze plenty of defendants in his day, and he knew the tricks and knew the effect these ploys had on juries, especially when the prosecutors got the defendants to half-agree with them. He knew, too, that this jury, a couple of thugs on the back seat, were listening intently and had heard what amounted to a confession. "You said it again, Sheriff,'' Pete repeated. "You wwwanted me to come here without a warrant. Did you or did you not?''

"Bilyeux, Bilyeux, I never said anything about a goddamn warrant and you fucking-a-john know it. Now I don't want you giving these fellas the wrong ideas.'' The sheriff's face had changed from Thursday's gray to Saturday's florid. He was bewildered and Pete could see his hands shaking on the steering wheel and the sweat soaking his collar in the Town Car's air-conditioning. "Now, Bilyeux, we're businessmen here, partners who are trying to run a business. Private business, Bilyeux. It's free enterprise, right in the Constitution!''

"But, uh, Sheriff, bbbecause you have a business interest in this place and you put me in charge, you must have had a good business reason for sending me here,'' Pete said. "Right?''

"Of course I put you in charge and told you to come here, Bilyeux,'' the sheriff sputtered. "But that gives you no right to complain about my business interests. Every man has a right to profit from business, every man, me too . . .''

And so Pete heard the sheriff blunder inanely into pronouncing his own death sentence. Perhaps it would buy time for Pete and Louise, perhaps not.

The car arrived at the mine. The sheriff parked it in the shade. Butterball used Pete's handcuffs to chain him and Louise to the steering wheel. Then he opened all the windows and winked at the two and sauntered casually away. Chandler ignored the sheriff and followed Butterball.

Pete watched Butterball and Chandler go to a clearing where they met a dark-haired man in a business suit a little too expressionist for Pete's taste. The man had emerged from the maroon Cadillac Eldorado. The sheriff tried to join them but was rebuffed and forced to wait out of earshot. The three engaged in a heated, if whispered, discussion. The man in the suit often looked at his watch and down the road, as if expecting someone.

"You deserve the Academy Award for that one, buster," Louise told Pete, who snorted appreciably at her appreciation of his prosecutorial performance. "Look at the way they're treating your pal, the sheriff. You know what that other guy is, don't you?"

"Who?"

"The guy in the suit."

"I've, uh, got a p-pretty good idea." Pete remembered reading many years before that the abandoned mine had been sold to a consortium of Atlantic City businessmen who wished to convert it to an archive for storing documents.

"The Mafia, La Cosa Nostra, the Black Hand, the mob, whatever you want to call it," Louise spat, "filth that runs rampant like cancer cells. Those pricks have their slimy, porcine paws into everything from dope to toxic wastes to crooked politicians. It makes me want to puke to see those scumbags romanticized with all that godfather crap. They're punks, pure and simple, and they'd pillage the world and plunder every baby's cradle in it if there were a sleazy buck to be made. Now even they're finding it tough to get recruits. So they're using these other zombies, these amoral motorcycle creeps, to do their enforcing for them."

"Uh, how dddo you know so much about them, Louise?"

"My maiden name is D'Alessio," she said.

"Oh," Pete said.

Pete confided to Louise his opinion that it was not the intent of this lot to permit the sheriff, him, nor her to complete the day alive.

'Yeah, but they'll do it in different ways,'' she said. ''Your pal the sheriff was in with them, so they'll use him to send a message. As for us, they don't like to get publicity for rubbing out people who aren't involved with them, so they either leave no trace or make it look natural . . . Oh, God! Our insect repellent's wearing off! We're in the shade!''

Surreptitiously, they got out their atropine kits and injected themselves. Louise warned of their impending symptoms and asked Pete if they should make a break for it now. Pete thought this impossible and implored her to do nothing and let him handle events.

''What are our chances?'' Louise asked Pete.

''That dddepends,'' Pete said, ''on what Charlie and your doctor friends can do, and that's not much. To get the state police they'd have to radio through the sheriff's office. And if the sheriff has left word that everything's okay, the office won't do anything. So I guess our chances depend mmmostly on us.''

''What can we do?'' Louise said.

''Uh, wait for them to make a mistake,'' Pete said.

''What if they don't?''

''I don't know. I guess I've bbbbbeen a, uh, f-f-f-fool.''

She thought she could see shame on his face. ''What the hell do you mean, a fool? Just what the hell do you mean? If you hadn't figured out it was the flies, people would still be dropping dead all over the landscape. If you hadn't figured out how to track this place down . . .''

''Right,'' Pete said, with irony in his voice. He began to feel flushed and a little ill from the atropine. His heart, beating hard enough already, began to beat progressively faster. He felt thirsty. He knew Louise must be feeling the same way and probably worse, considering her wound. He kissed her on the cheek and prayed silently.

They waited. They watched. The man in the suit kept looking at his watch and down the road. Chandler and Butterball stayed with him. The sheriff stood alone in the sun, his hands thrust dejectedly in his pockets. They noticed Butterball admiring Pete's gun.

"What did you say that gun was called, Pete?"

"A, uh, P-P-Python."

Louise chuckled.

"What's so funny?" Pete said.

"The python's a bigger snake than the cobra. Snakes and guns," she chortled, "they're so penile."

For the first time since Tuesday night, Pete laughed.

A large Mercedes limousine, also with darkly tinted windows, rolled up the road and stopped.

The man in the suit trotted toward it wearing an obsequious attitude. Butterball waddled toward it with Chandler. The sheriff followed them, waving and smiling and walking anxiously. Butterball gestured for a pair of King Cobras to detain him.

The man in the suit talked through a rear window at the opposite side of the car. His gestures were animated. He said something to Butterball, who waved a signal toward the woods where the trucks and Cadillac were parked. Some King Cobras ran out of it carrying wires and equipment toward the phony woods that Pete and Louise could now clearly see stood at the entrance to the mine.

"Hiya, Carlo," the sheriff called from a distance to the Mercedes, smiling his campaign smile. "Hey, Carlo, can I see you for a minute? Got to talk to you, old son. Carlo?"

The man in the suit pointed to the sheriff and then to Pete and Louise and listened to his instructions from the Mercedes. Finally, he nodded and with Butterball walked over to the sheriff. Butterball took the sheriff's gun from him and gave it to a King Cobra. Then he and the man in the suit walked to Pete and Louise.

"Hiya, folks," the man in the suit said to them. "Uh, folks, there's been a little problem, if you's know what I mean. A, like, business complication, little problem. We're going to ask you's to move inside and wait a few more minutes, if you know what I mean."

Pete knew what he meant and did not deem it salubrious.

Butterball unlocked the handcuffs and he and the man guided Pete and Louise into the mine. Louise limped

badly. Pete supported her and would have offered to carry
her but decided not to risk her wrath.

The sheriff was marched toward his car between two
King Cobras. He fixed his attention on the big Mercedes.
"Carlo," he called, "hey, old son, gotta talk to you for
a minute. Just gimme a minute, Carlo, just a minute!"

Some King Cobras sprayed insecticide in front of Pete
and Louise as they were led by flashlight into the dark
shaft. They could see they were in a huge cavern stacked
from floor to ceiling with containers and drums of many
sizes.

Butterball handcuffed Pete and Louise to a forklift. He
put the handcuff key ostentatiously in his pocket and
winked at them.

"Now don't you folks worry about a thing," the man
in the suit told Pete and Louise, smiling cordially. He
looked at his watch. The King Cobras inside were finishing connecting the wires. "Sorry about this, folks, if
you's know what I mean. But you're only going to be
here a little while, half-hour or so. Trust me."

Pete had learned never to trust anyone who asked for
trust. He realized this ruck was in a panic to blow up the
mine before everything was discovered. He would create
a small distraction. "Uh, 'scuse me," he said. "We're
thirsty, and Louise here c-c-could use some aspirin.
Could you, uh, boys help us out?"

"Hey, no problem," the man said. "I'll send someone
right back with ice water and aspirin, how's that? Now
don't you's folks worry about a thing, you'll be all right.
Trust me."

The man smiled cordially. Butterball winked and giggled, and he and the man in the suit and the King Cobras
left the mine. Pete and Louise watched the large entrance
door clank shut. Now they were in darkness.

"Hypocritical bastards," Louise hissed.

24

"Who are thou that cries out in the dark to beg relief from horror?" spoke the one.

"Call me humankind," spoke the other.

"Then perish anon. Wander false pathways. Beckon the skies to rain flames. Beckon the waters to vomit forth pestilences. Beckon the earth to harvest venoms. Go the way of the great lizards," spoke the one.

"Art thou the dread Lord Tezcatlipoca, he who sheweth his visage before none of my kind?" spoke the other.

"I am called by many names," spoke the one.

"Awful god, it is written that thou didst cast out thine enemy, Quetzalcoatl, from the land of the rich fields and the ripe fruits," spoke the other.

"So let it be written," spoke the one.

"Is it true, terrible 'Lord, that Quetzalcoatl be thine enemy?" spoke the other.

"He who would be mine enemy is enemy but to the law and himself," spoke the one.

"Dare I ask thee, dread god, if Quetzalcoatl also be that one known as Satan?" spoke the other.

"Speak not to me of contrivances, for they are of ye," spoke the one.

"Is not Tula that glorious place of sweet honeys, pure milks, and ready fruits on which we yearn?" spoke the other.

"Why should Tula be different from any other place?" spoke the one.

"Is it not written that Quetzalcoatl shall return to Tula and the glory of us all on such a day as the full moon sets under the sun?" spoke the other.

"Why should such a day be different from any other?" So spoke Tezcatlipoca, the one.

Adair Godwin was as amazed by the shoot-out as he ever allowed himself to be. He followed the sounds of the gunfire, suspecting that Peter Bilyeux was involved. To his surprise, he saw Peter and a woman with blood on her leg get in a Lincoln. He watched the car speed off and knew it could only be heading for the mine, as the road went no other place. He ran over hills and through woods in a direction that cut the distance and also helped conceal him. In the woods he found a dead motorcycle thug and relieved the corpse of a submachine gun and an extra magazine of ammunition. Adair thought the gun might come in handy, and marveled at his luck.

He got to the woods overlooking the mine in time to see Peter and the limping woman being taken into the mine entrance, which he was surprised to see was now hidden.

A fly landed on Adair's glove and burrowed. Adair swatted it dead and watched the sheriff being led to his car, as though to execution, and wondered just what in hell was afoot. The sheriff sat in the driver's seat and a motorcyclist sat next to him. Suddenly there was a shot. The cyclist got out of the car and walked around it, holding a revolver. He wiped the pistol with a rag and held it in the rag and opened the driver's door and the sheriff's body tumbled partly out, its head spattered with blood. Another cyclist picked up the body and dusted it off and held it while the assassin pressed the pistol into the sheriff's right hand. Then both cyclists shoved the body into the car and shut the door.

A man in a suit ran out of the mine and got into a parked Mercedes limousine with Rupert Chandler, the car dealer, and rode off. Also coming out of the mine was a fat blond motorcyclist wearing mirrored sunglasses. Adair recognized him as the man who had yelled at him when he distracted the rifleman near the house of Enid and Peter. This man then surveyed all the goings-on, gave his machine gun to a fellow, got a coil of rope, and ambled up the hill under which the mine lay.

Adair thought he knew where the blond man was going

and what he meant to do with the rope. The daylight moon began to set in the west and Adair followed this man and conceived an idea.

Josh Rosen had a terrible Friday night. The state police would not overstep the authority of the Elmsford County sheriff, and the sheriff neither took nor returned any more of Josh's phone calls. The commanding general of the National Guard was cordial and sympathetic and agreed to put some units on standby alert but could go no further without the governor's authorization. That priest/mayor and that mother superior kept calling Josh, but Josh could do no more, and the governor had not replied to his cable and would not arrive until Sunday morning.

Josh lay in his bed about ten-thirty this Saturday morning trying to make up for lost sleep. The phone rang again.

"Josh, where the hell is everybody?" the governor said.

"My God, where are you, governor?" Josh said.

"I'm at the goddamn airport, where do you think? Jesus, just because the plane was a little late, hell, you'd think people would make allowances for the governor of the state."

After some discussion, it turned out the cable the governor had sent saying he would be back day after tomorrow was meant to be understood as Pennsylvania time. When the cable company dated the transmission, they gave it Japanese time—a day later across the international date line.

Josh told the governor of the events in Elmsford County.

"Jesus Christ, this would have to happen in an election year," the governor said. Then he made a quick decision.

It takes more mature skills to define the frontier between democracy and anarchy than were possessed by the youngsters of Our Lady of Sorrows. As they ran lower on food, they ran lower on patience. At last it was decided to risk travel by day.

And so it happened that about eleven-thirty Saturday

morning they found themselves on the road that led eventually to the old mine.

"Isn't it a little late for Fourth of July?" Abe said.

"Man, I don't like the sound of that at all," Charlie Sevenpines said. "Sounds like tommy guns."

Drs. Knox and Applebaum, with Charlie Sevenpines, examined their own guns and kept them at the ready and trotted toward the sounds of gunfire. They were still several miles from the mine.

The sheriff's car had passed them in a tornado of dust just minutes before. The three would not know it, but had they rounded another bend they would have seen it pick up Pete and Louise.

Major Wilson Spreckels was an insurance agent in real life. One weekend a month and two weeks a year he was commanding officer of the 131st Mobile Air Support Team (MAST) of the National Guard of the Commonwealth of Pennsylvania, stationed at Indiantown Gap.

He had seen the movie *Apocalypse Now* some thirteen times for one scene that set his blood arush. Then he discovered that for a few hundred dollars he could purchase a videocassette recorder and a cassette of this film and watch the scene at home. This he did, to the dismay of his wife if not his two teenage sons. The scene, of course, was the one where the helicopters attack a Vietnamese village to the tune of Wagner's "Ride of the Valkyries."

It so happened he was inspecting his spanking-clean helicopters and the men who flew and manned them, many sporting varying degrees of hangovers, at about eleven-thirty on this Saturday morning. A lieutenant rushed up to him and saluted and reported the major was wanted on the phone by Harrisburg. The major returned the salute smartly and grumbled that it was probably some damned bureaucrat with some damned paperwork contrived to harass men such as he, whose hearts belonged to combat arms.

In truth, he should have got the message much sooner because for some time after getting the call from the governor, no one in charge at National Guard headquarters quite knew how to cope with an epidemic of poisonous flies. It was finally decided to send the nearest helicopter unit to have a look-see. This would be the 131st MAST at Indiantown Gap—Spreckels, Wilson, Maj., CO.

The major reappeared and with dewy eyes gazed upon his spit-and-polish team. With strains of Wagnerian music seducing his mind's ear, he put his hands on his hips, Patton-style. He blew the traffic policeman's whistle that hung on a braided cord from his neck, his only other fetish, and barked, "Mobilize!"

"Well, they didn't make any mistakes," Louise said.

Pete fumbled in his pockets with his free hand. "Uh, Scheherazade was only as good as her last story," he said.

"Damn," Louise said. "Not the CIA, not the army, nothing more sinister than a bunch of greedy geeks and crooked politicians. Now I guess they're going to blow up this place with us in it."

"Uh, right about the first pppart." Pete reflected that few perils are more pernicious than the banal. He unlocked the handcuffs.

"Jesus, how did you do that?" Louise said.

Pete explained that Butterball and his friends had indeed made some mistakes. No cop in his right mind goes without a spare handcuff key, he said, thankfully suggesting that organized criminals are not as organized as they could be. They had left him with the flashlight on his utility belt and both of them with their atropine kits. He calculated they wouldn't blow up the mine until Carlo, who was obviously Mr. Big, had time to get to a main road. Pete estimated that would take about a half-hour.

There was another exit, Pete said. It was a narrow angled shaft that had a pulley-operated hand car large enough for two people. He and his brother-in-law had played in it as kids.

The one thing wrong with this route was that they would have to ford a shallow, swampy pool created by ground seepage.

"So?" Louise said.

"Uh, I think it's the s-source of the flies," Pete said.

"Oh, Jesus," Louise said.

Pete thought they could make it in time and it would
be better than trying to storm the entrance and getting
shot down.

"Let's go," Louise said.

The small flashlight revealed thousands of containers
in various stages of decomposition. Some had rusted
through, some were corroded by acids, and some bore
the three-armed radiation symbol.

"My God," Louise said, "those bastards must have
been doing this for years."

They ran as quickly as Louise could go. Three times
she tripped and fell but did not complain. They fought
their way over several mounds of drums that had fallen
in the aisle created for the forklifts. They saw some wires
and explosive charges.

"Shouldn't we cut them or do something, Pete?"

"Uh, no. That might set them off."

They began to see flies, then progressively more of
them, darting and dancing in the beam of the flashlight.
They covered hands with sleeves and used their light
jackets to make hoods that covered all but their eyes.
Flies began to land on them and they began to swat them
away, a process that increased in intensity as the flies
increased in number. The mine was cool, but they were
hot and sweaty from atropine and exertion.

Pete looked at his watch and announced they had perhaps fifteen minutes left. The flies came now in swarms
so thick the beam of the light barely penetrated them.
And as the flies increased, so did the number of radioactive drums.

The flies were ever more aggressive. The place teemed
with them and the sound of their combined droning was
as moaning ejaculating from hell.

"Get off me! Get off me," Louise found herself
screaming aloud.

Get out of here, Pete could hear himself thinking to
the flies as they moved frantically closer to the source,
with quick futile gestures brushing at gluttonous insects
that clustered and clung to their garments—both now hot
to the point of feeling burned, sweat soaking the skin
beneath improvised protective wear, breathing in quick-
ening gasps, fearful that each breath might draw flies into

their very lungs. Pete knew Louise, nervy as she had proved to be, was starting to lose her nerve. He also knew he was starting to lose his. The place, to the two of them, was the underworld, nether region of nightmare. It threatened to savage the mind, sunder sanity, ravage soul and body with damnation before death.

"Oh, God, Pete, how much farther is it? Oh, God! I don't know if I can go on. Oh, Pete, oh, really, do we have to go on?"

"Get out of here!" Pete heard himself yell at the flies, in a voice that sounded to him shrill and plaintive, lacking in force or confidence. Yes, it was the underworld. A place where evil gods who had never worked their will in this part of the world were now conjured to foment agonies. Pete knew his mind was faltering. This had never happened to him before, ever. The Lord is my shepherd . . . he heard himself beginning to pray, beginning to cling to the only solidity many of us seem to have when chaos and evil doom our lives.

"Oh, God, Pete, do we really have to go on?"

The first time she said it had seemed rhetorical to Pete. Now he knew it was real, and that he was asking himself this question too. Why not just open a garment and surrender to the flies? From what he knew, it was a quick death, much quicker than being buried alive when the mine exploded and caved in, with your throat gagging for minutes on filth, your chest convulsing and suffocating in hot dusty darkness . . . But it also occurred to him that there were two of them. To be sure, it was two against literally millions of flies. But with two, one could falter while one could prevail, and then roles could be reversed. He tried to find an answer. "Uh, Louise, I was jjjust about to ask you the same qqqquestion. Uh, how's about when I ask you, you say yes, and when you ask me, I say yes. Deal?"

Louise laughed; nervously, but she laughed. "Deal," she said.

They stumbled on, each quaking physically with terror and revulsion and exhaustion and heat.

"Oh, my, God," Pete suddenly yelled. His flashlight had been pointing straight ahead and the howling flies swarmed so thick they all but stopped its rays. Suddenly

he felt the ground shiver beneath his feet and angled the
flashlight down. "There it is," Pete said at last, and
shone his beam on the source. "Oh!" he gasped.

"Dear God," was all Louise could say.

The pool was phosphorescent and, as oil on water,
colored in multiple hues; ocher, amethyst, bright orange,
aquamarine, viridian, ebony, but above all, emerald.
Everywhere the pool's surface moved, coruscated,
changed as a living thing, kaleidoscope of torture; and
everywhere the dominant hue of the abomination was iridescent green, Chrysops green, quetzal green, color of
the feathered serpent, ancient phantom in whose name
innocent millions had been mutilated to their deaths.
Here, truly, was the heart of evil in the heart of life. Just
above the pool wisped fingers of fog that rose to obscu-
rity among the masses of hovering vampire flies. Just
beneath, motor of its motion, the pool boiled under attack by thousands of adult flies who dived to devour their
own young, gobbling maggoty larvae and pupae. Looking down on this horror in this underworld, Peter Bilyeux
doubted his doubts and his mind turned to the hands of
wicked gods disjoined in time to wreak torments on a
place that neither knew nor feared them. Myths stole their
insidious ways into his inner resources. Not simply Toltec myths, but Norse, Greek, any that told of terror in
the dark pits of our worst imaginings. Here emerged
Charon, ferryman who for a price would row them abreast
the adamantine gates to the hovel of Hades, where
shrieked Cerberus, three-headed dog with dragon's tail,
sentry who admits all but permits none depart.

"Get away from me! Oh, God, get them away from
me," Pete heard himself crying out as much against superstition as against the flies. He noticed that nearby a
large drum bearing the radiation symbol had rusted
through at the bottom, trailing pellets into the muck at
the pool's edge and thence into the liquid itself. Other
barrels leaked other things, and so Pete wondered might
the lethal syrup have been brewed. Or might it have
sprung full-formed from the hand of a hating god?

Pete sucked in his breath and shuddered. He wanted to
scream, as if he had been propelled as a living subject
into a Hieronymous Bosch painting or had fallen among

rotting bodies in a mass grave. Still the pool undulated and the pupae wriggled and the flies droned, scambled, and glutted. Pete looked at his watch again and at the pool again. He wished there were some form of infallible prayer, secret oath, magic incantation, to ward this off. As a protagonist in a classic tragedy, he knew what he must do and knew it would likely mean his death. To do otherwise would breach his contract with God. Still, as all of us, he had somehow thought his death might be tidier when at last he looked upon it.

For minutes he was robbed of his will to escape the explosion. But he was also responsible for the life of Louise . . . and the respect of God. He must go out trying. His boots were supposedly waterproof and he prayed they would withstand the virulent liquid. Louise could not possibly walk through it. He told her this, and that he would have to carry her, and expected her pride to resist but it did not. All pride fled before horror.

"All right," she said, trembling. "Just this once. We may be dead already, even if we get out of this. You can't feel radiation, you know."

They kissed briefly through their covers and held each other's shaking bodies.

He helped Louise to sit straddling his neck and held her legs tightly and stepped timorously into the vile pool. He felt his boots sink in the mire. Deliberately, he set one foot in front of the other. He did not run for fear of splashing the poison onto her. His boots when he lifted them came out with amplified sucking sounds that echoed their fear and disgust. The droning of the flies accreted to a banshee wail. They flew angrily as he trod through their sacred ground. They gathered and burrowed on the clothing of Pete and Louise. One nearly flew into Pete's eye and he shook his head violently to be rid of it. So intent was he on getting through the pool that he did not realize that the female green Chrysops had remained on his naked left eyelid and had begun to do her work.

"Yaaaaaaaaaaaaa," he screamed. The pain was venom and electricity at once and in an instant washed his body with ineffable agony. His heart stopped. He gulped air. The air did nothing. He started to totter. "Ow!," he cried as something stabbed him deep in the chest. He heard her voice as if calling from a mountaintop about atropine. Then he knew she had given him another injection. The heart sputtered. He inhaled deeply. The heart seemed to be somersaulting. He felt dizzy and wanted to sit down. Oh, God, if he could just sit down for a second, just a second, his heart might start beating correctly again. No, he couldn't do that. It would kill them both. But his knees were betraying them both. It seemed the bones that held them rigid were dissolving. He strained his muscles and forced the bones to lock, but his legs now splayed apart. Suddenly he noticed that he felt no more pain. It had gone as quickly as it had come. He was all right except for the heart. It was spastic and not working at all well, but it was working. He would have to stumble to the other side, now only a few meters away. Yes, he would do it, be it the last thing he ever did. With the force of his mind, he stiffened the muscles of his legs and in doing so felt his teeth grind against one another . . .

"Oh," he said. His heart coughed and wheezed like a broken car motor trying to keep running. But it was running. He staggered forward across the pool, a dumb-struck Orpheus crossing his Acheron bearing the wrong Eurydice. Once, he slipped, top-heavy. He faltered, then caught himself in time to keep the woman on his shoulders from falling.

His heart was still erratic and frantic but he could feel it pumping. Now quite drugged from the venom of atropine, derivative of deadly nightshade coursing in his bloodstream, Pete wanted to stop and vomit, but having eaten nothing since the night before had no stomach contents to expel. So the stomach wambled and roiled along with the heart.

Then he was lurching on dry ground. He searched for the pulley car and found it and tumbled Louise onto it. He was now quite hot and weak and nauseated, and his heart still fluttered and protested. He had trouble climbing into the car. Louise tugged at him.

"Oh, Louise," he muttered. "Oh . . . oh . . . I'm sick . . ."

Suddenly there was a short muddled burst of machine-gun fire from overhead.

"I'm sick . . . I'm sick . . ." Pete gasped.

"That's the atropine fighting the toxin, honey," Louise said. "I had to give you an OD, but we'll get you to a hospital."

At last the two of them were in the car. Pete tried to tug on the pulley cable but had little strength. Louise jerked on it with all her might. Slowly, slowly, the car moved upward toward tiny chinks of light leaking through the hatch above.

They reached the hatch and Louise pushed on it. Nothing happened. Pete pushed too and still it would not budge.

"It's . . . locked," Pete said.

Then he heard a familiar and unexpected voice from just outside the hatch. It was huskier and less articulate than the last time he had heard it. "Peter, is that you?" the voice said. It had an edge to it that sounded elated and angry at once.

"Yeah," Pete said. "Adair . . . Adair, is that you?"

"Yeah," Adair said. "Now get your head down. I'm going to blow this lock."

"Okay. Adair . . . I'm sick . . ."

"Get your damned head down, Peter!"

He and Louise ducked and winced at the resounding plangency of the machine gun blasting bullets through splintering wood and hasp and lock.

The hatch was flung open. The tall figure stood over them silhouetted against the glare of day from which they blinked.

"I'm sick . . ." Pete said, delirious.

Adair reached his gloved hand down to pull him from the car.

"No . . ." Pete said. "Take, uh, tttake Louise first. This place is g-going to blow . . . Oh, I'm sick, Adair, Louise . . ."

Adair pulled Louise to freedom.

"Thanks, Adair, whoever you are," she said. "Thank you. That's an interesting fly suit."

"It isn't a fly suit, lady," Adair snapped. "Come on, Peter, hurry."

Adair and Louise yanked him out of the mine and Adair rolled him roughly onto his back on the ground. Adair shot a glance toward the west.

"Hey, be careful," Louise told Adair.

"Shut up, lady," Adair said. He stood over Pete holding an Uzi in one gloved hand and shaking a finger of the other down at him as if reproving a refractory child. "Now listen to me, Peter, there's no time. Now tell me one thing, just one thing: what was she holding when the lightning struck her?"

"Oh, I'm sick . . . Oh, Adair, oh . . . Enid's dead."

"I know, goddammit, what did she have in her hand, Peter, the metal thing, was it a knife?"

"I'm sick, Adair. Yes . . . yes, it was a knife . . . yes, a mmmelted knife was in her hand . . . Oh, God, oh, Enid . . . Enid . . ."

"Thanks, Peter," Adair said, and stalked away.

The alternate exit to the mine lay in a tiny vale a mile or so on the other side of the hill from the main entrance. A small pond with a stand of trees beside it also lay in this glade.

Louise got Pete to his feet and led him to the pond. There she would have to quickly soak the toxin off his boots. She did not notice what was going on until it was too late.

It had been Butterball's misfortune to decide to examine the hatch on the alternate exit and check its padlock and then rope it off to be doubly sure no one would get out. Adair had jumped him and held the Uzi on him. Butterball had tried to sneak Pete's Python out of his belt where he had tucked it. Adair machine-gunned his knees and kicked the pistol from his hand.

Now Butterball was tied securely with multiple coils of his own rope around a tree that stood in the shade. In front of him stood a statue of Quetzalcoatl, the twin of Enid's.

Louise soaked Pete's boots and began to unlace them. She would remove the clothes from both of them and scrub their bodies in the pond against residual radiation.

Adair said nothing when he reached Butterball. He pulled off Butterball's mirrored sunglasses and tossed them aside and looked into Butterball's small blue eyes.

"You hurt me, you cocksucker, and I'm going to kill you for it," Butterball said. "Motherfucker, I'm going to cut your heart out real slow . . ."

Adair un-wound the bandages over his face and showed Butterball his grin.

Butterball's eyes widened.

Adair did not notice the vampire fly land on his cheek. But Butterball did, and it was his turn to grin. He giggled through the pain in his knees as the fly bit down to feast.

But nothing happened. The fly bit, and shook itself, and flew away. Butterball gasped and his eyes dilated further.

The sharp knife sliced in a deep surgical incision from Butterball's sternum to his waist.

"Aaaaaaaaaaa," Butterball screamed, and looked down to behold himself disemboweled.

Louise turned to see Adair's bloody gloved hands pull out large and small intestines, liver, stomach, and spleen.

"Aaccchhh! Ggggooooood! Aaaaaaaaaaaaaaa!" Butterball shrieked and writhed against ropes cutting into his fat and muscle.

Louise jumped up. "Stop that, fella! Stop that," she yelled.

Pete rolled onto his side in time to see Adair's hands slice past Butterball's lungs. Then the hands groped inside the chest. With one hand Adair cut. With the other he yanked.

"Aaaaaaaaaaaa," Butterball screamed and squirmed against the cords. Then he choked and rattled as, in an effusion of blood that soaked both him and Adair, his eyes began to close on the sight of his living heart being torn from its body.

"Oh . . . my . . . God . . ." Louise said.

"It's not a god!" Adair bawled, turning toward the full moon setting in the west under the noonday sun. He held the heart dripping with gore in the direction of the moon. "There's your heart of evil in the heart of life, you damned lie . . ."

As Adair was baying at the moon, Pete and Louise saw his face for the first time. The nose was mostly gone, leaving cavities as those on a bare skull. The lips, too, were gone and the teeth sparkled where flesh belonged.

The face was covered with lesions and its flesh was utterly dead. Only the eyes were untouched.

Adair threw the heart down and stamped on it. Then he unzipped his trouser fly and urinated over it. Then he looked at the moon, only the tip of which could be seen over the western horizon.

"This is for you, feathered serpent. Are you pleased, you myth of Satan? Why don't you take it back to Tula with you? You killed my Enid! And now . . . now . . . now I've killed you! How does it feel to be a dead god?"

Adair picked up the defiled heart and hurled it in the direction of the vanishing moon.

Then he shuffled to the opposite side of the pond from Pete and Louise and tried to wash the blood from himself. He re-wound his bandages and put his face in his hands and wept.

"Uh, Louise," Pete said, "what . . . what's wrong with his face?"

Louise stroked Pete's hair. "Hansen's disease, honey," she said. "Leprosy. Poor man, I've never heard of it so advanced."

The doctors and Charlie were nearly run down by the Mercedes. The driver simply honked the horn and sped down the road, leaving the three men on it to scatter or be killed. Charlie wrote down the license-plate number.

The bus lurched and rattled to a stop at a place with a high hill on one side of the road and a sheer drop on the other.

"What the hell coming down now, girl?" Talmadge said.

"Shut your mouth," Irene retorted. Slab-sided Talmadge was beginning to wear badly on her nerves. She fiddled with the wires and cursed at being zapped. The starter worked but not the engine.

Some of the boys, including Albert Tipton, got out and opened the hood and peered at all the wires and hoses and greasy things.

Irene cranked to no avail. Albert came inside and looked over Irene's shoulder at the instruments. "It's out of gas, Irene."

"Oh, shit," Irene said.

They were all outside the bus milling in the sun and trying to think when the big Mercedes skidded to a stop in front of them and honked its horn.

A man in a suit got out and ran up to the bus. "Hey, kids," he shouted, "you're going to have to move your bus. We've got to leave. We're in a hurry for a business conference, if you's know what I mean, important business. Where's your driver?"

Irene would have to think fast. She decided to put on her Butterfly McQueen act. "Oh, suh," she said, "driver juss upped and runned away wif de keys, don't know what he have in mind to do."

"He ran away?" the man said.

"Yes, suh, just like dat." Irene wrung her hands and hung her head forlornly. "He mus've been smokin' dope or somefing 'cause he juss stop de bus and runned off and lef us wifout no food, no water, no nuffin'."

"Where did he go?" the man in the suit said.

"Down dat road dere." Irene pointed in the direction from whence they had come and in which the bus blocked the path of the Mercedes.

"How long ago was that?" the man said.

"Oh, long time, now, suh, long time. Mebbe a hour or two."

The man jumped when the horn of the Mercedes honked behind him. Irene looked at the deeply tinted windows and shrugged and sucked on her thumb and slid her toes lazily in the dust of the road in her best dumbass style. The man ran to the car and held a hasty conversation with someone in the back seat. Then he got in and the Mercedes backed up the road.

The young people heard the sounds of a number of airplanes approaching. Soon they saw they were olive-drab helicopters with white stars on them flying fast and low above.

"It's the army!" Irene said.

Major Wilson Spreckels could get no more information on the nature of his mission than that a bunch of deadly flies were raising hell in some hick town in the boonies and he was to offer assistance to local authorities and to keep an eye peeled. He had begun to suspect it might be some kind of trick played by the inspector general to test his team's combat readiness. Deadly flies, indeed.

Then all hell broke loose.

The doctors and Charlie had almost reached the mine skulking under cover of woods when they heard a terrible screaming on the far side of the hill.

They saw the King Cobras, who had been starting up trucks and motorcycles and a maroon Cadillac Eldorado, stop everything and get out to listen. Some of them began to walk around toward the sound.

Dr. Applebaum stood up from their covert to get a better view and in doing so made a good view of himself. A King Cobra saw him and opened fire with an Uzi.

The bullets cracked by him and he got their message and dived for the ground, having been preceded by Charlie and Dr. Knox.

"That was stupid, Doctor," Charlie told him.

"They're shooting at us," Abe said. "Jesus Christ, they're shooting at us! What do they have against us? We didn't do anything to them. My God, they're shooting at us!"

"We noticed," Dr. Knox said.

The King Cobras had stopped their quest for the origin of the screaming and concentrated all their attention, and their fire, on two homosexual doctors and an exasperated native American. Bullets crashed into trees and sent leaves spinning around the three with loud whipping sounds. One tree limb was severed and groaned toward the ground.

"Doctor, I gotta say that again, that was really fucking stupid," Charlie said. "Now those pricks are after us with tommy guns and all we got is lousy pop guns. Shit! Now I'm only going to tell you guys this once. Save your shots. Don't even *think* about pulling a trigger until those bastards are close enough so you could hit 'em with a stick. They got a helluva lot more firepower than we do. Jesus, that was stupid! Jesus! Shit! Now I know how Custer felt."

"I'm sorry, Charlie," Abe said.

"Man, I hope you ain't gonna be sorrier yet," Charlie said.

Only Dolores the tarantula remained unperturbed.

The electronic device that would detonate the explosives reminded itself that only a minute remained.

Major Spreckels' helicopters sent swift dragonfly shadows hurtling across the road where the kids waved and applauded.

"What the hell is that?" the major said, noticing the bus and the youngsters and the Mercedes limousine backing up the dirt road. The IG may have pulled a really tricky one here. "Matthews, Witkowsky," the major called into his radio, "get your butts down there and check it out. We'll stay in touch."

"Yes, sir," said Matthews, who was a black man, and hovered over the bus.

"Yes, sir," said Witkowski, who was not a black man, and hovered over the Mercedes.

The shadows raced across the landscape. The major noticed a group of large trucks beside a hill, alongside more than a score of motorcycles and a maroon Cadillac. Men in strange costumes were running around ducking their heads. On the far side of the hill, three people were loafing beside a pond, probably fishing.

Then out of the corner of his eye, Major Spreckels sighted some telltale puffs of smoke belching from the men near the trucks and motorcycles. The major craned his neck and stared. The calls of distant bugles blown past distant times in tunes of glory echoed in the major's mind with resonances of military triumph, even as Valkyriean choruses throbbed in his heart. To hell with selling insurance. "Men," he called into the radio, "this is a firefight. Fix bayonets, cock your weapons, and put 'em on safe. Fasten your flak jackets. Fire only if fired upon. Men . . . Matthews and Witkowski, do you read me?"

"Yes, sir," everyone said.

"Now listen, everybody," the major said. "All personnel on the ground here are to be detained pending the arrival of civil authority. Evacuate any sick or wounded."

The major's helicopter banked on its side and slipped

toward the firefight. "We're going in, men," he called. "Follow me!"

This helicopter tilted over Pete and Louise and Adair, followed by a dozen others. Louise laughed and Pete smiled.

The electronic device decided now was the time.

The top of the hill flew off as Krakatoa in eruption.

Shock waves, rocks, pebbles, and dirt beat upward against the helicopter of Major Spreckels They forced the ship into a quick downward slide with its rotor perpendicular to the boiling ground. The major bumped his head and held on for his life as they plummeted. The ship was righted mere feet above the turmoil.

"Just what in goddamn hell is going on down there?" the major boomed.

Matthews' helicopter landed near the bus and Matthews and his men clambered out and dashed toward the young people. "Hey," Matthews said to them, "what's happening, babes?"

Irene Byrne grinned at him. "Hallelujah," she said, clapping her hands together, just like a Protestant.

Witkowski had a little trouble with the Mercedes. When he went one way, the car went another. When he zigged, it zagged. Enough was enough, Witkowski thought, and bounced the runners of the helicopter several times on the roof of the Mercedes, for emphasis. The car stopped. Witkowski landed and he and his men in flak jackets, combat helmets, carrying M-16s with bayonets mounted, surrounded the car just as the mine blew its top. Witkowski was amazed by the explosion, and even more amazed to see three men in business suits and a uniformed chauffeur emerge from the limo with their hands up.

Charlie and the doctors watched as the mine exploded. They saw an army helicopter nearly crash into the devastation, then right itself and skim the ground to land in the no-man's-land between them and the King Cobras. The rotor of the machine was still spinning when a soldier with gold on his helmet jumped out and pulled a pistol and cocked it and pointed it at the heavens. With his palm flat and parallel to the ground, he waved the whole of his other arm in a signal for peace. Then he blew a traffic cop's whistle to the four winds to denote he was bent on restoring order. His voice bawled, "Settle down, everybody!"

Charlie and the doctors felt the wind beating down on them from many helicopters landing. Leaves waved, grasses bent.

"Yahoooooooo," Charlie yelled. "It's the last stand for the King Cobras!"

Soldiers came out and swarmed over the terrain.

The King Cobras, already the worse for their encounters with a feminist pathologist, a rural deputy sheriff, and his half-mad brother-in-law, offered no resistance. Most of them were on parole anyhow and were experienced enough to know when the jig was up. The national guardsmen eyed their Nazi helmets covetously, perhaps remembering the bygone booty with which their forebears had returned from the fields of Europe.

Dr. Frederick Knox put his pistol on the ground and lit his pipe and strolled up to a captain. "Good afternoon, Captain."

"Good afternoon, sir," the captain said.

"Uh, Captain, we're medical doctors and we're searching for a missing woman and man. Did you happen to see anyone from the air?"

"Well, yes, sir, there are two men and a woman by a pond on the far side that hill, sir," the captain said.

"Good," Dr. Knox said. "Can you give us directions? We'd like to have a look."

"Well, uh, sir, I'm sorry, but I'm under orders that all personnel be temporarily detained," the captain said.

Dr. Knox tamped the tobacco in his pipe with his index finger and puffed. He had not been a former army doctor for nothing. "Well, Captain, that being the case, uh, as I say, we're medical doctors and we have reason to believe there may be sick or wounded over there needing medical attention. Is there any reason why you and your men couldn't detain us over to that pond?"

The captain thought about this. "No, sir," he said, "we can do that if sick or wounded are involved. Climb aboard, sir."

When the mine exploded, Pete and Louise covered their heads and lay prone. The earth moved. The water of the pond rushed back and forth in waves as if carried by a giant drunken man. The explosion and its earthquake subsiding, they looked at Adair, who remained where he was, covered with dirt that stuck to the blood he could not rid from himself. Then they saw the hill slowly implode and fill the mine as sand pouring to the bottom of an hourglass.

"Well, that's the end of the flies," Louise said. "Damn, I don't feel too good myself. Shit. Oh, hell, honey, now we'll never know what the toxin was or the chemistry of its transmission . . . Damn, I feel lousy. Well, maybe it's for the best. Suppose the army or the CIA got a hold of—"

"Louise, I . . . really . . . sick, damn . . ." Pete babbled.

She put her hand on his face and felt his pulse and then his chest. The face was flushed and hot to the touch. The pulse was fast. The heart fibrillated. He complained of feeling excited and sick at once in his delirium. He said his throat was dry and he had a thirst but could not swallow his own saliva. She limped to get water from the pond to daub his face. "You're tachycardiac, honey, but you'll be okay. We'll get you to a hospital . . ."

The helicopter landed near them. The doctors and Charlie and some soldiers ran up to them. Smiles and greetings were exchanged.

Dr. Knox thought it prudent to get Geiger readings from them. Of course, a Geiger counter can only measure the radiation remaining on you. It cannot measure the radiation you have absorbed if it cannot measure the source. Only a dosimeter you had been wearing at the time of exposure, or the symptoms, or fate, can measure that.

Charlie did not notice the female green Chrysops fly that alit on his neck. But Abe Applebaum did, and grabbed it by the wing and with some ostentation showed it to Charlie and stamped it dead.

Dr. Knox played the meter over Louise and his eyes grew grim. Then he played it over Pete and bit through the stem of the pipe in his mouth. "Captain," he shouted. "Abe! Charlie! Soldiers! Let's get the clothes off these people and wash them in this pond now. Now! We have no time to spare, no time at all!''

Adair tested negatively for radioactivity. Pete and Louise were scrubbed and wrapped in blankets and brought into the helicopter that would take them to Hershey with Dr. Knox and Adair. The helicopter rose. Charlie Sevenpines walked over to Dr. Applebaum and shook his hand.

Aloft, Pete was no longer conscious. This was just as well. Had he been able to hear the urgent conversations in the helicopter, it would have given him little heart for the ordeal that had only begun.

Part Four

BEYOND THE SECOND SATURDAY

'Tis now the very witching time of night,
When churchyards yawn and hell itself breathes out
Contagion to this world.

25

Of all the deaths that came to this place at this time, that faced by Deputy Sheriff Peter Bilyeux threatened to be the worst.

But at least he no longer dreamed of the execution in Saigon. In his waking moments the first night in the hospital he concluded from the awful shootings and sacrifice that there was an immanent dimension of cruelty in the human heart, the depths of which he could not fathom and perhaps would be well-advised to plumb no further. After he had killed the first King Cobra, the killing of others became progressively easier, and remembering this frightened Pete. He began to see the metaphor of human sacrifice as equivalent to what we do daily for want of ethical restraint.

He was gratified in knowing that the horrors of the week past could be laid to powers neither greatly politic nor, as he now thought again, greatly mystic. It was a conspiracy of mediocrity, a nasty crime done by nasty people, a police matter. His principal professional regret was in not suspecting the sheriff from the time of the fluoride episode.

He awoke late on Sunday morning feeling refreshed and cured. He lay inside a plastic tent. Whatever they had done for him made him feel as if he had gone to a spa. His recovery had been miraculous, even the nurses said so. But he noticed they did not venture close to him or stay with him for long. Every hour or so an intern with a clipboard and a meter came in to take readings and jot down information. He also noticed there was no telephone in the room, and that when he asked for one, the answers were evasive.

He felt terrific and said so to anyone within earshot. The only thing wrong was that his lower legs hurt as though they had been badly sunburned.

Dr. Knox came by later and looked him over. He paid particular attention to Pete's legs and feet. Pete said he wanted to get up and go to Mass. Dr. Knox said he was looking very good and had fully recovered from the sting of the fly and the overdose of atropine. He was the only one to have been bitten by a venomous fly to live to tell the tale, Dr. Knox said. That was fine, Pete said, he would like to thank God for it at Mass. That was out of the question, Dr. Knox said. Pete asked of Louise and Adair. Both were doing well. Louise was in her own room. Adair was also in his own room, under guard, as the prosecutor had not yet decided to seek an indictment. Dr. Knox would get Adair a good lawyer. Pete would like to see Louise and Adair and talk with them. That would be impossible under the circumstances, Dr. Knox said. Pete would have to remain under observation in reverse isolation for a few weeks.

"Uh, a few *w-weeks?*" Pete said.

"Yes, Pete," Dr. Knox said, "maybe longer. There are, uh, complications from your exposure to gamma radiation."

"Oh. Bbbut, Dr. Knox, can I at least go to Mass?"

"I think we know each other well enough for you to call me Fred, Pete, and, no, you can't go to Mass. You can't go anywhere for a few weeks. I'm sorry to have to say it, but that's how it is. I'll see if I can get a priest sent up. How's that?"

Father Fierro came by late that afternoon wearing his sacerdotal robes. Pete had been dulling his mind with the remote-control television in the room and toying with the idea of escaping. He was glad to see the priest/mayor. They chatted and joked and exchanged stories of the flies. Only one person had been killed by a fly since the mine exploded—a tourist from Belgrade, who had apparently been hitchhiking. Abe Applebaum and Charlie Sevenpines, assisted by the volunteer firemen and auxiliary police and boy scouts, had begun a massive effort to trap those Chrysops flies not entombed in the mine. The national guard was also helping them and had flown in large shipments of insect repellent. News reporters from the big TV networks were there and their stories would break on the Monday-night news. Everyone considered Pete to have been the key person in cracking the case. The mayor in Father Fierro was there to convey the gratitude of all. The county board of supervisors, who knew nothing of the case until the mine blew up, had met in emergency session. A resolution commending Pete and the doctors and Charlie passed unanimously. The priest confided that the board was holding appointment to the unexpired term of sheriff open, pending Pete's recovery.

Father Fierro heard Pete's confession and gave him communion and said a short Mass. Pete noticed he left the wine and wafer on a nearby table and did not reach under the plastic of his tent.

That night his feet hurt more. He became violently ill and vomited and lapsed in and out of sleep. At dawn the pain in his feet was worse, but he felt fine otherwise. The stomach illness had gone, though he had little appetite.

By Wednesday the pain became intolerable and he was being sedated. Fred Knox brought a burn specialist into the room. The burn doctor was covered from toenail to eyeball with light plastic. He reached under the tent to work with Pete's feet. Pete sat up and saw flesh shine pink as hot ham from a microwave oven.

"Pete, please lie back down." Fred Knox said.

The doctors left and Pete was alone until a plastic-garbed, plastic-gloved nurse came in to give him one of his many injections. He had long noticed that anyone who ever reached under his tent was covered cap-à-pie in light plastic. He knew he had survived fly and atropine poisoning and knew now they feared he might not survive radiation poisoning.

But he didn't care all that much now that Enid was dead. He thought of her and grieved and prayed constantly for her.

The following Saturday, Pete woke late and felt sick again and rang the nurse and asked for something into which he might throw up, just in case. He noticed they had been taking more blood samples from him. He also noticed that his scalp felt tender and a few hairs from it had begun to fall on his sanitized pillows and sheets. He developed the habit of passing his hand over his head, yet each time he did it more hair came out. He was feeble and dizzy and fell back asleep after the needles had done jabbing him. He wondered how Louise was doing.

A few days later he felt better and had a surprise visitor. A nurse came in first. Then Adair ambled in, tall and easy and athletic, followed by Dr. Knox.

Adair wore white gloves and gauze taped to his forehead that fell over his face like the veil of an Arab woman.

"Hi, Pete," he said. "Long time no see."

"Hi, Adair," Pete said. "Uh, how you ddoing?"

Adair laughed his elegant laugh, the lord come to call on the stolid squire. "Oh, okay, considering," he said. "Leprosy's not very contagious, Pete, don't worry. You have to be around it for years before it catches you."

It was Pete's turn to laugh. "Uh, I wasn't really w-w-worried about that, Adair. I think I'm, uh, immune." Pete remembered how Enid and Adair had looked before. They were beautiful.

"Uh," Pete said, "what have you been up to?"

"No good, of course." Adair chuckled. He gave Pete a long explication of the studies of the ancient Mexican Indian civilizations that had so obsessed and invigorated him, of the mysteries of their revenances, and of his theories about the gods. Adair grew more excited as he talked and Pete could sense him beaming through his ruined face. Pete knew it had been a long time since Adair had relaxed and conversed with anyone in English.

"They're us, you know," Adair said. "I guess I just figured that out."

"Uh, uh, who are us?" Pete said.

"The gods. All of them. Quetzalcoatl, Tezcatlipoca, you name 'em, Pluto, Zeus, Cyprus, Athena, Onid, Vulcan, Apollo, Hades, Thor, Mars . . . they, they're just metaphors for ourselves. For our better and worse selves.

It's like we're all Manichaean heretics, with maybe a little Freud thrown into the bargain.''

Pete resisted the temptation to know what on earth a Manichaean heretic was. As to the pantheon of pagan dieties—with the exception of Tezcatlipoca, who seemed to growl good sense and may have come to some lonely ancient as an inspiration of incorruptible majesty; that is, God—they could dump the lot into the nearest bedpan, Freud included. Sure, Adair was probably right, they probably were projections of ourselves. We gave them our reality and they gave us license to indulge in fatuous pastimes, rather like people who accrue vast debt with nary a thought of paying it off. "Uh, what about G-G-G-God?'' Pete said.

"Didn't leave a trace, did He?'' Adair said. "I mean, archaeologically speaking, don't I?''

"Mmmm,'' Pete said.

As Adair talked, he revealed other things about the past few years. He had concluded that because the Huerta clinic had not arrested his disease, he was surely finished. Now the doctors at Hershey told him he had a chance of remission. None of them pretended to be experts on Hansen's disease, but they did what they could as swiftly as they could. They had phoned the National Leprosarium at Carville, Louisiana. The leprosarium advised Hershey to send Adair to them forthwith when they heard of his symptoms. Negotiations with the prosecutor had been lengthy, but were at last complete and Adair would sleep that night in Carville.

"Peter, I feel awful about killing that guy,'' Adair said. "I guess . . . I don't know . . . I guess my disease and Enid's death and the questions, questions, questions I've been trying to resolve about the allegory of human sacrifice, I guess they all got to me. I sort of look on that killing as a kind of accident. You know, one of those silly human accidents that make you feel so stupid afterwards. What do you think?''

Pete did not answer. Instinctively, he passed his hand over his head and was mortified when a patch of hair came off with it. He tried to secrete the hair under his sheet but suspected he was fooling nobody, surely not himself. He came to a private opinion about Adair's opinion. He thought in addition to leprotherapy, Adair could benefit from psychotherapy too, the right kind, if such there was for Adair. He changed the subject. "Uh, remember, Adair, how we used to cccatch crawdads?"

Pete could feel Adair smile. He fought back tears for the tragic family, ruined by powers they could not control. Perhaps there was hope in the children of Elspeth. If Pete lived, he would try to be an uncle to these children. He was no radiation expert, but he knew he would never, or should never, have children now. He passed his hand over his scalp again and it came away with a good part of his forelock in it and Pete tried to hide this, too, under the sheet. He spoke to distract as much as to converse. "Uh, well, Adair, I hear the c-crawdads in Louisiana are damn near as big as lobsters. They say they're, uh, delicious. Uh, maybe one of these days I'll get down there and we'll eat some."

"It's a deal, Peter," Adair said. "I'd shake on it but I guess your hands are in quarantine." He was trying to joke.

Pete tried to laugh.

"Oh, I brought you something," Adair said. "I won't be needing it anymore." He pulled out of a sanitized bag his statue of Quetzalcoatl and set it on Pete's table.

Pete restrained his hand from once more going to his hair. "Oh, uh, thanks," he said.

"It's valuable, you know, especially in a set of two," Adair said. "Just look at the workmanship."

"Oh, yes," Pete said.

Pete wished him good luck and they said their goodbyes.

Pete fell back in the bed exhausted and sick again and wondered why he felt this way and why his feet and legs now looked as though they had acquired a rich Florida tan.

The negative ions in the cells of his body had invaded the territory of the positive ions, and the positive ions retaliated by invading the territory of the negative ions. The war thus waged wreaked havoc on his bone marrow and its ability to infuse healthy corpuscles into his bloodstream. He worried about Louise and what had happened and would happen to the cells of her body. He knew he had come to feel something for her and also knew it could be nothing like what he had felt for Enid. But he liked and admired her, felt good about her, felt responsible for her, and in better times would like to compare forensic notes with her.

Pete had been reluctant to force any issue with Fred Knox but knew he was getting sicker and wished to compose himself and settle his mind while he could still think clearly.

He pressed Fred on the next visit. The doctor sat down in a chair. "I'm not really accustomed to being a personal physician," he said. "But I guess I've sort of assumed that role in your case, my friend." He paused and took a breath, then continued. "Physicians are of two schools of thought when it comes to telling the whole story to their patients. Some always do, some never do, and most make judgments of which patients can tolerate the knowledge and which can't . . ."

"Uh, I think you know what j-judgment I want," Pete said.

Fred Knox took the hint and another breath. "Okay. We're doing what we can, obviously. The critical factor in your case is the radiation absorbed dose, or RAD. We don't know how much you got and couldn't without measuring the source of exposure. In our lifetimes, we're all exposed to about eight RADs of environmental X or gamma radiation, both having the same effect on the body. Chest and dental X rays account for about eight more RADs. In an exposure of up to twenty-five RADs there's usually no illness but there may be some long-term effects. From twenty-five to a hundred RADs there are usually detectable changes in the blood, the lymph nodes, and spleen, which, of course, your system shows. From a hundred to three hundred RADs there are severe blood changes, nausea, and vomiting. From three hundred to six hundred RADs there are extreme changes in the blood and bone marrow, severe anemia, epilation or hair loss, anorexia, severe nausea, skin blotches, gastrointestinal complications, probable reproductive sterility, and often more symptoms, not necessarily in that order. At five hundred RADs, about fifty percent of patients survive. Above six hundred RADs, few survive—"

"Uh, how many RADs do you think I got, Fred?"

"Well, Pete . . . well, we just don't know. We can only extrapolate that, uh, based on the reading I took from you at the mine and your symptoms now . . . Well, I'd be less than honest if it were not my professional opinion that you took six hundred RADs or more. I'm sorry but not hopeless. You shouldn't be either."

"I see," Pete murmured. "What about Louise?"

"You're talking about apples and oranges, my friend, as they say. I'd guess her to be about three hundred RADs. She's been sick, but her blood count has improved to the degree that she's out of reverse isolation. She's sure to recover in the short run."

"Uh, what about the long run?" Pete said.

"We'll talk about that later," Fred said. "Let's get back to you. Right now, you're in one of the best medical institutions in the United States. I've been consulting with people all over the world who are experts in radiation sickness. Some of them got their feet wet—excuse me, that wasn't an intentional pun, in Chernobyl and Hiroshima and Nagasaki. In fact, since an incident in Brazil when some people were badly irradiated, a sort of informal nuclear-accident medical team has been forming. I've been in touch with some of its members, and to be frank, no one is euphoric about your prospects. But no one has pronounced irrevocable sentence of death on you either. Treatments will progress as they have been, well in advance of your symptoms. Starting tomorrow you'll be getting round-the-clock infusions of GM-CSF, a new blood-cell-stimulating factor that showed promise in Brazil. The biggest danger now and for some time is secondary infection. You'll be allowed no more visitors until your blood count and other functions show progressive improvement. That fellow, Adair, was an exception. There will be no more exceptions."

"Not even L-L-Louise?"

"No, not even Louise."

"How, uh, how long before we know for sure, Fred?"

"God knows, Pete. I'd say by fall, but that's just an educated guess. Now . . . now . . . I want to tell you one more thing. I've told you what I have because you have a strong mind. As I said, we're doing all we can. That's a two-way street, Pete. There's a dimension in medicine that we don't understand and may not understand for a long, long time, if ever. You've got to work too, you see."

" 'Therein the patient must minister to himself,' " Pete said.

"That's from *Macbeth*, right?"

"Uh, right."

"Well, you see," Fred Knox said. "Shakespeare knew as much about it four hundred years ago as we do now. You've got to really want to make it, Pete."

"Wh-what for?" Pete said.

Fred understood how he felt. Louise had told him about Enid. "I was shocked to hear about the loss of your wife. But I think the question you've got to ask yourself is whether Enid would rather you lived or died. I'm sure you don't doubt the answer. Besides, maybe there's work for you to do, my friend. I hope I can call you that even though you must think of me as a sort of evil oracle." He smiled and clapped Peter on the shoulder from outside the tent.

"Uh, Fred, can I ask you for a fffavor? Uh, I'd like someone to get a Thomas Valley deputy to go to my house and get the, uh, mate of this statue." Pete pointed to Adair's Quetzalcoatl. "Uh, would you have the sonofabitch disinfected and put next to his p-pal here?"

"Why?" Fred asked.

"Why not?" Pete said.

"Okay," Fred said, and left the room.

Pete was alone with his thoughts in a small room in a large place humming and thumping with its work of teaching, healing the sick, and comforting the dying.

He looked over to Adair's Quetzalcoatl. "Are you the one who caused all this?" he said, and thought not.

Now Pete knew it was time for him to be reconciled with Enid.

* * *

By the fourth week all the deadly Chrysops flies that could be found—along with a good many innocent ones—were captured and destroyed by Abe Applebaum, Charlie Sevenpines, the guardsmen, and volunteers. No more people had been killed by the deer flies, nor was it thought any more would be. The Elmsford County prosecutor gained national publicity by swiftly bringing indictments against Carlo Monreale and a member of his crime family, one Anthony (Tony Monkey) Mancusi, who owned a maroon Cadillac Eldorado. Rupert R. Chandler and three members of the Elmsford County Board of Health were also indicted. The surviving King Cobras were indicted too, and their paroles revoked. The badly decomposed body of Sister N'Teta was found in a brook by a boy scout. And Pete Bilyeux grieved for his dead wife and had lost all his hair. His skin broke out in ugly blotches and he bled often from his nose, and his teeth were loose in his mouth. This mattered little as he could no longer eat and had to be nourished intraveneously.

By the end of the sixth week, the charges against Carlo Monreale had been dropped for lack of evidence. The others would face trial. But the headlines had doomed Carlo's career. He could only hope that his peers would tacitly declare him Mafia chieftain emeritus and allow him to retire unmurdered. And Pete Bilyeux grieved for his dead wife and had lost fifty-one pounds. Despite the best treatments, his blood count plunged. He no longer had the strength to operate the remote-control TV. Nor did he care to.

All he could do was think, and even that he could not sustain with clarity longer than a few minutes at a time. He pondered the loose ends of the case, and those of his life.

He thought of the things that could have driven Enid to divest herself of the tiny myths by which we overcome our daily frustrations, and to invest everything in a vast allegory.

And so had Adair and Enid succumbed to follies ancient as man.

Myth need not be mere fable or metaphor, Pete thought. Mythology and ideology may also be close relatives. He reflected on the sheriff's professed political conservatism and concluded there was nothing conservative about poisoning the earth. And so had the sheriff used ideological myth to mask his avarice.

And so did Pete understand that the banners of whatever ideologies under which so much of our world paraded were diaphanous streamers designed to guise old passions; the unending human compulsions to glut the lust of greed and to oppress. Ideology was not morality, which Pete came to define as that which is not injurious to your world or fellow creatures. Ideology is often the strangler of ideas. Perhaps time spent on ideologies and myths would be better served in contemplating a new pragmatism, even a pragmatheism. Pete thought of the message of Jesus, the first pragmatheist, who taught of the advent of the Kingdom of God. Pete felt that kingdom to be here now and always, if shunned or unseen beyond mirages of myth, metaphysics, and mysticism.

By the eighth week, it was discovered Peter Bilyeux had pneumonia. His blood count had begun to show improvement. His isolation was impregnable. It should not have happened.

They worked frantically on him but he could scarcely feel aught but fever and acute discomfort and an irresistible tension that had been with him for a very long time.

At 2:43 in the early hours of a Sunday morning he lay alone in the room and felt this tension begin to depart.

A peace came to him such as he had never known nor imagined. At last he was free. He was somewhere in the room but no longer in his body. He saw the body lying thin and ghostly and still. He saw the wires leading from it, the tubes leading from arm and chest to the IV trolley. He saw somewhere a television monitor with movements on it that slowed and stopped.

He began to go to another place. He was being drawn through a tunnel and someone was standing in the light at the other end. It was Enid.

He held her and kissed her. Then she broke off the kiss

and put her hands on his shoulders and gently pushed him away. "It's not time, Peter," she said. "You have to go back."

Oh, no, he thought, oh, God, no, I don't want to go back.

"Go back, Pete," Enid said.

He was propelled backward through the tunnel again. He was in the hospital room again and he sensed the monstrous tension returning. They had torn the plastic from his tent and were doing things to his body. A man was pounding on the body's chest.

Oh, no, Pete thought. Oh, no.

The brilliance of scarlet, gold, and bronze leaves defied an ironclad sky where romped eddies of tiny motes of early snow. The people in the parking lot wore winter clothes zipped and buttoned against the first deep chill of autumn.

The plastic tent was gone and they were letting him onto his feet now. His blood count had shown steady improvement and they could give him food to eat again. He sat in a wheelchair by the window and looked out over the parking lot. He ran his hand over his head and felt the stubble of hair starting to return.

Flowers, notes, plants, cards, and sundry knickknacks littered the room. The twin Quetzalcoatls squatted on their table and he had come to like them now that they were truly stone artifacts, beautiful of craftsmanship, old friends. Next to them lay a single bald-eagle feather with this note from Charlie Sevenpines: "I snuck up on the bastard and pulled this out of his butt just for you. What do you say about a country whose national symbol has become an endangered species?"

Taped to the wall over the Toltec statues was a huge four-color picture sent by Abe Applebaum. It depicted Dolores the tarantula posing provocatively in the nude in the style of a *Playboy* centerfold.

Dr. Fred Knox came in and said good morning and sat down in a chair. It was time for their appointed talk.

The short run was over. The long run was about to begin. It would be any number of delayed effects, most likely cancer.

"You'll run the highest risk of getting it in about three to twenty years, Pete. It might show up earlier or later, maybe even never. But statistically there's a probability that you'll get it. Now, you don't have to be cancer-phobic. Lots of people survive it and go into remission and die of old age. The more we learn about it, the more able we are to cope with it. It just means you'll have to cope with the idea of being alert for the symptoms, and having a thorough checkup every few months for the rest of your life . . ."

"Uh, and when I get it I'll need rrradiation treatments, right?" Pete said wryly. He remembered a recent letter from Adair, who was quite optimistic now that he was in Carville. But the letter also said that Elspeth had died of her cancer. I'd rather have leprosy than cancer, Adair wrote. Well, so be it, Pete thought. "Mmmy, uh, my body is a living time bomb, you mean."

"Well," Fred said, "that's a little histrionic, but not altogether inaccurate."

"Uh, well, Fred, so what else is new?" Pete chuckled.

"That's right, Pete." Fred smiled. "That's right. You could be run over by a garbage truck the minute you step out the door here. We're all living on borrowed time, aren't we? Now for some good news. I think you'll be out of here by the end of next month at the latest. And, starting today, you can have visitors. I know someone who's been waiting to see you for a long time."

"I, uh, can ssscarcely wait," Pete said with mock sarcasm.

Fred grinned and got up and touched Pete on the shoulder and walked out of the room, leaving the door open behind him.

Louise stepped into the doorway wearing a business suit. She had lost a little weight but looked good. She walked in with no sign of a limp and sat in a chair opposite Pete.

She had not seen him since that day at the mine nine months before. She knew what to expect, but was still shocked by the sight. He looked to her like a navy flyer shot down early in World War II who had spent four years in Japanese prisoner-of-war camps. She tried not to let her eyes or tongue betray what her heart felt.

"Hiya, baldy," Louise said.

"Uh, Louise," Pete said, "jjjudging from your bed-side manner, it's, uh, easy to see why your most loyal patients are corpses."

Louise laughed. "Freddie give you the pep talk about cancer?"

"Yeah," Pete said.

"Well, join the club, kid," Louise said. "That makes two of us. I quit smoking, though."

They laughed and needled each other and talked over their experiences. Louise had been back at work since the month before and had wanted to see him since they had both been brought to the hospital but no exception could be made for her.

"Freddie tells me they may turn you loose by Thanks-giving."

"Yeah."

"Well?" she said.

"Well, uh, what?" he said.

"Your place or mine?" she said.

They looked at each other and smiled with closed lips. Each saw from the other's eyes that they knew a great deal about each other. Their eyes were moist.

A little embarrassed and both still hurt in different ways, they broke off this look and let their eyes wander over the parking lot lying beneath the heavy sky. They saw a young couple get in a car with a newborn baby. Louise wiped her glasses and shook her hair and replaced the glasses and watched the new parents leave.

"I guess that's not for either of us now," Louise said.

"No," he said. "No, uh, I guess not." Pete got up and shuffled to the table and turned the twin statues of Quetzalcoatl to face the wall. "Well," he said, "uh, at least we don't have pppoisonous flies to worry about any-more."

Louise watched him walk with difficulty back to the wheelchair. She wondered if she should help him and then thought better of it. "I don't know, honey," she said. "There are still a lot of toxic waste dumps out there."

"And, uh, Quetzalcoatl never got back to Tula," he said.

"What?" she asked.

"It was jjjust a story," he said.

About the Author

AN HONORS GRADUATE OF SAN DIEGO STATE UNIVERSITY, **Stanley R. Moore** has lived in Hawaii, on both coasts of the U.S., and in between. He had pursued such varied vocations and avocations as truck driver, Navy officer, Top Secret courier, auto race driver, mayor, skin diver, filmmaker, marketing analyst, consultant, and writer—when not working on novels, screenplays, short stories, and poems. An avid bicyclist and outdoors person, Moore hunts for wild mushrooms, and once hiked to the bottom of the Grand Canyon and back in a single day. NIGHTSHADE is his first novel.

There's an epidemic with 27 million victims. And no visible symptoms.

It's an epidemic of people who can't read.

Believe it or not, 27 million Americans are functionally illiterate, about one adult in five.

The solution to this problem is you... when you join the fight against illiteracy. So call the Coalition for Literacy at toll-free **1-800-228-8813** and volunteer.

Volunteer Against Illiteracy. The only degree you need is a degree of caring.

TERROR ... TO THE LAST DROP

☐ **SHADOWSHOW by Brad Strickland.** The midnight movies at the Shadowshow Theater offered savage sex and bloodcurdling violence that went beyond any "X" rating ... but no one warned the audience they'd see themselves acting out the horrors on the screen ... or that those horrors were only a preview of the living nightmare that would soon descend over the town.... (401093—$3.95)

☐ **BREEZE HORROR by Candace Caponegro.** They're not dead yet. They won't be dead—ever. They were going for her beautiful, blonde Sandy, and for all the others on the island who had not been touched. They were coming up from the beach where they had grown stronger instead of dying of their hideous wounds ... and nothing could stop them, especially death, for death was behind them.... (400755—$3.50)

☐ **SLOB by Rex Miller.** He thinks of himself as Death. Death likes to drive through strange, darkened suburban streets at night, where there's an endless smorgasbord of humanity for the taking. In a few seconds he will see the innocent people and he will flood the night with a river of blood.... "A novel of shattering terror."—Harlan Ellison
(150058—$3.95)

☐ **MOON by James Herbert.** Somewhere on the spinning, shadowed earth, a full moon was glowing, energizing a lunatic whose rage could not be sated as it struck again and again and again in an unending bloodletting of senseless slaughter and hideous savagery.... "VIVID HORROR ... TAUT, CHILLING, CREDIBLE..."—The New York Times Book Review.
(400569—$4.50)

☐ **MANSTOPPER by Douglas Borton.** Snarling, leaping, ripping, killing— the ultimate horror is coming at you! There are four of them in the blood-thirsty pack. They have been born and bread for one single purpose. To kill. And now they are loose and doing what they do best. (400976—$3.95)

Buy them at your local bookstore or use this convenient coupon for ordering.

NEW AMERICAN LIBRARY
P.O. Box 999, Bergenfield, New Jersey 07621

Please send me the books I have checked above. I am enclosing $_____
(please add $1.00 to this order to cover postage and handling). Send check or money order—no cash or C.O.D.'s. Prices and numbers are subject to change without notice.

Name_____

Address_____

City _____ State _____ Zip Code _____

Allow 4-6 weeks for delivery.
This offer is subject to withdrawal without notice.

**A RIVETING NOVEL OF TERROR AND
SUSPENSE THAT PERPETRATES THE
VERY CORE OF HUMAN FEAR . . .**

The Bestseller by
JAMES HERBERT

THE
MAGIC
COTTAGE

Gramarye. The ideal storybook cottage. But in
this masterful, spine-chilling novel, James Herbert
leads us to the place where horror dwells and the
blood runs cold . . . where nothing is what it
seems—and nowhere is safe. . . .